Flowers On The Mersey

Also by June Francis
and published by Bantam Books

A Sparrow Doesn't Fall

Flowers On The Mersey

June Francis

BANTAM BOOKS

TORONTO • NEW YORK • LONDON • SYDNEY • AUCKLAND

FLOWERS ON THE MERSEY
A BANTAM BOOK 0 553 40504 7

Originally published in Great Britain by Judy Piatkus
(Publishers) Ltd.

PRINTING HISTORY
Judy Piatkus (Publishers) edition published 1992
Bantam Books edition published 1993

This book is set in Linotron Times

Bantam Books are published by Transworld Publishers Ltd.,
61–63 Uxbridge Road, Ealing, London W5 5SA, in Australia by
Transworld Publishers (Australia) Pty. Ltd., 15–25 Helles Avenue,
Moorebank, NSW 2170, and in New Zealand by Transworld
Publishers (N.Z.) Ltd., 3 William Pickering Drive, Albany,
Auckland.

Printed and bound in Great Britain by
Cox & Wyman Ltd., Reading, Berks.

If they had been thinking of that land from which they had gone out, they would have had the opportunity to return. But as it is, they desire a better country, that is, a heavenly one.

Revised standard version of the Bible.

In acknowledgement of the special ties that exist between Liverpool, America, and that island across the Irish Sea.

Prologue

Esther Clark placed the letter from Ireland on the green chenille tablecloth and rested her chin on her hand. What to do? There must be something. She sat there for several minutes before rising to her feet, unable to stay still any longer, and went to the sitting-room door. 'Hannah!' She had to call several times.

'What is it thou wants?' The maid's voice was disgruntled as she came into the sitting room. She swiped at a fly with her duster and smiled with satisfaction as it zigzagged like a drunken man on to the floor. She picked it up and deposited it on the coal fire before looking at her mistress. 'If it's the shopping thou's after, then thee'll just have to wait. I haven't finished upstairs.'

'I'll do the shopping.'

'You! Thee, I mean.' Hannah looked startled. 'Are yer going on thy own then for a change? Thee hasn't dun that for a while.'

'Yes. I'm going on my own,' said Esther, despite being all of a dither but determined that Hannah would not have the upper hand for once. The maid had entered her life one stormy night when she had come into the Quaker-run St Anne's Citizen's Institute, situated in one of the worst slum areas in Liverpool. Esther had been a voluntary helper and had fed the hungry young woman. Now, fifteen years on, Hannah was supposedly one of the Quaker faithful.

'Thou's up to summit.' The maid scowled and folded her skinny arms across her chest. 'What is it?'

Esther drew a deep breath. 'I'm going to St Anne Street, and I want to go alone.'

'Whatever for?' Hannah's tone was curious. 'If thee'll just hold thee horses, I'll cum with thee. Don't want thee having one of thy queer dos.'

'I'll be all right,' insisted Esther, reaching for the letter on the table. 'I can always go to the Centre if I'm not. Tina will give me a cup of tea.'

'Hmmph!' Hannah's sharp eyes glanced down at the letter and her thoughts shifted. 'It says Dublin. Is it from that sister thee were speaking about?'

'Yes. Sarah hasn't been at all well.' Esther picked up the letter and placed it in her pocket.

'Not surprising,' sniffed Hannah. 'They should shoot the lot of them rebels. The way they snipe at our soldiers . . . hanging's too good for them.'

'Just thou finish upstairs and don't thee be concerning thyself with such things,' ordered Esther, her plump cheeks turning pink as she hurried out of the room. There were times when the struggle to impart pacifist beliefs into Hannah proved too much, but having said that the maid's words had given her something to think about.

Esther put on her coat, found her handbag, took a couple of Dr Cassell tablets to calm her nerves and stood quietly for a few moments in the lobby, aware of Hannah's over-whelmingly silent presence behind her. Then she opened the front door and went out.

Esther sat on the tram, her gloved hand nervously twisting the ticket between her fingers. It was twenty years since she had last seen her sister and in all that time her father had only mentioned Sarah's name once. Esther had watched him withdraw into himself, shutting even her out. It made it all the more difficult to understand why he had kept the letters her sister had sent and which Esther had not known existed. Yet she could only be glad that he had not got rid of them. Otherwise she would never have been able to trace Sarah after he had died. As it was her letter had needed to be forwarded because her sister had moved with her husband and daughter to a different address in Dublin. Esther now had a nineteen-year-old niece, a member of this wild post-war generation. A young mind whom she might be able to influ-ence as she had once tried to influence Sarah, ten years her younger. She looked out of the window, remembering.

Her stop loomed up and Esther got off the tram and walked quickly in the direction of St Anne Street which not only housed the Institute where she had met Hannah but also the wholesale and general merchant store which her father had once owned. It was here that Sarah had met the handsome young Irishman, who had swept her off her feet.

How contented Esther's life had been before he had come on the scene. Mama's passing had been a blow, of course, as had the deaths of the three tiny boys, at each of whose births Papa had dared to hope that here was a future heir to his tiny kingdom. He had borne each terrible death stoically and resigned himself to the care of his older daughter. As for Esther, she had known it was her duty to tend her father and small sister.

They had lived in rooms over the shop, sharing them with the stock that Papa imported on ships from every corner of the British Empire. Brought on horsedrawn carts from the Liverpool docks, the boxes, tins, bottles and casks had always provided an exciting diversion from her book keeping. Life had been busy and fulfilling so that sometimes there had been no time to give Sarah the discipline she needed. Her sister had got away with much that their mother would never have allowed. Esther's only excuse was that Sarah was always so cheerful and bright about the place that she and Papa found it difficult to scold her when she did do wrong. (There had been the episode with a bicycle and a boy.) She had been forgiven much but not falling in love with Adam Rhoades, a member of the Church of Ireland. He had refused to accept the tenets of the Quaker faith and Sarah had been lost to them. Esther's fingers crumpled the ticket. Adam had caused a lot of pain and she still had not forgiven him.

She reached the shop to notice that the partially black-painted windows still bore in gold lettering her father's name and the year in which he had established his business – 1870, the year of her birth. Despite Hannah's company in the house she had felt very alone since her father had died in the 'flu epidemic which had swept Europe last year, killing more people than the Great War had soldiers. It made it seem all the more terrible that across the Irish Sea the rebels and the Black and Tans were playing all kinds of dirty tricks on each other.

3

Esther thought of her sister's letter and the unexpected tone of it. There was no note of brightness in it at all. It was obvious that her sister needed looking after but it was no good going herself. Her nerves would never stand the terrible sniping and explosions. She pursed her lips. There was only one person who was fit to go and that was Hannah, who claimed to be scared of nothing and who had nursed her mistress through 'flu. Hannah who could wear you down once she was determined about something. It was very tiring but it was that trait that had made her a survivor and so suitable for the task Esther had in mind. Hannah was the second eldest of six children, whose mother had taken to the bottle after her husband left. Hannah had reared the younger ones in a filthy court in the vicinity of Gerard Street. Those houses were one room above another with an earth closet beneath the bedroom window shared between several families. For coping with such horrors Esther could not fail to admire her maid despite the underlying aggression in her manner. Hannah waged war on dirt, strong drink and men. Esther did not doubt that her nerves would stand up to bullets and bombs. There would have to be some extra money in her wages, of course. She was as sharp as a knife where money was concerned because she was saving for her old age.

But Hannah was not the only one growing old. Esther would be fifty in August and wanted her family near her. She would send a note with Hannah suggesting that as soon as her sister was fit to travel, she and her daughter Rebekah should come to Liverpool on a visit. Surely Adam would see no wrong in that? He would want his wife and daughter in a place safe from violence – and hopefully it would be the first step in persuading them to stay in Liverpool for good.

Part One

Chapter One

Rebekah Rhoades walked soft-footedly along the lobby and opened the front door as Hannah came out of the dining room.

'It's fellas, isn't it?' demanded the maid, bustling towards her. 'That's what's taking thee out?'

'I've told you where I'm going.' Rebekah's voice was controlled, not revealing the annoyance she felt. 'Not that it's any of your business, Hannah.'

She closed the front door and hurried down the street, her russet and black skirts flapping against her calves. How dare Aunt Esther in Liverpool send that self righteous, prying old . . . old harpy? As if Rebekah had not been able to cope since her mother took ill with her nerves. It was boring being stuck in the house at times but she had given up a job, working in her father's government office, to do the housework and look after Mother. Now Hannah had taken over and she was fed up with it. She glanced behind her, not putting it past the maid to follow her, but there was no sign of Hannah's bony figure.

Rebekah relaxed slightly, enjoying the sun shining through the autumn-tinted leaves in St Stephen's Green. She had arranged to meet Willie, one of the lads from the street, by Nelson's monument in O'Connell Street but first she had to pay a visit to an old lady, who was her excuse for escaping the house. Since Hannah had caught her passing the time of day with a boy by their front doorstep, she had watched her like a hawk. It maddened Rebekah and it was that more than anything that had caused her to take up with Willie. It was nothing serious but she needed some young company. The

7

worry over her mother and the fighting had got her down. Like most people in Dublin her nerves were stretched to the limit. She was convinced that those in authority had lost control of the lower ranks on both sides and anarchy had taken over.

She felt a familiar sense of apprehension as she went along the High Street, and tried to concentrate on thoughts of Willie. He was fair and good-looking; a would-be poet who considered himself another Yeats. He had a swaggering manner which sometimes amused, sometimes irritated, but she would not have to put up with it much longer. Besides, not every girl had verse written in praise of her eyelashes!

Going down towards the Liffy she passed a couple of Black and Tan auxiliaries, so named because of the combination of khaki uniform with police cap and belt. A number of them were ex-soldiers from the Great War. They looked at her and she stared through them, determined not to show nervousness or irritation at their scrutiny. She was doing her good deed for the day by visiting the elderly grandmother of a young Irish soldier killed on the Somme.

Aware that they had stopped a little further up the street while one of them lit a cigarette, Rebekah hesitated in front of Old Mary's door, which opened directly on to the pavement. The wide brim of her black hat with its rust ribbon blocked her vision slightly and with one hand she eased it back as she knocked.

The door opened quicker than was normal, but before she could take in that it was not Old Mary standing in the doorway, she received a push that felled her to the ground. Two shots rang out and she lifted her head in time to see one of the auxiliaries crumple in a heap while another pulled out his revolver and pressed himself against a house wall.

Scared to death, Rebekah buried her head in her arms as several more shots rang out. An angry voice hissed, 'You bloody fool, Shaun. You'll have a whole heap of them down on our heads now!'

'Not if I stop the other one getting away!'

Rebekah forced herself to look up as the gun fired again and she saw the Black and Tan fall. She wished she hadn't looked. A hand took her arm, lifting her to her feet and the

8

hat was removed from her head. She stared into the face of a dark curly-haired man, who returned her scrutiny with a mixture of annoyance and concern. 'Are you all right?'

She bit her lower lip. 'My knees hurt! And I think I've laddered my stockings,' she stammered.

'I'm sorry about that.' His gaze took her in slowly. 'You were coming to visit I take it?'

'Y-yes!' She smoothed back her hair nervously. 'I'll come back another time – when Old Mary's alone!'

'I'm sure she'd like that.' He handed back her hat and smiled.

'Danny, what the hell – !' The voice was angry.

Rebekah jumped and her gaze darted to the other, younger, face. It was spotty and there was a trickle of blood at the temple.

'Who are you? Speak fast and say the right words or I'll blow you to pieces,' said its owner.

'Shut up, Shaun!' ordered Daniel in a weary voice. 'Can't you see that she's terrified out of her wits.' He turned to Rebekah. 'You've got nothing to be frightened of. We won't hurt you.'

'You mightn't!' Her voice shook despite all her efforts to control it. 'But he'd kill me if he had half the chance. And I know why! But I only came to say goodbye to Old Mary. I'll be leaving Dublin in a day or two.'

'You're leaving?'

'Yes!' She did her best to infuse assurance in her voice. 'So you see, I won't be around to tell anyone.'

'She's only saying that,' interrupted Shaun, scowling. 'Listen to the way she speaks. She's one of them.'

'I'm half Irish,' said Rebekah desperately. 'My father's family have lived here for hundreds of years. We're for Home Rule! And Mama is too. Although she's from Liverpool and was a Quaker, so she hates the fighting.'

'A Quaker! Maybe you're one of Cromwell's soldiers' descendants?' Shaun spat on the ground at her feet and his eyes darkened. 'We haven't forgotten what he and his troops did to our ancestors, have we now, Danny?'

'You're not listening, Shaun,' said Daniel, frowning. 'Her mother's a Quaker and she's from Liverpool. Cromwell's men were mainly Puritans. There's a difference. She's not involved in our fight.'

'She's still a witness.' The other's expression was stormy. 'And how do we know she's telling the truth about her father? He doesn't sound like one of us.'

'She's not going to say anything.' Daniel's eyes met Rebekah's again. 'Are you?' he said softly.

'I'm leaving, aren't I?' she retorted swiftly, but determined to say what she thought. 'I will say, though, that I just can't understand why he had to fire on them first when there wasn't a fight. It'll cause reprisals, and you must know how savage and bloody they can be.'

Daniel's expression tightened. 'We've lost two brothers in an ambush. You'll have to forgive Shaun his desire for revenge.'

'It's not for me to forgive,' she said, flushing. 'But what about those two mothers in England who've now lost their sons? It's just so pointless.'

Daniel shook his head slowly. 'If you're a Quaker then you can't begin to understand what drives a man in such a situation. You'd best get going.' He turned away but Shaun made an exasperated noise.

'Are you bloody crazy, Danny? You can't take her word that she'll keep quiet. Let's at least tie her up until we get away. If she'd been one of our women caught by the Black and Tans, they'd treat her different. See the flesh on her!' His hand moved unexpectedly to squeeze her breast.

Rebekah gasped and instinct brought up her hand but she gained control of herself before the blow could land. Even so Shaun raised his gun, and she felt sure he would have hit her if Daniel had not turned and gripped the back of his collar, dragging him backwards. 'Go, girl!' he said, spinning his brother round and forcing him into the house.

She stared at him a moment longer then went off in the direction of the river. When she reached the quayside her knees gave way unexpectedly and she sank on to the ground. She felt sick, thinking of how close the bullets had been and of the two men's blood on the ground. Then she heard running feet and turned and saw Daniel.

'I just wanted to check you were all right,' he said.

'Of course I am!' There was a touch of anger in her voice as she began to struggle to her feet. He took hold of her shoulder and helped her up.

'Leave me alone.' She was near to tears as she pulled herself free. 'Why bother with me? You must see dead men all the time. What's one stupid girl, sickened by the sight of blood?'

'I didn't fire the gun,' he said in a low intense voice. 'And I don't see death as often as you seem to think. I've said I'm sorry. I can't do anything else, except perhaps see you home?'

'I don't want you to.' She turned her back on him and looked over the river. 'Just go away.'

There was a silence but she knew he was still standing there behind her. She was filled with a strong feeling of apprehension. He was not going to go away. Why? And why be scared? She only had to scream and someone would come to her help. 'Please go,' she whispered unevenly.

'I'll see you home,' he insisted. 'Could you wait here for five minutes?'

'No.'

'Why not?'

'That's a daft thing to say.' Her tone was incredulous.

'I suppose so. You could still wait. Or is it that you're going for the soldiers?'

'It's what my father would have me do.' She paused, thinking of the brutality of some of the Black and Tans. 'But I don't like what the soldiers do either.'

'Good.' There was relief in his voice. 'My brother's a hot head and he shouldn't have done what he did, but I'm glad you're not a girl who'd go screeching to the military.'

At that she turned and looked at him. 'Maybe I should have screeched when you brother first fired. Sniping at people is despicable! Or perhaps, when he touched me, I should really have yelled. He should not have hurt me – where he – ' Her voice tailed off and a line of colour ran up under her skin.

'No, he should not have,' said Daniel, shoving a hand into a jacket pocket. 'And I know it should be Shaun saying sorry, but I couldn't get him to do that. Surely you'll accept my apology?'

'I don't know why you think I should,' she said coolly. 'But it does say in the Bible that we should forgive our enemies, so I suppose I've got to accept your apology.'

11

A smile lightened his expression. 'I'm no enemy of yours. And I'm thinking that some girls would have made a worse shananakins of it all, but you're a rare one with a head on your shoulders.'

She frowned at him. 'If I had screeched like a banshee then I don't doubt your brother would have shot me.'

'Perhaps. He's more nervous than he appears, you understand.' His voice was serious.

She raised her eyebrows. 'He surely has cause to be if he goes shooting off guns! Someone else might have seen him.'

'They'll keep their mouths shut,' he said with a certainty that she understood.

They fell silent and she looked away, flustered by his stare. 'Your brother said that Old Mary was your aunt.' Her tone was stilted. 'She never mentioned having family alive.'

'She isn't a real aunt. Was it her soul you were after?'

Rebekah felt like laughing hysterically. 'That's the kind of thing you Catholics said to my great-grandmama who came over from Lancashire during the Great Hunger to help feed the starving! Your faith is priest-ridden so I know when I'd be wasting my time.'

He grinned. 'What's your name?'

She hesitated before saying clearly, 'Rebekah.' There was a hint of hauteur in the look she gave him. 'And yours, I remember, is Daniel – a good Bible name.'

'Aye. He had to go into the lions' den.' His smile faded. 'I've got to get my brother away, but I'd still like to see you home.'

Her eyes narrowed thoughtfully. 'You don't trust me, that's what it is. You want to make sure that . . . '

'No!' he interrupted. 'That's not my reason. Think, girl. There was no need for me to follow you here. I could have just run.' He added in a softer voice. 'Wait for me here by the river. Give me a quarter of an hour.'

She laughed sharply. 'You said five minutes, five minutes ago! There's no cause for me to wait. I can't wait! I'm meeting –'

But he was already running up the street. 'Wait!' he called.

For several minutes Rebekah stood looking after him. He was crazy to think she would hang about for him. Her father would be furious if he knew that she had said as much as a good morning to a rebel. He had been paranoid for months, fearing a shot in the back because he worked for a British civil administration in utter chaos due to Sinn Fein's refusal to accept the ruling of British law courts and the collection of taxes. Besides, Willie would be waiting for her. It would be sensible to go right now. She chewed a strand of her hair. He had probably only told her to wait to give him and his brother time to get away. She should have marched straight to the barracks and told the soldiers what had happened, never mind standing and listening to his excuses. He didn't fire the gun . . . So? He had still been there, and his brother had. Why had she stayed listening to him? He was not even what you would call devastatingly handsome or even very tall. The dark part she would grant him, and he had brown eyes that had a way of looking at her that made her – No, she would not think of how he made her feel. He was not worth wasting her thoughts on. She shifted her feet restlessly. He had a button missing from the top of his shirt and wore no collar. Wasn't there a woman in his life to sew a button on?

A tap on her shoulder caused her to whirl round. 'I'm glad you waited,' said Daniel. He had been less than ten minutes.

She tilted her chin. 'Who said I was waiting for you?' She turned and began to walk away.

He fell into step beside her. 'If you were waiting for someone else, he obviously hasn't turned up.'

'I wasn't meeting him here.' She did not wait for him to ask where but said stiffly. 'Is Old Mary all right? The Black and Tans will search the street and ask questions.'

'I doubt she'll tell them anything.'

'Probably not.' Rebekah pushed back a strand of blonde-streaked brown hair from her eyes and sought safety in thinking of the old woman. 'Her memory's queer. She can talk about the old days like they were yesterday, but yesterday might never have happened.'

He nodded. 'You must have a lot of patience. I found it hard going because she kept thinking I was a lad after I told her who I was.'

'I listen more than talk.' She glanced at him and then away. He looked like he needed feeding up.

13

'Why do you visit her?' His voice was curious. 'How did you get to know her? It couldn't have been through the priest if you're a Quaker.'

'Her grandson's name was on the list of those killed fighting for the British in the war,' she said in her quick, light manner of speaking. 'Mama and I started visiting. It was our bit for the war effort. We'd heard that the Friends – Quakers to you – were visiting families in Liverpool, you see.'

'I see.' He made no further comment as they came to O'Connell's Bridge with its customary collection of beggars, some with missing limbs. One was selling shoelaces. Rebekah paused and bought some and Daniel followed suit, murmuring, 'Bloody war. Why did they go and volunteer?'

She remained silent, although she could have said there had been plenty in Ireland glad to take the King's shilling during the Great War because they were unemployed and their families hungry. It made her angry that those in Ireland killing each other could not use their energies to join forces and fight those kind of evils in both countries.

Daniel said, 'Do we cross for where you live?'

'No,' she said shortly.

'Then are you really wanting to go straight home?' He smiled and she thought it was enough to charm crows from the trees and was suddenly wary. 'Why do you ask?'

'It's a fine day and I'm free for a few hours.'

People's suffering was still on her mind. 'Free from what – ambushing people?'

He frowned. 'Why go on about it? I didn't ambush anybody, as you know. If you feel that bad about me, why did you wait?'

'I don't know why I waited,' she said honestly.

His frown vanished. 'Don't you?' He seized her hand and pulled her on to the bridge. She had to run to keep up with him and was confused as to why she bothered. She was definitely annoyed at his presumption in taking her hand; it simmered just below the surface, but mingling with it was an unfamiliar excitement because what was happening was so out of the ordinary and he was so different from the boys she knew.

14

She sought for something to say to stop her mind dwelling on the effect he had on her. 'Do you know Dublin?' She asked that because he did not have the Dubliner's way of speaking.

'Sure. I used to come more often when Mam was alive.' He slowed down and matched his easy gait to her hurrying steps, guiding her round a mess on the ground. 'Would you like to go a different way than this?'

'No.' She glanced over her shoulder. 'Hannah just might come looking for me.' She did not like mentioning Willie now.

'Who's Hannah? Your sister?'

'I have no sister.' A grim little smile played round Rebekah's mouth. 'Hannah's a real live gorgon who'd turn you to stone as soon as look at you. She's from Liverpool and all she does is go on about the place. My Aunt Esther, whom I've never met, sent her because Mama isn't well. I think it's all a trick. For weeks she's worked on Mama until all she does now is talk about when she lived in Liverpool. You'd think the place was the promised land to hear her. And then doesn't Hannah suddenly start on Papa, but it's a different story with him! It's America, and the ships that sail from Liverpool to New York taking emigrants. You'd think she'd been there from her talk of what a great country it is. I've never known my parents to disagree but now, although they don't exactly argue, you can tell that one wants to settle in Liverpool and the other in America.'

'Who do you think will win?' He sounded amused.

Rebekah flashed him an embarrassed look and tried for a light note. 'Papa, of course. Doesn't the man always get his way? I take Mama's side, and maybe that's why Hannah doesn't like me. When she first came she was all smiles – but that was when she thought we were only going over to Liverpool for a visit. When it became a possibility that we might live there for good, she changed. For some reason she doesn't want us settling in Liverpool.'

'What reason can she have for not wanting you living there?'

She shrugged.

'Perhaps she's jealous of you?' he suggested with a smile. 'You're young.'

'Why should she begrudge me that?' Rebekah's eyes sparkled. 'No, it's because I don't behave as she thinks a good little Quaker girl should. In her opinion, I talk too much, I fidget, I've taken up my hems – that's the last word in flightiness according to her! I said I'd like to go dancing so she says it's because I want to flirt! She spies on me when I talk to the young men in the street.' She stopped abruptly and looked away over the glistening peaty waters of the river. She was talking too much. What would he think of her?

'Go on.' He was looking at her again with that expression in his eyes that made her feel – she wasn't sure exactly how she felt. It was odd.

'It's not important,' she murmured.

'What *is* important?'

'Mama getting better.'

'What's wrong with her?'

'The fighting's made her ill. She jumps if I drop a fork.'

'That's really why you're leaving Dublin?'

'Yes. Aunt Esther made us realise that there's no need for us to stay.'

There was silence and she was very aware of his eyes on her. 'I suppose you were against Pearse and the Easter Rising four years ago?'

She looked at him, puzzled by the question. 'Not really. I thought it wrong that the British executed him and the other leaders. It turned them into martyrs, and people felt sorry for them then and angry with the British Government. I wish Pearse and the others had been patient and then Ireland wouldn't be getting torn apart.'

His eyes narrowed thoughtfully and he kicked a pebble. 'Frustration. What do you do when you feel like you'll never get what you want? People lose patience.'

'They act stupidly instead, like your brother,' she said without thinking.

'We've lost two brothers,' repeated Daniel, his tone rebuking her. 'I'm sorry he frightened you.' His hand brushed hers and she drew back.

'Let's not talk about it.'

He nodded. 'Let's carry on talking about you. These lads – are you walking out with one of them?'

'Oh no!' she said quickly. Their eyes met and there was a churning feeling in her stomach. 'Have you a wife?' she blurted out.

16

He raised his eyebrows and his fingers caught her fingertips. 'I was thinking about marrying once but she married someone else. I'm glad now that I didn't.'

'Why? Has she changed? Is she not so pretty? Has she put weight on?' Rebekah freed her hand, but she was glad that he was not married.

'It had nothing to do with looks. But wouldn't you stop right now walking with me if I had a wife? That's why I'm glad.' He caressed her cheek with the back of his hand, causing her to jump. 'Your skin's so smooth and you're the pretty one.'

She blushed. 'You shouldn't say that. I don't need flattery.'

He looked disbelieving. 'Don't you like nice things being said to you? One of those boys must have said something?'

Rebekah thought of Willie and his poetry about the length of her eyelashes. 'They tease. One tried to kiss me but I didn't want him to.'

'Why?' His shoulder touched her upper arm and she looked away. 'Because I'm waiting for Mr Right to come along.' Her voice was deliberately firm. 'And Hannah was watching through the curtains, and she'd tell Papa.'

'Has Papa someone in mind for you then?'

'Not that I know of. He's just old-fashioned! You wouldn't think that him and Mama ran away. She says that he was very handsome when he was young, and although she was brought up to believe that it's more important to see the beauty of the soul shining through a person's eyes than for them to be good looking, she couldn't resist him.'

'Fancy that!' His face drew close to hers, almost touching it. 'I can see the soul in your eyes.'

Her heart suddenly felt as if it was beating on the outside of her body and she murmured, 'Hannah says that if a man kisses you, he can give you a baby.' She did not know why she said it.

'It takes more than a kiss to make a baby.' His voice was expressionless.

Colour flooded her cheeks again. 'I'm not stupid! Why are we talking like this?' She stopped abruptly, knowing that she should never have come with him.

'Perhaps because kissing is on your mind?'

She gave him a look. 'Only because we're talking about it.'

17

'Only talking.' His eyes gleamed. 'There's no danger in that, is there?'

Rebekah thought it wiser to remain silent and considered turning back but he made no more comments guaranteed to make her blush, and soon the sweep of Dublin Bay was before them.

Ships were at anchor and a lone yacht flew before the stiff breeze that whipped colour into Rebekah's cheeks and set her skirt flapping against her lisle-clad legs. She glanced at Daniel and surprised a grim expression on his face as he looked not at the sea but to the hills. 'What's wrong?' she demanded impulsively.

'I'm thinking of the blood that's stained those hills. And how it must tear at a man's heart to leave Ireland for good.'

She caught on to his last words. 'Are you leaving Ireland too?'

He did not answer but said instead, 'You said you were leaving. When?'

'The day after tomorrow. We'll be taking the steamer to Liverpool and staying with my aunt. Perhaps we'll go to America from there – who knows?' She shrugged.

'There's plenty of opportunities for a man to put the past behind him in America,' he murmured. 'Did you know that the old Celts believed that the Land of the Ever Young existed westwards across the Atlantic? There's a story about Oisin, a knight of the Fianna, who went there and lived with the beautiful princess of Tir na nOg, never growing old.'

She smiled. 'Everlasting life. It's what a lot of people are looking for.'

He dug his hands deep into his pockets. 'In this story it didn't do them any good. Their love couldn't be consummated because she was immortal, and he a man. If he left her world then he would die, while she carried on living forever without him.'

'What happened to them?'

He stared at her. 'It's a romance. Oisin was heartsick for Ireland. So he left her and they never saw each other again.'

How sad for the princess,' she said quietly.

'It was sad for both of them.' He surprised her by taking her hand. 'I wish you weren't leaving so soon.'

18

She did not know what to say to that or whether to snatch her hand back. His skin was warm and rough, his grip firm. 'I have to go,' she said at last.

'It doesn't give us much time to get to know each other better.'

'There's no point in doing that, anyway,' she said.

'You don't think so?'

'No.' Her tone was positive. 'I can't stay long. There's a hundred and one things to do before we leave.'

'And I suppose your papa wouldn't like you being here with me?'

'Yes.'

He toyed with her fingers. 'You won't want me to be seeing you home them?'

'I didn't say that. But maybe it's not sensible. If my father –'

He interrupted her. 'Then perhaps we'd better say goodbye here.' He leaned towards her and kissed her briefly. She stared at him. Part of her had been waiting for it to happen. Hannah would say that she'd been asking for it. Glancing about them she saw that there were only seabirds gliding overhead to take notice of them, so that when he drew her closer she made little resistance. She wanted him to kiss her again and for longer this time. It was foolish but that was how she felt. The next kiss proved more than nice and she responded, but not for long. She placed her hands against his chest and he lifted his head and looked at her. She found herself with nothing to say and he kissed her again. She was almost breathless by the time that kiss came to an end, and decided that it better stop now.

'It's time I was going home.'

He hugged her close. 'You don't want to go home?'

'No. But I'd better.' Her tone was grave.

A slight smile lit his face and he let go of her and sat on the grass. 'You liked it though.'

'Yes. But I wasn't brought up to think about my own enjoyment.' She knelt on the grass. 'It's different for girls.'

'Of course it is.' He stretched out. 'And as well as that, I'm Catholic and a rebel.'

'Yes.'

'You think they're insurmountable objects to our getting to know each other?'

'What do you think?'

He leaned on his elbow and his expression was thoughtful. 'They probably are.'

She frowned. 'Yes. Although you act like they're not there. It's the same with the shooting earlier. You seem to be able to brush it aside. I saw it and it's the kind of thing that makes me glad to be leaving.'

'You've made your point.' He looked over the sea, his expression sombre.

Rebekah's eyes followed his and she considered it wise to change the subject. 'Papa says that America has breathtaking scenery.'

It was a couple of minutes before he responded and then it seemed it was with a struggle. 'Would you mind going to America?'

'I haven't thought about it much.' She twisted her hat between her hands. 'Liverpool – Ireland – America,' she murmured. 'They have strong links. Mama was telling me about her side of the family. My grandfather had some kind of wholesale shop. He came down from Bolton in Lancashire during the American Civil War because thousands were out of work. The ships blockaded the Southern ports in America, which meant there was no cotton for the mills. They were hard times. So he went to Liverpool looking for work.'

'How did he make the money to buy the shop?' Daniel broke off a blade of grass and chewed on it.

She leaned towards him, her expression lively. 'He went to the Meeting House on first-day – that's Sunday to you – and the owner took him on. He worked hard. When the boss died he married his daughter. Papa wasn't so lucky. He'd hitched a ride on one of the wagons up from the docks to my grandfather's shop. He'd just got off the boat from Ireland after a quarrel with his brother. Till then he lived on the family farm. He came in looking for a job and met Mama. They married against my grandfather's wishes. Because he was Quaker, she was treated like she didn't exist by him and the Friends.'

'What made your father come back to Ireland?'

She smiled. 'Mama says it was to put the sea between them and her father. But his mother had written to him. He had two brothers and one had sickened and died. What about your family?'

He threw the grass down. 'There's only Shaun and me now, although we have relatives in Liverpool. My mam's sister's family.' He stared down at his hands. 'There was money once. My great-grandfather had land. Out of his own pocket he drained a marsh to grow more crops. The only trouble was that the landlord owned the land. During the potato famine he took it back.' His expression darkened. 'D'you know what it does to a man to lose his roots? The land which his family has farmed for generations?'

'It happens in Ireland.' Her tone was philosophical. 'Papa's family farm has gone now. I'm sorry that you lost your land.'

Daniel's eyes softened. He took her hand and kissed it. She ran her fingers over his mouth. The next moment he pulled her down and she sprawled on top of him. He kissed her forcefully and she responded with a slowly growing passion. His hands roamed her back, coming to rest on her covered bottom. Instantly she was alerted and attempted to push them away, aware of a hardness beneath her. She felt the sigh run through him and then he pushed her off.

'We'd best get back.' He stood up, holding out a hand to her.

She took it. 'I've been thinking that for the last half hour,' she murmured.

'I know.' He grimaced. 'Where do you live?'

She hesitated, considering how her father had always stressed not giving their name and address to strangers.

'You don't trust me, do you?' His dark brows drew together.

'My father – he's getting almost as nervous as Mama,' she excused. 'But if you still want to, you can walk with me as far as Trinity College.'

He nodded but his expression was angry. 'When I was a lad and we had nothing, I wished I could have killed that landlord who took our land. But now I'm just wishing that you could believe in what I believe. Understand why we have to fight against British Imperialism.'

'"Vengeance is mine saith the Lord,"' she murmured.

Daniel's laugh had a bitter sound to it. 'But who's to do His dirty work?'

Rebekah shook her head, feeling unexpectedly depressed. 'I only know that killing creates suffering and it is destroying

21

Ireland. Will that do for an answer?' She turned and walked away.

Daniel caught up with her. 'I hate violence as much as you do. It's just that there's no other way.'

'Don't lets talk about it any more. There's no point.'

'I suppose not if you're leaving. I'll walk with you as far as Trinity.'

She nodded and silently they began the walk back, side by side.

Chapter Two

Rebekah was out of breath with rushing by the time she reached the red-brick Georgian terraced house where she lived. Pausing on the step, she pressed the palms of her hands to hot cheeks in an attempt to cool them as she tried to empty her mind of Daniel and everything that had happened since she left the house, but he was still in her thoughts when the front door with its shiny brass knocker was pulled open.

In the doorway stood the tall, soberly clad figure of Hannah. Her coal black eyes bored into Rebekah's. 'So thee's come back after all. I bet yers been with a fella!' she declared triumphantly in her mixture of old-fashioned Quaker speech and Liverpudlian. 'It's written all over thee so don't be denying it! It's one of those lads from up the street, isn't it? One of those clothes horses! One of those strutting peacocks! Well, yer father's been home, and in a right mood he was – even before I told him that thou hast been missing all afternoon and still not home! He's gone to look for thee.'

'What did you tell him?' demanded Rebekah, pushed past the maid. 'Where's Mama? You didn't say anything to either of them about fellas? Because it's all lies.'

'Of course I did to yer father.' Hannah hurried in after her and would have closed the door but suddenly it was taken out of her hand and slammed.

Rebekah turned swiftly, her heart sinking at the grim expression on her father's still handsome features. 'Go and tell my wife that her daughter's home, Hannah, and then go to the kitchen.'

'Yes, Mr Rhoades.' Hannah shot a triumphant glance at Rebekah before disappearing into the dining room.

Her father's hand fastened on Rebekah's arm, causing her to wince. 'Up the stairs, miss. I don't want your mother hearing what I have to say. She's been worried about you.'

'But I told Hannah I was going to see Old Mary earlier on,' she said, almost tripping over her feet as he hurried her along the lobby past the solemnly ticking grandfather clock. 'Honestly, Papa, I did go there.'

'Old Mary didn't remember you being there – but then that's not surprising according to your mother, and considering the soldiers were searching the houses,' he muttered, dragging her up the stairs. He was breathing heavily and paused for breath on the landing, leaning against the brown-painted wall next to an oil painting of Kingstown harbour.

The painting instantly reminded Rebekah of Daniel kissing her and her cheeks warmed. She was aware of her father's regard. Had someone seen her with Daniel? 'Papa, I dawdled home,' she said hastily. 'It's been a lovely day.'

He straightened and his expression was thunderous. 'You weren't dawdling alone, though, miss, were you?' He pushed her with some force along the landing. 'I saw you as you came past Trinity College, his hand on your arm and you looking up at him.' His bedroom door yielded beneath his touch and sunlight touched them as it filtered through the lace curtains and heavy dusty velvet drapes that adorned the multiple paned windows that reached almost ceiling to floor.

Rebekah closed her eyes against the sun's brightness and sought for words. 'I can explain!'

'I'd be interested to hear a reasonable explanation for you being in Daniel O'Neill's company,' he said through his teeth, the palm of his hand in the small of her back sending her flying across the room on to the patchwork quilt of the old mahogany bed.

She gasped with shock, pushing herself up, and turned her head just in time to see her father take a switch from the wardrobe. Both belonged to the owner of the house and the switch had never been used on her, although her father had told her how he had been beaten as a boy. Her eyes dilated with apprehension. 'What are you doing?'

'Down, miss. This is going to hurt me more than you.' He swiped the air with the switch, making a whooshing noise, and took a deep breath. 'I should never have listened to your mother when she said that we shouldn't heed the scriptures where they say spare the rod and spoil the child, but I did because you were a girl.' He advanced towards the bed. 'But I never thought a daughter of mine would be cavorting with the likes of Daniel O'Neill! Didn't you think of the danger you could be putting us all in?' he shouted.

'He only walked with me to Trinity!' She struggled as he forced her face down on the bed and flung her skirts up. The first stinging blows landed on her cami-knicker clad bottom and she yelped. Never before had he raised a hand in violence against her.

'You should not be walking with him at all!' he cried. 'There's a price on his head, and if you had been seen by either side you could be dead! We could all be dead!'

The blows, and the words, sent shock waves through her. 'How do you know he's got a price on his head?' she gasped, trying to free her head from the folds of her skirts.

'How do I know? Because I've seen the poster. His brothers had prices on their heads. The whole family's rotten. His two older brothers are dead but he and his younger brother are wanted. One of the soldiers said the one you were with is like the bloody Scarlet Pimpernel because he keeps disappearing.' His swearing shocked her as much as being beaten. 'Have you been meeting him regularly? What have you been saying to him?' he panted. 'Is it you that has been providing the Sinn Feiners with information?'

'What information? I don't know what you mean,' she croaked, catching her breath as another blow landed.

Adam Rhoades leaned against the foot of the bed, the switch dangling from his hand, and said harshly, 'Did you know that another army barracks has been attacked and several men killed? Also a goods train has been disrailed. Becky, Shaun O'Neill is implicated, and if he's involved then it must go without saying that his brother is as well.'

Rebekah was filled with dismay. 'I don't know anything about that! I only met him today outside Old Mary's. She's an old neighbour of his mother's.'

There was a silence and she felt the bed give as her father sat on it. 'You're telling me the truth about only meeting him today?' His voice was a little more controlled.

'Yes!' She struggled again to free her head. How dare he degrade her in such a way at her age. She would never forgive him! Never!

'Perhaps it was him the soldiers were looking for?' he muttered angrily. She remained silent and when she did not answer the switch came down again but there was less strength in the blow. 'Don't you know better than to get involved with a man like that?' His voice trembled. 'Why was it you took so long to reach Trinity? Did you flirt with him?'

'No!; She stopped struggling and lay still.

'I can't emphasise too much, Becky, the danger you could have been in. We've had friends disappear. He could have known who you were and tried to get to me through you.'

'Papa, he didn't know who I was!' she cried, her fingers clenching on the bedspread as she searched for the right words to channel his thoughts into a different direction. 'It wasn't like you say at all. We walked as far as the bay because it was such a nice day, and he told me a story about the Land of the Ever Young.'

'What?' He sounded disbelieving.

'It's the truth.' She crossed her fingers.

Her father made a disgusted noise. 'Faery tales! The man's a dreamer and a fool. That's the trouble with some of these rebels. They lack a sense of reality.'

'Yes, Papa.' She was suddenly thinking that Daniel had seemed the most real person she had ever met.

There was a silence and she felt her father pull down her skirts. Relief made her body sag. Then he demanded, 'But why did you go with him in the first place?'

Rebekah tensed again but thought quickly. 'He wanted to know how Old Mary had been. He hadn't seen her for a while.'

The room was silent again but for the sound of his heavy breathing. 'I hope that's the truth, Becky. I've never known you to lie to me before, but – '

'It is the truth,' she said in a low voice. 'And don't be thinking, Papa, that he'll try and see me again because I told him that we were leaving Ireland.'

'Good!' He sighed. 'Thank God we're going at last. Your poor mother worrying about everything and everybody. The

26

never knowing who might be next.' He wiped a hand over his sweaty face. 'We should have gone years ago.'

'But we're going now,' she said. 'Mama will get better.'

'Yes. But there's nothing definite settled. There'll be uncertainties still, but I've been thrifty so that's in our favour.' He stared at the switch in his hand and violently threw it across the room. 'I shouldn't have hit you so hard,' he said jerkily. 'I'll send Hannah up and she can wash and anoint the weals.'

'No!'

He stood up, frowning. 'I don't want to be upsetting your mother. There's been enough of that lately due to that aunt of yours – so no mention of this, and I'll expect you down to dinner.' He held out a hand. 'I'll see you to your room.'

She ignored his hand, shrinking from physical contact with him, and got herself up.

He left Rebekah outside her room and within moments she was lying on her stomach on the bed, easing off her T-strap shoes. She was in pain, and her emotions were a tangle of hurt, anger, guilt and resentment. She could understand her father's fears but was still shocked by his violent reaction to having seen her in Daniel's company. He had never been an over-indulgent father but he had been approachable, if on the whole leaving most of the decisions concerning her upbringing to her mother. Only in the matter of religion had he insisted that she attend his church, although he had never quarrelled with her mother's insistence that teaching her something about Quaker beliefs would not harm her. Only in the last two years had father and daughter rubbed each other up the wrong way. He had found her a job in the tax department where he had a position of authority. (The previous man had left because of the tenuous hold the British government had in Ireland.) Making friends had not been easy and young men had been wary about approaching her. In a way life had become simpler when her mother had collapsed while shopping and she had to give up her job.

As Becky remembered the tedium of those earlier months of her mother's illness, she compared her life then with what had happened today. Her mother had been frightened to be in the house alone, and scared of going outdoors. Becky had been almost completely tied to her. She remembered how relieved she had been when Hannah first arrived, until she had got to know her better. As an example of a Quaker and Liverpudlian, Becky could have been put off both if it had not been for her mother. Being cast out of the Liverpudlian meeting house had not embittered her. She had a genuine love for her home town, a belief in the brotherhood of all men and women, and abhorred violence. If Becky had not met Daniel she would have had little to regret in leaving Dublin. It was no longer the safe place of her childhood.

Were her father's suspicions about Daniel true? She did not want to believe that he was a killer. The word sent a shiver through her, conjuring up images. Then she remembered his words and the feel of his arms and decided that it was a good job that they were going because she would have found it difficult to turn him down if he had asked her out again. She forced herself on to her knees. It would have been much more sensible if she had not waited for him and gone to meet Willie, who because he was unexciting caused little disturbance to her emotions.

As Rebekah began to undress, Daniel's words about the softness of her skin came to mind. She imagined his mouth on her naked flesh and grew hot and damp and tingly. She gave up undressing to reach for her brassbound leather Bible on the old-fashioned bedside cabinet. Her sleeve caught the angel holding a candle and she dropped the Bible quickly to save the candleholder from breaking. It belonged to the owner of the house as did most of the furnishing in the place. He had left for England when the troubles started and as they had been living in a small damp house, her mother had coaxed her father into renting this one, even though it was too large for them, the furniture old-fashioned, and only downstairs lit by gas.

Replacing the angel, she picked up her Bible again. She should be asking God's forgiveness for lying, seeking perfection instead of thinking thoughts which she felt sure her parents wouldn't approve of. She remembered the girls who had come to the house during the war to fetch their younger brothers and sisters whom her mother had taken in, fed with soup and bread, and attempted to teach them their letters. The girls had talked about boys and men, love, and how babies were made.

28

A door downstairs opened and Becky heard Hannah's sharp tones mingling with her father's deeper ones. Quickly the Bible was placed haphazardly on the bedside cabinet and she rushed over to the half-empty wardrobe and brought out a primrose-coloured georgette dinner frock, the only such garment she had. From the dressing table she took some cotton knickers and a scarf. For a moment she stood naked, twisting to see and gingerly feeling the weals across her lower back and buttocks. Then she dragged on a white cotton robe and went over to the mahogany and marble washstand.

By the time Hannah knocked on the door Rebekah was washed and dressed, with the scarf providing a little extra padding beneath her knickers. 'Come in!' she rose from her seated position in front of the oval mirror on the dressing table. 'What is it, Hannah?' she asked cheerfully.

The maid's face fell. 'I thought I heard – '

'Heard what, Hannah? The noise I made earlier because there was a spider in the room?'

'A spider?'

'Yes. I can't abide the creatures. All those legs!' She shivered.

Hannah sniffed and her dark eyes were disappointed. 'It's downright foolish to be scared of an insect. Just put yer foot on them and squash 'em – that's what I do.'

'You're so much braver than me.' Rebekah smiled sweetly, wondering how the Quaker maid taught to abhor violence could find pleasure in the idea of her suffering and the death of a spider.

The maid did not smile back. 'Yer father said that thee wanted me.'

'It's all right now, I managed without your help, but if you could take my dirty clothes, please?'

Hannah sniffed and did not move. Instead she folded her arms across her non-existent bosom. 'Talked thy way out of trouble after all did thee?'

Rebekah raised her eyebrows. 'What trouble, Hannah? I told the truth – that I went to see Old Mary and walked for a while in the fresh air. That was something you could have told Mama and Papa about earlier,' she rebuked gently. 'Now – my dirty clothes.' Adding, just to make the maid squirm a little,

29

'Watch out for lice. Old Mary isn't fussy when it comes to washing.'

The maid hesitated, then moved to pick up the untidy sprawl of clothing on the floor. 'Yer father's still annoyed about something,' she muttered, straightening. 'Came in earlier with his face all twisted and slammed his paper down on the hall table – nearly knocked off the lamp that I'd trimmed and filled this morning – but he keeps hold of a piece of paper and he was looking at that very letter when I left him just now. I wonder what's in it?'

'If it's something bad, I'll soon find out,' murmured Rebekah.

'I suppose so,' grunted Hannah, moving towards the door. Rebekah returned to twisting her heavy tawny hair in a coil at the nape of her neck. For a moment her fingers itched for the scissors before commonsense asserted itself. Papa would only see cutting her hair as an act of defiance and the thought that he might again respond violently was enough for her to put the notion aside.

He was standing on the landing when she came out of her bedroom. He had changed into grey flannel trousers and a clean shirt and collar. His dark hair was parted neatly on one side and he had shaved. For a moment she wondered if he was going to bring up the subject of Daniel again and tensed, but he said nothing, only flicking the embroidery round the neck of her frock before proceeding downstairs.

They entered the dining room, to find her mother fiddling with an arrangement of scarlet and lemon dahlias. The gaslight glowed on cutlery and glass and turned Rebekah's mother's complexion the colour of parchment. She wore an Edwardian dark green frock with a high neck, and a heavily fringed crochet shawl was draped about her shoulders. Her slender hand was cool where it touched Rebekah's. 'Such a worry you've had me in, Becky, but your father's explained that you were with Old Mary so let's eat. I suppose you're hungry as usual.'

Rebekah avoided looking at her father, trying to control the anger that rose inside her, and schooled her features as she seated herself on a balloon-backed chair.

Hannah bustled in carrying a tureen. 'Here's some pea soup for yer and I don't want it getting cold,' she grunted. 'It's full of the juices from the beef that I boiled yesterday.'

It smelt delicious and there was silence as Rebekah's father said grace. There was no conversation while they ate their meal. After the soup came cold beef, potatoes and mashed turnip. For pudding there was stewed plums and baked custard. It was not until tea was poured that her father spoke. 'I've had an answer from the agent, Sally.'

His wife looked across at him hastily. 'What agent?'

'The shipping agent.' His tone was irritable.

'Why should you write to a shipping agent?' Her voice trembled.

'For berths to America, of course,' he said in a tightly controlled voice, stirring his tea jerkily so that it spilt in the saucer. 'I wrote to Cunard's in Liverpool, thinking that way I could get preference and the most comfortable passage for you. No expense was to be spared. I even gave them a draft on my bank. Now they write and tell me that all berths on their ships were taken up weeks ago. That I should have booked a passage earlier.'

Rebekah exchanged glances with her mother, who was obviously trying hard to conceal her relief. 'Does that mean we won't be going to American then?'

'Of course it doesn't!' Her husband slammed the table. 'How many times do I have to tell you, Sal, it'll be a better life for us there. The Ireland we know is finished. And England's going to find it difficult financially. The war cost them! America's the place.'

'But if there's no berths,' murmured his wife, pleating a fold of the tablecloth. 'What can we do?'

'There's other shipping lines,' he said firmly. 'They probably won't be as comfortable but we'll have to put up with that.'

'Adam, if you're doing this for me,' she said hesitantly, 'as I've said before, there's no need. A new life in a new land is for those just beginning. I feel too old to start up again. Liverpool would suit – '

'No!' His mouth thinned and he scrunched the letter in his hand. 'I don't feel too old, and you only feel like that because of what it's been like here for the last couple of years. You'll

31

soon perk up once we're away from the fighting. There's lots of folk emigrating who are as old as us, and travelling further. Since the war they want to leave Europe. It's that sister of yours who wants you to stay in Liverpool. And why should we, Sal? For years, nothing! We were treated like lepers. Not a penny farthing did your father ever give you. We had to struggle when he could have made it a bit easier for you.'

'I know, I know!' She put a hand to her mouth and her throat moved jerkily. When she spoke again, her voice shook. 'Don't let's go over all that again, please. Will you still allow me some time with Esther? She was like a mother to me, if you remember?'

'Bossy enough!' he interposed.

'She couldn't help that.' A shadow crossed his wife's face. 'You had your mother to old age. Can we still stay with Esther? Once we leave for America, you know that it's unlikely I'll ever see her again.'

He nodded slowly. 'I won't deny you some time with your sister. But if she upsets you by playing her tricks, like she did when she tried to separate us when first we met, then we'll find lodgings elsewhere.' He patted her hand before taking up his teacup. 'It might be best for me to see if we can leave tomorrow.'

'But I haven't finished packing,' said Rebekah in a startled voice, her thoughts moving swiftly into the present instead of dwelling on her parents' past.

Her father's eyebrows came together. 'Then you shouldn't have wasted time visiting that old woman and going for walks,' he said fiercely. 'Get a move on, miss, because what doesn't get packed will be left behind.'

Rebekah decided it would be wisest to show willing and rose with stiff awkward movements, hoping that her mother would not see anything amiss. She was in pain and did not want to go to America. It would be even stranger than Liverpool and so far away from home. As for Daniel, there would be no chance of ever seeing him again. Her resentment against her father hardened as she went as quickly as she could out of the dining room, barely able to take in that such great changes in her life were happening. Soon they would leave Ireland for ever.

Chapter Three

The Irish ferry boat steamed up the Mersey, having safely manoeuvred the sandbanks in the estuary and avoided the numerous craft in the river. Rebekah had never seen so many ships and growing excitement now replaced the regret she had felt when she had seen Ireland becoming a tiny smudge on the horizon. They had not departed as early as her father had wished because there had been too much to do.

Yesterday tempers had been fraught and only Hannah had gone about her tasks with a smile on her face that had maddened Rebekah. She had handed back her discarded clothing, saying that there was no way that she could get them dry if she washed them. So Rebekah's dirty clothes had been stuffed in a cloth bag with her nightdress, tortoise and ivory dressing table set, her Bible, and an old doll given her by her dead paternal grandmother which she could not bring herself to part with.

Now her father's hand descended heavily on her shoulder and she tensed. 'You must stay close to Hannah. If you get separated in the crush, wait outside the Riverside Station and we'll find you there.'

'Don't thee be worrying, Mr Rhoades,' said Hannah with a satisfied smile. 'I'll watch her like a hawk.'

Rebekah contained her impatience. 'Papa, I do have a tongue in my head. I'm not a child.'

'It might be better if you were,' Adam said shortly, and before Rebekah could say another word he was gone.

She frowned, guessing that he was making an oblique reference to the episode with Daniel O'Neill. She had not been able to get him out of her mind but now she gave her attention to Liverpool. Along the seafront sprawled its famous docks and its bustling landing stage. It seemed enormous after Dublin.

'Soon be getting off now, and thou wilt be needing all thy wits about thee then,' said Hannah, picking up her bag. 'Babylon it is all around dockland. There's pickpockets and lads wanting to carry thy bag who'd have the last farthing off a one-legged beggar. Stick close to me as thy father said, and hold on to everything.'

Rebekah noted the change in the sound of the ship's engines and watched the sudden surge of foaming water about the hull. Now they were only yards from land, and ropes thicker than a man's arm were being thrown from ship to the landing stage. On shore, a little way back, she could see a roof with the words RIVERSIDE STATION painted on it.

Hannah seized her wrist. Irritated, Rebekah pulled herself free, not seeing any reason to hurry as she gazed on the people that crowded the deck. She spotted her mother, a little more colour in her cheeks than normal, who gave her a faint smile. 'Stay close to Hannah,' she called, before suddenly disappearing from Rebekah's sight as people surged towards the gangway.

No sooner did Rebekah and Hannah set foot on land than they were besieged by several youths. A huge burly lad, with a thatch of red hair, freckles, and an ingratiating smile which revealed several gaps where teeth were missing, shouldered his rivals out of the way and laid a hand on Rebekah's luggage. 'Carry yer bag, miss?'

'Thou wilt not,' Hannah intervened sharply, poking her elbow into his upper arm.

He barely spared her a glance but thrust a widespread hand on her face and pushed hard. She went toppling backwards. 'If yer in need of lodgings I can show yer a decent place,' he said, as if Hannah's interruption had not taken place.

Rebekah had no time to enjoy the spectacle of Hannah sprawling but had to tug hard on her bag. 'Will you let go? I can carry my own bag – and I don't need lodgings because I'm staying with my aunt.'

His smile slipped. 'That's alright, luv. I'll still get yer a cab.' And he gave a heave that took the bag clean out of her grasp.

'Hey, give me it back!' she cried indignantly.

He did not even spare Rebekah a backward glance but was away. Her temper rose and she gave chase. It was not easy keeping her quarry in view. The Prince's landing stage was a busy place at most times and it was worse today because several large ships had docked. Still she managed to weave her way through the crowd to catch up with him and seize hold of her bag. 'Got you.'

Several heads swivelled in their direction as he turned with an ugly expression on his face and surprised her by sneering. 'Hey now, what's this, little thief! Have yer seen this one, folks?' he yelled, looking about him. 'Real barefaced she is.'

'It's you that's the thief,' she panted, enraged, swinging her free hand and punching him on the nose.

Tears started in his eyes and a ex-serviceman, selling matches, chortled, 'Serves yer right, Joe.'

'Yer little cow,' he said in a muffled voice, covering his nose a moment before bringing down his fist. The blow would have stunned Rebekah if she had not swerved while tugging at her bag. The clasp gave and out tumbled a flesh-coloured lawn nightgown.

She snatched it up from the damp, dirty ground. 'Whose bag is it?' she cried triumphantly. 'Do you wear skirts?' Several people laughed.

'It's me mam's,' he snapped, obviously determined not to be bested as he struggled with her.

'Yer haven't a mam,' called a voice. 'Give the girl her stuff back.'

'That's right,' said Rebekah. 'Give me it back.'

Joe's eyes narrowed and he pulled so hard on the bag that she was catapulted against him. 'I take orders from no one. Yer've got a bloody nerve, girl,' he hissed in her face. 'I could squash yer as soon as look at yer. Yer don't think any of this lot'll help yer.'

'Get your hands off me.' She was proud that her voice did not betray her.

He stared at her, almost eyeball to eyeball, and laughed. 'Yer gonna make me?'

Before she could speak, a voice said, 'She mightn't be able to but I can.' The words uttered in the familiar Irish brogue

35

took both of them by surprise and Rebekah twisted in Joe's grasp.

Daniel did not pause in his advance on them. 'It's a fine mess your father's making of looking after you.'

Rebekah felt a lifting of her spirits. 'He's with Mama. I was with Hannah but this – this person pushed her in the face.'

'Hardly friendly.' He clenched a fist. 'If he doesn't take his filthy hands off you, I'll knock his block off.'

'I wouldn't try it, Paddy.' Joe eyed Daniel up and down uneasily. 'You might be taller than me but I've got the weight, see – as well as a pile of mates I can call on.'

Daniel shrugged. 'I don't like fighting a lad of your age but if you're so keen, boyo, I've got a few friends I could whistle up. So let her go.'

Joe reached for his belt but before he could pull out the knife that was there, Daniel made his move. Rebekah was forcibly swung out of the way and his fist made contact with Joe's jaw. He crumpled slowly to the ground.

'Let's get out of here,' said Daniel, seizing her wrist and getting them lost in the crowd in seconds.

'Where are we going?' Her grip tightened on her bag as she almost fell over her feet in her attempt to keep up, cram her nightdress back in her bag, and look at him at the same time.

'Out of sight, out of reach. Joe's a regular here. He's bound to have mates somewhere.'

'I shouldn't have got you involved in a fight,' she said, her breathing flurried.

He smiled. 'That was a good punch on the nose you gave him.'

'You saw it?' she gasped. 'Perhaps if I hadn't hit him, he mightn't have got tough with me. I lost my temper.'

'You've got to stand up to some people.'

She shook her head. 'I should have turned the other cheek.'

He ignored that remark and said, 'Where are your mama and papa?'

'Seeing to the luggage, I suppose. I'm to meet them at the Riverside Station if I get lost.' She looked about her. 'I *am* lost.'

'We're only going to the end of the landing stage.'

'You've been here before?'

'I told you, I've got relatives in Liverpool.'

There was a pause before she said, 'Why didn't you tell me you were coming?'

'I wasn't sure if it was the right thing to do.' He glanced at her. 'Mam always said, "When in doubt, say nowt." Besides, I had our Shaun to get out of trouble.'

'He's here?' Involuntarily she glanced about them.

He grimaced. 'Not right here and now. We came yesterday.'

She stopped abruptly. 'Then there is a price on your heads?'

He halted. 'Now who's told you that?'

'My father.' Her voice was low. 'I hoped it wasn't true. But it is, isn't it?'

Daniel was silent for several minutes, then he said vehemently, 'I'm no killer! My brothers gave the family a bad name. What made your father mention it? Did you tell him about us?'

'No!' She frowned. 'He saw us together. I got a hiding just for being in your company.'

'I'm sorry.' He squeezed her fingers.

'It's not your fault. He thought I'd been passing you information for I.R.B. activities. He's been overwrought lately. I told you that the other day.'

'I'm still sorry he hit you. What did you tell him about us?' They had halted almost at the far end of the landing stage and her gaze took in the khaki-coloured waters and beyond them Birkenhead and its new shipyards. 'I told him I'd met you at Old Mary's – that I'd walked with you because you wanted to know how she was.'

'He believed you?' His gaze followed hers across the water.

'I don't make a habit of lying. For the first time in my life he hit me – then asked questions.'

He held her hand tightly. 'I'm sorry again.'

'I know. You don't have to keep saying it. Will you be staying in Liverpool?'

'I'm not sure what I'm doing. You?'

'Father's determined that we're going to America.' She told him what had passed at the dinner table.

'He'll get berths,' said Daniel positively. 'There's other shipping lines.'

'I don't know how quickly, though. It could take time.' She glanced at him and he shook his head.

'You mustn't be thinking what you're thinking.' He released her hand. 'We both agreed that it's pointless us getting to know each other.'

She tossed her plait back over her shoulder, surprised at his perception. 'I know. And it would be difficult meeting.'

'It could be dangerous too.'

'Even here?' she whispered.

He added hastily, 'If your father saw us together again, it wouldn't be much fun for either of us.'

'Could he have you arrested?' She moved away from him and he followed.

'Probably.'

They were both silent, and she felt if he did not speak and say something positive then she would burst. He did not and she rushed into saying, 'Where are you going now?'

'To my aunt's. I only came to see if – ' He stopped and stared over the river.

'To see what?'

'The ships.' He glanced at her. 'What are you doing tomorrow?'

'I don't know,' she said quickly. 'If you wanted to – '

'Aye! I'm prepared to take a chance.'

'Where do we meet?'

'You don't know anywhere.' He smiled.

'Here?' Her eyes were bright.

He nodded. 'One o'clock?'

'Fine.'

He leaned towards her and their lips met briefly. 'Till tomorrow then,' he said, and vanished into the crowd.

Rebekah wondered if she was quite mad but she was smiling as she turned and ran towards the customs shed. She went through and headed for the railway station. As she neared it she saw her mother and Hannah waiting. 'Where have you been? We've been worrying, thinking you might have been carried off and shipped to China!' Her mother's voice was lively.

'China?'

'Tea clippers used to race there and back in the old days.' Her mother put a hand through her arm. 'Oh, it's so good to be home! Do you know, Becky, the Liver building wasn't built when I was last here. Isn't it grand? And the docks – they seemed to have spread out.'

Hannah interrupted her with a sniff. 'I was robbed lying on the ground. Sum things don't change.'

'Poor Hannah!' Rebekah could spare her a smile. She was thinking no further than tomorrow and nothing could cast a cloud on her spirits. 'Did you have much stolen. I got my bag back.'

The maid sniffed again. 'Me purse. Yer father and mother came before I could suffer any more insults from those black-hearted scoundrels. Not fit for mackerel bait, they ain't.'

'Where is Papa?' asked Rebekah, quickly changing the subject.

'Arranging transport for the bulk of our baggage,' replied her mother. 'He said that we were not to wait but to get a taxi to your aunt's. But I was just thinking, love, if your legs are like mine then a walk will do them good. Hannah can get the tram if she wants.'

'I will,' said the maid, and accepted her fare and left them.

Rebekah thought about warning her mother against walking too far, she had been resting a lot since her illness. But then Rebekah considered how useful walking about the town might be in getting to know her way about.

They went under the overhead railway and passed the sailor's church. Her mother told her that just over a hundred years ago there had been a terrible accident during Sunday service when part of the steeple had collapsed, killing more than twenty people. Further on she pointed out the town hall. 'When my father tried to stop me going out with your papa, he told me how there'd been a Fenian plot to blow up the town hall in 1881. You know that the Fenians were sort of forerunners of the Irish Republican Brotherhood?' Rebekah nodded. 'They caught the men, and thank God the town hall is still here. But Father thought the telling might prevent me wanting to marry your papa. He had a habit of tarring all the Irish with the same brush.'

Rebekah said nothing but she was thinking of what her father had said about Daniel. By the time they came in sight of the Graeco-Roman style St George's Hall, built during Victoria's reign, her mother was tiring so they caught a tram in

Lime Street. Rebekah asked about places and roads, some of which her mother did not know, although she pointed out the Royal Hippodrome in West Derby Road. 'When I was about twelve, my father's sister came down from Bolton. She took me to a variety show. It was a revelation. I enjoyed the acts and went again with a friend when I was older, but I never told Papa or Esther. Aunt Maggie wasn't a bit like other Quakers I knew. She had a yen for the stage, and soon after left the Society of Friends and went to London. The only time Papa mentioned her again was years later when he said I was as flighty as her. I remember I replied that I looked upon that as a compliment. That she was the best in the family.' Her eyes gleamed. 'He nearly hit me. Sad. I would have liked to have seen her again.'

Rebekah smiled. Liverpool seemed to be bringing out a different side to her mother and she was glad to see it.

They descended from the tram a couple of stops later and walked up a road of red-brick houses with long front gardens. Rebekah had visualised something grander because her father had told her that Aunt Esther had come into the family fortune and it had been quite substantial. They stopped at a house with a green front door with a black wrought iron knocker on it.

Footsteps hurried in response to their knock and the door opened to reveal Aunt Esther. She was small and round, with fluffy yellow-white hair. The three of them stared at each other then the two sisters flung their arms around each other.

'Oh, Sarah,' cried Esther, tears in her eyes as she crushed her against her black serge bosom. 'It's so good to see thee. If I'd know that thou were definitely arriving today, I would have come to meet thee.'

'It doesn't matter. We're here now.' Sarah's voice was unsteady as she disentangled herself from her sister's arms and seized Rebekah's hand. 'This is Becky. I think she's got a look of our side of the family, don't you?'

'Oh, yes!' She's got Mother's eyes. Thou art very welcome, Rebekah.'

'Thank you.' She suffered her aunt's embrace, then was pulled inside the house.

'It's been so long, Sarah,' said her aunt. 'I hope thee can stay for weeks and weeks. Hannah was saying something about America?'

'Yes,' Sarah sighed.

Rebekah squeezed her hand. 'It's Papa's idea, Aunt Esther.'

Her mother nodded. 'We've tried out best to dissuade him, but there's no moving him. He's adamant.'

'Adam always was,' said Esther, her lips compressing in an uncompromising line. 'Hannah said that he left thee to fend for thyselves at the Pierhead. No doubt it's his selfishness as well as the fighting that's worn thy nerves down. Did Hannah give thee the Dr Cassell's tablets I sent? I know plenty of people who swear by them, and I've taken them myself since Papa died.'

Sarah said warmly, 'I've taken the tablets, and I believe they have done me some good. It was kind of you – and to send Hannah too. She's such a good worker. But please don't speak of Adam in such a way.'

'Thou still won't have a word said against him,' said Esther in resigned tones. 'Such loyalty does thee credit, sister.'

'A wife has to stand alongside her husband.' Sarah smiled. 'Try and get on with him, Esther. I know the pair of you could never see eye to eye in the past, but do try now. Papa tried to browbeat Adam into doing what he wanted and it was the biggest mistake he ever made.' She paused long enough for her sister to nod, then added, 'Now how about a cup of tea? I'm parched.'

'Hannah will make us a cup,' said Esther, leading the way. 'It was quite a sacrifice sending her to thee. The girl I've had to put up with in her place doesn't do half the work, and walked out this morning just because I rightfully complained about the way she hung the clean curtains – she said she'd be happier working at that new Woolworths! Young girls these days! It's the war and this suffragette movement. It's unsettled them.'

'The movement was going in our day,' murmured Sarah, entering a back room and looking about her, before sinking into an armchair.

'Yes, but we didn't get involved. There was too much work to do.'

'That's true. But it's no different for women today. They still work hard.' She smiled at her daughter. 'Some have to work harder.'

'But there's many who are just out for a good time,' protested Esther.

'It's the war,' said Rebekah, who had knelt on a tiger rug at her mother's feet.

Her mother nodded. 'Thousands of women have lost the chance of marriage, and there's thousands more who have to be father and mother to their children. Even if more women get the vote, there's no easy cure for what ails most girls today.'

'Let's not talk about it,' said Esther, sitting in the other armchair. 'Instead tell me what hast thou been doing all those years in Ireland, and why that husband of thine wants to go to America.'

Sarah shook her head. 'I'm not ready to talk about Ireland. You've no idea how the fighting – ' Her voice trailed off.

'Thou should never have left Liverpool.' Esther's voice held a fierce note. 'Adam could have accepted our ways.'

'Don't let's go over that again.' Sarah's face stiffened. 'Why not tell me who bought the shop? And what happened to . . .'

Rebekah leaned back against the leg of her mother's chair and listened to the two sisters talk. They gossiped about old times and old acquaintances, and not for the first time she wished that she had a sister to confide in. To talk to about Daniel. She let her mind drift, wondering how she could escape tomorrow.

Hannah brought tea and toasted buns. The door knocker sounded and it was Esther who went to answer it because the maid was occupied. Rebekah and her mother exchanged glances and her mother put a finger to her lips.

Rebekah could hardly prevent a smile when she heard her aunt's disgruntled tones. 'It's thee! I suppose thou had best come in.'

'You always did have a warm welcome for me, Esther,' said Adam in a surprisingly pleasant voice. 'You'll be pleased to know that I won't be staying above a day or two.'

'Why is that?' Esther's dismay was obvious. 'I haven't said anything so terrible yet.'

'No, but you will,' he said grimly. 'I've booked berths for us on a ship going to America.'

'Not already,' cried Esther. 'Thou could have given Sarah and me some time. We've hardly had chance to – '

'There's been plenty of chances for you during the last twenty years,' he rasped.

'No, there wasn't. Thou never did try to understand our way. And now – '

Rebekah got to her feet at the same time as her mother, who called, 'Will you two please stop! My nerves can't stand it!'

Her father came into the sitting room. There was a sullen expression on his face.

Rebekah said quickly, 'When are we going, Papa?'

His expression lightened. 'I can see you're as impatient as I am to be on our way, Becky. I'm glad you're coming round to my way of thinking.'

'I didn't say that, Papa,' she murmured. 'I only asked when we were leaving Liverpool. And how did you manage to arrange it so quickly?'

He looked towards her mother. 'I put it down to the hand of God myself,' he said with heavy humour. 'No doubt, Sal, you and Esther will disagree.'

'Maybe,' said her mother, unsmiling. 'Just answer Becky's questions.'

Slowly he took his pipe from a pocket and placed it between his teeth. 'When I was seeing to our luggage I literally bumped into the son of the man who bought our old farm.' He paused to search for matches. 'The father's dead and the brother who inherited was killed in the war. The second son now owns the father's shipping line as well as the estate in Ireland. Joshua remembered me.' He lit up. The three women waited in silence for him to continue, and once he had his pipe going to his satisfaction he did so. 'We now have a cabin to ourselves on one of his ships. With a bit of luck we'll be leaving on Monday.' There was the slightest hint of defiance in his tones. 'The ship is still short of crew but they should be signed on over the weekend.'

Rebekah glanced at her mother and on seeing her expression, anger bubbled up inside her. 'Couldn't you have allowed

43

Mama a few more days?' she hissed. 'Why the rush to get to America?'

Her father turned on her. 'You wouldn't understand! It was bad enough when we left for Ireland twenty years ago. Your mother was homesick for ages. It's better my way, you'll see. Now how about a cup of tea?' His gaze passed over the three of them just as Hannah came into the room.

'Tea! I know what I'd like to do with you and a cup of tea,' said Sarah in a seething voice. 'How could you arrange everything without consulting me? You could have given me more time.' She swept out of the room. Esther glared at Adam and followed her sister.

There was a silence. 'Well,' he snapped, 'are you going to walk out too, miss, or are you going to show me some respect and gratitude by pouring me a cup of tea?'

Before Rebekah could say or do anything, Hannah chipped in 'I'll do thee a cup of tea, sir.' She picked up a fine bone china cup decorated with red-purple roses and filled it to the brim. There was a wide smile on her bony face. 'I'm sure thee's right and are only doing what yer think best for thy family. As yer know, two of me brothers are in America. It's a fine place. They never want to come home.'

'Who'd want to come home to you?' Rebekah could not resist saying, and walked out of the room. Her aunt's voice could be heard from the direction of the parlour, and although the door was shut Rebekah could clearly hear what was being said.

'There's no reason why thou hast to go to America, Sarah. I've got enough money to keep the three of us.'

'You're suggesting I leave Adam!' Her mother gave a sharp laugh. 'It's easy to see that you've never married, Esther.'

'I looked after Papa and that was no piece of cake,' retorted her aunt. 'I know what men are like. They like their own way. Only thinking of themselves. Papa treated me like a skivvy, and from the look of thee Adam hasn't behaved any better in that Godforsaken country.'

'You know nothing about my life there, only what I've told you of in the last year and that's not Adam's fault! You don't know him.' Her mother's voice had altered, and sounded weary.

'A handsome face and a beguiling way with him.' Her aunt sniffed.

'There's more to Adam than that but you never wanted to see it.'

'I'd brought thee up. I didn't want to lose thee.'

'I can understand that.' There was a pause. 'Don't let's quarrel. We have to make the most of the time we have.'

'Then thou art going to America?' The words were uttered in a disgruntled voice.

'I can't leave my husband just because you want me to stay here!' There was silence and her aunt murmured something Rebekah could not catch. Then her mother said, 'I'll try and make him change his mind but I think it'll be a waste of time.'

There was movement towards the door and Rebekah backed away and sat on the stairs as the two women came out. 'Hannah's making up to Papa,' she murmured.

Esther stared at her. 'Hannah! Not her! She doesn't like men.'

'I thought that myself but perhaps it's Papa's handsome face,' she said lightly.

Her aunt's mouth tightened. 'Handsome is as handsome does. He won't get much change out of Hannah, whatever he says and does. I'm not going back in there right now. If thou likes I could show thee thy rooms?'

'I think we could all do with time to calm down,' said Rebekah's mother. 'Come on, Becky. Grab your case.'

She nodded, considering it wiser to do as suggested, and followed the two sisters upstairs.

As Rebekah unpacked her nightdress, toothbrush and toothpowder, her aunt came back into the room. She sat on the bed, her expression determined. 'Thou doesn't want to go to America, does thee, Rebekah?'

'It doesn't matter what I want,' she said honestly.

Esther nodded and sighed. 'It's always been that way. Girls have to do what they're told. Duty – it's a burden. But thou cares what thy mother wants? Thou wants her to be happy?'

'She wouldn't be happy without Papa,' said Rebekah positively. She glanced at her aunt. 'I heard you and Mama talking. It's no use, Aunt Esther. If Papa has made up his mind, I don't think he's going to change it. Especially when he's already got the tickets.'

Esther played with the bobbles round the shade of the beside lamp. 'Thou doesn't think thee can change his mind?'

'Me?' Rebekah was startled. 'I doubt it.'

'Some fathers and daughters are very close.' A frown creased her plump face and she added with apparent difficulty, 'Papa was very fond of thy mother. As I was. The light went out of our lives when she left. If thou could persuade – '

Rebekah shook her head. 'I'm sorry, Aunt Esther, but Mama's your best bet. Papa and I aren't the best of friends at the moment. Now, is there any chance of my having a bath?'

Her aunt nodded and with a gloomy expression took her outside, indicating the bathroom before going downstairs.

Rebekah lay in bed, listening. Eavesdropping had always been the only way she could obtain the information that her parents thought they should keep from her. Even here in her aunt's house it did not seem to have occurred to them that they could be overhead. Her bedroom window was slightly ajar and theirs next door must also be open. Her father was speaking, stressing each word. 'Why did we leave Dublin, Sal? To get away from the fighting, that's why. And Liverpool isn't far enough away for me. Joshua Green told me that there's cells of the I.R.A. over here, causing as much trouble as they can by arson and cutting telegraph wires. You know the way they work to create chaos.'

'Esther hasn't mentioned anything about that,' responded her mother in that controlled way of speaking she had when her nerves were fraught and she was on the brink of tears.

'She wouldn't, would she?' he insisted. 'It's in her interests to keep quiet.'

'She wouldn't think of that!' Her mother's voice trembled. 'Esther might have her faults but she wouldn't deliberately keep something like that to herself.'

'Perhaps not,' he said mildly, before adding, 'What I'd like to know is, if she cared so much about you, why haven't we heard from her in all these years?'

'You know why! Father didn't tell her about my letters.'

'So she says. More likely she wanted to keep all his money for herself.'

'You can think what you like. I don't believe that.'

46

'You wouldn't.' His voice had softened. 'You like to think the best of everybody. Believe me, Sal, it's our future I'm thinking about in going to America.'

'I don't doubt that.' She sighed. 'But what if Esther takes ill? She has no one close.'

'She has Hannah. She'll be all right.'

There was a short silence and her mother said something Rebekah did not catch because she was distracted by her own thoughts about Hannah. When her father spoke again, his manner had changed altogether. He sounded excited. 'There's a good chance of my already having a position to go to in America, Sal! I'll be seeing Joshua Green tomorrow about it. You said that you wanted to do some shopping. Well, that fits in fine with my plans. I'll give you some extra money and you can go into town with Esther and Becky and buy some new clothes.'

'Becky does need some new things,' said her mother thoughtfully. 'She's had little chance in the last few years of going on a shopping spree.'

'Aye, well, there's been little chance for any of us to go on shopping sprees and have a good time. It'll be different in America, you wait and see.' The voices grew faint and Rebekah presumed they had moved away from the window. Everything else was inaudible.

She lay staring out the window at the night sky, thinking that it was a real shame they were not staying in Liverpool. Still, at least they were going shopping in town tomorrow. Surely there would be an opportunity for her to get away and meet Daniel? All she had to do was to watch out for it.

Chapter Four

'I'm sure Papa would be against you having your hair cut.' Rebekah's mother looked at her anxiously as they stood in front of Hill's Hairdressers in Ranelagh Street not far from Lewis's great store where Sarah had just purchased a pair of black glacé kid shoes with patent leather toecaps for her daughter.

'But everyone's cutting their hair now,' insisted Rebekah.

'You've got such lovely hair,' protested her mother. 'Your father wouldn't like it cut. Besides it would be such a shame to –'

'Please, Mama,' she said coaxingly. 'It's always braided and generally hidden under a hat so nobody sees it.'

'The girl has a point,' interrupted her aunt. They both stared at her. 'Why shouldn't she have her hair bobbed?' She bristled. 'If it's good enough for the upper classes, then who's thy husband to speak against it?'

'The upper classes!' snorted Sarah. 'That argument won't wash with Adam. You're a snob, Esther.'

'No, I'm not,' said she. 'The trouble is, Sarah, thou hast been in the backwoods in Ireland. If thou wants to find a husband for the girl, she has to make the best of herself.'

Her mother gazed at Rebekah and said softly. 'Of course I want a husband for her, but I don't think Adam wants her to marry just anybody.'

Her aunt sniffed. 'He's just the kind of father who doesn't want to see himself replaced in his daughter's affections!' Her gloved fingers twisted her handbag chain so that it dug into her hand. 'Let the girl get her hair cut if she can make an appointment today. If she can't – well, then, her hair will have to stay the way it is.'

Sarah's uncertain gaze went from her sister to Rebekah. She smiled at her mother. 'You can tell him that I went missing and did it without your knowing.'

'I'll do nothing of the sort,' said Sarah with an outward show of calm. 'We'll go and have another look in Lewis's windows while you find out if you can get it cut.'

'Thanks, Mama!' Rebekah hugged her and stared once more at the picture of a fashionable young woman with a cap of deeply waving dark hair before entering the hairdressing salon. If she was lucky then she would tell her mother and her aunt not to wait, that she would find her own way home.

An hour and a half later Rebekah came out of the shop, carrying her hat. Her head felt so light that it might not have been there. She had been told that if Madam was prepared to wait, then they would fit her in. Well, Madam had waited and they had done her a treat. And, she told herself with fingers crossed, she did not care if Papa hit the roof because she was certain that Aunt Esther would take her side.

Setting out for the Pierhead, and knowing that there was plenty of time, Rebekah enjoyed looking in the shops, not only at her new reflection but at the clothes and fancy goods. Her gaze was riveted by a French voile hand-embroidered blouse in George Henry Lee's window but she knew the chances of her buying it were remote. She turned away only to collide with two men deep in conversation. All her brave resolutions vanished and her heart sank as she recognized her father. She averted her face and mumbled an apology, and would have passed unrecognized if his companion had not seized her arm and enquired if she was all right.

Reluctantly she glanced up to see a man, probably of about thirty, pleasant-looking, fair-haired and moustached, with pale blue eyes. At the same instant she heard her father's quick intake of breath and knew him to have identified her.

'Rebekah!' His mouth pursed in the way that she had become familiar with during the last months.

'Yes, Papa?' She forced a smile and pulled her arm out of the man's hold. 'I'm in a hurry – to meet – Mama and aunt Esther in Kardomah's cafe.'

'Never mind that!' Her father's voice cut through her explanation. 'You've had your hair cut! Does your mother know about this, or have you – '

'I think it looks charming,' interrupted his companion, smiling. 'You never told me your daughter was so pretty, Adam. Introduce us.'

Grudgingly her father said, 'Rebekah, this is Joshua Green, the owner of the shipping line we're sailing with. Say your how do you does.'

Knowing that her father could hardly upbraid her in his presence, Rebekah held out her hand and said warmly, 'How do you do, Mr Green? I'm happy to meet you.'

He raised his hat and the blue eyes took on a look of startling awareness as his fingers fastened about hers. 'It's a pleasure to meet you, Miss Rhoades.' His voice was deep. 'It's a pity you're to be in Liverpool such a short time because I would have asked your father's permission to show you the sights.'

'That's kind of you,' she said, surprised.

'I would have enjoyed it.' He smiled and pressed her fingers.

'It's nice of you to say so, but I must go. Thank you.' She withdrew her hand and before her father could say anything else she hurried away, resisting a backward glance to see if they were watching her.

The exchange had wasted time and then she had to stop and ask someone if she was going the right way for the Pierhead. They said she could not miss it if she kept walking straight ahead and down towards the river.

Rebekah did just that but was getting anxious as she neared the Mersey. She glanced up at the Liver clock. It was five past one and immediately she made haste, running up the covered passenger way that led to the landing stage. She need not have worried. Daniel was waiting.

'I thought you mightn't have been able to get away.' His eyes searched her face and she knew it had been right to come.

'I almost didn't get here.' Rebekah took off her hat and shook her head.

50

'You've had your hair cut!'

'Don't you like it?' Her voice was anxious. 'It was my excuse for getting rid of my mother and aunt. And, besides, I've wanted to get it cut for ages. Long hair is a nuisance.'

'I thought you were perfect as you were. But, yes, I like it.' He smiled as she blushed.

'Papa almost didn't recognise me. I bumped into him in Church Street. Now I'm in trouble! If he had known I was coming to meet you, he'd have gone up in smoke!'

'Then we'd best avoid Church Street if we don't want to see a fire-breathing papa,' he said, offering her his arm. 'Where would you like to go?'

'I'm still only a little the wiser about places,' she murmured, taking his arm. 'All my family seem to be in town so window shopping is out.'

'Best get out of Liverpool then,' said Daniel. 'I'll take you on the Overhead Railway to Seaforth Sands. It's the fastest electric train in England, and the first. We'll be there in no time and you get a great view of the docks and the river.'

'That sounds fine. I've never heard of Seaforth.' She was very aware of the muscular arm beneath her fingers and the smell of his shaving soap. He was all spruced up – clean collar, blue tie, well-brushed dark jacket and grey flannels. She was glad that she had on her best yellow organdie frock and her only pair of silk stockings. They made a fine couple, she thought, feeling warm inside.

'It's a good place for an outing,' he said. 'The tide's out so we'll be able to stroll on the sands.'

'You know it well?'

'Well enough. I've been coming on and off since I was thirteen. Liverpool has some nightmarish spots but I like the place. There's always something going on. But I was telling you about Seaforth – Prime Minister Gladstone lived there for a while, you can see his family house, and a ship called the *Dicky Sam* went aground on the sands during Victorian times. Straight from Virginia it was, and full of tobacco.'

'Was anybody drowned?'

'I don't know about that. Only that the villagers stripped the ship of its tobacco.'

'They stole it?'

'What the tide washes up and leaves – ' He smiled.

'It's still stealing,' she said slowly. 'The shipowners and the merchants would lose money.'

'They can afford it.' He glanced at her. 'Sweated labour, Becky, that's how they use the poor. A working man isn't paid what his labour is worth.'

'I know that. Are you a union man?' She hoped he would tell her more about himself.

'To be sure I am when I get the time. You're not against the unions?'

'I know hardly anything about them. What union?'

'I'm a seaman,' he said. 'What other job would keep bringing me back and forth to Liverpool and Ireland?' He took her hand and led her up the steps to the station as she digested the unexpected information, considering how it put a different light on things.

'I suppose your being a sailor is what makes the soldiers think you're like the Scarlet Pimpernel,' murmured Rebekah, as they settled themselves in a second class carriage.

He stilled. 'What makes you say that?'

'My father said it.' She cleared her throat. 'He also said that the I.R.A. have cells in Liverpool. I wasn't sure if he was saying it just to make Mama not want to stay here. Do you know – ?'

A frown creased his forehead. 'Look out of the window, Becky. You'll be getting a good view of the river and the ships. As well as that, there's the warehouses for storing the cargoes to see. They're enormous, aren't they? They hide some terrible housing. As bad as any you'd see in Dublin.'

'You don't want to talk about the I.R.A.?' she said quietly.

'No.' He looked out of the window. 'Did you know now that Liverpool has the biggest tobacco warehouse there is?'

She recognised his determination not to talk about the troubles, but his involvement was there between them even though they were away from Ireland and it bothered her, really bothered her. 'I thought cotton was the biggest commodity Liverpool handled?'

'Sure it's huge.' He glanced at her and the frown was still there. 'But there's more than that to the Port. You have your rubber – your timber from Canada – vegetable oils for soap.

52

And there's granaries for the cereals from Canada and America.'

She looked down at her hands. 'I have to know, Daniel. Have you come to Liverpool because of the I.R.A.?'

A muscle tightened in his cheek. 'And there's the emigration trade. It's bigger than cotton now.'

'I suppose you think it's none of my business,' she said.

'I wouldn't say that exactly. But can't you allow me to forget that side of my life? I thought meeting you was the best thing that ever happened to me. That's why I wanted to see you again. Now – ' He shrugged. 'I didn't know you wanted to pump information out of me.'

Rebekah felt awful. 'I'm not trying to get information,' she murmured. 'I came because I wanted to be with you. Do you think I'd have bothered otherwise?'

His face softened. 'Then why go on about the – ' he hesitated ' – the organisation.'

'That's what you call it?'

'It's safer.'

She raised her eyebrows. 'And you ask me why I go on about them! I don't want you hurt.'

He smiled. 'I'm not going to get hurt. If I tell you that I'm not as involved as Shaun – that I've never killed a man in ambush – will you believe me and drop the whole thing?'

'I'll try.'

'Good girl. Now tell me what your father's doing about going to America?'

'He's got tickets on a ship.' She pulled a face. 'It's probably sailing the day after tomorrow. Aunt Esther was livid, and I wasn't too pleased as you can imagine.'

'Damn!' he exclaimed in a low voice. 'It doesn't give us much time.'

She shook her head. 'And I daren't be away too long. I'm a coward, you see. I can't imagine how Papa could get to know I'm with you but it worries me in case he does.'

Daniel's hand tightened about her fingers. 'He won't get to know. Stop worrying.'

She smiled and gave his hand a squeeze in response. For several minutes they did not speak and she was content just to be in his company. Then he began to talk about Seaforth again.

'The Marconi Wireless Company was stationed there, you know. It was there that the captain of the *Montrose* radioed the information about the murderer Crippen being aboard his ship. Unless you've been aboard ship and in trouble, you can't imagine the difference radio makes to being at sea.'

Rebekah was interested. 'I heard someone once say that it was love that got Crippen hanged.'

'They must have thought what they had was worth murdering for.'

'Love does strange things to people.'

'Sure does.' He smiled and she smiled back. She felt happy just looking at him and listening to his talk about Seaforth and his relations in Liverpool.

They clattered down the steps from the station and immediately felt the breeze from the river blowing sand into their faces. The sun had come out from behind white clouds and there were lots of blue patches. It was turning out to be a lovely day and Rebekah tried not to think that it could be the only one they had.

Daniel ran her down to the beach and she laughed for the sheer pleasure of being in his company, out in the fresh air with no fear of snipers or bombs going off.

He brought her to a swinging stop when they reached the shore, pointing out the high tide mark at the foot of the cobbles. 'The tide comes sweeping in fast all along the coast for quite a way. There's sandbanks so you have to be careful.'

They strolled along the deserted beach. The tide was way out and sky and sand seemed to stretch for miles. Her nerves were soothed. Across the water she could see the low green Wirral coastline and the hills of Wales. It was different to Ireland and yet in a way similar. There was a joy inside her that she had never experienced before and every time she looked at Daniel, her heart seemed to swell.

The sun grew warmer and they took off their shoes and stockings and paddled in water in a shallow gully left behind by the tide. They did not talk about anything serious, only of shells, crabs, fishing and swimming. He told her tales that made her laugh. Uncomplicated laughter, but at the back of her mind all the time was the knowledge that there was little time for his tales and the simpler things that couples did

54

together. Probably they would never do this again and she could not bear the thought.

They walked on, barefooted, and when Daniel's arm slid about Rebekah's waist, she leaned against him. 'There's sinking sand somewhere,' he murmured. 'My cousins used to warn me about it. They told me that a donkey was swallowed whole into a pit of black mud.'

She shivered. 'If you were wanting to bring me down to earth then you've done it, Daniel O'Neill. Imagine losing someone you love in such a way!'

'Do you love anybody that much, you couldn't bear to lose them?' He turned her towards him and his expression was intense as his eyes scanned her face.

'Do you?' she whispered.

'I'm starting to think I might.' He stroked back her hair.

'Me as well. But what can we do?'

'I don't know. But don't you be worrying about what I said about the mud. It's probably not true. My cousins are terrible exaggerators. If they caught a tiddler it would end up a whale.'

She smiled as he had intended and he kissed her open mouth, long and deep. They both dropped the shoes they carried and their arms went round each other. She rubbed her cheek against his and kissed it, tasting the salt on his skin. Then she pressed her mouth against his and he pulled her against him with insistent hands, and kissed her back. His passion dissolved any sensible thoughts she might have had and she responded with hungry enthusiasm. For what seemed ages they only kissed. Then, 'You're lovely,' he said, 'I want to make love to you.'

He pulled her down on to the sand and her heart pounded. Their hands explored, undoing buttons. He had hair on his chest and his skin was cool with the wind from the sea. He touched her breast and a few moments later there did not seem anything terribly wrong about him rubbing his chest against her breasts. It was at least five minutes before he stroked her skirts up above her thighs. For a moment she did think that really she should say something to stop him but there was such desire inside her that although she protested and he hesitated, removing his hand, it was not long before he was back again and caressing between her legs. She was surprised at how pleasant it was and how weak was her resistance. She did not want him to stop. Her pleasure was growing, overwhelming her, until she had no control over the movements of her body. When he stopped she wanted him back and said so. 'If you're sure,' he murmured, and took off his pants. She stared up at him from dazed eyes, not so certain when she saw him naked. She liked the look of the strength of him, but before her mind could touch on the consequences of what might happen next, he was besides her again. His fingers touched her and she quivered with anticipation, closing her eyes and her mind as he straddled and slowly penetrated her. It barely hurt, and as he moved the pain mixed with the pleasure that still lingered, and her desire for more caused her body to match his movements. Her arms went round him but he removed them one at a time and withdrew quickly. She reached up for him and his mouth touched hers briefly.

Luxuriating in a sense of relaxation that she had never felt before, it was several minutes before she opened her eyes and saw for the first time what had entered her. It didn't look as big as it had felt inside her and now her mind took over. 'Will I have a baby?' Her voice was low and slightly apprehensive.

He shook his head. 'I made sure I wouldn't do that to you.'

'How?' She sat up.

'Just take my word for it.' He pulled on his trousers, then passed shoes and stockings to her.

She stared at him. 'We can't just say goodbye,' she insisted.

He wiped sand off his foot with his sock, not looking at her. 'I've nothing to offer you, Becky.' His voice was taut. 'I'm a man with a price on my head.'

For a moment she could think of nothing to say. All the pleasure had dissolved and all she could feel was a great big lump in her throat. 'I don't know what to say,' she gasped. 'After what we've just done, how can you just leave me?'

'What else can I do?' He glanced at her, frowning. 'I'm sorry.'

'Sorry?' She put a hand to her mouth and closed her eyes, forcing back tears.

'Becky! Becky, don't cry.' He dropped his sock and put his arms round her. 'This ship you're going to America on – '

She rubbed her eyes against his bare chest. 'I don't know the name of it.'

'God, you must!' he said urgently. 'Think!'

'It's no use my thinking,' she cried, pushing herself away from him. 'We were all so annoyed with Papa that we never asked!'

'The line – what's its name?'

'I don't know that either!' She hunched her legs, aware of her nakedness, and dropped her chin on her knees.

'Don't you know anything about it at all?'

'Only the name of the owner.' She lifted her eyes and looked at him.

'Well?' he said, smiling.

'Joshua Green.'

'Hell!' His smile faded, and reaching out for her clothes he threw them at her. 'It just would have to be Green's, wouldn't it! He sank back on to the sand, a moody expression on his face.

'What is it?'

'It's him, that's all.' He looked up at her. 'He has land in Ireland, you know.'

'I know. Apparently he owns the farm that was once my grandma's. I don't know the hows and whys. It was years ago, when I was a child.' She bit her lip, clutching her clothes to her breast. 'Does it matter to us?'

'It matters to me.' He picked up his sock again. 'Can you find out the name of the ship and meet me at the Pierhead about two o'clock tomorrow.'

'I'll try.' She began to dress. 'It won't be easy getting away.'

'If you can't make it, you can't,' he said grimly.

'But that would mean we wouldn't see each other again,' she stammered.

'You really do want to see me again?'

At a look from her a slow smile lit his face. 'Trust me, Becky. I'll think of something. Now hurry up! There's a man with a dog coming along the beach.

She hurried.

Rebekah walked swiftly up the road in the direction of her aunt's house, hoping her father had not arrived home yet.

Hannah opened the door and sniffed. 'Thee's here at last, are thee? Yer hair's a mess.'

'It's because of the wind.' Rebekah flashed a honeyed smile and pushing past her went on into the house.

Her mother and aunt were having tea. 'Sorry I'm late,' she said breezily, pulling off her gloves, hoping that they couldn't tell anything from her face. 'I'm completely windblown because I've been down by the river watching the ships. Is Papa in?'

'Not yet.' Her mother stared at her, fidgetting with the neck of her dress. 'I hope he's in a good mood.'

'I saw him in town. He was with that shipowner he mentioned – Joshua Green.'

'Green's?' Her aunt shook her head and picked up her knitting. 'Such a small company. I hope his ships are up to scratch.'

'Oh, do stop going on, Esther!' Sarah's attention was still for her daughter. 'What did he have to say about your hair?'

'What you'd expect.' Rebekah took a scone from a plate. 'Mr Green said he liked it.'

'I doubt that would weigh with your father.' Her mother bit her lip.

Rebekah shrugged, and tilted her chin. Being with Daniel had put strength in her somehow. She was ready to confront her father, and anyway doubted he would hit her while staying in her aunt's house. Anyway, she intended to be nice to him because she needed the name of the ship and a chance to get away tomorrow.

It was not long before he came in. 'Well, miss, I can't say that I liked it at first sight,' he muttered, accepting a cup of tea from Hannah and standing in front of the fireplace.

'I consider she looks extremely neat,' put in Esther, her blue eyes determined.

'It's tidy, Adam,' said his wife quickly, 'and will be easier for Becky to take care of on the voyage.'

His gaze fell on his wife. 'No doubt she did it without your approval?'

'Yes!' said Rebekah swiftly.

Her mother shook her greying head. 'No, Adam.'

'I persuaded her to let the girl get it done,' put in Esther. 'Lots of women are having a bob these days. I've been thinking of it myself.'

His mouth thinned. 'They say there's no fool like an old fool, but for pretty young things I suppose it's acceptable.' He looked in Rebekah's direction. 'Joshua Green's sister has had hers done recently. She's not very well apparently since her husband was killed in the war, and lives quietly. For some reason Joshua believes that a visit from you would cheer her up. As I've some business to discuss with him, he suggests that we spend the afternoon at his house and have tea with him tomorrow.'

'Surely if you've business to discuss you'd be better going alone,' said Rebekah swiftly, her heart sinking. 'There's things I'd much rather be doing than visiting strangers.'

Her father's mouth pulled down at the corners. 'I said Mr Green's sister is ill,' he said emphatically. 'Surely if you had time in Dublin to visit that old woman, Mary, you can spare time to relieve the monotony of the day for a sick young woman? I insist on your coming with me.'

'Mama, couldn't you?' Rebekah sent her mother a look of entreaty.

Sarah shook her head. 'Your aunt and I are visiting an old friend. I would gladly take your place otherwise.'

'That's settled it then,' said her father, his eyes steely. 'You come with me, Rebekah, and I want no arguments or trying to get out of it. I'll be keeping my eye on you.'

'What time is this visit?' Her hand curled tightly in her lap.

'After lunch.'

Rebekah could have screamed. She was already missing Daniel. 'Where do they live?'

'Not far. The other side of Newsham Park. Joshua's brother made the move out of the town centre for his sister's health a couple of years back.'

She tried one last time. 'If she's been married, Papa, then she must be a few years older than me? She might not want my company.'

'She's twenty-two.' He gulped his tea and reached for a scone. 'Young to have suffered so much. But perhaps Joshua's right and you can cheer her up. Whatever you do, don't be talking about the fighting at home. It could upset her.'

'Perhaps you'd like to tell me what I can talk to her about?' Rebekah said acidly. 'I doubt we'll have much in common.'

His mouth tightened. 'I'm sure you'll find something. Now let's drop the subject. Tell me, Sarah, did you get all that you went for in town?'

Rebekah went out of the room and up to her bedroom. What was the point of asking her father the name of the ship now? Was it worth her trying to get out of the house earlier in the day? She thought of his expression and voice when he said, 'I'll be watching you.' He would too. She sank onto the bed. She could only put her trust in Daniel as he had said she should.

Joshua Green's house fronted an expanse of green parkland. A gravelled path flanked by rhododendrons wound round the side of a large red-brick porch, and there were several steps up to the entrance. A ship's bell swung from a wrought iron hook.

Rebekah watched, one white-gloved hand clasped about the Barker & Dobson chocolates that her mother had insisted she took for Joshua Green's sister. This was more the kind of house that she had thought Aunt Esther would have. Her father pulled the short rope that set the bell clanging. Nothing happened. She felt fidgety and checked that the yellow ribbon threaded through her short hair was lying flat and fastened the top button of the brown jacket over her primrose-coloured frock. Adam rang the bell again and for good measure banged the knocker. Moments later the door was opened by an elderly maid.

The hall seemed dark after the brightness of the sun and their feet made a ringing noise on the tiled floor as they followed the maid to a back room where she announced them. A yawning voice bid them: 'Come in.'

Warmth hit them and Rebekah's eyes went involuntarily to the fireplace where one of the latest gas fires burned. Then her gaze moved quickly to the woman lying on the sofa with her mousy head nestling against several cretonne cushions. On the plaid rug that covered her legs lay the magazine *Vogue*, a blue-black Persian cat and a half-empty bowl of grapes.

'Josh shouldn't be long because he's been gone ages,' she murmured, staring at them. 'The vicar rang up, wanting something or other, and he said it would be easier if he went round to sort it out.' She sat up and Rebekah was able to gain a better view of the pale face and nondescript features of their hostess. 'You don't mind waiting for tea? If you're hungry help yourself to a grape.' Limpid grey eyes seemed to gaze past them as with a slender hand, adorned only by a wedding and an engagement ring of rubies and pearls, she offered them the bowl of black grapes, still with the bloom on them.

Her father declined politely and nudged Rebekah's arm. She hesitated before refusing. The girl shrugged. 'We grow them ourselves – or at least Fred the gardener does.' She gathered the bowl to her beige jersey-clad bosom and lowering her head too a grape from the bowl with her teeth.

Involuntarily Rebekah glanced at her father, who nudged her again. 'Give her the chocolates,' he muttered beneath his breath.

'Chocolates?' Their hostess stared vaguely at them. 'For me? What sort are they?'

Rebekah handed them to her and she smiled, gazing down at the box. 'How kind! I'll eat them now.' She dropped the bowl of grapes on the Indian carpet, then opened the box of chocolates. She bit into one before looking up abruptly and saying, 'I've forgotten to ask you to sit down, haven't I? Do sit and have a chocolate.'

Adam refused but this time Rebekah did not. She was hungry. Her father sat ramrod straight in an armchair, his expression unusually blank. Rebekah, who was finding their hostess more interesting than she had expected, relaxed in a leather-upholstered chair, and waited for her father to speak first.

There was a silence while Mrs Richards ate the chocolates, flicking over the pages of the magazine, giving them only a perfunctory glance. Rebekah decided to break the silence and sought for something safe. 'Does your cat have a name?'

Joshua's sister looked up at her from beneath pale lashes. 'Bloody foreign moggy,' she said, seeming to relish the words. 'That's what Fred calls him when he mucks up the garden. My name's Emma. Dicky calls me little Emma. His proper name is Richard Richards. Silly, isn't it? He'll be coming home soon now the war's been declared officially over.'

'The war finished ages ago,' said Rebekah, startled. 'In nineteen-eighteen.'

61

'No!' said Emma softly, her hands moving restlessly. 'Not properly it hadn't, and Dicky signed up for the duration. The other day I read in the paper that officially it's over. You'll see – he'll be back soon.'

Rebekah glanced at her father and saw that his colour was high. He looked away and stared out of the window. Oh Lord, she thought, what do I say next? 'Your hair's nice. I had mine cut at Hill's yesterday. Where did you get yours done?'

Emma did not answer right away but ate another chocolate before saying, 'Upstairs in my bedroom. A man came. He had dark shiny hair and talked and talked until my head started aching so much, I threw the hairbrush at him.'

Rebekah was startled into asking, 'Did you hit him?'

'Yes.' A mischievous expression suddenly lit Emma's face. 'He said that he wouldn't come again and I said good. That I would let my hair grow and grow until it reached my bottom.' Her mouth trembled and an apprehensive expression replaced the mischief in her eyes. 'Josh was annoyed and lost his temper. He said that it's all gone on too long – that I've got to pull myself together or else. Or else what? I asked, and he said that I'd soon see.'

'He probably didn't mean anything by it,' said Rebekah, suddenly feeling out of her depth and wishing that Joshua Green would come back.

There was a silence which seemed to stretch and stretch. Her mind drifted to thoughts of Daniel, hoping that he had been disappointed when she had not turned up and that he would think of something so that they could be together again.

Suddenly there was a sound of the front door opening and the murmur of voices in the hall. There came hurried footsteps and several seconds later Joshua entered the sitting room. He was dressed in grey flannels and a navy blue blazer with silver buttons. His pleasant face clouded as his eyes flickered over his sister's prone figure. 'Still resting, Em?' he said lightly.

She murmured indistinctly but his attention had already passed to the others. 'I hope you haven't been waiting long?' He bowed slightly in Rebekah's direction, and smiled. 'I was unavoidably detained. After persuading me to let him have one of my boats for a day's cruising on the Mersey next year for some of the orphans, the Reverend droned on and on. He's a real windbag but not a bad chap as clerics go.' He waved a hand in the direction of the window. 'Let's go outside. Because it's such a fine day I've told Janet to serve tea outside.' Moving swiftly, he crossed the room. As he passed his sister he murmured, 'I presume you are joining us, Em?' He switched off the gas fire before going towards the french windows, opening them and beckoning the others out into a large walled garden.

Rebekah was glad to be outdoors. The room had been stifling hot. She paused on a paved area where a white table and four chairs stood close to the wooden figurehead of a mermaid from which the paint was peeling.

'Once she graced the first sailing ship that my grandfather commissioned,' said Joshua, coming to stand at her shoulder. 'Andromeda, my brother called her.'

She looked up at him. 'I doubt if Perseus will be coming to her rescue.'

He nodded seriously. 'Too late for the old girl. I suppose I should really get rid of her but father was a bit superstitious where Andromeda was concerned. He reckoned that she brought the family luck.'

Rebekah placed her hand on the mermaid's dirty yellow hair. 'You should give her a new coat of paint. I'm sure she'd enjoy that.'

He smiled. 'You think so?'

'If I was her I would.' She ran a finger over the beautifully carved tresses and facial features. 'I'd want golden hair, bright blue eyes, red lips – and a sea green tail.'

'What nonsense you talk,' said her father, coming up to them. 'Take no notice of her, Joshua.'

The light died in Rebekah's eyes. 'It was only a bit of fun,' she murmured, turning away from the two men and walking over to where Emma stood with the cat bundled in her arms. The fragrance from some late-flowering roses filled the air.

'They smell nice, don't they?' said Emma, her expression sombre. 'I had some in my bouquet when I married Dicky before he went to France.'

Rebekah could think of nothing to say but felt deeply sorry for her. To lose someone you love, so young – no wonder she'd gone funny. Daniel came to mind and she stood close to Emma, absently stroking the cat up the wrong way until Joshua called them to come to tea.

Emma ate little which was not surprising, thought Rebekah. Conversation between her father and Joshua seemed to be about politics and shipping. Afterwards they disappeared inside the house and Emma unexpectedly gripped her hand tightly and stared at her with dilated dark blue eyes. 'It'll be our fifth wedding anniversary next week. Perhaps Dickie will be home for it,' she whispered. 'Will you remember me when you're out in the middle of the Atlantic, and pray?'

Startled, Rebekah replied, 'If you want me to.'

'Thanks.' She wandered back into the house.

Rebekah followed. Not long after that her father called that it was time to go. She walked down the front path to where he waited with Joshua, who held out his hand. 'The *Samson* will be sailing tomorrow. Until next we meet, Rebekah.'

'What?' she asked in a vague voice, thinking that it was too late to get the name of the ship to Daniel. She could only hope.

'Sometimes I come over to America on business,' he answered, squeezing her fingers.

'Oh, I see!' It seemed ages since she had actually thought of what it would be like in America. 'That will be nice,' she added politely, freeing her hand and moving to the other side of the gate.

He raised an arm in farewell and as they turned the corner into the main road she was aware that he still stood at the gate, watching them.

Chapter Five

Daniel had not been on the landing stage and although Rebekah scoured the decks, staring at every sailor she encountered, she had not seen him anywhere on the ship. As she gazed at coasters and dredgers, ferry and cargo boats, tall liners and tiny river craft, her vision blurred. He must not have been able to find the right ship in time. Or else – terrible thought – he had not wanted to. She felt quite desperate, especially when she caught a glimpse of Seaforth. The tide was in and although she could not be sure of exactly where they had walked and made love, she had not forgotten what it felt like. She tried not to think of never seeing Daniel again but could not stop. She scrubbed at her eyes and was aware of her mother weeping by her side. She could no longer bear her own thoughts. 'Mama, shall we go to our cabin?'

'In a minute.' Her mother wiped her face with a handkerchief and then blew her nose. 'I'm sorry to be such a misery but it's just really hit me that I'll never see Liverpool again. When I went to live in Ireland, I always believed that one day I'd return.' The tears flowed again and the next words were muffled by her handkerchief. 'But America, Becky! We'll never come back from there!'

'We might,' said Rebekah in bracing tones, determinedly quashing her own misery and slipping a hand through her mother's arm. 'Never say never, Mama'.

Her mother sniffed and dabbed at her nose and eyes again. Rebekah thought of Daniel's words about leaving Ireland and wondered sadly if the Americas were full of emigrants still mourning the countries they had left behind.

They passed down a companionway and Rebekah barely noticed that her mother's colour was changing until she felt her pressing her arm and saw that her face looked clammy and pallid. They managed to reach the cabin before Sarah was sick in the basin. Rebekah helped her to undress and soon had her lying between the sheets in the bunk bed. She rang for the steward and cleaned out the basin before sponging her mother's face and hands. The steward came and soon her mother was comfortably settled with a couple of arrowroot biscuits and a cup of weak tea.

Her father arrived from seeing one of the officers. 'Not feeling so good, Sal?' He patted the hand lying on the cover. 'Don't think about it. Mind over matter and you'll soon feel well enough to see over the ship,' he said cheerfully.

'Not yet I won't,' muttered Sarah, giving him an exasperated look. 'You've never been seasick, you've no idea. Pass me my bag, Becky. There's a book I can read. And I need my glasses.'

Her husband frowned and sat sideways on the bunk. 'Joshua arranged with the captain for us to see over the ship. One of the perks of my new job, Sal. I'd like you to come.'

'Well, I'm not.'

'It's not until after dinner. You might feel better then.'

'I won't,' she said determinedly.

'You're not sulking, are you?'

She looked at him. 'What would be the use? Take Becky.'

'Me!' Rebekah had no desire to be in her father's company.

Her father glared at her. 'And why not, miss? If you think you're going to be let loose on this ship to flirt with all and sundry, then you've got another think coming! You'll come with me and like it.'

'I might come but I certainly won't like it!' retorted Rebekah, handing the book to her mother.

'Like it or lump it,' muttered her father, his eyes narrowing. 'You are definitely coming. It could be useful to you in the future. Mr Green bought the ship from one of the big companies and changed her name. She was designed and built at Harland and Wolff's Belfast shipyard and used to carry first and second class passengers.' His voice had risen as if he was trying to impress the knowledge into her. 'He's had her converted to transport single class emigrants, knowing he couldn't compete for the upper-class tourist trade. He's just had oil-fired boilers installed. It's a good investment! Coal's a bulky, dirty fuel to load and carry. Try and remember all that, daughter! It might come up in conversation in shipping circles and you'd know what a man was talking about. A man likes a woman who can listen intelligently, instead of babbling on about mermaids wanting to be painted.'

'Mr Green knew it was a bit of fun,' she said hotly. 'He probably hears enough about boilers and engines in his office.'

Her father stared at her and there was that pinched look about his mouth again. 'This is one of the times when I wish you'd been a boy!'

'Being a girl was hardly my choice,' she said, tilting her chin. 'You can blame that on God.'

'That's enough, Becky,' murmured her mother, without lifting her head. 'Go with your father and give me a bit of peace.'

Rebekah wanted to say more but considered her mother was upset enough at leaving Liverpool. She went with her father to dinner and ate the soup, roast lamb and tapioca pudding with a lack of her customary enthusiasm for food, taking little notice of the company at their table. Afterwards her father steered her hurriedly to the bridge.

It soon became obvious to Rebekah that the officer, Mr Eaton, who was acting as guide on their tour of the ship, was out to please her father. He listened with flattering attention to all his questions and she wondered what the job was that her father had mentioned. The way Mr Eaton was behaving, her father could have been buying the ship!

They climbed down into the engine and boiler rooms. The pumps were slightly noisy and there was a strong smell of steam and oil. It was hot and Rebekah felt a bit sick as she politely tried to pay attention to the conversation between her father and the second engineer as they discussed valves, pistons, pressures and boilers. Depression clouded her spirits. As her eyes roamed the pipes which seemed to snake everywhere they fell on one of the overalled men. His eyes were fixed on her, the whites gleaming in a face that was shiny with sweat and smeared with grease. A smile drew oily lines in the grease and her misery evaporated. She could hardly believe it but she had found Daniel!

Rebekah glanced at her father and jumped when she realised he was watching her. Quickly she looked away and smiled at Mr Eaton, praying that she had not given the game away. She forced herself to look subdued and followed her father up the ladder out of the engine room. Even so, her mood was buoyant. Daniel had done it! He must really care! He had told her to trust him and backed his words up with action. Hallelujah!

As she stood in the tiny space that housed the ship's wireless she wondered how he would be able to get in touch with her. It had to be soon! Mr Eaton, who it turned out was a cousin of Mr Green, was at her shoulder, telling her about the advantages that a smaller ship could have over the larger liners when it came to knots per hour. They could be in New York within the week. Rebekah had expected it to take much longer and the news gave a greater sense of urgency to thoughts of seeing Daniel.

When the tour came to an end her father gave Rebekah no chance to escape but took her upper arm in a grip so tight that she winced. 'I saw the way you were looking at Mr Eaton, my girl, and I'm telling you now that I have someone better in mind for you.' He gave her a shake. 'Just behave yourself! I haven't forgotten what happened in Dublin and I'll not be having you making a name for yourself among the crew!' He slackened his grip slightly. 'Now let's go and have our tea.'

She stared at him defiantly. 'I'm not hungry, Papa.'

'I've paid for this food so you'll eat it,' he said, his fingers tightening again on her arm. 'Now, move.'

She moved, realising that it was unlikely that Daniel would have left the engine room yet.

She was toying with a smoked herring, thinking of how she was to get away from her father, who was talking engines to the man opposite him, when a pleasant-looking girl with auburn hair twisted in a knot on the top of her head, grimaced and said, 'All this talk of engines is double dutch to me, even though me brother Pat's a deckhand on the *Gideon*. A sister, or brother, whatever you call it, to this ship. Yer'd sure and think I'd have picked up some knowhow, wouldn't you?' she said in a Liverpool accent.

'I beg your pardon?' said Rebekah, gathering her wandering thoughts.

'My name's Brigid O'Shaughnessy.' The girl's eyes were warm. 'The trouble is I never listened to Pat when he chunnered on. All I need to know about a boat is that it'll get me to where I'm going. Not that I was in any rush to leave Liverpool, but as my Keith said, they promised him a land fit for heroes. And while round Mere Land isn't too bad, it's hardly Paradise. Even so I kept telling him it was home, but he wanted a better future for our kids when we have 'em, so I had no choice but to pack me bags and come.' Tears welled in her eyes and her voice wobbled when she spoke again. 'He might be right but I'm already missing Mam and me sisters.' She sniffed and wiped her eyes with the back of her hand. 'He'd like a bit of land to farm, and a cow. I'm not keen on cows. I've lived next door to the dairy all me life and the smell was something awful at times. They're dangerous as well.' She nodded sagely. 'One of the cowmen had his eye flicked out by a cow's tail. That wasn't much fun for him, I can tell you.'

Rebekah suppressed a giggle. 'Do you have to keep cows?'

Brigid raised her eyes ceilingward. 'It's what he wants! But I'll get to work on him. You can change a man if you go the right way about it, so Mam always said.'

Rebekah gave up all pretence of eating the smoked herring. 'Are there lots of things you want to change about him?'

'There's never been a perfect man.' A dimple appeared in Brigid's cheek. 'Are yer leaving someone behind?'

Rebekah glanced in her father's direction. 'There's someone. Papa doesn't approve.'

'Dads are like that.' Brigid's tongue darted out, licking the jam at the side of her mouth. 'I used to nip down the yard to the lav meself and sneak out the back way.'

'Not a bad idea.' Rebekah smiled and stood up, murmuring her excuses to her father. He nodded but told her that he'd expect to see her back in the cabin in ten minutes. She smiled a goodbye to Brigid and left.

Rebekah walked the promenade deck but saw no sign of Daniel. He was not in the general saloon either. She wondered whether the crew were allowed in such places. Continuing her hunt she gazed through the door of the smoking saloon and withdrew her head, coughing, after a hurried review of the few men's faces present. She was starting to believe she was wasting her time and that Daniel must still be down in the engine room when he came up a companionway, talking over his shoulder in an emphatic voice. He stopped in mid-sentence when he saw her and there was a brightness in his eyes.

She felt as if the whole of her body was smiling and without hesitation flung her arms around him. 'I'm so glad to see you!'

'Same here.' He hugged her.

'I was so worried Papa might have recognised you.'

'I'd heard he was coming so I had my disguise ready.'

She spoke against his shoulder. 'Your own mother would hardly have recognised you.'

'But you did.' He held her off from him and her smile deepened.

'You were staring at me.'

He grinned. 'You had the best legs in the engine room!'

'You shouldn't say things like that,' she said demurely. 'You'll have me blushing. How did you find the ship?'

'I had a mate check the passenger list – then I signed on. Crazy though it might be.'

They continued to stare at each other, smiling until a voice said, 'Danny, isn't this the girl who was in Dublin? Did she tell her father about us and that's why you said – ?' Rebekah jumped. It was Shaun.

Daniel frowned. 'No, she didn't. Her and me are none of your business. Go for a walk and I'll find you later.'

Shaun did not move. 'Mam would want me to be looking out for you, and I know for sure your taking up with a Quaker wouldn't be to her liking.'

Daniel's mouth tightened. 'Go away, Shaun.'

His brother jingled the change in his pocket. 'I knew she was trouble as soon as I saw her.'

'It's you that's trouble,' said Daniel grimly. 'Now, go.'

He scowled. 'What about our business? I hope she's not going – '

'She has nothing to do with our business,' said Daniel emphatically. 'And if anyone was going to get us into trouble, it would be you!'

Shaun's face reddened and he scuffed his feet before turning and walking away. He looked back several times with an angry expression.

Daniel pulled Rebekah down on to a bench. 'I'm sorry about that.'

'It's all right,' she said in a low voice. 'I understand why he doesn't want me around. But what's he doing here?'

'He's the only brother I've got left. I thought it less likely that he'd get into trouble if I brought him.'

'Papa might recognise him. You'd better warn him.'

He nodded. 'I never thought.'

'It doesn't matter,' she said softly, squeezing his hand.

'Let's forget them both. I'll enjoy seeing your pretty face after being down in that hellhole every day. But don't expect to see much of me. We work long hours.'

'I'm just glad you're here.'

'Me too.' He stared down at her and she wondered what he was thinking, just before he kissed her in a manner as starved as her own.

It was the sound of children's voices that caused them to draw apart. As soon as the girls and their mother had passed they turned to each other again, but the sight of a man coming up the companionway to stand at the rail, puffing his pipe, was enough to make Rebekah draw back. 'You'll have to go,' she whispered. 'It's my father.'

Daniel looked down at her. 'D'you think I'm the kind of man to run from your father?'

She lowered her gaze. 'Do it for me. If he discovers you're on this ship, there'll be terrible trouble. I know him, you don't.'

There was silence and her father turned his head and glanced idly about. She pressed herself against the back of the bench, hoping that Daniel's bulk would conceal her, and did not dare look in her father's direction again.

'I'll go,' murmured Daniel. 'I've a few hours before I've to be down in the engine room again. If you can make it, we can meet on the boat deck after supper.'

She nodded. 'I'll find a way.'

He turned up his jacket collar and went in the opposite direction from her father. She watched him go, thinking that some women were being emancipated but that didn't make most of them any freer than in Victorian times.

Her heart thumping, Rebekah rose to her feet and went over to her father, standing at the rail.

He turned and frowned at her. 'Your hair's a mess. What are you doing here? I thought you were going to see your mother.'

'I got lost.' Relief lightened her voice.

'After having a tour round the ship?' he said sarcastically. He prodded the hollow beneath her collar bone with the stem of his pipe. 'If I catch you flirting, you're in trouble.'

'You won't catch me, Papa,' she retorted.

'What's that supposed to mean? That you think you're too smart for me?' His eyes narrowed as he put his pipe back into his mouth and his teeth bit into the end.

'No, Papa. I mean that I have no intention of flirting with any man,' she said, adding with a self-assurance that she was far from feeling, 'You should trust me, Papa.'

'Hmmph!' he grunted. 'Let's go and see your mother.'

Sarah still showed a wan face. 'Was it a good tea?'

'Kippers, and bread and preserves. I didn't eat much.' Rebekah sat on her bunk and spoke about the people at their table but it was not long before her mother's eyes closed and she dozed off. Rebekah sighed and hoped that she would be able to get away after supper.

At the dining table Rebekah got into conversation again with Brigid, who asked her, 'This fella you spoke about, will he be following you out?'

Rebekah whispered, 'I'm seeing him after supper. He's one of the engineers.'

Brigid's brows arched. 'Oh! So you haven't left him behind.' Her voice was low. 'Is he your first boyfriend?'

Rebekah's head lifted. 'My first real boyfriend.'

Brigid smiled. 'Well, yer probably in luv with luv, as me mam used to say. Enjoy it while it lasts, but be careful because yer know what they say about sailors.' At that point in the conversation her husband nudged her arm and she turned to him.

Rebekah noted that her father was talking to someone else and swiftly left the dining room.

Up on the boat deck she looked about for Daniel. The wind was cold and it was almost dark. She shivered and huddled inside her coat. Suddenly a hand seized hold of her shoulder and she was pulled into the space between two lifeboats. She trembled as she held up her face to Daniel's kiss. Was this being in love with love? Would it pass as Brigid had warned her? She did not want it to because it was wonderful.

His head lifted and he rubbed his cheek languorously against hers. 'You had no trouble getting away?'

'No. Although –'

'Good.' He undid a couple of buttons on her coat and she remembered what Brigid had said about sailors. He looked down at her, and there was the slightest gleam in his eyes. 'You don't mind?'

'No,' she whispered. 'Although with Papa aboard, I'm a bit nervous.'

'I don't plan on taking any risks with you.' His arms slid about her waist beneath the coat. 'It's just that it's warmer this way.'

It was, and she snuggled her head against his shoulder, breathing in the mingled faint odours of oil, soap and damp wool. 'When do you have to go on duty?'

'An hour or so.'

'It's not long.'

'No.' His mouth moved over hers with a sensuality that was enjoyable. As their kisses grew more torrid, she forgot everything but the physical sensations she was feeling. His hands shifted until they rested just beneath her breasts, which seemed to be swelling, and her breath caught in her throat as his fingers explored them. Then came the sound of footsteps, a man's cough, the smell of pipe smoke. She stiffened and Daniel's hand pressing against her breast seemed to be attempting to stifle the heavy beating of her heart. Neither of them moved or spoke until the footsteps retreated.

Daniel took her hand and began to walk with her. She was glad of the chance to let herself calm down. Her blood still seemed to be pounding in her head but as they slowly walked, the sea breeze cooled her hot cheeks and gradually she felt more in control. She sought for something to say that would take her mind off her father and what he might say when she got back to the cabin. 'What made you become an engineer?'

'It wasn't anything I planned.' He squeezed her fingers. 'Life was awful at home, despite Mam trying her best. My brothers were always fighting so I ran away to sea when I was thirteen. I wanted to see the world.'

'And have you?'

He smiled. 'You don't see much of it from an engine room. And one port's pretty much like another when a ship's only turning round.'

'You sound disillusioned.'

'It's not as bad as I make it sound,' he drawled. 'A ship's something special.'

'Do you have a woman in every port?' She had heard that about sailors.

'What a question!' He brushed her cheek with his fingers.

She caught his hand and suddenly remembered Shaun. 'Is it a taboo like the I.R.B.? The business with your brother – '

His brows furrowed. 'Forget what Shaun said. Forget them. I never go to any of the meetings. It's Irish people having a complete say in their own country that's important to me.'

'Why don't you get out then?'

His mouth twisted. 'You've lived through the last few years in Dublin and you ask me that? When it's all over and Ireland's free, there won't be any need for killing or secrecy.' He hugged her to him. 'Talk of something else.'

'Tell me more about yourself. Did you go to school?'

Daniel stared past her at the sea. 'Sure. But my brothers were there before me and a priest decided he was going to beat the wickedness out of me before it got a firm hold.'

A shudder ran through her. 'Don't talk about it if you don't want to.'

He shrugged. 'The parents of another boy complained. He was replaced. My mam, though, would never go against the priests, whatever us boys said.'

'It's a wonder you learned anything,' she whispered.

Daniel smiled. 'I liked learning once I was allowed to do just that. The priest that replaced Brother Jerry was well read and had been about the world a bit. Spent time in Africa and

South America. He liked nothing better than to talk about travelling and ships. It sounded like a different world.'

'That's what made you run away to sea?'

He nodded, remembering the horrors of that first ocean voyage. The seasickness and the yearning for home. The hard work and the men who had wanted sex with him. At first that had terrified him more than any beating but he soon learnt from a couple of seamen that he did not have to use his fists and feet. 'Sod off, mate, I'm not that way made,' caused them to back off.

Rebekah nudged his arm, sensing his withdrawal from her. 'Was it what you expected?'

'Is anything,' he said drily. 'And why are we wasting time talking about the past?'

'Because I want to know more about you, of course. Have you had many girlfriends?' she blurted out.

'I've had other things on my mind each time I've docked in Liverpool and New York, so there's no need for you to be jealous.' He sounded amused.

'I'm not jealous. It's . . . I don't like to think that I might just be one in a line. You could have had more than one in each port?' she said jocularly.

'I could have half a dozen, but I haven't!' He pulled her into his arms but she warded him off.

'What do you have on your mind?'

He sighed. 'I've never known anyone like you for asking questions – except perhaps our Shaun.'

She did not enjoy being linked with him, and thought of what her father had said. It made her uneasy. 'I'm not likely to tell anyone.'

'I'm not giving you the chance.' His face was set. 'I'll not be having you knowing anything about that side of my life. It's safer for you and safer for me, as I've told you before. Just take my word that I'm not involved in anything violent.'

'You said New York. Eamon de Valera, the President of Sinn Fein, is in America.'

He frowned. 'Don't pry, Becky.'

She was silent, but all the fear and anger of the last year or so bubbled up inside her. 'I don't know why, when he was legally elected, he couldn't have taken his seat in Westminster.'

His arms dropped. 'You must know!'

She shrugged. 'Because he wants an all Irish parliament – Dail Eireann.'

'There you are then. Having Irish M.P.s in London hasn't done us much good, so we have to take the other way however much I hate it.'

'But why be involved?' she said urgently. 'You don't have to be! There's no need for you to set foot in Ireland ever again. What's to take you back? You have no mother and your other brothers are dead.'

He stared at her. 'You know what takes me back. Have you no feeling for the place at all? I seem to remember your saying that you believed in a Free Ireland.'

'I do.'

'But you're not prepared to help bring it about.'

There was silence before she said, 'I pray. Isn't that what women have always done when men went off to war? Violence is what drove my parents out of Ireland, and I'm past caring if I ever see the place again.'

He looked as if she had smacked him in the face but she could not stop. 'It'll be a half empty country Dail Eireann will be ruling over, the way things are going.'

'But you believe we'll win?' His voice was strained.

'I believe that the British will hand over some kind of self-government because they're fed up to the back teeth with the Irish problem. Shall we not talk about it any more?'

'That's all I ever asked,' he said intensely. 'Not to talk about it.' He stared at her a moment, and thrust his hands into his pockets. 'I'm going to have to go. Maybe I'll see you tomorrow.' And without touching her, he walked away.

Rebekah wanted to call him back but she had a feeling it would be of no use right now. A shiver went through her. If he was not careful he could end up getting himself killed.

As quietly as possible Rebekah entered the cabin. Her mother looked up from her knitting and her father from a sheaf of papers. 'Where've you been?' he demanded.

'Walking,' she said shortly.

'I didn't see you and I've been over most of the ship.'

'You can't cover the whole ship at one time.'

'Don't be impudent, Rebekah!' He flung the papers aside. 'I've warned you – if I catch you up to anything, you'll regret it. If this happens again you won't get off so lightly.'

'Don't you think you're over-reacting, Adam?' murmured her mother. 'It's Becky's first night at sea, and if I was her age I might find it exciting and not want to go to sleep yet.' She smiled at Rebekah over her glasses. 'But there are men about, love, and lots of them have probably been drinking. We worry about you. Now get into bed and think about what we've said.'

Rebekah nodded, and before her father could say any more she dived under the bedcovers to change. She wriggled into her cambric nightgown as the light went out. Years ago she had longed for a sister to talk to, and cuddle up with, when night terrors held her frozen between chilly linen sheets. She had made do with a dog when staying on her grandma's farm. She sometimes dreamed of the summers spent in Wicklow. That had been Ireland at its best. If only it could always be like that. But it was not, and Daniel's wanting to go back scared the life out of her.

'Now I'm feeling better, you can accompany me round the promenade deck,' said Rebekah's mother, tucking her hand into her arm. 'Your father's having a word with one of the officers but we must get exercise and fresh air while the weather's not too bad.'

'What's this job he mentioned?' Rebekah began to work out the odds of seeing Daniel on their tour of the decks, or the possibility of him attending the entertainment in the General Saloon that evening.

'Mr Green has asked him to replace the shipping agent, whom he considers too old for the job. It's quite an important position, with the emigration and tourist trade getting into its stride. It'll keep him very busy. What we're supposed to do while he's busy I've no idea!' There was an unaccustomed hint of sarcasm in her voice.

'You still don't want to go to America?'

Her mother shrugged. 'I know it's not my fault but I feel mean leaving our Esther the way we did. She's not getting any younger.'

'Papa would say – '

'I know what your father would say. "She hasn't bothered with us for years and she's got Hannah." Hannah's a worker, all right, but she's not family.'

'I think she's after Aunt Esther's money,' murmured Rebekah.

Her mother halted and stared at her. 'What makes you say that?'

'She was glad to get rid of us and annoyed that Aunt Esther bought us presents.'

'The presents were nice,' said her mother. 'You must write to your aunt – keep in touch. We never saw much money from your father's side of the family so I'd like you to get some of your aunt's. You have a right to it.'

'What happened that Papa never got any money?'

'His older brother drank and gambled all the money away. That's how your father's Mr Green got his hands on the farm. I've told him if we do ever get rich and influential from this job he's got, I'd like a ship named after me. In my younger days –' She did not finish because a sudden gust of wind took her old-fashioned, wide-brimmed hat from her head and sent it careering along the deck, bringing the conversation to an end.

It was evening and Rebekah had not seen Daniel all day. She frowned as she fastened a white belt about her hips and smoothed the tan dress of cotton and silk down over her thighs. She was supposedly going to the Entertainment. Her father had left her and her mother, saying he was going to the smoking saloon to see a man from Manhattan. Presumably he believed her mother would not let her out of her sight, but Sarah had tired of her fidgetting and told her to go out but not be late.

Rebekah took a brown handbag by its chain and twisted it round her wrist. Her mother looked up from a book. 'I suppose I've got to accept that fashions change. When I was young – '

'When you were young – I know, Mama – your skirts were down to your ankles.' Her eyes softened. 'I won't be late.'

She looked in on the Entertainment – a girl singing, "I'm forever blowing bubbles" – but there was no Daniel. She found him on the boat deck, leaning on the white-painted rail, gazing out over the dark sea. She took a deep breath to steady herself as he turned and looked at her. 'Daniel, I'm sorry about last night. What you do is your business.'

'Thanks.' He was still smarting from her words. 'Do you really mean that about not caring if you never saw Ireland again? Don't you have any feelings for your birthplace?'

'Of course I do. But my future's in America now.' She hesitated. 'Yours could be, too. I don't like thinking that you might be killed.'

He turned slowly. 'No one can be completely immune from suffering and death. It's all around us.'

'That's not quite the same.'

Daniel put his arm around her. 'Don't look so sad, Becky. Let's forget about Ireland and America and live life while we've got it.' He turned her towards him.

'That's easily said,' she murmured. 'But you want to live in Ireland. You're like that Oisin in the legend.'

'But you're no princess.' He kissed her neck. 'You're real, thank God.' They kissed once, twice, and before long were back to where they had been the evening before, except this time no footsteps disturbed them. In an atmosphere of dark skies and slapping waves their passion for each other seemed at one with the elements.

She gasped as his tongue ran over her nipples and her fingers laced through his curly hair and held his head against her breast. With her other hand she pulled out his shirt and stroked his bare back. She wanted to be part of him just as she had been on the beach, and pressed against him.

A soft sigh escaped him. 'Becky, love, do you know what you're doing to me?'

'Tell me,' she whispered. 'Tell me that you love me, that you want me.'

He lifted his head and gazed into her face. 'I love you, I want you.' His voice was husky. They kissed and she could feel the heavy thud of his heart against her bare beast as his hands took hold of hers and guided them to his trouser buttons. He nuzzled her neck and with an accelerated pulse and shaking fingers she forced the first three buttons through holes, brushing the swelling beneath with the tips of her fingers several times. Abruptly he pressed her hand so that she could not move. 'Keep still. Let me calm down,' he said against her ear.

'What do you mean?'

A chuckle sounded in his throat. 'It's too nice.'

'What is?'

'What you're doing.' He took her hands away and held her at arm's length. 'I don't know what we're going to do. I want you, but we could end up in trouble.'

'Can't we get married?' She struggled to get close to him again but he continued to hold her off.

'It's not that easy and you know it,' he murmured. 'I'll have to do some thinking. It's getting late. I'll have to go.'

'Already?' She could not hide her disappointment.

He kissed her and she clung to him. He released her with obvious reluctance. 'It's time you were getting back or we'll have your father breathing brimstone and fire.'

'Shall I see you tomorrow?'

He nodded. 'I'm on in the early hours but I'll hope to see you here towards the end of the morning.'

They parted at the head of the companionway that led to her parents' cabin. Rebekah began to think up excuses.

She was not far from the cabin when she collided with a staggering Shaun, who stared at her from bleary eyes. Thinking that in his drunken state he had not recognised her, she would have passed without speaking but he dragged on her arm and stuttered, 'Why don't you leave my brother alone?'

'I don't think it has anything to do with you.' Rebekah's voice was curt. She made to pull away but he stumbled into her and she fell against the wall. Suddenly his hands and mouth seemed to be everywhere and she was slapping at him. 'I'll scream,' she hissed, 'if you don't stop it!'

'And wake everybody?' he sneered, and rammed her against the wall.

She screamed.

A couple of doors opened and Shaun removed his hands as if she was a burning chestnut.

'Rebekah!' It was her father's voice.

She turned on Shaun quickly. 'Go! Or you'll get what for!'

Her father had seen them and was hurrying along the corridor.

'I'll bloody get you,' said Shaun, before making a stumbling retreat.

Her father would have pushed by her if Rebekah had not seized his arm. 'Papa! A complete stranger, and he wouldn't let me past.'

He wrenched his sleeve out of her grasp. 'A stranger?' he said sardonically. 'I thought I recognised him as one of those damned O'Neill boys.'

She felt a chill of apprehension, realising her mistake in screaming. 'How could it be?' she said, her voice quivering. 'You've got O'Neills on the brain, Papa!'

'Don't be impudent!' His eyebrows hooded suspicious eyes. 'I'll check the lists – and if it is him, I'll have something done. It's a good job it's not nine o'clock yet or you'd be in worse trouble. Now get into the cabin.' He gave her a push that sent her stumbling along the passageway.

. That night she dreamed of Trim Castle in Ireland where her father had taken her as a girl. It was large and forbidding and frightening. She was looking through an opening at the sea far below, knowing that Daniel had gone somewhere far away while she was locked in a tower. It was all her father's fault and she had to get out before he came back. Suddenly the window wall vanished and she was airborne, flapping her arms as she sped over the sea, but there was someone behind her. That someone took on the shape of a banshee and her fear grew into an overwhelming panic. It would catch her and she would never see Daniel again!

Chapter Six

Scared by her dream, Rebekah could hardly wait to meet Daniel the next day and she was halfway up the companion-way to the boat deck far too early when she heard footsteps behind her.

Daniel took her hand. 'I nearly bumped into your father. He came into the smoking saloon so I made a quick exit.'

'Shaun wasn't there?' Her voice was strained.

'He told me what happened,' said Daniel, his expression suddenly vexed.

She felt certain his brother had not told him everything. 'This morning Papa's going to check the passenger list to see if you're both on it,' she said quietly.

'He'll find no trace of Shaun. I smuggled him aboard.'

'Papa's very determined.'

He nodded. 'He'll still have difficulty. I wish I'd left Shaun at home now. He's always been trouble. I spent more time getting him out of fixes than myself when we were kids.'

'I thought it was your older brothers who were the troublemakers?'

He grimaced. 'They were, but Mam always said it was Daddy's fault. When he got drunk he was like a mad hog. I remember kicking him back once when he hit me. I was about five, and he landed me such a clout that my ear swelled up and I couldn't hear properly for days. It got so bad in the end that I was glad when he became ill and died.'

She was horrified. 'Papa was never like that! It's just lately that – '

'He's frightened and worried,' interrupted Daniel in a positive voice. 'He's not young to be taking such a big step as emigrating.'

'He doesn't seem to be bothered about that,' murmured Rebekah.

'He wouldn't tell you.'

'No.' She was silenced for a moment, then she murmured, 'What will we do if he does find out you're on the ship?'

'He hasn't yet. Let's worry about it another day.' He pulled her towards him and for a while there was no more talk.

They resumed talking about her father when some people came up on deck. 'If you weren't a Catholic and a rebel, he might accept you,' said Rebekah.

'But I am,' Daniel said emphatically.

She stared at him. 'People do get round the religious thing. My parents did.'

'Nobody's ever done it in our family.'

'There's always a first time.'

Daniel shook his head at her. 'Do you realise me mam would spin in her grave? She was always wanting me to settle down with a nice respectable Catholic girl, schooled by the nuns and as innocent as a newborn chick. In fact I know one in Liverpool. A friend of me cousin. She'd bear me numerous children, all to be raised as good, clean-living Catholics.'

Immediately Rebekah felt threatened. 'What's this girl's name?'

'Marie. She's got the softest brown hair and goes to mass every day.' His eyes twinkled. 'She knits me socks and prays that I'll be a reformed character. Me cousin Maureen told me that's so.'

'Her prayers don't seem to be working very well,' said Rebekah, raising her eyebrows. 'Have you kissed her?'

'Only the once.'

'Oh?'

'She didn't take to it like you. All screwed up for it she was. It was like kissing a prune. But I'm sure she'd make a faithful, dutiful wife.'

'She sounds too good to be true.'

'Sure, and she's an angel.'

83

Rebekah looked him squarely in the face. 'Then she should be in Heaven – with your mother, if she's the kind of girl she wants.'

He shook his head at her in mock reproof. 'If I had any sense and was a good, clean-living Catholic, she's the girl I should think of marrying. But when a man's in love it's not clean living he's thinking about. It's kissing and cuddling, and – ' His look said the rest and she could only agree with him because inside she had that physical ache for him again. She tried not to think about the future but went into his arms.

It was on the way down the companionway that they met Rebekah's mother going up. She wished desperately that she could have escaped with the barest, 'Hello, Mama.' And she did press Daniel's arm, hoping he would take the hint and go ahead, but he did not.

'I've been wondering where you were,' said her mother, addressing Rebekah but staring at Daniel.

'I'm hoping you won't mind my walking with your daughter?' he said, taking off his cap. 'It's nice and fresh on the boat deck. Unlike the engine room.' He held out a hand. 'I'm – '

'This is – Willie Smith, Mama,' interrupted Rebekah. 'I met him at the Entertainment. He asked me to walk round the deck with him.'

Her mother shook Daniel's hand. 'How do you do, Mr Smith?'

'Very well, thank you.' He avoided looking at Rebekah and she did not look at him as he exerted his charm. 'And yourself, Missus? Miss Rhoades was telling me that you haven't been well.'

'I'm much better, thank you.'

'I'm pleased to hear that. If you aren't minding, I'll be leaving Miss Rhoades with you as I'm on duty within the half hour. It's been nice meeting you.' He looked in Rebekah's direction. 'I enjoyed our walk.' She murmured polite agreement and did not watch him go.

'A nice-looking and polite young man, but not Mr Eaton,' said her mother calmly.

'I never said I'd been with Mr Eaton.' Rebekah fiddled with her glove, and looked down the steps.

'So you didn't. Shall we see if the air is still fresh on the boat deck?' Her mother ascended the stairs.

Rebekah followed her. 'Where's Papa?'

Her mother ignored her question. 'I presume that you were with Mr Smith last evening?'

Rebekah was about to tell a lie but changed her mind. What purpose would it serve. 'Yes, Mama.'

'Your father's worked up about some young man.'

'Mr Eaton?' Rebekah picked a piece of cotton from her sleeve.

Her mother looked at her severely. 'I was your age once, Becky. I saw the way the pair of you didn't look at each other.'

Rebekah dropped the thread. 'Didn't look at each other?'

'Yes! It's in case you give anything away. If two people like each other, they can't easily hide it. They try. How your father and I tried to keep it from our Esther and my father!'

'Mama – ' began Rebekah.

'I won't say don't see him,' interrupted her mother, clasping her hands. 'In fact, I won't even say bring him to meet your father.'

'I wouldn't,' said Rebekah quietly. 'We've made no arrangements. He has duties.'

'Duties.' Her mother smiled. 'Of course, he's a sailor. I used to adore sailors. We had plenty of them coming into our shop, trying to sell us things. The ones I met always had exciting tales to tell. The only trouble was that our Esther would always hover. But he seems a decent enough young man. Irish blood somewhere, I think.'

'He has family in Liverpool,' said Rebekah quickly.

'Don't half the Irish?' Sarah hesitated. 'Anyway, next time you see him, if it's evening have him escort you to our cabin. That way you'll be safe from drunkards. Now let's go and have some of that fresh air.

She put her hand through Rebekah's arm and urged her out on deck, changing the subject to talk of apartments in New York. Rebekah let her talk flow over her, trying not to worry whether her mother would tell her father about the meeting with Daniel.

'Well, Becky, there aren't any O'Neills down on the passenger list,' said her father, at the lunch table. 'But don't be thinking I've given up. They could be using a different name. Or they could be crew working as deckhands.'

85

Trust her father to put them down as deckhands, thought Rebecca mutinously, aware of her mother's gaze.

'Who are these O'Neills, Adam?' asked Sarah.

'Bloody rebels,' he muttered, putting down his teacup.

'Language, Adam,' murmured Rebekah's mother. 'What would rebels be doing on a ship going to America?'

'Their president's in America. They could be taking messages.'

His wife's hand slackened on her fork. 'I don't think that's going to affect us, Adam. Shall we talk of something else.'

He changed the subject and Rebekah breathed easier. She caught Brigid's eye but the Liverpudlian remained silent and later followed her out of the dining room. 'I take it,' she said, 'that the fella you told me about, and one of the O'Neills yer dad mentioned, are one and the same person?'

Rebekah leaned on the rail, and put her chin in her hand. 'How did you guess?'

'I know a Daniel O'Neill.' Brigid's elbow nudged hers. 'His auntie lives in our street.'

'That's a coincidence,' said Rebekah, not sure whether she was pleased or not that Brigid should know Daniel.

'They happen. He's a nice bloke. Friendly like. No sides.'

Rebekah sighed. 'We bumped into my mother and I wanted him to make a quick exit, but he didn't budge and had to go and be nice to her. I'm worried in case she tells Papa.'

'I presume he didn't use his own name.'

'I introduced him as Willie Smith.'

'Smith? Real original.'

Rebekah allowed herself a smile. 'It was the best I could do on the spur of the moment.'

'What are yer going to do? Yer dad seems pretty determined to find Danny.'

'I know.' Rebekah bit on a nail. 'I'll have to wait and see.'

'It might be best if you stopped seeing him.'

Rebekah's eyes clouded and she took her finger out of her mouth. 'I can't! I just can't! Even if Papa beat me – ' The words were low and intense.

Brigid's expression was concerned. 'I'd think about it if I were you, luv.'

'I already have,' said Rebekah, and walked away to make a fruitless search of the decks for Daniel.

Supper passed without incident and she decided after listening to Brigid's talk about the Entertainment and the dancing that followed, she might as well go along and see what went on. She changed into a new skirt and the eau-de-nil crêpe-de-chine blouse her aunt had bought her. On her way in she met Daniel, who immediately led her outside.

'Why did you have to interrupt me when I was talking to your mother?' he demanded.

'I thought – '

'I know what you thought.' He pulled her hand through his arm. 'If you'd waited for me to finish, Becky love, you'd have heard me tell your mother that my name was Peter Riley. You saying Smith complicates things. There isn't one on this ship.'

'I'm sorry. Papa said that you might be going under another name, and that you could be members of the crew! He's not going to give up, Daniel.'

'Well, he's not going to find an O'Neill amongst the crew.'

'If he gets at the truth – ' Her expression clouded.

The corners of his mouth tightened. 'I don't want you getting hurt because of me.'

'He mightn't hit me,' she said with difficulty. 'He could just try and make sure that I don't see you again.'

He nodded. 'I'd prefer that.'

'You would?'

'There's always a way round things. Didn't I get on this ship?' He pulled her into the shadows and into his arms.

Rebekah held him tightly, still scared. 'It'll be New York soon and Papa'll make sure he keeps me away from you.'

'I'll think of something.'

She hoped he could but was still worried. She kissed him with a desperation she had never felt before.

Their kisses became more passionate, grew wilder, and his hands began to roam her body. He unbuttoned her blouse and eased the garment down to her waist, flicking off the straps of her underskirt. She looked into his face and it was soft with desire. She felt a quivering sensation in her stomach and a rush of anticipation. His mouth was on her neck, throat, breasts, covering her with little kisses, sending tremors through her. She felt like a volcano on the simmer and was aware that he was trembling with desire too.

Then unexpectedly he drew away and turned to the boat on their right. He climbed up and began to unfasten its covering, threw it back and pulled her up and inside the boat.

It was not the most comfortable place she had ever been in, but she rid herself of her clothes. Her breasts tingled as they brushed his bare chest and then his mouth was fastened on hers again and he began to explore and caress her all over as he had done once before. They moved together as if their bodies were moulded out of the same clay and she held on to him with all her strength. When she finally arched against him, he kissed her to drown the cry that rose in her throat and then withdrew quickly, moaning.

Afterwards they lay in each other's arms. 'We can't risk that again, Becky love,' murmured Daniel. 'It was a near thing. I wouldn't shame you.'

'It might mean that they would have to let us marry.'

A sharp laugh escaped him. 'He'd lock you away first. It's not going to be easy.'

'I know.'

'I have to go back to Ireland.'

'I'll go with you.' She hesitated. 'There or Liverpool.'

'You still don't want to go back to Ireland.' His voice suddenly sounded weary.

'I'll go wherever you want me to.'

He sighed and sat up. 'I should give you up.'

'But you won't?' There was a note of panic in her voice.

'Not if I can help it,' he said soothingly.

They kissed and got out of the boat. He fastened the cover back. His hand caressed the side of her face. 'I love you, Becky.' He kissed her again. 'I've got to go. I'm on duty soon. I'll see you early tomorrow evening. Perhaps we can go dancing? It would be more sensible.'

She nodded and they parted.

Rebekah had hoped that her father might still be in the smoking saloon when she returned to the cabin but he was lying on his bunk, fully dressed, filing his nails.

'Where were you, miss, when I looked in on the Entertainment?'

'What time was that?' She slipped off her jacket and placed it on the top spare bunk.

'It doesn't matter what time it was, you weren't there. With Mr Smith, were you, on the boat deck?'

She glanced quickly at her mother, who did not lift her eyes from her book, but Rebekah could tell from the stiff way she held her shoulders that she was no longer reading. She moistened her mouth. 'I was with Mr Smith. He's good company.'

'He isn't on any of the lists!' Her father flung the nail file on the bed and sat up. 'Perhaps it was Mr Jones? Maybe Mr Riley or Mr Merriman? Then again it might be none of them but Shaun O'Neill's brother!'

Rebekah cleared her throat. 'I thought you said there were no O'Neills on this ship?'

'That was before I saw one of them standing at the bar in the smoking saloon. He had gone before I could get to him but I'm sure it was the younger one.' He slid down from his bed. 'If I find the other one, I'll have them both clapped in irons.'

Rebekah moistened her lips. 'You're being melodramatic, Papa. We're not in England now. You can't just arrest people!'

'I have influence on this ship,' he said in a manner that was very convincing.

She threw a look at her mother, who had put down her book and was twisting a long strand of her loosened hair in an agitated manner.

'Come here, miss.' Her father's words were quietly spoken.

To Rebekah they seemed all the more threatening than if he had shouted, and she stayed where she was.

'Don't provoke me, Becky,' he said. 'I only want to ask you a question and get an honest answer from you.'

'Adam, don't you think it's a bit late – ' began his wife.

'Don't interfere,' muttered her husband, covering the couple of feet that divided him from his daughter. His expression darkened as he seized hold of her arm. He fingered her blouse, which was open at the neck, and pushed her head to one side. He prodded his thumb against her skin. 'What's this? And where did you get this thing you're wearing?'

'It's a blouse that Aunt Esther gave me, Papa!' She attempted to pull away.

89

'I know it's a blouse,' he whispered. 'D'you take me for a bloody fool. But what's the mark on your bloody neck? You look like you've been bloody bit.'

'It was an insect.' It was the first thing that came into her head.

'At sea? You wore the blouse for him, I suppose?' he said in a seething voice, and caught her a blow across the side of her head. 'Get it off and don't let me see you wearing it again. It's cheap and it's nasty and makes you look common.'

'It is not cheap,' said Rebekah, suddenly firing up. 'It cost Aunt Esther a lot of money!'

'Esther!' He seized on the word. 'It's her influence that's caused you to defy me. She's never liked me.'

'Can't this all wait till in the morning?' said his wife in a trembling voice. 'You'll be waking people.'

He stared at her and visibly controlled himself, releasing Rebekah's arm. 'You get ready for bed, Sally. She can go to bed too, but she can give me that blouse first. It's too provocative.'

Rebekah rubbed her arm. 'What are you going to do with it?'

'Just give it to me,' said her father.

She eased her throat. 'It's mine. Aunt Esther bought it for me. You've no right – '

Adam's face began to change colour. 'Don't tell me I have no rights! Women have got too much to say for themselves these days. Now give me that blouse,' he thundered.

The colour ebbed from Rebekah's face and she went behind the bunks and, turning her back on him, took off the blouse. With one hand she reached under her pillow for her nightdress. Expecting her father to do something at any moment she quickly exchanged one garment for the other before sitting on the pillow.

'Well, miss?' he said, ducking his head under the top bunk and thrusting his face close to hers. She drew back hurriedly and pulled her nightgown down over her underwear. He slapped her face. 'I said, where is it?'

She said nothing waiting for the next blow. He thumped her on the upper arm, and she would have fallen off the bed if she had not clutched the post that held the bunks together. The patter of bare feet sounded on the floor.

'Adam, what d'you think you're doing?' His wife heaved on his arm. 'Can't we talk about this sensibly?'

'Let go, woman!' He tried to shrug her off but she hung on grimly and their struggles took them further from Rebekah's bed. She watched them until they broke apart and began to argue in fierce whispers. She could not make out what they were saying but hated to see them arguing and slid beneath the bedcovers, pulling them over her head. Eventually they both fell silent.

With a thumping heart Rebekah waited for her father to make a move towards her. The bunks creaked. She held her breath for what seemed an age but he did not come. Slowly she relaxed and her fingers gingerly touched the sore part of her arm. It could have been worse. She supposed it had been stupid not to give him the blouse and she did not really know why she had been so stubborn about hanging on to it. He would not forgive her nor would he forget that he had seen Shaun.

She fell asleep, only to dream about Trim Castle and escaping the banshee again. She woke with a headache and a nightmare feeling still in her limbs. She tried to rationalise the dream, remembering that outing to Trim Castle again. It was huge and grey and her father had told her that during the Middle Ages the Anglo-Normans had kept hostages there.

And damsels in distress, she supposed, when knights were bold and their menfolk locked their women in chastity belts! Oh God, she was no longer a virgin! What would her father do to her and Daniel if he knew that? Irish rebels were sometimes hung for treason against the British Empire. In the grip of her dream, her fear of her father's power was beyond sensible thought or reason.

Chapter Seven

'Your father has Joshua Green in mind for you.'

Rebekah stared across the cabin at her mother. It was the next day.

'He wants you to be comfortable,' Sarah said earnestly.

'Joshua Green!' Rebekah laughed sharply and lifted her gaze from the magazine she was trying her best to read. 'So he's acting the Victorian papa! It's outdated, Mama. This is the twentieth century.'

A look of resignation crossed her mother's face. 'You might as well say it's what my father did, and perhaps if he hadn't behaved in such a way, we might not have run away the way we did. Believe me, I sometimes wonder whether it was worth it.'

For a moment Rebekah was dumbfounded. She had always believed that her mother thought the world well lost for love. 'You love Papa!'

'Love doesn't pay the rent.'

'Daniel's got a job.'

'I know. He's a sailor. Which means bringing up children on your own. Catholic children.'

'At the moment I don't care about any of that.'

Her mother's mouth firmed. 'Well, you should!' She got up from the bunk. 'Think! And do the sensible thing before your father does something we'll all regret.' She packed up her knitting and left her daughter alone.

Rebekah did not want to think, and hoping that maybe Daniel had got off duty earlier than he had said, she hurried up to the boat deck. She walked up and down, gazing at the single funnel which was almost midship. There was little wind and smoke hung in the sky, its acrid smell tainting the chill salty air. She counted the lifeboats. Daniel had told her that since the sinking of the *Titanic* the safety regulations had changed. Once it had been the ship's tonnage that decided the number of lifeboats, now it was how many passengers were aboard. She paced the deck several times, exchanging greetings with other people taking the air, but did not see Daniel. She did not go back to the cabin, though but walked around despite the cold.

It grew misty and she turned up the collar of her coat, hoping that Daniel would not be much longer. He wasn't.

Rebekah took his arm. 'Let's not go to the dance. I've got a feeling that Papa might turn up.'

He nodded. 'We don't want a confrontation on the dance floor.'

'Definitely not!' She shivered at the thought.

He glanced down at her. 'New York doesn't mean the end of everything for us. You might want to pretend to play it your father's way, for safety's sake. We could give things time. In a few months the fighting could have finished.'

She gripped his hand and said forlornly, 'I don't want to play it his way. Anything might happen. I'm prepared to turn round as soon as we get to New York and go back across the Atlantic. I can get a job. I have worked. I can type! We can save up.' A flush darkened her cheeks. 'When you dock, I'll make a home for you. I'm not asking you to marry me. There's the religious thing, and I'm not twenty-one.'

Daniel stared at her, a gleam in his eyes. 'Just like that, you'd live with me? I can just see me going to confession and saying, "Father, I have sinned by not only falling in love with a *Protestant* girl, but living with her as well." The priest would love that!'

She stared at him and smiled. 'Would you really say that to the priest? What would he say back?'

'Never mind. But we couldn't do it. It's a mortal sin and so is preventing babies.'

'But we did it and you said I'll be all right. We don't have to have babies until we get married. We could still do it lots of times.'

He grinned. 'You're a terrible girl, Becky. We'll have to wait and get married properly, but I don't know when.' He frowned. 'Your father's been asking questions in the crew's quarters.' He fell silent.

'And?'

'He's offering money for information about two Irish brothers. A couple of the lads know about Shaun. Any time now they're going to take the money.'

She was scared for him. 'What do you want to do? Papa's planning to take over Green's agency in New York so you'd know where to find me if – '

'That's why you had the guided tour?'

'Yes. Papa's going to be Joshua Green's agent. He took me to see his house in Liverpool.'

His eyes flickered over her face. 'A huge place, is it?'

'It's nowhere near a mansion. It's not as big as the houses in Merrion Square in Dublin. He has a sister living with him. Widowed. She's a bit – queer. I felt sorry for her.'

'Who wouldn't.'

'What do you mean?'

'It doesn't matter. Green and I were on the same ship once, that's all. It was torpedoed.'

'And?'

'It has nothing to do with now,' he said softly. 'Can you hear the music? Shall we dance here on deck?'

'I can't.'

'I'll teach you.'

She wanted to ask more about Joshua Green but was wise enough to know he did not want to talk. She wanted to go on about marrying but knew that would have to wait too. She gave herself up to the moment.

Despite the cold and the mist which had thickened she enjoyed learning to dance with him as teacher. Everything seemed unreal, including the mournful sound of a foghorn in the distance. They were so wrapped up in each other that at first the footsteps coming in their direction did not register. As they drew closer she opened her eyes and looked over Daniel's shoulder. Instantly she recognised the shadowy figure behind. 'It's Papa,' she said through lips that quivered.

Daniel looked down at her and for a moment his hands held her tightly. 'It's all right! Don't look so scared. It's happened now. There's nothing we can do.' He dropped his arms and they turned around.

For a moment nothing was said. Then her father addressed Rebekah. 'Your mother's in the cabin. You can go there.'

She shook her head. 'No. I want to hear what you say to Daniel.'

Her father's expression seemed to set like stone. 'You will do as you are told,' he said, stressing every word. 'I told you to have nothing to do with this man.'

'Papa, I'm nearly twenty. I'm not a child to be ordered around.' Her voice shook with sudden anger. 'The world has changed since the war. Women – '

'I don't want a lecture on emancipation.' A tic twitched his left eye and his fists clenched. 'This man's a traitor and a murderer, and you'll do as I tell you.'

'He is not a murderer!' she said hotly. 'Just because his brothers – You judge him without knowing him!'

'I don't have to know him!' Her father's voice rose. 'You're talking to a man who belongs to an organisation that wears a mask to cover up its activities.! So get away from him and go to your mother!'

She tilted her chin. 'No.'

Daniel spoke. 'Becky, go.'

She looked at him but before she could speak or move, her father's hand shot out. The force of the blow knocked her head back against Daniel's shoulder. 'I will not have you speak to me like that!' Her father's whole body seemed to loom larger with uncontrollable rage.

Daniel steadied her. 'Don't you ever hit her again!' His voice shook with fury.

'Don't you tell me what to do with my own daughter, you filthy rebel.' Her father's fists clenched.

'Papa, please!' Rebekah held a hand to her head in an attempt to stop it spinning. 'I'll stop seeing him. Just don't hurt him.'

'Hurt me!' cried Daniel, putting her on one side. 'It's me that'll bloody hurt him. Hitting you! He's a coward!'

'I'm no coward, you turf hopper!' Her father swung his arm.

Daniel easily parried the blow before lunging forward and catching him a punch on the chest. 'You're a bully. One of Green's yes men!'

Her father staggered slightly before making a recovery and coming forward with surprising speed. 'I'll have you know, boy, that I have shares in the company,' he panted. 'I'm one of the bosses. I'll have you fired! I'll see you never work again!'

Daniel was so surprised that he dropped is guard slightly and was caught a clout across the mouth. He began to bleed.

Now the two men grappled with each other, trying to throw each other off balance. Her father caught Daniel a vicious kick in the shins and he stumbled backwards. The blood from the blow on his lip was running down his chin. He prevented himself from falling and ran at the older man with his head down. Her father doubled over but soon straightened up to ram his fist at Daniel's mouth again. More blood!

Rebekah screamed. She had had enough. 'Stop it! Stop it!' She jumped on her father's back but he flung her off. Daniel's fist caught him on the jaw.

She drew back, her heart pounding. She would get Mama! She would stop Papa before either of them did each other a real injury.

She fled along the deck, only vaguely aware of a flurry of whistles blowing somewhere nearby. A foghorn sounded, then came what seemed to be an answering blast of sound. Her hands shook as she sought to open the cabin door but her fingers were shaking so much that it took her longer than usual.

At last it opened. 'Mama!' she cried. 'Come quickly!'

Her mother's pale face stared at her from the bunk. Rebekah took a few steps forward. 'Mama?' The eyes were red-ringed, as if she had been crying. Suddenly they widened as there was a noise like an explosion and then a dull, roaring sound. The whole ship seemed to shake. Next came a tearing and rending, a crunching and rippling noise. Rebekah wanted to call out but was abruptly flung to the floor. Her bunk crashed down on her. A dark object came through the side of the ship and crushed her parents' bunk beds against the wall.

Chapter Eight

Daniel became aware of the fog whistles at the same time as he noticed that Rebekah had gone. He swung her father round by the lapels of his coat and brought his fist back ready for the blow that he hoped would finish the fight. Then suddenly he saw, terrifyingly close, the prow of a ship looming up through the fog. 'Holy Jesus!' he whispered, crossing himself and taking a step back.

'Ha!' exclaimed Rebekah's father triumphantly through swollen lips, and punched him with the last of his strength.

Daniel staggered back as the ship hit, lost his footing and went head over heels backwards. Momentarily he rested on his haunches, trying to get his breath back. Then he sprang to his feet as the other ship crunched its way through steel and wood along the side of the *Samson* towards him. He turned and fled from its destructive path, down the nearest companionway. He had to find Rebekah! Thank the holy mother she had left! Her father . . . He didn't want to think of that. Where they had fought was just a tangled mess.

The lights had gone out and doors were opening. There were shouts. A woman screamed. People were running along corridors in panic, fighting to get past him as he searched and called, went up and down corridors, feeling his way. He realised that what he was doing was crazy. He presumed that Becky had gone back to her cabin but didn't know where that was exactly.

A light from a torch suddenly shone in his face, half blinding him. 'Is that you Riley?' The voice was incredulous.

'Yes!' He knocked down the torch with bloodied knuckles.

'You look a mess. Not that it matters. Come with me!'

'What?'

'Yer wanted, mate! In the engine room! It's flooding down there and there's a boiler making a funny noise. They need your expertise.'

'Hell!' Daniel groaned, and clutched his hair. 'I have to find someone.'

'You won't be finding anyone if you don't come. That boiler could blow.'

Daniel took a deep breath and told himself to calm down. The odds were that Becky was all right. There were a heck of a lot of people running around.

'Well! Are you coming?' demanded the mate, shining the torch into his face again.

Daniel nodded and went with him.

For a long while Rebekah lay stunned, her thoughts incoherent. She was aware of a crushing weight on her right arm. Then there was a babble of voices outside along the passageway, hurrying footsteps and the sound of rushing water.

Fear was blighting her courage and it took several deep flurried breaths to calm her nerves and enable her to try and move her legs. At least they seem uninjured. She tried freeing her arm but the pain was excruciating and caused sickness and dizziness. Dear God, was she going to die? No, please! What had happened to Mama! She called to her mother but there was no answer.

Lifting her head she stared in the direction where she had last seen her mother and slowly, as her eyes became accustomed to the dark, could just make out the shambles that was her parents' bunk. She did not want to believe that her mother could not have survived. It was a nightmare. What about Daniel? What had happened? She must get out of here.

She screamed and carried on yelling for help until at last someone did come. The door was forced open and two men came in. One picked her out by torchlight and came over to her.

'You all right, luv?'

She laughed weakly. 'Oh, yes. I'm just lying here for the good of my health.'

'Glad you've still got your sense of humour.' He turned to his companion who had gone over to the other bunk and was trying to prise it away from the wall. 'Give us a hand here vicar.'

The parson delayed several moments and could be heard praying. Then he came over, still in his pyjamas. Rebekah cleared her throat as the two men began to lift the weight from her. 'Mama's all right, isn't she?'

'Sorry, my dear.' The parson's hand was gentle on her cheek. 'It must have been almost instantaneous if that is of any comfort to you.'

She did not answer but a sob swelled her throat and tears blurred her vision. A few moments later she was free and one of the men was saying that her arm was broken. The parson was wrapping her in a blanket. The other man lifted her and she recognised him as their steward. 'I have a friend. He's an engineer. Da – No, Peter Riley,' she croaked. 'He's one of the engineers. He was with my father.'

'The engine rooms are flooding but they're getting it under control,' the steward answered. 'He should be all right. Ain't seen no sign of your father, though, miss. But that's not surprising, the panic everyone's in with the dark and all.'

She closed her eyes briefly, pressing down *her* panic, and said huskily as he helped her up, 'What happened?'

'This other ship came out of the fog and hit us. It's ripped this side open, but there's nothing for you to worry about. We're in no immediate danger.' His voice sought to soothe.

'No. I've got nothing to worry about.' she whispered before bursting into tears. He patted her shoulder and the parson told her that she would be all right. They would see that she was taken care of.

The passenger alleyways were still in darkness. 'Why aren't the lights on?' she stuttered.

'Water's short-circuited the dynamos,' said the steward cheerfully, flashing his torch. 'We'll take you on top. Don't worry.'

She wished he would stop telling her not to worry. What was happening to Daniel? Where was her father?

The decks were crowded with people in various states of dress. Some were crying. One man sat calmly playing solitaire, sitting on a lifebelt. An elderly woman was putting up

99

her hair. It was still foggy and the ship's whistles played a mournful tune. The doctor came and put her arm in splints and a sling; gave her a couple of tablets. She asked him about the water coming into the engine rooms and he said he knew nothing about it. She looked round for a sign of someone she recognised and a few feet away saw a white-faced Brigid with a blood-stained bandage tied round her bright hair.

Rebekah struggled to her feet and stumbled light-headed over to her friend. She slumped down next to her and put her free hand through Brigid's. 'Mama's dead and Papa's missing.' She barely recognised her own voice. 'Are you badly hurt?' Brigid shook her head. 'Keith?' asked Rebekah. There was no answer but the Liverpudlian's eyes were filled with tears.

'Oh God,' whispered Rebekah, and gently drew Brigid's head down on to her shoulder.

She did not know how long they sat there while the deck started to empty. Mr Eaton came up to them. 'Miss Rhoades, will you and the other lady come with me, please? We want to get you off the ship.'

She stared up at him in a daze. 'Off the ship?'

'Yes. It's sinking. But you don't have to worry,' he said quickly. 'It'll take some time and the wireless operator's wired for help. There are several ships on the way. It shouldn't be long before you're picked up.'

Rebekah nodded and took a deep breath. 'Daniel O'Neill . . . no, Peter Riley! He's one of your engineers. Is he down in the engine room?'

His smile fixed, he said reassuringly, 'Yes, he is. It's a bit fraught down there with the pumps being worked overtime, but I don't think any of them are in danger. There was a bad moment I believe when the boiler could have blown, but Riley managed to turn some valve or other and prevented it happening.' He hesitated. 'He said when I found you – that he's sorry, but your father didn't see the ship coming. I presume – '

'He knows I'm all right?' Rebekah whispered.

He moved his shoulders in a gesture that revealed his discomfort. 'Not yet.' He offered her his arm and she accepted it with gratitude.

'What happened to the other ship?' she stammered.

'What?' He seemed distracted but answered, 'She drifted off, but we've had a message from her. Her bow's badly damaged but she'll keep afloat.'

'Was there anybody hurt?'

'Several of the crew were killed.' He hesitated. 'I'm sorry about your parents.'

'Thank you,' she said woodenly. They both fell silent.

It was no simple task getting on her lifebelt. Neither was it easy or pleasant having to climb down the ladder into a small bobbing boat.

Rebekah and Brigid cuddled up to each other because it was freezing cold. The fog lifted a little, and although their boat had been rowed away from the *Samson* they could still see the great rip in her side. She was listing badly to port and Rebekah felt taut with apprehension. It began to rain.

People moaned and groaned and Rebekah felt she had never felt so miserable in the whole of her life. Time passed slowly and pictures from her childhood drifted through her mind. It occurred to her that now her father was dead, he could not stop her seeing Daniel. She tried to draw comfort from the thought even as she wept.

It grew lighter, and although there was no sign of the sun several people said they felt better. After what seemed hours someone said the crew had begun to leave the ship. That it could not be long before the *Samson* went down. An exhausted and soaked Rebekah peered through the rain, trying to make out the faces of the figures climbing into the boats. Water was washing the ship's decks and some of the men jumped into the sea. A cheer went up suddenly and the sound of the ship's whistle and siren were heard. Distracted, she turned and saw a steamer looming up through the downpour. When next she looked at the *Samson* there were only two figures clinging to her rigging. She presumed one of them was the captain. The next moment they were in the water – had gone under – came up. Under – up. They were swimming for the nearest lifeboat. There was a great cracking and a gurgling sound as the *Samson* sank, and for a while the sea was a great churning mass.

101

Brigid sobbed, clinging to Rebekah, who clung to her just as desperately. Had Daniel got off? How could she find out? Dear God, please let him be safe?

Within half an hour they were taken aboard the *S.S. Reliant* and wrapped in rough warm blankets. Rebekah's teeth chattered so much against the rim of the cup of hot sweet tea that she spilt it. Her head felt as if it was splitting and her throat felt raw. She fought to keep burning eyes open for sign of Daniel. Then she saw Shaun.

Three times she had to call his name before he showed any sign of hearing her. Then he sauntered over, cup in hand, blanket about his shoulders. Close up, she could see the strain in his face.

'Is Daniel all right?' she stammered.

He scowled. 'Didn't you see him in the water?'

'No.' She felt as if her heart was being squeezed and she feared his answer. 'He was rescued?'

There was a pause. 'If he was, I didn't see it,' said Shaun with a tight smile. 'He could be drowned. All I do know is that he's not on this ship.' Without another word he turned and walked away.

Rebekah stared after him. She felt as if *she* was drowning in a sea of misery, pain and discomfort. It couldn't be true! It just couldn't be true! He was meant for her. God couldn't take him away. That wasn't fair. She loved him, needed him, wanted him above anything else in the world. She would die without him.

'I don't know if I can bear it.' Brigid's voice was low. 'Keith, your parents, Daniel. I think I'll kill myself.'

'Don't say that!' Rebekah eased her throat and attempted a smile. 'I think I'm going to die anyway.'

A corner of Brigid's mouth lifted wearily. 'I won't kill myself if you don't die on me.'

'Is that a promise?' A cough was tickling her throat.

'Cross my heart,' Brigid's voice wobbled.

'Right. That's it, 'murmured Rebekah. 'We stay together.'

Brigid nodded and the pair of them sat on, sipping their tea with the tears dripping into the cooling liquid.

A doctor came and spoke kindly to them. He examined their injuries and told Rebekah to follow him. Brigid went with her.

Rebekah watched as he sprinkled plaster on strips of bandage then dipped them in water before wrapping it around her broken arm. She was a mass of aches and her throat and head felt worse. Her heart felt like a lump of stone. After the plaster set they were taken to a cabin and given warm clean nightwear, a hot milky drink and some tablets.

The last memory in Rebekah's mind before the tablets took effect was of Daniel saying, 'I love you, Becky.' Then it was overlaid by the grey rain-splattered scene of men struggling in the water while Shaun's words ran through her head.

Rebekah woke in a small room to a conversation going on in the distance. Her head turned on the smooth cool pillow and for the first time in what seemed forever there was no pain in her chest or her head. Where exactly was she? Who was talking? The memory of her arrival was hazy but she did remember that she had seen Brigid since coming here. Was that her she could hear talking? She tried to call her friend's name but her voice was only a whimper.

There was a glass of water on the cabinet by the bed but it was an enormous effort to hold it, and then another to lift it to her lips as she sagged across the bed, her broken arm held awkwardly against her chest. She sipped slowly. That was better. She cleared her throat. 'Brigid'. The voices stopped abruptly and there was the sound of heavy footsteps and lighter hurrying ones moving towards the door.

Rebekah squinted at the door, trying to recall who had brought her to this clean blue-painted room. One of the voices had said something about nearly dying. Were they talking about her? She had been having terrible dark dreams. Daniel and water . . . the ship . . . Mama and Papa! It was as if there was a blizzard in her head. A moan issued from her lips and her face turned into the pillow.

The door opened. Rebekah's wet cheek rubbed against the white cotton before she twisted to see who had entered.

'How are you, Miss Rhoades?'

She made no answer, staring at the man. He was familiar but she could not place him.

'Becky, Mr Green says he wants to take you back to England.'

'Who? What?' Rebekah's gazed shifted to Brigid's pale thin face.

Joshua, who was wearing a black suit, removed his hat before approaching the bed. 'Surely you haven't forgotten me? I've come to help you.'

There was a brief silence before she murmured. 'I haven't forgotten. You're the owner of the *Samson* . . . or you were.'

His expression was grave. 'It's a sorry business. A terrible thing to happen. I don't know what to say – '

'I don't think you can be blamed for the fog or for the other ship hitting us, Mr Green,' she said quietly, easing herself up against the pillows with difficulty. Brigid rushed forward to help her.

He looked relieved. 'I'm glad you can look at it like that, Miss Rhoades. We are, of course, taking legal action against the other ship. We want damages for the loss of the *Samson* and her cargo – as well as for the lives lost and passengers' belongings.'

She eased her throat. 'I would like to go to church.'

He nodded. 'We'll have a memorial service for them.' His voice was sombre. 'And for the others who died . . . as soon as you feel able to cope with it.'

Rebekah looked at Brigid. 'You do know that Mrs O'Shaugnessy's husband – '

'Yes. We've been talking.'

'About going back to England?' she asked.

'I didn't think you would wish to stay in New York.'

'No.' She stared down at the bedcover and her fingers plucked at the sheet. 'Mr Green, one of your engineers helped save a boiler from blowing. He was Irish and I knew him in Dublin.' Her pleading eyes were lifted to his. 'His name was Daniel O'Neill but he went by the name of Peter Riley. Last I heard, he was in the water. I don't know if he was rescued.'

For several moments Joshua did not speak. Then, 'I knew an O'Neill in the war, if it is him you're talking about. We were on the same ship for a while, I haven't had time to see if there's been any losses among the crew because I've only been in New York a few hours, but I'll certainly find out for you.'

She smiled faintly. 'Thank you.'

'It's the least I can do.' He returned her smile. 'I was told by the nurses not to stay long so I'll leave you now but I'll be back later.' He held out his hand. She took it, comforted by its strength and warmth.

The moment he left Brigid came and sat on the bed. 'Well that's that,' she said.

'What's what?' murmured Rebekah.

'Him! His lordship coming to see yer. Apparently it was on his orders that yer got moved from the hospital to this rest home. They only just about allowed me in.'

Tears filled Rebekah's eyes. 'I'm glad they did.' Her voice was unsteady as she squeezed Brigid's hand, noticing how bony it felt. The bandage on her head had gone but there was a yellow bruise and a healing cut on her forehead. She wore a black coat which hung on her. 'How are things? It's the first day I've felt enough myself to consider you?'

Brigid's eyes, with the dark pouches underneath, avoided hers. 'I'm surviving. But don't let's talk about it.' There was a pause while they sought strength from the other's presence. Then the Liverpudlian said in a bright voice, 'I haven't told yer but me brother came in on the same boat as his lordship.'

'Your Pat?'

'Yeah! We'll probably go back on the *Gideon*.' She hesitated. 'How d'yer feel about going on a ship?'

'I haven't thought about it.'

'I don't like it,' said Brigid bluntly. 'But if it's the only way to get back home, then I'll just have to put up with it.'

Rebekah rested her head against the pillows. 'At least you've got a home to go to . . . and your sisters and your mam.' It hurt when she thought of her own mother and she wanted to weep.

There was another pause. 'What about that posh aunt of yours?' asked Brigid.

'Aunt Esther?' She supposed that she had to consider living with her aunt. 'She's family, of course.'

'Better than none.' Brigid hesitated. 'D'yer really believe that Daniel could be alive?'

'You think I'm clutching at straws?'

Brigid's answering silence was frustrating.

'His brother didn't see him drown,' said Rebekah, tilting her chin. 'He could be alive.' Her mind refused to accept that she would never see Daniel again.

'I'm not saying he couldn't be,' muttered Brigid as if the words were forced from her. 'But don't build up yer hopes.'

'Have you seen any sign of Shaun?'

Brigid shook her head and freed her hand. 'I think yer'd be better resting. Short visits – that's what I was told. Yer haven't been well and yer don't want to have a relapse.' She hugged Rebekah and went out.

For a long time Rebekah lay there, fighting back tears and a terrible sense of desolation. Then two nurses came in, one carried a basket of fruit which she said was from Mr Green. The other brought a bowl of broth. She had a nasal twang to her voice and spoke cheerfully about the visitors and how lucky Rebekah was to have an excuse to stay in her nice warm bed as it had begun to throw it down outside. Rebekah let the words flow over her as she drank several spoonfuls of broth voluntarily, and was coaxed into swallowing the remainder. Afterwards, she was left alone, which was the last thing she wanted as thinking only served to depress her spirits further. What if Daniel was dead? How was she going to live without him?

The morning sun put a bit of heart into her and Rebekah felt less inclined to accept the worse. She managed some porridge, a cup of coffee, three grapes, and a trip to the lavatory on her own. Joshua came to visit, and because everything and everybody else was unfamiliar, he seemed to represent reality.

'Did you find out anything about Daniel?' she demanded as soon as the pleasantries were observed.

He paused in the act of sitting on the chair beside the bed and said in deep tones, 'No. I can't find anyone who has seen him since the *Samson* sank.'

'Oh!' She almost fell back into utter despondency, but not quite. 'Have you seen his brother?'

'Brother?' He seated himself, his expression severe. 'Should I have?'

His reaction gave Rebekah pause for deliberation and she lowered her gaze. 'I suppose not. Have you seen Brigid since yesterday? She won't have to pay to return to England, will she?' Her voice was concerned. 'They didn't have much money, and now she has nothing.'

'You're very friendly with this woman?' There was a note in his voice that caused her to slant him a challenging look.

'Mama and Papa didn't object to our friendship and I don't see why you should. Or that it has anything to do with you, Mr Green.'

There was a silence and she saw a brief flicker of annoyance in his face. 'Your father named me as your guardian.'

'You!' She was dismayed and the fingers of her left hand kneaded the sheet as she remembered what her mother had said about her father's plan for her. 'I thought my aunt – ' She stopped abruptly. 'No! Of course not Aunt Esther.'

'I know it will come as a shock to you, but it seems there was no one else.' His expression was affable once more as he withdrew an envelope from his pocket. 'I went to see your aunt as soon as I had the news about the *Samson*. She was concerned for you and gave me this note. I was to tell you that her home is now your home, and I consider the way matters lie at the moment, that's not a bad idea.'

Rebekah took the letter and placed it on the bedside cabinet. 'When can I leave for Liverpool?'

He turned his hat between his hands. 'I've arranged the memorial service for the day after tomorrow. You'll need some clothes. I've asked for some to be brought in for your inspection – and some footwear as well. We'll be leaving the day after the memorial service.'

'Thank you. How long have I been here?'

'Two weeks.'

'Two weeks!' She was aghast. Surely if Daniel was alive she would have heard from him? The realisation sapped her newfound strength and she sank back against the pillows, closing her lids tightly on the tears of weakness.

Joshua leaned forward and took her hand. 'There now, Rebekah. Don't be upsetting yourself. The service will be an ordeal, I know, but I'll be with you. Don't be worrying about anything.'

Her wet lashes lifted. 'I wish people would stop telling me not to worry,' she said through gritted teeth. 'I'm frightened, and terribly unhappy, and I don't know what I'm going to do with the rest of my life. I've got loads to worry about!'

'You're overwrought.' He patted her hand. 'You've suffered a great shock as well as your injuries. It's natural you'll

107

feel this way. What you need is building up. I'm certain your aunt will see to that.'

'Aunt Esther?' Rebekah laughed slightly hysterically. 'She'll expect me to become a Quaker. And I'm not a good girl.'

'Shh! I'll get the nurse and she'll give you something to calm you down,' he said soothingly, dropping her hand and going out of the room.

Rebekah sobbed into her pillow. What was life going to be like with Joshua Green in charge of her affairs, and her having to live with Aunt Esther? She could not see it being exciting or fun. All her dreams had sunk beneath the stormy waters of the Atlantic. She wanted to die, die, die. She thumped the pillow and unexpectedly remembered that was what Brigid had said too.

By the time Joshua and the nurse entered the room Rebekah had gained some control over her emotions. Willingly she took the tablets that would give her brief respite from her misery. 'Good girl,' she heard Joshua say as her eyes closed, and then she drifted, was whizzing across what appeared to be a misty sea. For an instant she recaptured the dream in which she had escaped from the castle and her depression was if anything worse than it had been waking. Then unconsciousness claimed her.

Chapter Nine

Daniel was tired when he alighted from the train at Penn station in New York City but a restless anxiety drove him on through the bustling sidewalks to the vicinity of West 19th Street. It was a fortnight since he had been plucked half drowned and concussed from the sea to be laid in the bottom of a lifeboat by one of the passengers. He could remember little of what had happened after that but later was told in hospital that the wind had risen and they had lost an oar. The boat had drifted but eventually they were picked up by a liner heading for Philadelphia. The captain had refused to take them to New York, saying his first duty was to his own passengers. He would wire to Green's agency in New York that they were safe, and once they were fit for travel they could make their own way there.

Daniel reached the agency with its rather pretentious frontage and went in. A fiercesome-looking female stared at him over steel-rimmed spectacles and he wished he had taken time to freshen himself up. 'Can I help you?' she said frostily.

'I'm looking for a Miss Rebekah Rhoades and Mrs Rhoades. They were passengers on the *Samson*.'

Suddenly it appeared that she knew whom he was talking about because her expression thawed slightly. 'Are you a relative? Because if you are you've just missed the memorial service. It was this morning. Perhaps you'd like to talk to Mr Green?' She stood, and before he could answer, hurried through a doorway behind her.

Memorial service! Daniel sat on one of the chairs in the reception area and put his head in his hands. Dear God, he

109

hoped that was just for Mr Rhoades. He had heard that several passengers had been killed but had hoped . . . could not believe that . . .

'Oh, it's you, O'Neill. Or is it Riley? What can I do for you?'

Daniel lifted his eyes and met Joshua's cool gaze. 'Miss Rebekah Rhoades?' He stood up.

Joshua feigned surprise. 'You knew her?'

'Yes. From Dublin.' He cleared his throat. 'That woman said something about a memorial service.'

'That's right. Friends of yours, were they, O'Neill?' There was the slightest hint of derision in his voice.

Daniel's back stiffened. 'I wouldn't be saying that of Mr and Mrs Rhoades. But Rebekah – '

'The daughter? She's dead,' said Joshua, watching him intently. 'They're all dead. The cabin was smashed to bits. I'm sorry, O'Neill, if she was a friend of yours. Tragic. But there it is. I knew them myself, you know.'

For a moment Daniel just stood there, his face quivering, then he turned and made for the door. Joshua hurried after him and thrust an envelope in his hand. 'Here's you pay, O'Neill. I'm sorry I can't offer you another berth right now.'

Daniel thrust the envelope into his pocket without looking at it or Joshua, and walked out. He had not gone far before he heard the women from the agency calling after him. 'There was a message for you, Mr O'Neill. From a Shaun Riley. He said that if you turned up, to look for him at Kelly's place.'

Daniel gave no sign of hearing but carried on up the street. He could not get the image of Rebekah out of his mind. God, God, God! He wanted to smash something! Anything! Anyone! He wished now he had hit Green's smirking face. The coward didn't give a damn that he was suffering, and Daniel had known it. Aye, he'd known the pain he'd been inflicting, Daniel thought grimly. Becky! Oh Becky, love! That swine didn't care that you were dead!

A long time ago, he had liked Joshua. Funny, that. They had been on a ship leaving Pennsylvania then, carrying a cargo of horses, wheat and oil. It was 1916 and they had been intercepted south-east of Cape Race by a German submarine. They had taken to the lifeboats – or what was left of them. That was when Daniel had discovered a different facet to Mr

110

Joshua Green. If he hadn't been so bloody-minded then, they wouldn't have lost so many men. It had all come back to Daniel when he had been struggling in the water.

Becky . . . Funny, lovely, warm, sexy Becky! He could hear her now saying that she loved him – offering to live in sin with him. He scrubbed away the tears with his coat collar. He would find his brother and get rotten drunk. His fingers searched for the hip flask in his pocket. He hoped that Shaun had not drunk any of the so-called whisky on offer at Kelly's. Some of it could blind a man. He had given his brother fair warning.

Daniel carried on through the wet streets, shivering with cold and shock, until he came to Kelly's. Inside there was a strong smell of sweat and wet wool but the room was warm, if smoky and crowded. Daniel's eyes scanned the room and saw his brother over in a corner with another man. He pushed his way between tables until he reached them. 'So you survived then,' said Daniel, in a voice slurred with grief and weariness, looming over his brother.

Shaun slowly got to his feet, his face alight with relief. 'I knew you weren't fish food! I just knew it!' Awkwardly the brothers hugged each other and then sat with knees touching in the confined space. Daniel exchanged greetings with the other man, whose name was Brendan O'Donovan.

He was a large man with a balding head and several chins. 'Tell us what happened to you, Danny boy.'

Daniel told his tale succinctly. 'Green told me that the Rhoades' cabin was really smashed up. That they were all dead. Did you see it, Shaun? Did you see any sign of Rebekah?' His voice shook. 'Did she suffer, would you say?'

Shaun's throat worked and he avoided his brother's eyes. 'Are you meaning that Quaker that you'd taken a fancy to?'

'Aye.' Daniel's mouth set in a hard line. 'You're knowing right enough who I'm talking about.'

Shaun swirled the beer in his glass. 'I'm knowing nothing about her. I was worrying myself enough about you without caring about her. If Green says she's dead then she must be. Will you have a drink?'

Slowly Daniel shook his head. 'And rot my guts? Get me a coffee.' He took some coins from his pocket. His brother sloped off. Daniel sat, staring at nothing in particular, his thoughts turned in on his own misery, until Brendan jogged his elbow.

'A beauty was she, Danny? English?'

'I'd rather not talk about her.' Daniel's eyes focussed on the American. 'How are things with you? Did Shaun manage to save the goods?'

'He got them to me. Although how much longer De Valera will be exchanging Irish Republican Bonds for dollars, I don't know. Word's out that he's fallen out with the I.R.B. and Devoy. And he didn't do well politically in Washington, as you know. He's not liked for whipping up enthusiasm for the interests of what many in the Senate see as a small, unimportant country on the other side of the ocean.'

'You think there might be a chance of him returning to Ireland?' Daniel frowned and gnawed at his inner lip. 'God knows, from what I've seen of the mess everything's in, they need him. It's anarchy there, and something's got to give. You can't govern a country by bullying methods and the law of the gun. In the end it's got to be done above board. I think it's time de Valera went home.' Daniel stopped abruptly as his brother placed his coffee in front of him. He took out his flask and poured Irish whiskey into the dark liquid. It felt good going down.

'What's this about going home?' asked Shaun eagerly, seating himself. 'I'm game if you are.'

Daniel exchanged glances with his brother and forced a smile. 'I'm all for going home. But I won't be trying for a berth with Green's again. I'll get us on another ship. I've friends.'

Brendan shook his head. 'Well, boys, don't go getting yourselves into trouble.'

Daniel laughed harshly. 'Perhaps this time I will.' He gulped at the hot drink and started to feel the sharp edges of his grief change shape. The room had begun to spin slightly already. He had not eaten all day but it did not seem to matter. He was thinking that at least talking about Ireland, he had found some outlet for his anger and sorrow. Hadn't he spoken to Rebekah about Oisin and his love for his princess and country? Loss of love might break your heart but the land was

112

always there. Rebekah had said it was sad for the princess but Oisin had gone back to Ireland – found faith, only to die.

Life was bloody unfair! Just when you started to believe there was a chance of something different – something sweet, something good – it all went bloody wrong. Rebekah was dead and nothing seemed to matter any more.

Part Two

Chapter Ten

'I never thought I'd cry my eyes out at the sight of the Liver birds.' Brigid wiped her damp face with the back of her hand as she hung over the ship's rail.

Rebekah smiled faintly. 'What are they supposed to be?'

'Our Pat says they're cormorants. I wouldn't know. I always thought they were mythical.' Brigid switched her attention from the Liver building to the waiting crowd below, and suddenly her face brigthened and she waved madly. 'Me mam's down there, and our Kath and her kids!' She put a hand over her mouth. 'Oh Mary, mother of God, they're all there! I think I'm going to howl again.'

'What's wrong with that?' Rebekah straightened her shoulders. 'Of course you're pleased to see them, and I hope they spoil you soft.' She moved away from the rail. 'We'd better say goodbye now.'

Brigid stared at her and said unsteadily, 'Yer'll be all right? You have me address?'

'Yes!' Rebekah hugged her awkwardly. 'Now go to your family.'

'They'll probably be fed up with me by Monday and Mam will be brushing me out of the house, saying that hard work's the cure for all ills . . . to go and get meself a job,' said Brigid in a muffled voice against her shoulder. 'What about that aunt of yours and his lordship?'

'What about them?'

Brigid held Rebekah off from her and said sternly, 'Yer not to let them boss yer about.'

'Fat chance,' said Rebekah.

'Hmm!' Brigid frowned. 'Yer not as tough as yer make out.'

'I'm tougher than you think.' She smiled. 'Now are you going or not?'

Brigid grinned. 'I suppose I'd better go and show me face.'

'And I'd better find his lordship.'

'He's got his eye on yer, so watch yerself.'

Rebekah grimaced. 'He's got no hope.'

'Good.' Brigid gave her one last hug. 'Keep yer chin up.'

'And you. Now go or you'll have me crying.'

'It'd do yer good to cry.'

'I've cried enough to fill an ocean. Go!'

Brigid went but kept looking back and waving until out of sight. Rebekah knew that she was going to miss her terribly but also that it was wrong to depend on her when she had her own family. She blinked back tears, tilted her chin and went in search of his lordship, Joshua Green, who was escorting her to her aunt's house.

'Thy father should have listened to me,' said her aunt, standing in the doorway looking like a plump blackbird in mourning clothes.

'So you said three times in your letter,' murmured Rebekah.

'It's because I felt it so deeply.' Her aunt dabbed at her eyes. 'My poor Sarah. Men! They think they know it all.'

'Some think they do,' agreed Rebekah, remembering how she had struggled against blaming her father for what had happened all the way back across the Atlantic and the Irish Sea. 'But Papa couldn't have forseen the other ship ramming us,' she added. 'And anyway it's no use going on about it. Think about how now you've got to bear with me. I'm sure Hannah's told you just what you're letting yourself in for.'

'Fellas,' muttered Hannah, glaring at her.

'Hundreds of them,' said Rebekah drily, noting Joshua's look. 'I eat them for breakfast.'

'Now thou art just being plain silly.' Her aunt blushed.

Hannah grunted. 'Thee'll rue the day, Miss Esther. Trouble, that's what thee's taking in.'

'Mind your place!' intervened Joshua in a sharp voice. 'You have no right to speak like that about Miss Rhoades. She has been through a lot and needs sympathy and care.'

118

The maid sniffed and without another word went back indoors.

'I've had to speak to her severely myself the last week,' murmured Esther, looking at nobody in particular as she picked up Rebekah's bag. 'Perhaps thou would like to come in, Mr Green, for a cup of tea?'

'Some other time,' he said brusquely. 'Your niece is tired and I have to get home.'

The blush which had just begun to fade in Esther's cheeks surged up again. 'Suit thyself. Rebekah shall we go inside?'

Rebekah nodded but held out a hand to Joshua. 'Thank you for looking after me. Could you let me know when everything is sorted out?'

He inclined his fair head and from his pocket took several banknotes, pressing them into her palm and folding her fingers over them. He held her hand longer than was necessary. 'I'll be in touch.' His voice was warm.

'I'll look forward to it,' she said politely. He hesitated, then kissed her cool cheek before striding off in the direction of West Derby Road.

Rebekah quickly dismissed him from her thoughts, pocketed the money and followed her aunt up the dark lobby into the sitting room. Somehow she had to cope with the next few weeks. The minister who had taken the memorial service had told her to think no further than one day at a time. Good advice, when even the simplest tasks were made difficult due to her broken arm! She struggled to undo her coat and her aunt hurried to help her.

Hannah stood watching them. 'At least that broken arm will stop thy gallop.' Her small dark eyes were unsympathetic. 'That is, unless we're gong to be having Mr High and Mighty Green calling every hour God sends.'

'Hannah,' protested Esther. 'That's uncalled for.'

'Don't worry, Aunt, we understand each other.' Rebekah smiled at the maid. 'Your condolences are really appreciated, Hannah.'

'Hmmph!' The maid turned her back on them and began to make tea.

Esther stared at Rebekah and shook her head. 'I'm sorry, dear. But do sit down and tell me if we will be seeing much of Mr Green. He told me that he's thy guardian. Is it true?'

'It seems so.' Rebekah prepared herself for another attack on her father.

'It's all wrong,' cried her aunt, folding her arms across her bosom. 'I'm thy next of kin! If my dear Sarah had had any say in the matter – '

'If you go on about Papa again, I'll scream,' interrupted Rebekah in a firm voice. 'And I can really scream if I want to. Ask Hannah! If I see a spider I scream. If a man attacks me I scream. Moaning and groaning, nagging and lectures, make me scream and want to carry on screaming. What I need is to be looked after, as Mr Green said.' She sat in an armchair. 'Am I allowed any of that food? I'm hungry.'

Her aunt appeared dazed. 'Of course thou art, dear. Help thyself.'

'It's difficult with my broken arm,' she said softly.

'I'm sorry. I wasn't thinking.' Her aunt placed a couple of sandwiches, a slab of gingerbread and two scones on a plate, putting it on Rebekah's lap. 'What thou needs, my dear, is God in thy life. I remember going through a time when there was a big scream inside me.'

'What happened to it?' said Rebekah, forcing herself to eat a sandwich. Brigid had told her that she had to build herself up, although she had little appetite. 'Did you let it out or did you swallow it?'

'I am a Quaker,' Esther said proudly. 'Due to meditation and prayer, it went. We'll take thee to Hunter Street, Rebekah, and there thou wilt find consolation. Then perhaps thou might wish to help out at St Anne's Centre?'

'Hunter Street?' Rebekah's eyes lifted from contemplation of her plate. 'That's the Friends' Meeting House?'

Her aunt nodded, blue eyes fixed on her niece's face. 'Thy mam spoke of it?'

'Yes. I don't exist in their eyes, do I?' said Rebekah, biting into a scone. 'Mama went and did wrong, and was thrown out.'

'I wouldn't have put it quite like that,' said her aunt, going red again. 'Besides – that's in the past. Thou can start with a clean slate.'

'That's nice.' Rebekah's voice was emotionless.

Her aunt seemed disconcerted and there was silence while she ate a scone. She dabbed her mouth with a napkin.

120

'Perhaps thou would prefer going to the adult class in Breck Road?' she suggested. 'Thou could learn more about our ways there, and of the Bible.'

'I know my Bible, Aunt Esther. Mama and Papa read it to me when I was young, and I also went to church. What I need at the moment is a bit of peace.'

Her aunt took a quick sip of tea before saying, 'Peace! Thou should have been at the Peace Conference of all Friends in August. Rufus Jones gave the lecture. He compared the conscience to a lantern. Emotions upset our judgment – but we must see the light from God.'

'God gave us our emotions,' countered Rebekah.

Her aunt ignored her remark. 'Thou must meet Ellen Gibbs who's the same age as thee. She's very keen on fighting for peace. She and her mother attend my sewing circle on Monday afternoons. I take it thou can sew?'

'I don't think I'll be sewing on Monday.'

'We make garments for the poor but I presume from the only baggage thou hast, thou must be short of clothing. Perhaps thou can sew for thyself? I have some material. Thou wilt need some good combinations. It's almost November and we can't have fires in every room. Good thick wool will keep the draughts out and will see thee through more than one winter.'

'I've silk underwear,' murmured Rebekah, gazing down at her silk-stockinged legs and her small neat feet in the black crocodile skin boots with the tiny buttons up the side. 'Mr Green had some brought into the nursing home for me to choose from.'

'Silk! Mr Green!' Her aunt's brows shot up. 'Thou wilt catch thy death of cold!'

Hannah tutted. 'Disgusting! I told thee what she was like with fellas, Miss Esther.'

'My knickers were bought with my money,' said Rebekah, flashing them both challenging looks. 'Papa purchased shares in Mr Green's shipping line. They're worth something . . . and not everything was lost when the ship went down. There was time to recover some property from the ship's safe. Apparently Papa had been thrifty all his life.'

'He had?' Her aunt looked startled but her expression soon changed to one of satisfaction. 'That explains a lot!'

'What does it explain?'

'It's in Mr Green's interests to be nice to thee if he knows all this.'

'Of course it is,' said Rebekah, determined to behave as if she had already thought of that herself. 'And it's also in my interests to be nice to him if I want money to spend. Until I'm twenty-five he controls the purse strings – but he seems a reasonable man so far, and charitable. He was telling me about the Seamen's Orphanage that he takes an interest in.'

Her aunt seemed lost for words for a moment but not for long. 'He wants to appear in a good light to thee.'

Rebekah took a firm hold on her patience. 'He only told me about the orphanage because I asked about the collection box on the ship.'

Her aunt sighed. 'It wasn't right thy father leaving him – almost a stranger – in charge of thy affairs.'

'I suspect Papa had an ulterior motive.' Rebekah rose and went over to the window.

'He did it to annoy me,' said Esther.

'I don't think so,' murmured Rebekah, remembering a conversation with her father on the ship. 'There'll be insurance as well, Aunt Esther. I could be a rich woman one day so I think Papa thought it best to have a man in charge of my affairs.'

'Fortune hunters!' exclaimed her aunt. 'And if they knew about my money – '

'I told thee, Miss Esther,' grunted Hannah, 'just like wasps round a jam pot the fellas will be. We'll have no peace.'

'There'll be no fellas – fellows, I mean – coming here,' said Esther. 'Does thou hear that, Rebekah?' Her expression was severe.

'I heard.'

Her aunt's face softened. 'My poor dear, thou can find satisfaction in other things. Perhaps it would help if thou involved thyself in the peace movement? I have a book written in the last century, called *Wanderings in War Time*. The author visited the Franco-Prussian battle fields. It'll make edifying reading for thee when thou goes to bed.' Rebekah murmured a thank you.

That night she found it difficult to sleep as she had on board ship. The mattress was as lumpy as ever and the room was decorated with heavy floral wallpaper that looked as if it had been there since Queen Victoria's Jubilee. Her mother had said that the furniture had come from the rooms above the shop. She decided that as soon as possible she would buy a new bed.

Her gaze washed over the ceiling and she was wishing that time could be switched back . . . that she was with Daniel gazing over Dublin Bay. Had he thought of her or never seeing Ireland, when he had been swamped by the freezing waters of the Atlantic? Oh God! Her sorrow seldom ended in tears now. It was as if frost had blighted her capacity to cry. She picked up the edifying book on battle fields, began to read, was depressed even further, and threw it across the room.

Despite her aunt's coaxing words Rebekah did not go to the meeting house the next day. She had no desire to be welcomed back into the fold of the Quakers in the manner of a prodigal daughter. She doubted her ability to cope with people's sympathy and well-meant suggestions. It was difficult enough dealing with her aunt's overwhelming desire to have her as one of them. Nor did she attend the sewing circle. Instead she went walking in the park.

Her aunt was annoyed with her. 'Ellen wanted to meet thee. She suggests that thou joins the Women's International League for Peace and Freedom.'

'Not now,' said Rebekah in a lifeless voice. 'I just want to be left alone. Can't you understand that, Aunt Esther?'

'No. I can't,' retorted her aunt, pursing her mouth. 'I would have thought it easier to forget in the company of others.'

'I don't want to forget,' said Rebekah, hugging her broken arm to her chest. 'However much it hurts, I want to go on remembering.' She walked out of the room, wishing she had Brigid to talk to, knowing that she would understand.

Yet over the next weeks Rebekah did not get in touch with her friend, believing that she might not want her company now she was back with her family. The fact that Brigid did not write or visit only seemed to confirm that belief. Neither was there word from Joshua Green which surprised her.

Rebekah's arm was freed from plaster and to her relief she was able to use it without much difficulty. She helped with the housework which did not please Hannah.

'Always under me feet thee are,' muttered the maid, giving her a look that was positively poisonous. 'Why don't thee get yerself a proper job or go and see that man? No doubt he'd enjoy looking at thee legs. Short skirts! Sinful I call them. But some girls would go to any lengths to get a man.'

'I don't want a man,' said Rebekah, outwardly calm as she polished the walnut sideboard.

Hannah's look was disbelieving and she sniffed in a way that expressed exactly what she was thinking.

Rebekah was determined not to let the maid drive her out of the house but even so she began to scan the columns of the local paper in search of a job.

'Housekeeper wanted.' Pity she couldn't send Hannah after that. 'Situations required by ex-officers and other ranks.' Poor soldiers! At least she was not desperate for work because she had a family dependent on her. She read on. Charlie Chaplin was getting divorced from Miss Mildred Harris, who was not to use his name in her profession. What happened to a marriage to make the scandal of divorce more preferable?

A couple more weeks passed and Rebekah continued to look in the *Echo*. Joiners throughout the country went on strike. The papers said that it was a bad look out for Christmas. She was terribly lonely and despaired of ever feeling normal or even mildly cheerful again. The days stretched ahead of her like a dark tunnel with only night at the end.

December came in and she read that there was talk of an Irish truce . . . that there could be peace. She considered how she and Daniel had spoke of such an event and could have wept. In the same paper there was an article about the funeral of a Sinn Fein victim. A young man had been shot dead in Liverpool when the Sinn Feiners had set fire to buildings. Hundreds had attended the requiem mass despite the gales that had swept Merseyside. Rebekah remembered the day in Dublin when Shaun had shot the Black and Tans and she experienced a heaviness that seemed to weigh her down. Even in Liverpool people were not completely safe. She was filled with a sense of restlessness and a need to talk about Daniel. Her aunt was no use. She would surely disapprove. Brigid! She had to talk to her. Before the doubts started crowding in again, she wrote to her.

Brigid replied by return of post. 'Of course I want to see you, you dafty! I thought you'd found some posh friends and didn't want me.' She gave arrangements for a meeting, and for the first time in a long time Rebekah looked forward to the days ahead.

At breakfast three days later, and two months to the day since the *Samson* had set off to America, Esther voiced her plans for the day. 'We'll go shopping, just for a few essentials. Then after a quiet time and dinner, we'll walk in the park. Exercise is essential for a healthy body.'

Rebekah had heard similar sentiments every day for the last few weeks. 'No thank you,' she murmured. 'I'm meeting a friend.

'A friend?' Esther stared at her.

Hannah paused in doling out the porridge. 'It's a fella.'

'It's half a dozen,' said Rebekah mildly. 'We're going to dance ragtime in Woolworth's threepence and sixpence store.'

'I don't believe it,' said her aunt, obviously startled.

'I do,' said the maid in a satisfied voice, slamming a dollop of sticky porridge on to Rebekah's plate.

Rebekah's smile was genuine for the first time in weeks.

Chapter Eleven

'Where next?' Rebekah put her arm through Brigid's and smiled at her. They had done some of Brigid's Christmas shopping and then had coffee and cakes in Cooper's café before strolling round the Bon Marché where Rebekah had paid twenty-one shillings for a jade crêpe-de-chine blouse – all due to Brigid's persuasive tongue, and the fact that she had spent little of the money Joshua Green had given to her. 'Yer looking real drab,' her friend had said, and Rebekah, who had stopped feeling drab from the moment her letter had arrived, agreed and bought the blouse. Now she was wondering why they had stopped in front of the flower girls outside Central Station.

'D'yer realise it's two months to the day since we sailed for America?' said Brigid.

'Yes.' The smile faded from Rebekah's face.

'I want to buy some flowers. I'm going to throw them on the Mersey.'

Rebekah stared at her. 'It's a lovely thought, but won't the tide wash them back?'

Brigid shrugged. 'I know it's daft but I want to do something.'

A sharp laugh escaped Rebekah. 'But I thought you'd lit candles in church and had masses said?'

'I have.' Brigid's voice was fierce. 'But it's not enough! I feel so frustrated, Becky. So angry with God.' She fumbled inside her handbag. 'He could have allowed me at least a grave to tend! But then, I suppose I'm no worse off than the thousands of women who lost their men in the Great War. Although they do have the new cenotaph.'

'We'll have a whole armful!' Rebekah found her own purse. 'I think lovely big yellow chrysanths are best.' She pointed out the flowers to the woman wrapped in a thick black knitted shawl. 'Yellow's for remembrance, you know, Brigid.' Her tongue was almost tripping her because she felt like crying. 'Not that I've forgotten Daniel or Mama or Papa – or your Keith.' She handed a pound note to the woman.

Brigid took some of the flowers and dropped a halfcrown in Rebekah's pocket. 'Yer don't have to pay my share.'

She shook her head but it was no use saying anything to Brigid. She was proud, and as she had a job as an all-purpose maid for a doctor with an invalid daughter, Rebekah presumed she must have some money.

They dodged a horse drawn wagon and a delivery bicycle as they crossed the road, laden down with parcels and flowers.

They walked in silence, deep in memories. 'I see in the paper the troubles in Ireland might be over,' said Brigid at last.

Rebekah nodded. 'I wonder if Shaun's back in Ireland or whether he stayed in America?'

'I haven't heard anything. D'you want me to find out?'

'No,' she said shortly. 'I never did care for him and I don't know why I'm bothering my head thinking about him now. Let's get a tram to the Pierhead. I don't know about you but my feet are killing me.'

As the Birkenhead ferry discharged people at the landing stage, throwing flowers into the Mersey did not seem such a good idea.

'People'll think we're mad, won't they?' said Brigid.

Rebekah looked at her, pinched with the cold, miserable of face, and was angry. 'Who cares?' She began to run and Brigid followed her.

Rebekah stopped on the spot where she had stood with Daniel a little longer than two months ago. Was it crazy to feel so lonely for someone she had known so briefly? She looked up at the sky, searching for she did not know what. God could not be pleased with her. She had broken his rules. He was supposed to be a forgiving God, but was she sorry for what she had done with Daniel? Did she have any regrets about defying her parents? She bit her trembling lips. She and

Daniel had become part of each other and she could not be sorry about that, though she did regret hurting her parents. For a moment longer she searched the clouds, needing reassurance, but there was no sign from the heavens. Stupid of her. God's spirit was within you. It was an inner voice that she needed to listen to, but how did one know what were just one's own thoughts and which God's? She sighed, then put down her parcels and cast the chrysanthemums one by one on to the water.

It was the first of many outings with Brigid and when Rebekah mentioned that it was her birthday the week before Christmas, her friend said, as she paid twopence for *The Penny Magazine* in the newsagent's: 'You can't just let your birthday go by.'

'What's there to celebrate?'

'Yer aunt not doing anything special?'

'She hasn't mentioned it, but that could be because she's cross with me. She thinks I've got a fella.'

Brigid's eyebrows shot up. 'Why does she think that?'

'Because I pretend I have – just to get Hannah going. She was actually croaking around the house yesterday. You couldn't call it singing. Besides, Quakers don't sing. Nothing would please her more than to see me married off – preferably to someone not of the Quaker persuasion. You're tall, dark and handsome, and after my fortune.'

Brigid grinned. 'Yer joking!'

'She believes it because she wants to, of course. Aunt Esther doesn't know what to believe. I've denied that you're a man but she's not sure because Hannah's gone on at her about my flirting with boys in Dublin. I'd ask you to visit, only she'd bombard you with questions. Wanting to know about your family and all that. Religion, you know.' She smiled. 'I think on my birthday I'll tell them that we're going to the theatre.'

'Are we dollying ourselves up?'

'Of course! We've got to put a good face on things.' Rebekah held her head on one side. 'Where shall we go?'

Brigid hesitated. 'If yer like – instead of doing that – yer could have a birthday tea in our house. Mam would like to meet yer and she'd be pleased to do it.'

Rebekah stared at her. 'What does she feel about my not being a Catholic?'

'As long as yer not Orange, that's all she cares. If yer were a fella, of course, it'd be different.'

'That's reassuring,' murmured Rebekah.

'Our Pat'll be home.'

'It'll be nice to see him again,' said Rebekah politely. She had little recollection of what Brigid's brother looked like, despite having met him aboard ship.

Brigid put her hand through her arm. 'He'll cheer us up. Even if he has yer crying at the same time. He left the money for our Kath's kids to go the grotto last time he was home so I'm taking them next week. Would yer like to come? I've got a half day off.'

'If I haven't found a job by then,' said Rebekah, not having much hope of doing so.

'Right! It'll soon be Christmas.' Brigid sounded cheerful but Rebekah knew exactly how she was feeling. She watched her open her magazine and start reading as she walked. 'What's so fascinating?'

'It's the new Ethel M. Dell romance.'

'Will there be any kissing?'

Brigid gave her a mock disapproving look. 'If you want lots of kissing you should read *The Sheik*. Although they do more than kissing in that! Mam sez it's immoral. She's read it because she sez it's her duty to know what kind of rubbish us girls read.'

Rebekah smiled. 'Ethel M. Dell's not immoral?'

Brigid returned her smile. 'They pray and struggle with their consciences. Yer should read Elin Glyn's *Three Weeks* if yer want immoral. Not that there's anything real descriptive. She's a princess and older. He's young and handsome. They're not married and they make love on a couch of roses. Have yer ever heard the like?'

Rebekah thought of a sandy beach and the hard wood of the lifeboat. 'It's not realistic.'

Brigid's glance met Rebekah's and her voice quivered when she said, 'Who wants realism?'

Rebekah squeezed her arm and wondered if the pain would ever go.

The days passed less slowly. Rebekah went with Brigid and her niece and nephew to the grotto to see Father Christmas. Afterwards she took them to the cocoa house on the corner of the Haymarket and Manchester Street. They had hot drinks and Wet Nellies, a sort of stale bunloaf, which dripped treacle. In their company she momentarily forgot her grief. On the way home Brigid told Rebekah that she had met Daniel's cousin and mentioned Shaun to them. 'They hadn't heard nothing from him! The news about Daniel came as a terrible shock!'

That night Rebekah could not get to sleep at all and in frustration picked up Florence Barclay's *The Rosary* which Brigid had lent her. It was said to have been read and wept over by every housemaid in the British Isles. Even Hannah had read it and told Rebekah that it would do her soul good – which had not particularly recommended it to her. Rebekah wondered if there was something wrong with her because she was already bored with the lovers and their blindness to each other. When it came to the end, with the hero on his knees in front of the heroine, Becky wanted her to pull him up and have him demanding her all!

She put the book down, remembering the passion there had been between Daniel and herself. It seemed evil that it should have been suppressed so soon. Evil because that passion still existed. The yearning to give herself – to be taken. She turned off the gaslight and remembered that first meeting with Daniel. Had she fallen in love with him then? She recalled all their meetings. Her eyelids dropped and she dreamed that he was alive again, that they were making love on a bed of roses. Stupid! Roses had thorns. Even in dreams she could not escape reality. She woke up and wondered if the day would ever come when being alive did not hurt.

Chapter Twelve

It was one of those glorious winter days, crisp but sunny, that catches at the throat, and is all the more welcome because one knows that the bad weather will soon be back. In a few days it would be Rebekah's birthday and she felt older than her twenty years. She almost wished herself as young as the girls, who could not be more than ten years old, importantly wheeling baby sisters or brothers in high prams. Several boys, on the way to the park not a couple of hundred yards away, kicked a ball up the middle of the road. A horse waited patiently between the shafts of a coal wagon as the coalman heaved a hundredweight sack of coal on his back and carried it up the long path to a house. Steps were being sandstoned and brass knockers polished as Rebekah walked past gardens where a few chrysanthemums still bloomed. A middle-aged man tying up flowers called, 'Good morning.' He had given her a friendly wave in the past but her aunt had always hurried her past.

Rebekah stopped. 'It's a nice day.'

He grinned. 'It is that. I'm Mr McIntyre. You're Irish? Never knew there were Quakers in Ireland until I heard about you.'

Rebekah returned his smile. 'There's a few but I'm not really one of them, although Mama used to be. It's nice to meet you, Mr McIntyre.' She held out her hand. 'I'm Rebekah Rhoades.'

He hesitated and wiped his own hand on well-worn grey flannel trousers before taking hers. 'It's terrible the things that have been going on over there, and it doesn't look like the

131

peace talks are getting anywhere. They say that peace would be more likely if Lloyd George's didn't expect them to lay down their arms before handing only part of Ireland over to them!'

'Unconditional surrender,' said Rebekah. 'I can't see it coming off.'

He nodded and leaned on the gate. 'I see they've got two sisters on conspiracy charges to do with that Catholic lad's murder in town. Apparently there was a framed Irish Republican Declaration in their house in Seaforth, as well as lists of arms and explosives. I ask you, Women! I thought our Edwina was mad enough when she got herself involved with that suffragette movement before the war. You've never been involved in anything like that, Miss Rhoades?'

'No, but I admire her courage. I read some of my mother's leaflets about what was done to Emily Davison.'

He nodded, his expression grim. 'They force fed my daughter once. That was enough for her. It was peaceful means after that.' He nodded vehemently. 'But I shouldn't be keeping you if you've the messages to get. You aunt'll be after me.'

He moved away and she carried on up the road, stricken with pain at the sudden memory of that afternoon with Daniel in Seaforth.

The smell of freshly baked bread did not rouse Rebekah from her thoughts but as she entered the bakery she collided with a young woman in a brown tweed costume. Around her neck she wore a complete fox stole with glassy eyes that seemed to fix on Rebekah's face at the same time as the woman's. She looked to be in her late twenties. 'You're the Irish Quaker,' she said.

Rebekah grimaced. 'No, I'm not. My mother was, and so is my aunt. I'm not sure what I am.'

The woman raised thick eyebrows. 'My mistake. I'm Edwina McIntyre.' She possessed her father's strong bone structure and squarish face. 'Has your aunt been saying anything about me?'

'Nothing,' said Rebekah, taken aback. 'But your father's been telling me about your being a suffragette.'

Edwina's smile became fixed. 'Oh, that! Being in prison isn't seen as so bad by your aunt because some of the Quaker men were jailed for being conscientious objectors during the war. It's my having had a baby and not being married that makes her look on me as a scarlet woman.' She paused. 'Am I shocking you?'

'Are you trying to because you don't like my aunt?'

Edwina laughed. 'How clever of you. She makes me squirm, the way she stares. You'd think I was the serpent in Eden.' She pressed Rebekah's arm. 'You must come and have a cup of tea with us one day. You can tell me all about yourself.' She waved a hand and strode off.

Rebekah stared after her. She could not see herself and Edwina having much in common, and the other woman had shocked her a little by her openness. Although who was she to judge? How would it have been if she had had Daniel's baby? How would her aunt have reacted? Perhaps she would have taken her in still, but a baby? And Joshua Green, what would he have said and done? She fancied a scandal would be the last thing he would wish for. Probably he would have sent her away to a quiet discreet Home and had the baby put up for adoption. Hers and Daniel's baby – how would she have felt about that?

It was strange, never having met Edwina before, that Rebekah should bump into her that evening when buying the *Liverpool Echo* from the newsvendor. Edwina was reading the front page. She looked up. 'Oh, it's you again. I'm just reading about that poor woman they pulled out of the Mersey. I bet some man's behind it. They've named her as Emma Richards. Her brother's a shipowner and lives not far away. He goes to our church.'

'What!' Rebekah handed over the money for a newspaper and found the article. She began to read: 'According to her brother, Joshua Green, his sister had been staying with friends in Formby-by-the-Sea. She had been unwell for a while. They had not become worried immediately as she often wandered off on her own.'

'You look like you've seen a ghost,' said Edwina, staring at her.

'I've met her,' murmured Rebekah, folding the paper. 'Her brother's my guardian.'

'Her brother is – not your aunt?'

'My father and aunt never got on.'

Edwina nodded, but asked no questions as they began to walk. 'I see there's to be an inquest. Do you think it was suicide?'

'You mean, did she kill herself?' Rebekah's back stiffened.

'That's what suicide is,' said Edwina drily. 'And you can't exactly fall into the sea at Formby. Of course she could have been trapped by the tide on a sandbank if she'd gone paddling – but the time of year's all wrong.'

Rebekah said woodenly. 'It's been a lovely day today.'

'Cold, though. It's been quite a year for the poor man.'

'You mean with one of his ships sinking, and now this?'

Edwina wrinkled her nose. 'I meant his being jilted at the altar last April. They make jokes about that sort of thing happening but he was actually left waiting in the church. I mean, men can be swines – but to humiliate someone like that is all wrong.'

Rebekah nodded. 'I'll have to go and see him.'

'I don't envy you.' Edwina smiled. 'By the way, that invitation still stands. Just drop in when you feel like it.'

'Thanks.'

They parted at her aunt's front gate.

Rebekah told her about Emma. 'I'll have to go and see Mr Green.'

Esther looked up from her sewing. 'Not a nice thing to happen. Couldn't thou just send a letter and flowers.'

'There's to be an inquest, which means funeral arrangements won't have been made yet.'

Her aunt sighed. 'Well, if thou must, thou must. But don't linger.'

Rebekah said that she had no intention of doing so and went out of the room before her aunt could say more.

Rebekah stared at the ship's bell on the side of the red-brick porch, and then at the cat miaowing on the doorstep. She remembered how her father had tugged on the rope and set the bell clanging. She thought of Emma and her cat, and a heavy sigh escaped her. 'Bloody moggy', that's what Emma called it. So wrapped up in herself had she been during the last weeks, she had almost forgotten that Emma existed. She pulled on the rope and knocked on the door. Twice. Then she picked up the cat which was winding about her legs, and stroked it. Bloody Moggy began to purr.

Joshua opened the door. He looked angry and seemed about to say something but checked himself when he obviously recognised Rebekah's slight figure in the shadows. He said lamely, 'It's you, Rebekah. What are you doing with that cat?'

'I've just come to say how sorry I am. About your sister, I mean.'

'That's kind of you. I intended coming to see you this week. It's your birthday on Friday, isn't it? You'd best come in.'

'I expect you're busy,' she said, suddenly nervous.

'Don't be foolish.' He smiled and put his hands on her shoulders. 'I should have come to see you sooner but I've been busy organising new schedules and trying to buy another ship. I have the chance of purchasing an elderly lady with a good record and having her overhauled. Now the joiners have gone on strike and messed matters up. Put the cat down and let me take your coat.'

'I think he's missing Emma.' She released the cat which ran inside the house.

'I'm trying to keep him out!' Joshua made an exasperated sound which he turned into a laugh as he hung her coat on a stand. 'Sorry. It's not your fault. It's just that it miaows all round the house and drives me mad.' He led her into the front room where a fire burned in the grate. He remained standing, resting an elbow on the mantleshelf.

'Poor cat!' Rebekah looked up at him from beneath her lashes and said impulsively, 'Can I have him if he's a nuisance?'

'He has a pedigree, you know.' He hesitated. 'But I'll be glad to get rid of the creature, if I'm honest.' He pressed an electric bell on the mantleshelf. 'We'll have a cup of tea and I'll take you home in the car afterwards.'

'Thanks.'

There was a discreet knock on the door and the maid entered. She glanced at Rebekah as Joshua asked her to bring tea. Rebekah remembered her from last time. Janet, that was her name.

135

After she left there was a short silence before Joshua said, 'I was going to suggest a visit to Crane Hall to see "The Gondoliers" on your birthday, but under the circumstances I suppose that's out of the question.'

She smiled. 'I would have had to refuse, anyway. I've been invited out.'

He lifted his head. 'Oh? By whom?'

'My friend Brigid. I'm having a birthday tea at her house.'

'You're still seeing her then?' He frowned into the fire. 'I would have thought – '

'What?' He did not answer and she added in a light voice, 'I like Brigid. She's gutsy and makes me laugh. I wondered if there was any news about the compensation?' She had not intended asking.

'These things take time.' His fingers toyed with a porcelain shepherdess on the mantleshelf. 'I will say, though, that it's unlikely there will be any.'

She stared at him, unable to conceal her disappointment.

'I'm sorry.' His expression was bland. 'I'm likely to receive the value of the *Samson* and its freight, but passengers will probably only receive the price of their fare.'

'But that's unfair!'

'It's a disgrace, but that's the way things are. We do urge people to get themselves insured.' He moved to stand in front of her and bent to peer into her downcast face. 'It's not my fault, Rebekah. If I could afford it I'd pay the compensation myself. As it is I need the money to buy a replacement for the *Samson*.'

'I understand that, but what about Brigid's husband and the crew who were lost?' She lifted her head and caught his change of expression.

His eyes glinted, 'I presume we're talking about O'Neill?'

'Daniel,' she said firmly. 'He has a brother, Shaun.'

'He's the one you mentioned in New York?' He moved back to the fireplace. 'Haven't been able to trace him, I'm afraid.'

'He has relatives in Liverpool. They live in the same street as Brigid's family.'

'Do they now?' His hand stilled as it reached for the silver cigarette box on a small table. Then he took out a cheroot and lit it from the fire with a spill from a jar in the hearth. 'Have they heard from the brother?'

'No.' Rebekah sat on the sofa. 'Would it be worth telling them if they do hear anything, to get in touch with you?'

'Definitely,' he said without hesitation. 'Not that I can do much. Still – ' He shrugged and there was a pause before he murmured, 'I suppose you learnt about Emma from the newspaper?'

'Yes. I wondered when the funeral would be, and where?'

'It depends on the findings of the inquest.' He sat down on the other end of the sofa. 'If you were thinking of attending, I don't consider it a good idea. You've been through enough.'

She swung one leg, gazing down at her foot, finding it difficult to say what she wanted. 'I felt sorry for your sister. A woman I was talking to thought it unlikely that she could have drowned by accident.'

There was a pause as he inhaled deeply before letting the smoke drift slowly out through his nostrils. 'And what do you think?'

Rebekah moistened her lips. 'She was very confused.'

He gave a high laugh. 'She was crazy! Living in a different world to the rest of us most of the time. I find it quite believable that she could go walking on the sands and forget how swiftly the tide comes in.'

'But what about her friends?'

'Friends?' He looked startled.

'Didn't they warn her of the danger?' Rebekah was puzzled by his reaction.

He shrugged his shoulders. 'I should imagine so. But Emma could easily forget what she was told.'

'When you say it like that, it sounds the most likely explanation.'

'It's what I'll be saying at the inquest.' The creases about his pale blue eyes deepened. 'I want my sister buried in holy ground. No scandal.'

There was another discreet knock at the door and the next moment Janet entered with a tray. Rebekah did not press the subject further.

While the drank tea and nibbled chocolate biscuits, they discussed the weather and how she was settling in Liverpool. 'I've been looking for a job,' she murmured.

'What kind of job?' He leaned towards her. 'Perhaps I can help you?'

'I was thinking of office work. I can type and know a little shorthand.'

'I'll ask around.'

She was surprised. 'You aren't against women working?'

He laughed shortly. 'What's the point of swimming against the tide? If my sister had found herself a job, then maybe she wouldn't have ended up the way she did. A child would have been best for her. Anyway, I'll see what I can do for you.' He put down his cup and stood up. 'I'll have to take you home now if you don't mind? I'm expecting callers.'

She got to her feet. 'The cat?'

'The cat.' He sounded amused and put an arm about her shoulders. 'I'll get Janet to find it while I bring the car round.' He kissed her forehead. 'Wait for me in the porch, and while I'm driving you home perhaps we can make some arrangements for having your birthday treat in the New Year.'

'That would be very kind,' she said in a polite voice before hurrying out of the room.

It was Rebekah's birthday and she was getting ready to go to Brigid's. She gazed at her reflection, remembering how thrilled she had been with her appearance after her hair was cut. Now it gave her no pleasure. The ends were straggly. She should have gone to the hairdresser's and had it trimmed. The jade green blouse made her skin look pale, almost translucent. She wondered about touching up her cheeks with rouge but decided to leave them alone. Standing, she smoothed the black serge skirt over her hips before picking up a black hat and cramming it on to her head. She pulled a face then smiled as Moggy bumped noses with his reflection in the dressing-table mirror and miaowed. She blew him a kiss. He had cheered up her life, despite Hannah's moans about: 'The lazy do nothing cat!' and 'Feeding it on best cod's head, are we now? I could make soup out of that!'

Rebekah put on a coat and kid gloves, and went downstairs.

'Dressed to kill,' sniffed Hannah.

'I suppose thou wilt be going out with him on Christmas Day?' muttered Esther, pleating a fold of her skirt.

'No.' She deliberately looked pensive. 'I said I'd be spending it with my rich aunt.'

Esther looked startled. 'Thou means that?'

'Of course. You're my only close kith and kin, barring grandpapa's relatives up north – or so you keep telling me. Who else should I spend Christmas with?' She smiled and went out through the doorway.

Rebekah was not so cheerful as she walked the dark streets, passing children swinging on a rope tied to the bars of a lamp post on the corner of a street, and others chasing and hiding up entries and garden paths. Should she tell Brigid about the compensation or leave it until it was official?

She caught a tram and got off near the Mere Lane cinema. A week or so ago she and Brigid had seen 'When Men Betray'. The poster had proclaimed it: 'A stirring drama of women's frailties!' The film had made a couple of girls behind them in the cinema say, 'It makes you wonder if yer should ever trust a man.' How trustworthy was Joshua Green? Her father must have trusted him but Daniel had not liked him. She felt the familiar aching emptiness. Had that been only because Joshua owned property in Ireland? Or was there something else?

She peered at the numbers on the houses and began to count. Her nervousness grew at the thought of facing Brigid's family. What did they really feel about Brigid's friendship with her?

A cow's lowing startled her, as did a series of yells. She realised that she was passing the dairy. The next moment out of the darkness hurtled Brigid's niece and nephew, Jimmy and Veronica. The boy skidded to a halt inches from her but the girl flung her arms about Rebekah's skirts. 'We were told to watch out! Jimmy's shouted to them yer coming.' Rebekah swung her off her feet and round and round until they were both dizzy.

Jimmy seized her hand and pulled, causing her almost to fall over her feet in sudden haste. 'Happy birthday to you! Happy birthday to you!' he chanted. 'Me mam had the shop make yer a cake and Auntie Bridie paid for it! But there's only one pink candle on it. Me Uncle Pat said it's just as well because we didn't want to set fire to the house. That's a joke,' he said earnestly, his eyes shining in the lamplight. 'It's a joke because he said yer only a chicken yet. Scarcely out of the egg!'

Rebekah laughed because she was so relieved by the warmth of their welcome. The next moment Brigid was on the doorstep and pulling her inside the house. 'Yer found us! I was just saying to our Pat that yer might find it difficult in the dark. I never thought. I should have gone to meet yer.'

'I was all right. Jimmy's been telling me about the cake. You shouldn't have gone to all that trouble and expense, with it being Christmas soon and all.'

'Nothing's no trouble, girl.' A thin figure wrapped in a flowered pinafore came bustling across the kitchen floor. Her face still bore traces of the pretty girl she must have been. The tightly curled reddish hair showed few grey hairs.

'This is me mam,' said Brigid, the affection clear in her voice.

Rebekah was momentarily struck dumb, never having known Brigid's maiden name. Then she held out her hand. 'Hello, Brigid's mam. It's really kind of you.'

Her hand was taken and shaken vigorously. 'It's sad times we've living through, girl, and if we can't do a kind deed, then life's not worth living. Some people call me Ma Maisie, so you might as well. I feel like I know yer already through our Bridie.' She released Rebekah's hand but urged her over to the fire. 'The table's already set. I've done us something hot as it's a real cold night. Now get yerself warm. Our Pat's just making us a toddy. Yer'll take a drink with us?'

'Thank you.' Rebekah did not like saying that she had never touched alcohol before.

A man was standing on the rag rug before the glowing fire. He was good-looking with wide-set brown eyes and very white teeth. Rebekah remembered Brigid's brother Pat. 'It'll warm the cockles of yer heart,' he said. 'Bridie, have yer got the cups ready?'

'I got them ready, Uncle Pat.' Veronica came dancing into the kitchen from the scullery where she had vanished immediately on entering the house. She was followed by Kath, a ginger-haired woman, who nodded in Rebekah's direction and murmured what she took to be some kind of welcome.

There was a subdued air about her. Brigid had said that her husband had died last year as a result of wounds inflicted during the war.

Pat poured the steaming liquid into the cups standing on the white tablecloth. 'Lots of water in that drop I've given the kids, Ma. A toast and then we'll sit down and eat. You've never lived, Miss Rhoades, till you've tasted Ma's spareribs and cabbage.'

'Call me Becky,' she said, warming her hands on the cup.

'Becky it is then.' He chinked his cup with hers and smiled into her eyes. 'Drink up! I hope you'll be having lots more birthdays.' She drank up, determined to try and enjoy herself.

It was a birthday like no other that Rebekah had ever had. Nothing exciting but she felt part of a real family. Although if she had known that she would have to join in taking a turn to entertain the rest of the gathering, she might have had second thoughts about accepting Brigid's invitation. But not knowing, and the drink, and the fact that Jimmy could do a fair imitation of Charlie Chaplin and Veronica recite a skipping song 'Eeper-weeper chimney sweeper' about a man who shoved a wife up a chimney, made her feel that she had no choice but to sing a rather shaky 'Keep the Home Fires Burning' – the only song she could think of on the spur of the moment and one which Old Mary had once sung.

'Not bad,' said Pat, who played the piano.

Rebekah flushed. 'I'm not as good as Kath. She sings lovely.'

'Mam could have been on the stage,' stated Veronica proudly.

'No,' protested Kath. 'I only came second in a talent competition, and I couldn't have done that if it hadn't been for our Bridie, who pushed me into it.'

'Never mind that now,' said Pat, holding up the jug. 'Who's for another drink and a game of snap?'

Jimmy held out his cup but was refused. 'You've had enough me lad. Go and get the cards.'

The boy went and they settled round the table. It was soon obvious to Rebekah that the game was played so that the children could win. By the end of the evening her heart had warmed to the whole family and she was sorry when it was over.

She walked home arm in arm with Brigid on one side of her and Pat on the other. All the way he bellowed at the top of his voice, 'Swanee, how I love you! How I love you! My dear old Swanee!' It did not seem to matter that it was December and freezing cold. She suspected that they were all slightly drunk but did not care. It took the edge off her grief.

When they reached Aunt Esther's house she thought of asking them in but before she could voice the words, they both said they would have to be off home. 'See you New Year's Eve,' said Pat, tickling her under the chin. 'We'll have some fun then.'

'I'll see yer on Monday,' said Brigid, hugging her. 'I'm working all weekend. There's a dinner party on.'

They both waved and left her standing at the gate.

The week before Christmas passed swifter than Rebekah had hoped. There were sad moments. Shopping in town she was conscious of the constant trickle of people laying flowers in front of the new Cenotaph in Lime Street for their dead loved ones.

She bought *The Boy's Own* for Jimmy and a doll for Veronica. There was a tin of Mackintosh's toffee de luxe for Ma Maisie and perfume from Luce's perfumery in Ranelagh Street for Brigid. A scarf for Kath, cigarettes for Pat, and several sets of the best woollen combinations for Aunt Ester. She did not dare to forget Hannah and bought her one set of the thickest, itchiest unmentionables.

In the *Liverpool Echo* it was stated that a verdict of accidental death had been passed on Mrs Emma Richards. Rebekah was relieved. She ordered flowers to be sent and remembered to buy Joshua a present just in case he called. He came when she was out and left her a silk scarf.

Christmas was quiet and Rebekah was glad when it was over. Ireland's Yuletide had not been so peaceful. A constable in plain clothes had been set on outside the Gaiety Theatre in Dublin, and the Hibernian Bank at Drogheda had been robbed of thirty-six thousand pounds on Christmas Eve. Rebekah was glad that she was out of it all, and vowed to stop reading the newspaper, as well as deciding to look forward to the January sales. She would allow having money to go to her head.

New Year's Eve started quietly but her aunt was not pleased when at nine o'clock in the evening Rebekah started getting ready to go out with Brigid and her brother. 'If thou art not in by midnight, I'll lock thee out,' threatened Esther.

'But I'm twenty now – and midnight is when the fun starts,' insisted Rebekah, with her shoulder wedged against the front door as she pulled on her gloves. She was not really worried because she had had a copy of the front door key made. 'Don't be a spoilsport, Auntie,' she said in a coaxing voice. 'There's lots of Scots in Liverpool and first footing is popular, as you should know.' She straightened. 'You need all the good luck in this life that you can get.'

'Superstition!' said Esther, a worried frown puckering her plump face. 'Thy grandfather would turn over in his grave! What would thy mother think? Thou art supposed to be in mourning! That frock thou art wearing – it's green.'

'Green for grief, some people say, Auntie dear,' retorted Rebekah, her eyes shining with sudden tears.

'Oh, Rebekah!' exclaimed her aunt in a despairing voice. 'I hope thou doesn't come to grief.'

'I won't.' She suddenly felt sorry for her aunt and kissed her cheek before hurrying down the path.

Ma Maisie's kitchen and parlour were crowded and the party had spilled out into the street. People were dancing to the tinkling ragtime piano music of Scott Joplin. Rebekah had watched for a while but then Pat had partnered her. He was a showy dancer and because of that she had to concentrate on her own steps – steps taught her by Daniel. Then he handed her over to a shipmate at ten minutes to midnight, saying, 'I've got to first foot. I'm the only dark-haired one in the family.'

The blast of hooters and whistles from the ships on the river, and the clanging of church bells, heralded in the New Year. Pat reappeared, carrying a slice of bread, a piece of coal, a lump of salt and a shiny sixpence, which he handed to his mother standing just inside the front door. Then he kissed every woman and girl at the party, including Rebekah whose head felt airy despite the aching regret gripping her. Glasses and cups were filled again and toasts drunk.

'You're still looking bright-eyed,' said Brigid, yawning and coming to lean against the railings next to her. 'I thought you'd be ready for yer bed. It hasn't been too much for yer, then?'

Rebekah rested her head on her friend's shoulder. 'It's better than sitting at home, moping. But I suppose I'll have to make a move.'

'Stay here,' said Brigid. 'Doss down with Mam and me. It'll be a squash, but snug as a bug in a rug.'

Reluctantly Rebekah shook her head. 'Aunt Esther just might be waiting up.'

'I'll get our Pat.'

'No.' Rebekah seized her arm. 'He must be tired.'

'Aren't we all? I've work early this morning. Nineteen twenty-one! Another year to get through.' She squared her shoulders. 'Our Pat won't mind, and I wouldn't trust yer with anyone else. At least he's not lying down drunk.'

Rebekah resigned herself to being seen home by Pat, not so certain as Brigid that he could be trusted. She was proved right when he pulled her into a doorway halfway along Breck Road, holding her so that her arms were wedged against her sides and kissing her in a far from brotherly fashion. She stamped on his feet twice before he released her. They looked at one another. His teeth gleamed in the dark. 'So it's true yer still carrying a torch for Daniel O'Neill then?'

'Is that what Brigid told you?' she parried.

'Who else?' He shook his head sorrowfully. 'You women! Yer not like our Bridie now, and believing you're a one man woman?'

'I could be. Besides, it's only three months.'

He smiled. 'Early days. Yer'll get over him. In the meantime there's plenty of other pebbles on the beach I could pick, yer know.'

'Pick one up then!'

'I could do that.'

'You're handsome enough.'

He grinned. 'That's right enough. But if yer wanting the truth I'm not after getting meself shackled and there's too many girls since the war who are desperate – if yer peck them on the cheek they think it's a proposal of marriage. I've no mind to settle down just yet. And I'm not wanting the kind of girls who hang around Lime Street because yer never know what yer going to catch.'

Rebekah knew from Brigid about the women of the streets and did not know whether to be shocked because he had mentioned them. 'Should you be talking to me like this?'

'Why not?' He took her hand. 'Yer a woman of sense. I've heard yer talking. You've got a head on yer shoulders.'

'Is that supposed to be a compliment?' She was amused.

'You got it first time.' He squeezed her fingers. 'We could have a good time when I dock.'

'I'm not so sure,' she said, considering it might be worth experimenting to see if she could feel anything for another man. 'Besides, what about Brigid? I go out with her.'

'I've friends,' he said softly. 'Yer both need cheering up. Laugh all your troubles away, that's what I say.'

'Smile though your heart is aching?'

'That's the ticket.' He pulled her hand through his crooked arm and she did not desist. They went on their way, with Pat insisting on arranging to meet when next he docked.

Although Brigid was dubious at first about the whole idea of going out with a shipmate of her brother's, her own philosophy was similar to his: Pack up your troubles and smile.

Rebekah's life took on a different colour. She was often out and her aunt moaned that she never saw her – said that she was becoming flighty. Joshua called but Rebekah was not there to see him. Her aunt complained on his behalf even though she was still annoyed that he was Rebekah's guardian. She shrugged the complaints aside because, like keeping Pat at arm's length, it was good practice at hardening her heart against other people – that way you didn't get hurt so easily.

If sometimes she wanted to cry when waiting for Pat's ship, because this would have been the kind of life she would have had to get used to with Daniel, she never spoke of it to anyone. She was too busy pretending that she was coping with life.

Chapter Thirteen

'So I've caught you in at last,' said Joshua, one foot jamming the door open. 'About time too! It's been months!'

'Time does fly,' murmured Rebekah, opening the door wider. 'You never did take me out for my birthday.'

'No,' he said shortly. 'Your aunt was saying you've been burning the candle at both ends.'

'Aunt Esther would.' She deliberately put an amused note in her voice. 'Did you want me for anything in particular or just to tell me off?'

'Something in particular!' The lines about his mouth and nose deepened. 'Can I come in or are you going to keep me standing on the doorstep?'

'Come in by all means.' She led the way into the sitting room. 'Aunt Esther's at one of her meetings and Hannah's out, so you'll be able to scold me in peace.' She plumped up a cushion and removed the tin of Mansion polish and a duster from the arm of a chair, putting them on a shelf.

He took off his trilby. 'You're expecting me to scold you?'

'I knew you'd catch up with me sooner or later,' She waved him to a chair but remained standing herself. 'I suppose it's about money?'

Joshua's eyes narrowed. 'There's something different about you. You've changed.'

She shrugged peach cotton-clad shoulders. 'I've had to grow up quickly over the last few months. Come to terms with life.'

He nodded. 'That's a pretty frock you're wearing.'

Rebekah raised finely drawn eyebrows. 'It's going to be the soft soap first, is it? Thank you, kind sir.'

He smiled. 'You are pretty and I don't begrudge you buying new clothes. But little as I like to say this, Rebekah, you can't carry on the way you have been. The letter you sent me two days ago requesting an advance on your allowance – I can't let you have it. What are you doing with your money?'

'I gave some away.'

'What?'

The corners of her mouth lifted. 'Don't look so shocked, Mr Green. I can give my own money away, can't I?'

He had been in the act of sitting down but straightened up again. 'No, you can't! I do have a say in the matter. Who did you give it to?'

She hesitated. 'A good cause.'

He stared at her and Moggy, brushing past the fire irons, made their clatter sound loud in the silence. 'What good cause?'

Rebekah sighed. 'Brigid's mother took ill unexpectedly and had to have an operation. If Brigid had had the compensation money, it would have paid for it. I thought it only fair that – '

He made an exasperated sound. 'She talked you into it, I suppose? Made you feel guilty!'

Rebekah fired up. 'No, she didn't! If she'd known it was my money she wouldn't have taken it. I told her that it was the compensation. The operation was serious and it's still dicey whether her mother will pull through.'

'Even so – '

'Even so nothing!' She slammed her hand down on the mantleshelf, her expression mutinous. 'What's the use of having money if you can't help your friends?'

'You won't have any money to help yourself if you don't stop spending it,' he said stiffly. 'It doesn't grow on trees, you know.'

She brushed his words aside. 'You care about those orphans of yours, don't you? Surely you understand – '

'Yes, yes,' he said impatiently, looking down at the carpet. His head lifted. 'But you're too soft-hearted, my dear. That's why your father made me your guardian. I'm going to have to be firm for your own sake. If you want any money you'll have to apply to me in person – no letters – and I'll want to know exactly what you're spending it on.'

147

'What?' She was filled with dismay. 'I'm not a child!'

'Don't I know it.' His glance flicked over her body.

She had seen that look often in Pat's eyes but so far had managed to keep him under control, his kisses doing little for her. 'Well then?' she murmured. 'Can't you trust me to act like an adult?'

'I'd like to,' he said softly. 'But you are still a comparative stranger to Liverpool, and if your aunt can't keep a proper watch on you, then I'll have to do so.'

'I've already decided that I'll spend less,' she insisted. 'I'm really quite sensible. You shouldn't take any notice of what Aunt Esther tells you.'

'I'd expect her to see things differently so I don't take everything she says to heart.' He took a cheroot case from his pocket. 'I presume that you haven't found a job yet?'

'No.' Rebekah was not going to admit that she had not bothered looking for a few weeks. Instead she had been spending a fair amount of time at Brigid's, looking after the children while their mother was at work.

'Perhaps I can help you with a job.' Joshua lit up. 'Sit down, Rebekah, and let's talk.'

She shook her head. 'I'm in need of a drink. Would you like one?'

'Thank you.'

Rebekah made a pot of tea and placed on a plate some jam tarts that she had baked. After she had poured the tea, she murmured, 'Now tell me about this job.'

He patted the arm of his chair. 'Come and sit here.'

'I'm quite comfortable here, thank you,' she said.

Joshua shrugged. 'It's a very worthwhile job but there's not much money in it.'

'Aunt Esther hardly takes a penny from me so the money isn't my main concern. Although – '

'If your aunt is supporting you, that's good.' He looked pleased.

Rebekah grimaced. 'Let me finish. She has threatened several times that if I don't pull my socks up – '

'I can't see her being other than pleased with you if you take on this job. It's to do with the Seamen's Orphanage.'

'That's in Orphan Drive on the other side of the park.' She leaned forward eagerly. 'Not too far. Good.'

He held up a hand. 'Wait until I've finished. You wouldn't be working at the Orphanage. The job I'm talking about involves visiting the widows and children of men who lost their lives at sea. You can find out what financial help is needed so the children can remain at home.'

She nodded her head slowly. 'I'd like to help. As long as they don't look upon me as a snooper.'

'You're too young and pretty for anyone to see you in such a light.'

Rebekah avoided looking at him. It seemed Brigid, and her father, had been right and his lordship did fancy her, but she would not let that influence her decision. 'When do I start?'

'I'll have to find out.' He sipped his tea. 'Remember I was going to take you to see "The Gondoliers" at Crane Hall? Well, it's being performed once again. We could have supper afterwards if you'd like to come? I could let you know then.'

'All right.' She tried to sound enthusiastic. 'That would be lovely.'

Joshua arranged a time and soon afterwards left, saying he did not want to have to listen to a sermon from her aunt again on the folly of her father leaving a young girl in the charge of a bachelor.

After he had gone Rebekah stood with Moggy clutched tightly in her arms, staring into the fire, thinking about Daniel, Pat and Joshua, and how she would not mention the job to her aunt yet. Then resumed her polishing.

'I don't know why yer have to go out with his lordship,' said Brigid, frowning, as she and Rebekah left the Royal Infirmary in Pembroke Place.

'Money and a job.' Rebekah smiled. 'Honestly, Brigid, I'd sooner go out with the Emperor of China! But Joshua holds the purse strings.'

'He's after yer. I've said it before and I'll say it again.'

'I hadn't seen him for months,' said Rebekah impatiently. 'Talk sense.'

'But that's not his fault.' Brigid tucked her hand in Rebekah's arm as they crossed the road. 'You've been gallivanting with our Pat. Does his lordship know about that?'

'Why should I tell him? Your Pat's intentions are perfectly dishonourable, as your Mam was relieved to hear tonight.'

Brigid grinned. 'If you'd said it like that she would have worried.'

'I guessed she was going spare every time Pat came home and we went out.'

'Well, she's not going to be worrying now,' said Brigid positively. 'I told her that there was no need . . . that you're still carrying a torch for Daniel.'

Rebekah sighed. 'If you know that I don't see how you can go on about his lordship, although I think my father had him in mind for me to marry. I feel bad about my father now. I wish we hadn't been out of friends when he died.'

Brigid squeezed her arm and her voice was brisk when she spoke. 'There's nothing you can do about that now. So let's go for a walk in the park before it gets dark and forget our problems.' Rebekah agreed and they went on their way.

Despite what Rebekah had said to Brigid about the outing with Joshua, she began to look forward to it. She had never seen a Gilbert and Sullivan performance. Her aunt, though, was not pleased about her going.

'I don't know why thou hast to go out with the man.' Esther agitatedly plied her needle through the hem of a plain brown skirt.

'It's having her hair cut – it's given her brain fever,' interpolated Hannah. Rebekah and her aunt stared at her. 'Tis true,' added the maid, a gleam in her eye. 'Head feels cold, blood rushes to it to warm it.'

'That would mean a good half of the women in the British Isles have brain fever then,' said Rebekah, a smile in her voice.

Her aunt sighed. 'Let's not get silly, Becky dear. Do consider. Thou'd be more inclined to stick to the straight and narrow if thou came to the meeting house instead of just enjoying thyself gallivanting here and there.'

'I'll go tomorrow,' murmured Rebekah in an attempt to placate her, and swallowing her annoyance. First Brigid and now her aunt! Why couldn't people just let her make her own decisions?

Her aunt looked at her. 'Thou means it?'

She nodded. 'Cross my heart.'

Esther smiled but Hannah, who was clearing the table, grunted. 'I'll believe it when I sees it. All this dollying thyself up for a man. Thee'll cum to a bad end.'

'Didn't you ever dolly yourself up, Hannah?' inquired Rebekah, experiencing another flash of annoyance. She was not dollying herself up for a man but for herself. She smoothed the boat-shaped neck of the mauve georgette dress, and glanced at Hannah who had not replied. 'Well? Didn't you ever walk out with a young man in your day?'

'I could have,' said Hannah gruffly, staring down at the white starched tablecloth and brushing crumbs off it on to a plate. She flung them on the fire, then looked at Rebekah, a hard glint in her eyes. 'But we's had no muny and I had thems that relied on me. Thou knows nuthing about such things, Miss Fancy Pants. Going here, going there. Thee thinks thee has suffered. Thee knows nuthing about real suffering and what it is to do without!'

'Hannah!' Esther's voice was sharp. 'That's enough! Miss Rebekah isn't to blame for thy misfortunes.'

'Aunt! It's all right!' Rebekah shrugged herself into her coat. 'I'm sorry, Hannah, I shouldn't have said what I did.'

'No, thee shouldn't.' Hannah glared at her and went out of the room as the knocker sounded.

'I really should get rid of her,' said Esther, shaking her head and wincing as she got up. She rubbed a knee.

'Don't do it because of me,' responded Rebekah swiftly, picking up her handbag and wondering where Hannah could go. 'Better for us to suffer her than to inflict her on someone else.' She kissed her aunt's cheek, who followed her slowly up the lobby, gave a barely civil greeting to Joshua, and stood watching her get into the car before she turned and went back into the house.

'Poor Aunt Esther,' murmured Rebekah as they drove off.

'Why do you call her poor?' asked Joshua sharply. 'She looked blue murder at me. I wonder if she realises I could take you away from her.'

Startled, Rebekah looked at his nice-looking, clean shaven profile. He was wearing a navy lounge suit and oozed masculine power. 'I don't think the thought's occurred to her.' She paused, wondering why he had said what he did, and added in

151

light tones, 'When it does, she might just beg you to take me away. I'm not the easiest person to live with. At the moment she considers it her duty to care for me because I'm her only sister's daughter.'

'You want to keep reminding her of that,' said Joshua in a pleasant voice. 'She must have some money tucked away from when your grandfather died. You don't want that prune-faced maid getting it all.'

Rebekah's hands tightened on her handbag. 'Money's useful but it's not everything,' she murmured.

He glanced at her. 'That's a nice sentiment but it's not true. If you hadn't a penny you'd realise that there's nothing lovely about being broke. Be nice to your aunt.'

She looked out of the window, so that he would not see her expression. 'I'm as nice as I can be. If I was any nicer she'd smell a rat.'

'Not her. She'd believe her influence was having a good effect on you.'

'You're probably right.' Her voice was non-committal and she changed the subject, asking where was Crane Hall.

'Near the Bold Street end of Church Street. If you know the Lyceum News room, it's not far from there.' He added good-humouredly: 'I keep forgetting that you're a foreigner. Your accent's so faint.'

'I've been mistaken for English in Dublin.'

He flashed her a look. 'Do you miss Ireland?'

'Sometimes.'

'I have a place there.'

Rebekah swallowed an unexpected lump in her throat. 'Your father bought Grandmama's farm.'

'You know about that?' He sounded surprised.

She wondered why he should be and how he would respond if she told him about her conversation with Daniel concerning him, but thought it wiser to say, 'My father told me. I remember Grandmama always trying to build me up on buttermilk and porridge.'

He frowned. 'She was a fiercesome woman. She made up for what your uncle lacked, so my brother said.'

'I was fond of her.'

'Why shouldn't you be? Family.'

152

She hesitated before saying, 'You must miss your family. Your sister, your brother – '

'Of course,' he said in a voice that did not encourage further questions.

They fell silent and did not speak again until they came to Crane Hall where Joshua tried to explain the plot of 'The Gondoliers' as she attempted to read the programme. She was glad when the music began and she could give all her attention to the entanglements of the various lovers.

When they came out of the Hall she was humming beneath her breath 'Take a pair of sparkling eyes'.

'You'll have some supper?' Joshua helped her into the car and she was conscious of the warmth of his fingers through the thin silk of her stockings when they brushed her leg as he moved her skirts out of the way of the door. She thought of Daniel and how the least touch of his hand could make her quiver.

'I'm not hungry.' She shrank back against the cool leather seat. 'And I'd better not be back late.'

The light from a street lamp reflected in his unusual pale blue eyes. 'You're not frightened of me, are you, Rebekah?' he surprised her by saying. 'I know I'm a few years older than you.'

'Frightened?' Was she? If she was it was only a fear of being pressurised into doing what he wanted just to keep on the right side of him. She closed her eyes. 'Why should I be? I'm just tired that's all. I'm not used to all this excitement.'

'I thought you had been having an exciting time lately.' He straightened. 'Your aunt said that you've been going out with some man for ages.'

She stilled, wondering if – as her guardian – he could stop her seeing Pat. 'It was a joke at first,' she murmured, 'Hannah has this thing about me and fellas so I pretended I was meeting someone.'

'Your aunt says that someone has been seeing you home,' he said emphatically.

'Does she?' She opened her eyes. 'He's Brigid's brother. His mother insists he sees me safely to the doorstep.'

'You don't find him exciting?'

She looked at him. 'Haven't I just explained?'

153

He stared at her and said abruptly, 'Did you find O'Neill exciting?'

'What?' Her heart gave a peculiar lurch.

'You heard me, Rebekah.' He vanished out of sight to crank the car, leaving her wondering why he had to mention Daniel right now. What was the point? He slid into the driving seat and drove away from the kerb. 'Well?' he murmured.

'Well what?' Her pulses were beating uncomfortably fast.

'O'Neill? You were very concerned about him in New York.'

'I don't want to talk about him.'

'Why? He didn't do anything to you, did he?'

Rebekah felt heat rising in her face. 'Why are you talking like this?' she whispered. 'He's dead.'

His gaze was on the busy street and she thought that was why he did not answer immediately. 'I believe he had a way with women. Irish charm, I suppose. You'd appeal to him. Young! Innocent! You're lovely, you know. I bet he told you that.'

Suddenly she experienced a deeper darkness than she had suffered since first hearing that Daniel was dead. 'You're trying to turn me against him – why?' Even to her own ears she sounded bewildered.

'Because I don't want you wasting your thoughts on him,' he muttered, his neck reddening. 'I could tell you things – '

'No!' Her voice trembled. 'Please take me home.'

'I'm only thinking of you.' The tone of his voice had changed almost to a caress. 'If you can't accept the truth you won't get far in this life, my dear. You're so trusting.'

She stared at him and then away. 'I loved Daniel but he's dead. I accept that and don't need to know what you want to tell me. Can we talk about something else? What about the job you mentioned?'

For a moment she thought he was going to ignore her words then he shrugged. 'You can start on Tuesday, seeing as it's Whit this weekend.' He told her where and what time, and after that did not speak but drummed the fingers of one hand on the steering wheel. She sensed he was still annoyed because she refused to listen to what he wanted to say about Daniel but she was determined not to revert to their previous conversation or to begin a new one.

At last he broke the silence. 'Are you sure you wouldn't like some supper? I don't like eating alone and it hasn't been easy since Emma died.'

Rebekah was uncertain whether he was attempting to elicit sympathy but she was in no mood to feel sorry for him. 'I'm not hungry.'

He sighed heavily. 'What a pity. I was going to take you to the Oyster Rooms. You'd have liked oysters.'

'I hate the thought of eating them.'

'Do you hate me as well? Just because – '

'Don't say it,' she interrupted wearily. 'Talk about something else. Ships! Or what about Andromeda – your good luck charm? Is she still languishing in the garden?'

'I've had her repainted.' His expression brightened. 'That should please you.'

'It does.' She smiled. 'I hope she does bring you luck. I reckon you could do with some.'

'There's always an element of luck in life. Look at the *Samson*. A few minutes either way could have made a tremendous difference. You wouldn't be sitting next to me now.'

'No.' The word was muted.

There was a silence but she could imagine his thoughts. You could have been with O'Neill. Or could you?

He glanced at her. 'Sailors are notoriously superstitious. I know because I've lived among them. I'll take you to see Andromeda.'

'Not now,' she said, relieved that he had not mentioned Daniel but alarmed at the thought of going back to his house at this time of night.

He patted her hand where it rested in her lap. 'Forgive me, Rebekah, if I've upset you. It's just that I have your welfare at heart.'

'Apology accepted.' She removed his hand. 'But can I see Andromeda another day?'

'Tomorrow,' he said firmly. 'Why don't you come along to church? It's time you got yourself known and involved in the community. There's people worth your while getting to know. We could have dinner afterwards and – '

'I told my aunt I'd go with her to the meeting house in the morning.'

155

He scowled. 'I really do think you should do what I say.'

'I promised. Would you have me break a promise?'

'Of course not,' he said dourly. There was a short silence. 'I suppose we could go to church in the evening and have supper afterwards?'

She supposed that she should do something to please him and she was interested in seeing Andromeda. 'Okay.'

'Good girl.' He drew up outside her aunt's house. 'I'll see you tomorrow then.' He leaned towards her but she retreated.

'Tomorrow.' She gave him a sparkling smile from the other side of the gate and waved but did not stay to watch him drive away.

Chapter Fourteen

The church in Anfield was a beautiful building but Rebekah was more conscious of its being High Anglican with its confession boxes, priest in fancy vestments, an incense-swinging choirboy and a highly decorated altar, than of its stonework. What would her parents have thought of it all? What would Aunt Esther think? The Quaker meeting house that they had attended was a plain brick building in a run-down part of the town off Byrom Street, not far from the notorious Scotland Road. There had been a scripture reading meeting half an hour before the meeting proper with no more than eighty people attending the main service, which concentrated on silent communion with God. Her aunt had told her that once numbers had run into the hundreds and the meeting house had been on the edge of town, but as Liverpool's prosperity had grown so had the population risen. Housing had spread into the surrounding countryside enveloping the villages of Walton, Kirkdale and Bootle. Many of their members had moved out of the city centre and once smart districts of Liverpool had turned into slums housing the poorest of the poor. She had pointed out to Rebekah the area where Hannah had once lived and for the second time that weekend she had experienced a flicker of sympathy for the maid.

Rebekah rose and went up the long aisle alone, Joshua having left her to her so-called prayers. At the door she exchanged a few words with the vicar and came out into a warm spring evening.

'God in Heaven, fancy meeting you here!'

Rebekah turned and was surprised to see Edwina McIntyre with her father.

'Hello,' she said, feeling instantly guilty. 'It's my first time. There was quite a crowd, wasn't there?'

'Too many to know everyone,' said Edwina briskly, clutching a large handbag. 'You never did have that cup of tea with us.'

'I'm sorry.' Her expression was contrite. 'I've been busy.'

'Come back now,' said Mr McIntyre eagerly. 'I want to know what you think about the meeting between Sir James Craig and Mr de Valera?'

She stared, barely able to believe what he was saying. Sir James Craig was Premier Elect of Ulster. 'Is Mr de Valera back from America then? I haven't been reading the papers.'

Mr. McIntyre nodded with obvious satisfaction. 'Sir Edward Carson of the Ulster Unionist Party says that de Valera could do something to bring North and South together.'

Before she could respond Joshua came up to them. 'Rebekah, I was just coming to find you.'

She touched his arm. 'Joshua, this is Mr McIntyre and his daughter. They're neighbours. Mr McIntyre's just been telling me that President de Valera's met with Sir James Craig. Perhaps the fighting will stop at last?'

Joshua smiled but did not shake hands. 'It's nice to meet you. I'm sorry I've got to drag Rebekah away but there's someone I want her to meet.' Before another word could be spoken he hurried her away.

She turned on him. 'Didn't you hear what I said?'

'About Ireland? Of course. I hope there will be peace. Then I can sell my place over there.'

'Sell it?' Rebekah stopped abruptly. 'You mean – get rid of Grandmama's farm?'

'Not your grandma's, Rebekah. Mine,' he said with a smile. 'And what's the point of keeping hold of it now? Ireland will never be what it was in the days my father used to talk about. Now let's forget the place. Liverpool's your home.'

She could have said more and asked who was this person she was supposed to be meeting, but he was talking about Andromeda as he led her across the road in the direction of the park, and she guessed that it had been a means to get her away from the McIntyres in a hurry.

'She's lovely,' said Rebekah, stroking the green tail of the mermaid figurehead.

'She looks a lot better than she did,' agreed Joshua, hovering behind Rebekah. 'Let's hope she works some magic. I could do with it.'

She glanced over her shoulder. 'Has something else gone wrong?'

'You may well ask,' he said, his mouth tightening. 'The ship repairers are on strike over wages and the Stewards' Union are threatening to come out over a pay cut.'

'Does that mean your ships won't be sailing?'

'It means that no liners will be sailing if the stewards refuse to sign on this week. Although, if they signed their articles on Friday they're bound to go. Unless the union can be persuaded there's no money available, we're in trouble.'

'It must be hard on the men having their wages cut.' She moved away from him and down the garden.

'Life's hard for all of us.'

'It's harder for some. We have it easy in comparison.' She stood on tiptoe to inhale lilac blossom.

He broke off some for her. 'My family worked for what I've got.'

'They had more luck than others, perhaps?' She eased the lilac stem through a button hole.

'It's not all luck,' he said shortly. 'And the men should be glad to have jobs when times are hard.'

Rebekah frowned. 'I'm sure they are glad. But after all, they are only asking for what's theirs. How much is this pay cut?'

'Something like eight shillings a week.'

'Eight shillings! That's a lot for a man with a family to feed!'

'It's happening all over the country.' He scowled. 'You don't have to glare at me like that, Rebekah! There's troublemakers stirring up the men and it's not only in shipping. It's the miners and the railwaymen. Nobody seems to be content with what they've got anymore.'

'Times are changing in England just as they are in Ireland,' she retorted. 'The working classes no longer believe what the so-called upper classes tell them about their place in life. The war saw to that when it killed and maimed thousands of men! And for what?'

He seemed about to blurt something out but instead compressed his lips. After several seconds his expression relaxed and he placed his hands on her shoulders and shook her gently. 'You're a woman and can't begin to understand these matters. But you're more of a fighting Irish colleen than I credited. It's a wonder you're not over there battling against the so-called president of the Dail in Dublin. A schoolteacher for a President, I ask you! What can he know about governing a country?'

'He knows more about Ireland than Lloyd George,' murmured Rebekah, concealing her impatience. 'There's nothing wrong with its being a republic if that's what her people want.'

His smile faded and his eyes glittered. 'I suppose it was O'Neill who filled your head with such nonsense? Your father wouldn't have liked your supporting terrorists.'

She pulled away from him, her anger barely under control. 'Not all those who want an independent Ireland are terrorists! Lots of honest decent people want it too! And they want to keep the ties with Britain strong. When were you last in Ireland that you're such an authority on the subject?'

For a moment she thought he was going to strike her and drew back, watching him struggle with his emotions. At last he said in a tight voice, 'You're right of course. I haven't been to Ireland for a long time. At most I've spent two years there and I did meet honest, decent people. Your grandmother was such a one.'

She recognised the olive branch. 'I wish I'd known her better.' She sighed. 'Just as I wish I'd known my mother's mother. I kept the doll Grandmama Rhoades gave me for years – in memory of her – but it went down with the *Samson*.'

Joshua put his arm around her. 'We'll get you another.'

She forced herself not to stiffen and gave him a look. 'I'm too old for dolls. Besides, it wouldn't be the same.' she hesitated. 'There is something you can do for me, though.'

'Tell me.' He pressed his lips against her left eyebrow.

She wanted to move away but realised that would not improve her chances of getting what she wanted. 'The ship that's replacing the *Samson* – you'll change its name, won't you?' He nodded. 'Could you change it to the *Sarah Jane*? It was my mother's dream and I'd like to see it come true.'

'You don't know what you're asking,' he said bluntly. 'I'd be breaking with family tradition. All our ships are named for biblical heroes.'

160

'Sarah's biblical.' Determinedly she put her hand through his arm and said in wheedling tones, 'Please, Joshua.'

He stared down at her. 'I'll have to think about it. How about coming out with me tomorrow? We could go for a spin in the country.'

'I can't. I'm meeting Brigid.'

'Don't go.' He squeezed her hand against his side. 'We could discuss your idea.'

'I can't let Brigid down.'

'Oh, come on, Rebekah!' he exclaimed impatiently. 'You're going to have to cut that connection sooner or later.'

'Am I?' Apprehension tightened her stomach muscles.

'Dammit, of course you are! And better sooner than later.'

'Better sooner than later, you say?' Her brow furrowed.

'Yes. You can't move in two different worlds,' he muttered, and kissed her with a passion that took her completely by surprise.

Early on Monday morning Rebekah gave a threepenny bit to one of the boys who played in the road, to take a note to Brigid. She leaned on the gate in the sunshine, not wanting to go back inside the house to face her aunt's long face because she was going out with Joshua. As she waited for him to come, her feelings were mixed.

His desire to blacken Daniel in her eyes upset her, and yet she thought she understood it. After all, she had told him that she loved Daniel so that went some way to explaining it. Yet she felt there was something more. She frowned and shook her head and passed on to the next aspect of his character which she did not like: his attitude towards the men who worked on his ships. She had seen for herself how hard they worked, and surely so must he. He ought to realise they deserved what they earned. Neither did she like his insistence that she keep the right side of her aunt for mercenary reasons. Although she had no intention of allowing Hannah to get her hands on what she considered was rightly her own inheritance. But back to Joshua . . . She did not like his wanting her to cut her connections with Brigid. It was something she just could not do.

Yet he had his good points. There was his interest in the Seamen's Orphanage and the fact that he had given her the money she had asked for last week. He had found her a job and taken note of what she said about Andromeda. And he did have some kind of physical attraction for her, although she had resisted him when he had kissed her yesterday evening. He had apologised, saying that she had gone to his head. She pulled a face at the very idea.

There was the hooting of a horn and a motor car drew into the side of the road. Rebekah opened the gate, went over to the car and got in. She noted that Hannah was watching through the net curtains and waved to her. Her eyes gleamed as the maid's face quickly disappeared.

Some twenty minutes or so later they were rolling along the cobbled Walton Road with the hood of the Oxford Morris down. 'I thought I'd take you north of Liverpool,' said Joshua. 'It's nice countryside and coming this way I can show you where part of my family originally came from.' He waved a hand in an easterly direction. 'See that old mill? It's mentioned in a diary of my great-great-grandfather's. Springfield Mill, it was called. He passed it when he came to Liverpool seeking his fortune.'

Rebekah tightened the scarf to secure her new cream straw hat against the wind and gazed at the decapitated mill. In another age it would have been picturesque with its sails turning but with them missing it had a forlorn air about it. 'I take it he made his fortune?'

'He became a deckhand, but worked hard and was eventually the captain of a slave ship. He just about managed to make some money before slavery was abolished.'

'Did you know that the Quakers were involved in slavery at one time?' murmured Rebekah. 'I discovered that yesterday. And that they had dummy guns on some of their ships to trick privateers into believing that they were armed.'

'Never heard of that. But getting back to my family – even though slaving finished, there were still plenty of other cargoes to carry across the Atlantic. Earthenware, steel, glass, machinery, fish hooks, chemicals – you name it, we shipped it.'

Rebekah listened as he continued to talk about ships and cargoes, interspersing it with information about various landmarks. They passed a church. 'That's St Mary's. This is Walton-on-the-Hill where my great-great-grandfather came from. There's been a church here for over a thousand years. Well before Liverpool was more than a dot on the map. Now this place is a backwater, while Liverpool's thriving and a good place to live.' He smiled at her and drove on, humming.

He was full of smiles today, thought Rebekah, obviously enjoying driving and being away from his office. She had to admit to feeling some excitement herself, finding the speed of the car exhilarating. It was fun bowling along the road faster than anything else on it. She watched Joshua's hands as they moved from steering wheel to different levers and wished she could have a go.

Soon there was little else on the road. Housing became sparse and after Joshua pointed out Aintree Racecourse where the Grand National was run, it almost petered out altogether. As they travelled along country lanes where the hedgerows were white with hawthorn blossom and fields showed cowslips and daisies, he said, 'My grandmother on my father's side was Anglo-Irish, you know. Her family bred horses. That's how she and my grandfather met – at some horse race in Ireland.'

'You've never mentioned that before,' she said, surprise in her voice.

'Never saw the need.'

'But it explains why your father bought land in Ireland.'

'It would have been better if he'd ploughed the money into the business,' he said in clipped tones. 'Are you hungry?'

'Yes.' She would have liked to have asked him more about his family but now received the impression that he did not want to talk about them.

'Janet made us up a picnic. I thought we'd have it on top of Clieves Hill. It's not a difficult walk and there's a good view.'

He brought the car to a halt and lifted the picnic basket from the back seat, telling her to get the rug. She did so and followed him up the hill. They could have been the only people in the world. She stared at the view. The flatlands of coastal Lancashire spread below them and the dark huddle that was Liverpool was visible far away, as were the Welsh Hills and the Irish Sea shimmering in the distance.

Suddenly Joshua's arms slipped about her waist from behind and she realised that subconsciously she had been waiting for it to happen. She attempted to release herself but he laced his fingers and she could not unlock them. He said against her ear, 'Isn't the view worth coming all this way for?'

163

'Yes. But can we look at it while we eat, please?'

'Give me a kiss first.'

'Mr Green, you're taking advantage of me,' she said indignantly, digging her fingers into the backs of his hand. 'Now let me go at once.'

'Don't do that.' His voice held a warning note. 'Just one kiss, Rebekah. It's not much of a reward for bringing you all the way out here.'

'I didn't know that I'd have to pay!' she said. 'I thought you brought me out of the kindness of your heart.' She twisted in his hold, trying to free herself, and ended up facing him.

He smiled. 'That's a good girl. I like you. That's why I brought you. Now be a sensible child and kiss me.'

She frowned but puckered her lips, thinking it quicker to get it over. She suspected he would spend time arguing with her rather than give in. He laughed, brought her close and almost ate her. Her mouth felt bruised and she was trembling when he released her.

He rubbed his hands together in a satisfied manner. 'Now food Spread the rug, Rebekah.'

She did as she was told, watching him as he unpacked the picnic. There was tongue and beef sandwiches, homemade meat patties, fruit cake, scones, apples, and a bottle of white wine.

They did not speak while they ate. He filled two glasses with wine. It was sweet and she enjoyed it but refused a refill. 'Come on, Rebekah!' he said. 'It'll relax you.'

'I'm relaxed enough,' she murmured, determined that he was not going to get her drunk. Her gaze took in the view again and the car below them on the road. 'I enjoyed the drive. Do you often come out here?'

He shrugged and filled his own glass. 'I go to different places. I enjoy driving.'

'I wouldn't mind learning to drive.'

A little of his wine spilt as he turned and stared at her. 'But you're a woman.'

'So? I didn't imagine you'd have brought me out here if I wasn't. I imagine it's not that difficult. I'm sure I could get someone to teach me. In fact, I wouldn't mind having my own car.'

His expression grew wary. 'They're expensive. You can't afford – '

She knew that but was determined not to give up her idea. She wanted to drive. It would be exciting. 'I could ask Aunt Esther about buying one. I've noticed lately that her knee hurts her. Probably rheumatism. I could take her places.'

His mouth tightened. 'I don't know if it's a good idea, your having a car.'

'Why? Saying I'm a woman isn't a good reason. Women drove during the war, trams and all sorts of vehicles.'

'That was different,' he muttered. 'There weren't the men.'

She stared at him. 'That's no excuse. I'll ask Aunt Esther and I'm sure the dealer could arrange for me to have a few lessons.'

He stuck out his lower lip and it was several seconds before he said, 'I'll teach you.' He drained his glass.

'You?' She laughed. 'Wouldn't it go against the grain? You don't want to teach me.'

'Better I do than someone else.' He refilled his glass. 'Besides, your aunt mightn't buy you a car.'

That was true, she thought, but to go out with him again in his car was asking for trouble. He would probably believe that she did not mind his kissing her, and she did mind his presumption that he could kiss her when he felt like it. 'I'll think about it,' she said.

'You'll come.' His tone was positive. He flicked her cheek with his finger.

She rubbed her cheek but made no reply and began to collect the remains of the picnic together, aware that he watched her as he drank his wine. She was half expecting him to attempt to embrace her again but he did not. Soon afterwards he led the way down the hill and she followed, wondering whether he would suggest a lesson next weekend. She would have to make up her mind whether to go with him but before then she had her new job to think about, which started in the morning.

Chapter Fifteen

Rebekah hesitated at the foot of a flight of well-worn stone steps at the end of a row of dilapidated landing houses in Everton. She was aware of the curious stares of several small children sitting on the edge of the pavement. They had their bare feet in the gutter and were playing with stones. A couple of women who had paused in mid-gossip outside a front door set in the wall beneath the outside landing, watched her. She smiled but they looked through her and carried on with their conversation. She shrugged and looked up. Level with her head was a window with the curtains drawn. One of the panes of glass was missing and the space was blocked with a sheet of grubby cardboard. She glanced down at the paper in her hand and read the name and address again then began to climb the steps.

As she reached the landing a boy, whom she estimated to be twelve years old, came out of the second house. He leaned his back against the wrought iron railing opposite the front door, coughing and wheezing. He was pale and thin and wore grey trousers too short for him and a darned V-necked sleeveless pullover next to his skin. His eyes were unfriendly as they took in her appearance. She had dressed in her plainest and cheapest black frock but realised that here it would not be regarded as cheap. 'I'm looking for Mrs Rimmer,' she said, determinedly controlling her nerves.

'Ma's out.' He moved in one fluid movement back in front of the doorway from which he'd emerged. 'Yer'll have ta cum back tomorra.' His chest heaved.

'I can't,' said Rebekah, remembering how in Dublin there had been occasions when she and her mother had been informed that Mam was out while she had been in. 'If I can't see her today then I'll have to go to the next name on my list.'

'She's norrin, I tell yer! Why can't yer go away and leave us alone?' He coughed and twitched a shoulder in the direction of the floor inside the entrance. 'We've even had to sell the oilcloth,' he spluttered. 'There's nuffin else we got to pay yer.'

'Who said I want paying?' she said grimly. 'I've come to see your ma about giving her money.' She glanced down at the paper again although there was no need, she knew the words off by heart. 'Your father was drowned when an enormous wave swept over his ship, dismantling its steering apparatus and considerably damaging the deck,' she recited.

The boy nodded. 'The *Magnifique* the ship was called. Ma's inside with the baby. Me brothers and sisters are at school. Wait here.' He vanished inside the house to reappear a few minutes later, smiling. 'Ma said to cum in but don't go expectin' anythin' fancy.'

Rebekah went inside expecting nothing at all in the way of frills and she was not disappointed. The room she entered was furnished with one chair and a rickety card table. In a corner a couple of grey and black army blankets lay on the bare wooden floor. A woman in a grubby blue frock nursed a whimpering baby. She stood next to a grate in which the fire was dead. From the ashes it looked as if it had been made up mainly of cardboard, paper and wood.

'Billy sez yer from the Seamen's, miss,' said the woman eagerly. 'Will we get summit? Yer see, I need muny for medicine for Billy's chest. Bad it is still, but always wurst in winter. Goose grease me cousin gave me to rub on it after Christmas, and I'm sure it must have dun it sum good.' She paused for breath.

Rebekah nodded. 'I'm sure we can give you some money for medicine. I take it Billy hasn't seen a doctor?'

'Doctor!' A harsh laugh escaped her. 'Can't afford doctors. Daisy needs shoes and I owes the corner shop. Never clears that amount, but Mrs Murphy's got a good heart. As long as I pays summit she lets us buy on tick. If it wurn't for that swine of a man of mine, we'd never have got inta this state.'

'That's me dad,' said Billy, nodding. 'Always in the ale house. Never saw hardly any of his money, did we, Ma?'

'No, son.' She smiled at him and then at Rebekah as she continued to rock the baby which had fallen silent. 'He's a good lad. If his chest wasn't so bad he'd gerra job. Fourteen he is but nobody'll take him on. Andy cud have dun more for him but all he ever had on his mind was bed and booze. Eight kids I've got. Lost three.' Her expression turned ugly. 'Bed and booze. He was a bluddy animal.'

'No use my offering you condolences then,' said Rebekah as cheerfully as she could.

'What?' Mrs Rimmer stared at her. Then she began to laugh. 'Best bluddy thing that ever happened to me!'

Rebekah lay in the lukewarm bathwater, thinking of Mrs Rimmer and the lives different people lived. Her story was nothing new to Rebekah. Living in Dublin had accustomed her to inebriated men and worn down women, and she had seen more than a few drunken sailors since living in Liverpool where pubs were as plentiful as pigeons. She had slipped the woman a pound of her own money to tide her over until her application went through, and had gone on to the next family, glad of the street map book her aunt had given her, and thinking about what Daniel had told her of his own childhood. Poverty was a terrible thing. She had been a fool saying to Joshua that money was not important.

She pulled out the bath plug and with a towel wrapped about her went into her bedroom, thinking about her next port of call. She had felt sorry for Mrs Brown who ran a small shop wedged in a row of houses in Edge Hill. It was obvious that she missed her husband, that money was tight, but also that the family of four were managing. Mrs Brown worked long hours and the two boys, although only ten and twelve, helped with deliveries. The eldest girl of eight was already a good little housewife, according to her proud stepmother. Mrs Brown had married late in life, the widower of her best friend who had died in childbirth. Only the youngest child belonged to her but she saw it as her duty to do her best for all the children. They were not in dire straits so Rebekah could not recommend their receiving much financial help, but what she did so was put in for new boots for the boys. With that small offering their mother had seemed grateful. Tomorrow Rebekah would work in the office, writing up her reports.

168

She frowned at her reflection as she rubbed her wet hair, glad that it was short but knowing it needed trimming again. She smoothed merculised wax on to her face and tried not to dwell on thoughts of the place that the Rimmers lived in or on meeting Joshua next weekend. Liverpool, as Brigid had once said, was no Paradise. Its people were no angels, but Rebekah was starting to feel at home in it. She glanced at the clock and realised that she had better hurry or she would be late meeting her friend outside the Olympia.

Rebekah was surprised to see Pat and Joey when she reached the theatre on West Derby Road. 'What are you two doing here?'

'I thought you'd have heard from the bossman,' said Pat, the slightest sneer in his voice. 'The blinking stewards are on strike so we're not sailing.'

'I heard that the *Aquitania* had sailed,' said Rebekah, ignoring the tone of his voice. 'There were orphans on it who have been adopted by some rich Americans.'

'They were taking bets on the *Aquitania* going out, and the owners went and got a volunteer crew,' said Joey, Pat's mate, in a gloomy voice. 'Some of the stewards signed on at the lower rate of pay when Cunard's own clerks rushed to fill their places.

'You're going to be short of money.' said Brigid thoughtfully. 'We'll go Dutch if we go out again.'

Joe shook his head. 'I'm not having you paying for yourself. If I can't afford to take yer out, I won't go at all.'

'That's stupid!' said Brigid in a low voice. 'I'm earning so it makes sense I pay my way.'

'So I'm stupid,' said Joe, his thin face set stubbornly. 'That's the way I am and you won't be changing me.'

'Oh, Joe!' cried Brigid, giving him a gentle punch.

'Shut up, you two,' muttered Pat, taking some change from his pocket. 'Are we going in or not? The queue's moving, so make up your minds.'

'We're going in,' said Rebekah, putting her hand through his arm. 'I'm in need of a good laugh.' She knew better than to offer to pay for herself.

'You've been with his lordship today and all, have you?' said Pat, his mouth tightened.

'No, I haven't.' She squeezed his arm. 'I've been working.'

Brigid smiled. 'So yer got the job? Difficult day, was it?'

'Not really but it makes you glad of what you've got.'

Pat glanced at her and his face softened. 'What is it you're doing, luv?'

'I'm working on Outdoor Relief for the Seamen's Orphanage.'

'You're joking!'

'What's there to joke about?' Her look was puzzled.

'You're a blinking do-gooder!'

'You'd rather I was a do-badder?' She was irritated.

'You know what I mean,' he growled. 'You're working for the bosses. They give to salve their consciences. Do you realise, Becky, if they paid the workers decent wages, there wouldn't be any need for charity. We could look after our own.'

'You might look after your own, Pat, but not all workers do,' she said indignantly. 'A family I visited today were that poor you would have wept for them. And most of their poverty was because the blinking husband drank his wages away and she had too many kids. Nearly every time he docked she was off again. What chance has she of coping without help? He wasn't looking after his own, only satisfying himself!'

He flushed. 'Hey, come on now, luv! That's life. Most women expect to have babies when they get married. You're sounding like – '

'Women don't went ten and twenty, though,' interrupted a female voice from behind. 'If you men had the babies it'd be different, I bet.'

Several people looked in their direction and Pat's face went redder. 'See what you've started,' he hissed.

'Me started!' Rebekah's eyes sparkled. 'It's you that thinks women should produce babies like a baker turns out loaves.'

'That's a good one,' approved the voice from behind. 'Even when love goes out of the window, sex never goes stale on men. Even if they're a hundred and two!' There were several titters from the queue.

'Mother of God!' said Pat through gritted teeth. 'Women! A man's better off without them. I'm going.'

170

His sister seized his arm. 'Now yer'll just stay here! You started this, our Pat, by calling Becky a do-gooder. What's wrong with helping people? Yer just downright jealous if the truth's known.'

'Jealous? Of Mr Bloody Green!' He gave a strangled laugh, dragged his arm out of his sister's hold and walked away.

Rebekah stared after him. 'What do I do, Brigid?'

'Go after him,' intervened Joe in an earnest voice. 'Prove to him that yer didn't mean any of it. Kiss and make up, luv.'

'But I did mean it,' said Rebekah, her expression fixed.

'Too right, yer did, love,' said the voice from behind.

'Oh shut up, yer old bag!' shouted the normally passive Joe, and seizing hold of Brigid's hand he marched her out of the queue. She turned and called, 'I'm sorry, Becky, but it looks like it's not on tonight. I'll see you on Thursday. Meet you outside Lyons in Church Street at seven o'clock.'

'Oh, all right!' Rebekah was annoyed with her friend. She moved out of the queue.

Her supporter, a plump woman with a feather in her hat, patted her arm as she took her place. 'He'll come back, luv. Jealous as hell. Not the easiest type to live with but I bet you know that.'

'I didn't but I'm learning,' murmured Rebekah, and went in the direction of the park, deciding that she had better kill some time, otherwise Aunt Esther would be asking questions.

She walked to Newsham Park boating pond, and paused to watch boys send small yachts skimming across the water. At that moment she wished that she had never agreed to go out with Pat and felt like never bothering with him again. Maybe she would not have the choice. Did she care? She shrugged. Was he really jealous of Joshua Green? Damn! The two men were creating complications in her life that she would rather live without. If only Daniel . . . The ache which never completely left her made itself felt. Why had he had to die? Oh God! There was a lump in her throat and she wanted to hit something or throw things.

She went home and asked her aunt about buying a car.

'What for?' said Esther, stabbing herself with a needle.

'To ferry you around,' retorted Rebekah, leaning against the mantleshelf, her hands in her pockets.

171

'Chariots of the devil, that's what them motors are,' said Hannah, her dark eyes darting dislike at Rebekah as she poured the tea and spilt it in the saucer.

'Rubbish!' Rebekah glared at her. 'You just don't like the thought of Aunt Esther spending money.'

'A motor car would cost a lot of money,' said her aunt, sucking her finger. 'And who'd drive it? I don't want to hire a man?'

'I can learn.' said Rebekah, her anger lifting. 'Would you buy one? I could take you shopping and for drives in the country. I've noticed your knee – '

Hannah interrupted her. 'A bit of rheumatism, that's all. She doesn't need mollycoddling. Needs to keep it moving or it'll seize up.'

I'm not suggesting she glues herself to the car,' retorted Rebekah, glaring at Hannah again.

'I'll think about it,' said Esther hurriedly before Hannah could respond. She looked at her niece. 'It's not a decision to be made in a moment, dear. It would be nice to visit the country but aren't cars dangerous?'

'It depends who drives them,' said Rebekah.

'Exactly,' muttered Hannah, thrusting a cup at her. 'And there's them that thinks they knows it all and knows nothing. When has thee ever driven a car, miss?'

'Starting from next week I'll be learning.' She smiled sweetly. 'So put that in your pipe and smoke it! Mr Green is going to teach me.'

'Perhaps thee'll crash it,' said Hannah, and walked out of the room.

'Oh dear,' said Esther looking dismayed.

'I won't crash it,' murmured Rebekah, passing a plate of scones to her aunt. 'Just you wait and see. I'll show her.'

'Oh dear,' said her aunt again, putting down her sewing. 'I really do need a bit of peace at my time of life.'

'Sorry,' Rebekah said meekly, and put a scone in her hand. 'I'll change the subject.' She sat and began to talk about Mrs Rimmer and her family.

When Thursday came Rebekah made her way to Lyons cafe with only seconds to spare to seven o'clock. Brigid was not there but someone else was waiting for her.

'I hope you don't mind my coming instead of our Bridie,' said Pat, running a finger round his collar and moving his shoulders awkwardly. 'We'll be sailing soon after all – and she said I had no right to say what I did.'

'She was right.'

'I'm sorry,' he muttered.

Rebekah had been feeling annoyed two seconds ago but his apology changed that. 'I forgive you,' she said with a smile.

He grimaced. 'It's just that I didn't realise what I felt towards you.' He looked down at his well-polished shoes.

'Let's forget about it,' she said, choosing to ignore what he had just said. 'Will we have a cup of tea?'

He lifted his head. 'I thought you might like to go to the pictures?'

'No,' she said hurriedly, considering the cosy intimate darkness inside the picture house. 'Just a cup of tea.'

'Okay.' He sighed and stared at her, his brown eyes reminding her of a pony she had once ridden on her grandma's farm.

They went inside Lyons and she asked him whether the strike was over. He told her that most of the stewards were signing on, with only the chief stewards holding out and talking of forming their own union. Then he fell silent. She forced the conversation, enquiring after his mother and whether Brigid had given him a message for her. 'Ma should be out soon. We're thinking of throwing a party to celebrate. You will come?' he said eagerly. 'Ma thinks a lot of you.'

'Of course I'll come.' She smiled and he placed his hand over hers on the table.

'Mr Green – you and him aren't – ?'

She withdrew her hand, feeling irritated again. 'You asked me once whether I was a one man woman – I am! Shall we go now?'

He sighed, nodded and rose. 'I'll see you home.'

'There's no need. Just tell me what Brigid said.' He told her. 'Fine,' she replied, impulsively kissed his cheek, waved a hand and walked away, not looking back, and uncertain as to whether she was relieved or sorry about the way things had changed between them.

The weekend arrived and Rebekah was waiting outside the gate for Joshua to arrive. Her aunt had not made up her mind yet about buying a car but Rebekah was working on her, telling her how useful it would be. They would not have to get groceries and goods delivered but pick up what they wanted themselves. Hannah had grunted that they'd be putting people out of work. Rebekah could not see how just having a car could do that.

There was the tooting of a horn and Joshua drove up. This time they travelled south out of the city. He stopped near some stones. 'They're called calder stones,' he said. 'They're believed to be very old. Probably Neolithic. See the engravings on them.'

Rebekah peered closely at the weird rings and cuplike marks. They remind me of some of the old stones to be seen in Ireland.'

'Probably not as old as these,' he said dismissively and ushered her back to the car.

They travelled a couple more miles and still he did not mention anything about driving lessons so she did.

'I thought you might have changed your mind,' he muttered.

'No. I've mentioned about buying a car to Aunt Esther and she's thinking about it.'

'Hmmph!' He frowned.

She glanced at him and smiled. 'Are you scared of being in the car with me driving, Joshua?'

His expression sharpened. 'Too bloody right I am,' he said, but without any more preamble began to explain to her about steering and gear levers. She listened intently, waiting for the moment when he would move out of the driving seat and let her have a go. Eventually he did so and after a jerky start they were off. At first she went much too slowly because she was nervous about damaging his car. It was *his* car all the time he spoke about it. Be careful of *my* car . . . If you damage *my* car . . . She could understand his feelings but at last she went a bit faster. He did not allow the lesson to go on too long and it came to an end all too swiftly for her.

'Another one tomorrow?' she said.

'We'll see.' He pulled her towards him and kissed her. After a minute she disengaged herself. He laughed but did not persist. He drove back to Liverpool, telling her on the way about the day out they were having for the orphans on the river. 'We're taking them to Eastham on the other side of the Mersey. You must come. You'll enjoy it.'

'What day is it?'

He told her and she agreed to go, and he said that he would give her another lesson after church tomorrow.

On Sunday they went north again, out past Litherland where the smells from a tannery impinged on the country air. They picnicked on the bank of the Leeds-Liverpool canal and afterwards he allowed her to drive round the quiet lanes near the medieval church of Sefton and Ince Woods. He asked her how she was finding her work.

'I enjoy meeting the families.'

'You don't want to be too soft with them,' he said absently. 'Some of them are up to all kinds of dodges.'

'Perhaps you'd be crafty if you had nothing,' responded Rebekah. She had thought of talking to him about Kitty Dodds, whom she had met a couple of days ago, but changed her mind. It was her problem.

'Just be careful who you recommend. Money doesn't grow on trees,' he murmured, pressing her knee.

She said nothing, only removing his hand and changing the subject.

On Monday she met Brigid. Her friend looked relieved. 'I wasn't sure if yer'd be here,' she said, putting her hand in her arm as they walked towards the cinema. 'Our Pat couldn't make up his mind to whether yer'd said yes or no. He's been real moody and got drunk a couple of times.'

'I'm sorry about that.'

'It's not your fault.' Brigid frowned. 'I'm fed up with him. I have enough on me mind with thinking about Mam coming out of hospital. Did Pat tell yer about the party?'

Rebekah nodded. 'Have you a date?'

'Yeah.' Brigid told her.

Rebekah barely hesitated before saying. 'No problem.' It might be, though, because it was the day of the orphans' outing but she could see no way of saying no to Brigid or Joshua without offending one or the other.

Chapter Sixteen

The day of the outing dawned bright and clear and Rebekah, wearing a lemon wash frock and a broad-brimmed white hat to keep off the sun, and with a jacket over her arm in case it was cool on the water, met Joshua down at the Pierhead. 'You look stunning,' he murmured, as he took her hand and led her up the gangway and on to a crowded upper deck.

He ruffled several children's hair and one lad said, 'Is she your girl, sir?'

He laughed and said, 'Yes.' He introduced Rebekah to several of the teachers, not mentioning that he was her guardian and giving the impression that they were sweethearts. She was not prepared for events to move so fast and when he pulled her down on a seat beside him and slipped his arm round her waist, she removed his hand.

The Mersey glistened like a sheet of crinkled silver paper. Rebekah only half listened to Joshua. Her thoughts were of Daniel and the time they had spent on the *Samson*. She was betraying what was still in her heart by being with Joshua, and yet her father would have approved. Strangely, that mattered. It was as if by doing what he wished now she was making her peace with him. She thought of how he and Daniel had fought as the ship steamed across the water and only put it out of her mind when she left the ship.

Eastham Woods rang with the children's shouts and Rebekah smiled, finding pleasure in their enjoyment.

'Miss, miss, come and see this?'

'Miss, look at this bird's egg. Can I keep it? Can I, can I?'

'Miss, what's this animal?' A pair of huge dark eyes gazed up at Rebekah.

'It's a squirrel,' answered Rebekah. 'It eats nuts and hides them away in winter when it goes to sleep.'

'It sleeps the whole winter!' exclaimed the boy. 'Bluddy hell, fancy that! I wouldn't mind doing that meself.'

Joshua gave him a clip over the ear. 'You don't use that language in front of ladies, boy! I'll have a word with the matron and see you get your mouth washed out with soap.'

'Sorry, miss,' said the lad cheerfully, following them. 'I forgot meself. But if I was one of them squirrels I wouldn't have to worry about feeling the cold in winter.' He frowned. 'How does it survive if it sleeps for months? What does it do about them nuts?'

'It wakes up now and again when it gets a little warmer and digs them up,' informed Rebekah, aware of Joshua's scowl.

'Bluddy hell! That's clever! How does it know where –' The lad stopped abruptly as Joshua raised his hand, and fled.

Rebekah laughed but Joshua shook his head. 'You shouldn't have encouraged him.'

'He was trying to learn.' She gazed up at the leafy green branches above them and breathed deeply of the woodland smells. Suddenly Joshua's hands gripped her breasts and she gasped. 'What do you think you're doing?'

He looked at her but did not stop. She attempted to slap his hands away but he caught hold of her fingers and said huskily, 'Isn't it what you expected me to do?' He forced her into his arms. 'You girls like to play the temptress and then pretend you're doing nothing of the sort! But I'm on to you, Rebekah. I'm willing to go along with whatever you wish. I want you, you see.' His mouth came down over hers. She struggled but it was no use. He only let her go when she kicked him on the shins.

He rubbed his leg but smiled up at her. 'That was naughty but I forgive you.'

Rebekah touched her throbbing lips. 'I don't care if you forgive me or not,' she said. 'You hurt me.'

'Sorry.' He pulled her hand away from her mouth and pressed his lips lightly against hers. 'There. I've kissed it better. D'you want to kiss my leg?' he said in a teasing tone.

'Certainly not!' She remembered how Daniel had kissed the insides of her thighs and suddenly shivered. Did she really given the impression of being a tease? If so it must be unconsciously because she was lonely for Daniel's arms. She sighed. 'Shouldn't we be going back now? It must be time for the picnic.'

He nodded. 'I suppose so. Besides, there's a couple of children watching us. Put your hand through my arm and smile.'

Rebekah saw the sense in what he suggested and after that the afternoon passed off smoothly. It was only when they reached the Pierhead and he wanted to make an evening of it in town that there was a little unpleasantness. She stated that she was too tired to go gallivanting round the nightspots, and he sulked. She pretended to doze off in the cab and that seemed to convince him that she was definitely too tired to paint the town even a delicate shade of pink.

As soon as he was out of sight, Rebekah stopped waving at the gate, pulled a comb through her hair and then ran up the road in the opposite direction. It was still light.

'You're late,' said Brigid as soon as she opened the door. 'Our Pat said yer weren't coming.'

Rebekah was surprised. 'Why should he think that? I said I'd come.'

Brigid shrugged. 'Come in anyway. The men have gone to the pub. We've done the butties and everything. There's some of the neighbours in, and me aunts and a few cousins.'

'Come in, girl, and have yourself a shandy,' called Ma Maisie, beckoning to her. 'I'm on the tonic wine to build meself up.'

'You should be drinking Guinness,' said Rebekah, fishing a bottle from inside her jacket. She had bought it on the way. 'Best that Ireland can produce.'

'Now there's a good girl!' Ma Maisie's lined face eased into a big smile. 'Get me a glass and we'll drink to the Emerald Island – that her troubles will soon be over and there'll be peace between us.'

'Amen to that,' chorused several of the women.

Kath handed Rebekah a cup of shandy while Brigid forced off the jink from the bottle of Guinness. They all drank to peace in Ireland and afterwards Rebekah told Brigid about the outing with the orphans, without mentioning Joshua. By the time she had finished, the men were filling up the room and one of the woman was coaxing a tune from a concertina. Rebekah caught a glimpse of Pat across the crowded room. He was swaying and there was an idiotic smile on his good-looking face. 'I'll take you home again, Kat'leen,' he bellowed off key at the top of his voice.

'Oh, shut up. Uncle Pat, that's terrible,' said Jimmy, appearing from beneath the table with his hands over his ears. 'It's enough to kill the cat.'

'Are yer saying I can't sing, lad?' Pat squinted at him.

Veronica bobbed up beside Jimmy. 'Yeah. It was awful. Yer'd be better letting Becky sing. She sings real gud!'

Pat scowled ferociously. 'She's not here! And she's not one of us! Becky has a fancy man and thinks she's too bloody good for the likes of me.'

'Yer drunk,' said Brigid in disgust. 'Where's the eyes in yer head? Becky's here and she does sing better than you!'

'I'm not singing,' said Rebekah in a low voice to her friend, making up her mind to leave as soon as possible. She didn't know why Pat had said what he had but her feelings were injured at that 'She's not one of us!' Besides, she nurtured healthy suspicion of drunks and having Pat offer to see her home in this condition was the last thing she wanted. As well as that she was tired after her day in the fresh air. She picked up her empty glass from the table and took it into the back kitchen. She rinsed it in the sink and stood for a moment, thinking, and then went out through the back door and down the yard. Explanations could wait until next time she saw Brigid.

Running up the back entry, she was glad that it was still only dusk. With a bit of luck she would be home before dark.

It was as Rebekah came out into the road that she collided with Pat. 'How did you get here so quickly?' Her pulses were beating in her ears and she was in no mood for a tussle or an argument.

'Why are yer leaving so soon?' he demanded in a slurred voice, seizing her arm.

'I didn't want to stay.'

'Because of me?'

She sighed. 'If the cap fits – I'm not one of you, remember?'

Pat's eyes darkened and his throat moved. 'I saw you with him down at the Pierhead. I'm bloody surprised at you for spending today with him. I thought you'd come early to Ma's do. He's a bloodsucker, living off the backs of the poor. I thought that you and me – '

'It was the orphans' day out,' she interrupted. 'And there's no you and me! I didn't pretend anything different. You're Catholic, remember, and your mam wouldn't like there being anything serious.'

Pat scowled and his fingers tightened on her arm. 'Daniel O'Neill's being Catholic didn't stop you fancying him.'

'Daniel was Daniel and you can never fill his place.' Her voice was low and unsteady.

'Can Mr Bloody Joshua Green fill it?' He attempted to kiss her – a big slobbery kiss.

With all her strength she pushed him off and backed away. 'I don't want to go out with you any more! You're not my friend! And it's nothing to do with your boss. You've spoilt everything. Goodbye, Pat.' Turning she ran, tears rolling down her cheeks, and did not stop until she was nearly home.

She let herself in with her key as Hannah came charging up the lobby. 'Where hast thee been to this hour?' she demanded.

'It's nothing to do with you,' said Rebekah wearily, pushing past her and entering the sitting room.

'Thou art later than I thought, Rebekah,' said her aunt, struggling to her feet.

'I'm sorry.'

'It's that man, Miss Esther,' put in Hannah. 'He's a bad influence. No meeting house last week and now this! He's leading her astray! She'll be getting a name for herself in the neighbourhood. And we know she drinks.'

'That's enough, Hannah,' snapped Esther. 'Shall we be a little more charitable? It was the orphans' day out. And didn't Paul, in the Bible, say that a little wine is good for the stomach.'

'Always excuses for her,' muttered the maid and went out of the room.

'Oh dear,' said Esther, 'I don't know what to do about her, Becky.'

'Ignore her, and me,' said Rebekah. 'I'm going to bed.' She kissed her aunt and went upstairs. Enough was enough! Pat's mention of Daniel had brought him alive that day for the second time and she wondered what she had been playing at, going out with either of the men. But what was she to do? Shut herself away from male company for ever and turn into another Hannah, frustrated and bad-tempered, because it was obvious her religion didn't give her much joy? She thumped the pillows and that night cried herself to sleep.

Early Monday morning she wrote a letter to Brigid, explaining why she had left the party, and posted it on the way to visit Kitty Dodd for the fourth time.

'You're back, are you?' said Mrs Dodd. She was large, middle-aged, and had her hair in plaited coils about her ears. 'You might as well come in now you're here. Are you going to take them?'

'I've explained, Mrs Dodd.'

The older woman's mouth tightened and she reached for her coat and handbag. 'Well, I'll be leaving you with them, then, and maybe you'll change your mind and they won't be here when I come back.'

Rebekah stared at the four children. There were two sets of twins, three boys and one girl, all under seven, and their parents were dead. Their father had been Mrs Dodd's son. He had been killed, playing football on deck after his ship had docked in Montreal. He had not looked where he was going and fallen down an open cargo hold. His mother wanted his children placed in the orphanage 'You're a stubborn woman, Mrs Dodd. They're lovely children. How can you bear to be parted from them?'

'I can't cope,' she said, not meeting Rebekah's eyes but checking her handbag for her purse. 'I'm over forty. I'm too old. Even with her help next door they're too much of a handful, and it'll get worse.'

'I've told you we'll help out.'

'Financially, girl, but children's needs can't all be met with money. It's time they need, and someone with plenty of energy.' She pulled on black gloves. 'I don't mind keeping the girl.'

'The boys are still too young,' said Rebekah, the tension inside her easing. That was something at least. 'What if I take

181

them out for a while?' she suggested. 'It'll give you time to get your work done or put your feet up.'

Mrs Dodd stared at her and shook her head. A slight smile lightened her stern face. 'You're a right Miss do-gooder, aren't you? Why aren't you married with a baby of your own instead of bothering with other people's?'

'Perhaps I might have been,' Rebekah's voice was low, 'but he went down with his ship last year.'

There was silence except for the noise of the two older children whispering, then Mrs Dodd took off her coat and sat down. She waved Rebekah to the chair opposite hers the other side of the fireplace. 'I lost my man years ago but I had my lad. When the war came I thought I'd lose him but he came through.' Her throat moved. 'Then for him to be killed in a stupid accident – I just couldn't accept it. It seemed unbelievable.' She drew in a shaky breath and when she spoke again her voice was brisker. 'Well, no use us crying, girl. You're only young and have your life ahead of you. You'll find someone else. Have children. That'll help you over it. Now if you want to take them out, I'll appreciate it, and maybe I'll have a cup of tea for you when you come back.'

Rebekah nodded, emotion making it too difficult for her to speak. She picked up the two younger children, Stanley and Lily, who were three years old. Their grandmother told their five-year-old brothers to stop messing about with chalks and put pullovers on them. Rebekah fastened the others in the large twin perambulator kept in the lobby, and with the elder boys holding on the pram handle, they walked the short distance up Farnworth Street in the direction of Kensington Gardens.

'I felt like I won a battle this week,' said Rebekah as she and Joshua came out of Crane Hall after a Chopin recital.

He pulled her hand through his arm. 'I see the police in London have captured a gang of Sinn Feiners. There were women involved too, carrying revolvers inside their blouses which they handed to the men to fire.'

Rebekah's stare fixed on his satisfied expression. 'Why are you telling me?' She attempted to suppress the annoyance in her voice because he had shown no interest in what she said. 'Perhaps you think I've got a gun up the leg of my knickers?'

'My sweet!' He raised his eyebrows. 'Is there really any need for that kind of talk?'

'I suppose not,' she said stiffly. 'But think why I don't like you telling me things like that! I want to forget about anything to do with the struggle in Ireland. I know there were elections yesterday. That in Belfast the streets were festooned with red, white and blue, and that there was trouble. But I don't *want* to know! Instead why can't you tell me about the hundreds of unemployed who are rushing to sign ships' articles and your taking them on so your ships can sail?' Her tone was disparaging as she remembered Joe's talk a short while ago. She presumed that he and Pat had gone back to their ship. She had not seen them since the night of the party and she had received no reply to her letter and was feeling hurt.

'Rebekah, it's in your interest that my ships sail.' Joshua was frowning down at her. 'And you should be glad that at least some of the unemployed are getting work.'

'I am.' She closed her eyes briefly. 'But I bet you'll be paying them less than you were the chief stewards.'

'That's business, I'm afraid.' He sounded almost regretful. 'I would have preferred to pay it to the chief stewards. They're better at the job but proving stubborn. They've formed their own guild with some of the higher ratings of the catering staff.' He kissed her lightly on the cheek and smiled into her eyes. 'Let's forget about all these troubles and talk about us.'

'What about us?' Her voice was wary.

'You must know I'm mad about you.'

'Do I?'

'Of course you do.'

She moistened her lips. 'Say that I do?'

'You can't like living with that aunt of yours.'

'She's not so bad,' she said promptly. 'It's Hannah who drives me mad. She'd love to get me out of the house.'

His eyes narrowed. 'It's like that, is it? Can't you persuade your aunt to get rid of her?'

'She's been with her for a long time. Better the devil you know, I suppose.'

He stared into the distance. 'Does your aunt still resent my being your guardian?'

'Yes.' Rebekah glanced at him. 'Understandable, don't you think? She is my closest relative and you were a stranger to me.'

He smiled and patted her hand. 'But not now. I want to marry you, my sweet, but we don't want to alienate your aunt.'

Rebekah's heart had already begun to race because she had sensed what was coming and wanted to shout, No, no! But all she could say was, 'Marry you?' because it was what her father had wanted and she still felt bad about him, but it was all happening too swiftly.

'Yes, marry,' he murmured, squeezing her arm against his side.

She cleared her throat. 'It isn't a year since Mama and Papa died.'

'I don't want to wait.' His tone was determined.

'I'd need time to get Aunt Esther used to the idea,' she said in a rush. 'She's not going to like it. She might cut me off just like Grandpapa cut Mama off.'

He tapped a nail against his teeth. 'That is a thought. Do you know if she's made a will?'

A small laugh escaped Rebekah. 'It's not something you bring up in everyday conversation! Am I supposed to say, "Dear Aunt, have you left everything to me?"'

He frowned. 'It would make sense for her to tell you, seeing as how you are her next of kin. Anyway, even if she hasn't, everything should come to you, and by my reckoning she's the type who doesn't give business matters the due attention they deserve. I don't think we really have anything to worry about.'

Anger suddenly flared inside her. 'I know that money is important but do you really have to speak about my aunt in such a way? I don't want to think of her dying. Enough people I love have died already. I'm still mourning although I know I'm not dressed for it. I'd have to wait at least a full year before considering marrying!'

'A year!' He stared at her and she was surprised at how anxious his pleasant face looked as he clutched at her free hand. 'I had hoped – I do love you, Rebekah. I couldn't bear it if you said no.' His tongue stumbled over the words. 'Please do say you'll at least think about us being married?'

Still she hesitated but her heart softened at the sight of this different side to him. 'I'd like to know you a bit longer,' she said warmly, 'and then maybe the answer will be yes.'

His relief was obvious. 'Thank you. You won't regret it if you do decide to marry me.'

She said nothing only smiled. Nothing definite was settled and a year seemed a long way off. But the topic of marriage was to recur a couple of weeks later from a different source.

'Miss Rhoades! Miss Rhoades!' Mr McIntyre waved a newspaper in the air, signalling Rebekah to his doorway.

She was wilting from the heat and wanted nothing more than to get indoors, have a cup of tea, a bath, lie down on her new bed, but she pushed open the gate and went up the path past drooping marigolds. 'What is it, Mr McIntyre?'

'They've declared a truce!' His strong-boned face was bright. 'It's been signed by General Macready and Michael Collins!' He nodded his head sharply. 'You'll know him? One of the leaders of the Sinn Feiners. Had a price on his head.'

'Ten thousand pounds at one time.' She was relieved and pleased even though she had tried not to care about what was happening in Ireland. 'It's marvellous! When did it happen?'

He grinned. 'Come inside, have a cup of tea, and you can read it for yourself. I reckon it's all down to that Brigadier-General Crozier, who was the leader of the Black and Tans. He resigned because he didn't like what was going on.' Rebekah followed him up the lobby. 'A week or so back he said that you can't outmurder the murderers, and a whole lot more besides. It looks like the High-ups might have taken notice of him.'

'It seems like it.' Rebekah smiled at Edwina.

'So you've come for that cup of tea at last,' she said, returning her smile.

'Yes.' Rebekah took the newspaper thrust under her nose and read quickly of soldiers and civilians discussing peace prospects in Dublin. 'There's still difficulties ahead,' she murmured. 'The Unionists in Ulster have already set up a parliament. They want to stay in the Empire. President De Valera doesn't want any part of it.'

'The North and South will have to agree to differ,' said Mr McIntyre firmly.

Rebekah frowned. 'They might yet. But Lord Midleton is elected as a Unionist in the South, so there's going to be differences of opinion in the Dail.'

'I wish you two would stop talking politics,' chided Edwina, putting the teapot on the hob. 'I'm fed up of hearing about Ireland. Father, go and fetch me a lettuce from the garden so I can chat with Rebekah.' Mr McIntyre protested but was shooed out, and Edwina turned to Rebekah. 'Sit down and tell us about the job.'

Rebekah sat. 'How do you know about that?'

Edwina winked. 'I heard it on the grapevine. Most reckon that you won't be working for long, though.'

'Why do they say that?' she asked as casually as she could.

'Because they reckon you'll be getting married. They're not sure who to, though. Is it the shipowner with the motor or the dark handsome one they don't know much about? They're rooting for the shipowner because he's your guardian and has money. They say your aunt doesn't like either of them.'

'I suppose it's Hannah who's been gossiping.' Rebekah sipped her tea. 'The dark one was the brother of a friend but we don't see each other any more. Joshua has asked me to marry him but I haven't said yes. If I do marry him, at least with plenty of money I can be miserable in comfort.'

'Miserable?' Edwina pulled up a chair close to Rebekah. 'Tell Auntie Edwina all your troubles, love. Is it that you're wanting to get out of that house?'

Rebekah smiled. 'Aunt Esther I can cope with.'

'Is it a lover's tiff with this Pat then? Sounds Catholic. Is it religion?'

'I don't love Pat,' Rebekah said in a low voice. 'There was someone else but he died.'

'You'd only be young in the war,' said Edwina, her brow thoughtful. 'I presume that is – '

'It wasn't the war. He was an engineer on the *Samson* and was lost when it sank.'

Edwina pressed her hand and it was a few moments before Rebekah said, 'I'm not going to spend my life thinking "if only". With plenty of money I can have fun and do some good with it!' She could hear the defiance in her voice. 'I like my work with the Royal Seamen's Orphanage Outdoor Relief. I like children.'

'And you'd like some of your own?'

Rebekah was silent. 'I have thought about it. There's this family I visit. They're orphans but live with their grandmother. I take them out and give her a break sometimes. In their company it's easier not to think of yourself. Otherwise I do think far too much about my future.'

Edwina looked down at the floor. 'I had my daughter adopted,' she said quietly. 'Sometimes I wish I hadn't.' Her mouth tightened. 'My brother went on and on about my having already brought enough shame on the family by having gone to prison. Father had stood by me through all that, although many others would have given up on me. That's what my brother wanted to do.'

'Your brother doesn't believe in women having the vote?'

'Does he hell!' Edwina's eyes glinted. 'His poor wife is right under his heel. And, of course, getting pregnant was all my fault! I must have led the fellow on! You can imagine the type, can't you?'

'Did you love the father? Was he killed in the war?'

'Love?' Edwina shrugged. 'Not enough to want to marry him. He was exciting and all for women having the vote. He knew Bertrand Russell and believed in free love. I did at the time. I never told him about the baby.' She smiled. 'But that's all in the past. I wish you luck with your shipowner.'

'Thanks,' said Rebekah politely.

Over the next few weeks she began to view marriage with Joshua differently – to dream of having a family. She would have several children and take them to the farm in Ireland. She asked Joshua about the farm and the animals as they walked past the Floral Pavilion in New Brighton, a seaside resort across the Mersey.'

'I've no idea what animals we have.' His voice was disinterested. 'Father tried his hand at farming, but I put a man in and left him to it. Anyway, I told you, I'll try and sell the place when I know where we are with Ireland.'

'I'd love to visit it one more time before you sell it,' said Rebekah.'

'If that's what you'd like,' he said good-humouredly, 'I'll take you there as part of our honeymoon.'

'I haven't said I'll marry you yet,' she murmured.

The humour vanished from his eyes. 'No, you haven't. But I was presuming you would say yes.' He lifted her hand and kissed her fingers. 'Do say yes now, Rebekah,' he pleaded, 'and we could get engaged on your birthday and married in spring. You'll be wanting a fancy wedding, I suppose?'

'The whole works,' she murmured, trying to imagine what it would be like going to bed with Joshua. He could be passionate, and had it not been for Daniel she might have been able to view marriage with him as exciting and right, because she would be obeying her father's wishes at last. As it was she still had vague doubts, but supposed that since Daniel she would have them about marrying any other man.

'Well?' he said impatiently.

She decided and kissed his cheek. 'Yes. I'll marry you.'

His face creased into a smile. 'In the spring? By then Lloyd George should have sorted out De Valera and you can have your visit.'

Rebekah hoped so because the peace talks had been in danger of breaking down.

There seemed to be unrest everywhere in the following months. In September there were riots in Liverpool when the growing numbers of unemployed staged a protest and charged the Walker Art Gallery. They came up against the police who used their truncheons. Blood splattered the walls of the foyer but no one was killed. It was horrible, thought Rebekah. Violence did not solve anything. A meeting between leaders of Sinn Fein and the British government took place in October despite there still being disturbances, but at last it seemed that a Free Ireland was in sight.

Rebekah, remembering conversations with Daniel, experienced a deep sadness. But there was something else that was causing her sorrow. She had still heard nothing from Brigid and could only presume that her sympathy was with her brother and therefore she did not wish to see Rebekah. She was too proud to write again or to visit. She did miss the whole family but realised with the changes soon to be made in her own life, the split might well have been inevitable.

In December Joshua bought Rebekah a diamond and ruby ring on her twenty-first birthday and took her to Lyon's State restaurant where they dined and danced.

Her aunt bought her a secondhand car. A Tin Lizzie four-seater, it had side and rear lamps, which frequently went out because they were oil lit. The headlights, though, were electric and ran directly off the engine. When it was revved up they were bright but when it idled they only let out a dull glow. Rebekah loved it and immediately took her aunt for a drive, having a little trouble with the gears. There were two forward ones, bottom and top, operated by a pedal. Neutral was halfway, but she soon learnt she could only stay in neutral if the handbrake was on. Still, it was her very own car. Her aunt enjoyed the drive but was not pleased when Rebekah told her about the engagement and when she was getting married. 'I had hoped you would have stayed with me longer. He's marrying thee for thy money, my dear.' Her voice was agitated.

'He's got money,' responded Rebekah, sitting on the rug in front of the fire. She added in exasperation: It's what Papa would have wanted! He mentioned it the last time we spoke. It's the least I can do to make amends for the worry I gave him. I nearly ran away with someone, just like Mama!'

'But he stopped thee?' Her aunt's cherubic mouth pursed. 'He would, the hypocrite! Who was it? What happened?'

'He was a sailor and went down with his ship,' murmured Rebekah briefly, not wanting to go into further explanations.

Esther's hands paused on her knitting and she surprised Rebekah again by saying, 'I loved a sailor once but he was utterly unsuitable. It didn't need my father to tell me that. He came into St Anne's Centre and was different to anybody else I knew. He was a charmer and I thought I might have been able to change him, but he didn't want to be changed and I wasn't going to.' She smiled grimly and started knitting again. 'Sometimes I wonder how it would have been if I hadn't been me but thy mother. Still, that's the past and I can only hope thou won't rue the day thee marries Mr Green.'

She could not hope it any more than Rebekah as the days passed. In January a Free Irish government was set up and the keys of Dublin Castle handed over to the Dail. A peace treaty was confirmed under a new President, Arthur Griffiths. All seemed to be going well.

As winter turned to spring there was one person in the household happy about the approaching wedding day, although neither her aunt nor Hannah was attending the ceremony because it was in an Anglican church.

'We'll have a bit of peace at last,' said the maid with obvious satisfaction as she wielded the heavy iron on Rebekah's silk underwear.

'I'm not going to America, dear Hannah,' murmured Rebekah, hurriedly removing her knickers.

Hannah gave her an ugly look. 'He'll soon stop thy gallop, miss. A couple of babies and thee'll know what life's about.'

'I already do. Did you ever have any children, Hannah?' asked Rebekah with an innocent air.

Hannah's dark eyes glistened. 'Thee thinks thee's smart. But if thee dies in childbed, I'll have the last laugh.'

Rebekah smiled twistedly. 'You don't pull any punches, do you, Hannah? But I'll survive, just to spite you, and visit often just so we can stay friends.' She blew her a kiss and left the room, wishing the maid did not hate her so much.

Rebekah chose Edwina for her bridesmaid. Her aunt did not approve of the choice. 'She's no maid,' she muttered. 'Surely thou can find someone else more respectable?'

'There is no one else,' said Rebekah, controlling her impatience and thinking that at least once she was married she would be mistress of her own home, though deeply regretted that Brigid was not her bridesmaid and Daniel her groom, but there was no getting out of it now. Joshua had been jilted once before and however nervous she was she could not serve him such a turn. For better or for worse, in a few days' time she would marry him.

Chapter Seventeen

Rebekah was feeling faint, unreal, wondering if anyone had ever passed out at their own wedding. That morning she had wanted to run away but Edwina's timely arrival with the bouquet of spring flowers had caused her to pull herself together. Her white-gloved hand tightened on Mr McIntyre's arm, because it was he she had asked to give her away, despite Joshua's disapproval; he had offered an elderly uncle whom she had never met. To her surprise Aunt Esther had changed her mind, almost at the last minute, about coming to the wedding, and now sat as stiff as a poker in a sparsely populated pew as the organ played "Here comes the Bride". Some of the older children from the Orphanage – boys in sailor suits and girls in blue dresses and white pinafores – sat a few rows behind her.

It was after all not a splendid social affair because Joshua had come round to mentioning his being left at the altar before. 'I'd rather not have exactly the same crowd,' he had muttered. 'Just a few selected people.' So there were to be only twenty at the Breakfast to be held in his house. Rebekah had considered asking him about his first fiancée but he had frozen her off. She wondered if he had really loved her and was curious enough to want to ask questions but did not care to insist when it was obvious he did not want to talk.

The aisle was longer than Rebekah remembered but still not long enough. A few more seconds and she would reach Joshua, where he stood with his best man, David Beecham, who was prematurely bald, and owned a shipyard. She wondered why he had not asked his cousin, Mr Eaton.

She was there and her knees were knocking. After a brief glance at Joshua, handsome in his morning suit, Rebekah turned and gave her bouquet to Edwina, who winked at her. Suddenly it did not matter what she did or said, she thought vaguely, deep inside she still belonged to Daniel.

Conversation bubbled, hissed and buzzed about Rebekah's ears as, champagne glass in hand, she circulated among her guests, heedless of the fact that the trailing lace veil she wore was in danger of being trodden on.

A grey kid-gloved hand suddenly gripped her duchesse satin sleeve, causing her to stop, and she found herself being scrutinised by a pair of reptilian eyes. 'I hope you're not too young.' The voice was gruff. 'The other one seemed sensible enough and able to handle Joshua, but she let me down. It was Emma, no doubt. Their mother was never strong and could behave very strangely. Emma was like her, and one can't blame Joshua for putting her in that place in Formby-by-the-Sea. It was just as well she went the way she did, leaving the field clear for you.'

'What place?' asked Rebekah.

The woman ignored her question. 'Give him a few children and I'm sure he'll be all right. War unsettles men. You read about it in the newspapers all the time.' She patted Rebekah's arm and before she could recover from her astonishment, the elderly woman had crossed over to Esther who was peering curiously at a china statuette.

Edwina suddenly appeared at Rebekah's elbow. 'That was Amelia Green,' she marvelled. 'I never thought of her being related to the shipping Greens.'

Rebekah thoughtfully sipped her champagne and gazed at the old lady and her aunt. 'They're a pair of characters. They'd look good on the mantleshelf if you could shrink them.'

'Shrink your Aunt Esther and Amelia Green!' Edwina grinned. 'She'd knock you out with her umbrella first. She was a suffragette. What advice was she giving you? To stand up to your man?'

Rebekah shook her head and surprised her friend by saying, 'What's at Formby-by-the-Sea beside the sea?'

Edwina shrugged. 'I've seldom been there. There's a village and a lighthouse . . . woods and fields. They grow asparagus. Why? You're not going there on honeymoon, are you?' she said jokingly.

'The honeymoon is a secret,' said Joshua, making them both jump as he came up behind them. He filled both their glasses.

'What's so secret about Ireland?' said Rebekah, raising her glass to him.

'Ireland!' Edwina spluttered out champagne. 'If you heard Father on the subject you wouldn't be talking about going to Ireland. It's still much too dangerous for a honeymoon.'

'My sentiments exactly,' said Joshua, putting the bottle on a convenient occasional table.

Rebekah's smile faded. 'But you promised! You said – '

'My dear, you said when the fighting ends,' he interrupted in a gentle voice. 'The fighting still goes on and it's not just in Belfast, where it broke out first after the truce. It's happening all over the place because North and South can't agree where the borders should be. It could end in civil war because the Dail is at outs with itself. It's what one expects of amateurs in government. But at least if there's a civil war they'll be killing each other and not British soldiers. My man's already been threatened and we had a fire at the farm.'

'You never told me,' stammered Rebekah, her fingers tightening on the stem of the glass. 'How much of it was destroyed?'

'It's still standing but that's all I know. Now let's change the subject. We'll be leaving soon and I want to have a few words with David.'

He left Rebekah and Edwina staring at each other. 'It's for the best,' said the older woman weakly.

Rebekah swore and downed her drink in one go.

'Where are we?' Rebekah stretched and yawned. Disappointment and doubt had crowded in once she had known there was no Ireland at the end of the journeying and she had drunk too much champagne. Only vaguely did she remember boarding the train.

'Chester, my dear.' Joshua's gaze washed over her. 'I'm sure you'll like it. It's very attractive – medieval in places. The

Romans were here, and it has some decent shops. If you're good, I'll let you have some money to spend.'

'If I'm good?' She stared at him.

'Don't look so frightened, darling. I'm sure you will be.' He smiled and took their cases from the luggage rack, leaving the carriage.

Rebekah's throat tightened with nerves but she held her head high, wrapped the white fox fur around her shoulders and concentrated on walking in a straight line as she followed him.

Joshua's choice of honeymoon hotel could not have been more perfect if your taste ran to oak beams and white-painted plaster, luxury and a view of the tree-lined River Dee. She wondered whose money they were spending, his or hers.

As she stood gazing out of the window, steeling herself to make a move to take off her clothes and don the white silk nightdress, he said, 'Come and undress me.'

'What?' Her voice came out as a harsh whisper.

'You heard me, my sweet. Come away from the window and do as I tell you.'

Rebekah turned and looked at him. He had taken off his jacket and was in his shirt sleeves. There was a glass of whisky in his hand. 'I'm tired,' she stammered.

'Of course you are. The sooner you're in bed the better.' He crooked his finger. 'Come, my darling. It's natural that you'll be a little nervous but I'll be good to you.'

Her hands curled into fists. 'Can't I have a drink?'

'You've drunk enough.'

'But it's our wedding night.' She cleared her throat. 'A drink to celebrate?'

Suddenly the smile was wiped from his face. 'I want you to remember this night, not be in a drunken stupor! Now come here, or must I fetch you?' he barked.

Rebekah moved, frightened by Joshua's change of mood. It was all right for him to drink but not her it seemed. There was a glitter in his eyes that reminded her of her father when he had beaten her that day she had walked to the bay with Daniel. She stopped a foot away from him, her eyes fixed on his tie. How she wished he was Daniel.

Suddenly Joshua's arm shot out and his fingers fastened on the front of her peach chiffon blouse, pinching her skin so that

194

she cried out and struggled. Relentlessly he pulled her against him. 'What is the matter with you?' he said through gritted teeth. 'Although you shyness does you credit, it's a bit late. You weren't averse to my attention before. I hope it's for the right reasons, my darling, and that you are a virgin? That O'Neill didn't have you?'

'Why do you have to bring up Daniel now?' said Rebekah unevenly. 'Why won't you let him lie in peace?'

'Because I hate him,' said Joshua, emphasising every word.

'What? Why do you hate him?' Her voice had risen. 'What has he ever done to you?'

'Keep your voice down!' he muttered. 'O'Neill turned against me like the others! Dared to tell me, "You're making a mistake, sir!" Called me a coward!' His chest heaved. 'Rebekah, don't you see what that does to a man?' His pale eyes widened. 'I thought he liked me! Even my father was the same. My brother was first with him, and he spoilt Emma soft. I was sent to Ireland to learn about farming and hated it. I wanted to come back but he said no.'

'You said you knew nothing about the animals on the farm – that you'd spent hardly any time in Ireland.' She was puzzled. 'Why lie?'

His mouth tightened. 'I didn't want to talk about it. The war came and I joined the navy. I'd always loved ships. I met O'Neill when the government requisitioned his ship. We were friendly at first.' He took a deep breath.

And?' she demanded.

'He questioned my judgement. My knowing what was right. He was as bad as father, not believing I could have done better by Green's than my brother. He made a right mess of everything. It was a good job he died when he did or we'd have been bankrupt. Then I met Muriel and fell in love.' He laughed. 'She left me a note saying that she had only been going to marry me because she thought she needed a man after her fiancé was killed in the war, but at the last minute she couldn't go through with it. If she hadn't gone to Africa as a missionary, I would have cooked her goose.' He smiled. 'Now you're a sensible girl, my darling, so you'll do just what I say, won't you?'

'Will I?' she stammered.

'Of course. Come here.'

She stared at him, suddenly too frightened to move. What had he meant about cooking Muriel's goose? She jumped when he caught hold of her arm and instinctively tried to pull away but he seized her other wrist and, crossing her arms, twisted her round and flung her on to the bed. She rolled over and almost managed to get to her feet but he was too quick for her. He pushed her down on the bed, leaning over her and gripping her with his knees one either side of her. He tore open her blouse and despite her attempts to free herself, dragged it off. 'Joshua, please don't be so rough,' she cried.

'Why? I thought you girls liked being manhandled. You read about it all in *The Sheik*,' he said in a clipped voice, and hit her arm away.

'That's only a book,' she stuttered, on the edge of a scream, as he forced her to part with her chemise with a couple of slaps. 'I don't want to do it,' she stammered. 'I don't – '

'It's too late for that.' His eyes sparkled. 'You're my wife and I can do what I want with you. Fight as much as you like, I quite enjoy a struggle.'

She suddenly remembered how it had been with Daniel and could have screamed. 'I won't fight you.'

'What a pity, but perhaps wise.' He smiled as with one hand he kept both of hers imprisoned over her head. She did not move as he forced up her skirt and took off her cami-knickers. She would lie as still as if she was dead. Her eyes closed as Joshua fondled her breasts and crushed her with his weight. A sob bubbled in her throat as he poked at her down below, was pushing, forcing his way inside her. Her whole body tensed. It hurt! She had not expected it to hurt. Her fingers and toes curled, teeth clenched. She bit back a scream but could not prevent a groan. Dear God, make it be over soon! He ground his way into her. Up down, up down, up down! His stomach slapped against hers and he was moaning. A scream broke from her as he pressed down on her with terrible force. A few minutes later she realised what Daniel must have done to prevent her having a baby, and also that she no longer wanted a child by Joshua.

The breakfast tray had just been taken away. Rebekah had managed half a slice of toast and a cup of tea but Joshua had eaten a full English breakfast. Now he lay back against the pillows, smoking. 'You were a virgin. I'm glad you didn't cheat me,' he murmured, opening the morning paper.

Rebekah wanted to say, Yes, I did, but dare not. 'You hurt me,' she whispered. Down below she throbbed as if that part of her had a pulse of its own. Her nipples were sore and her ribs felt as if they had been crushed in a vice. He had taken her twice more during the night and that morning.

'It was inevitable. I didn't really expect you to enjoy it. Some women don't. Especially at first.' He tapped ash into the ashtray.

She thought how she had enjoyed that very first time with Daniel. 'You made sure I wouldn't enjoy it by mentioning Daniel and treating me like an object for your pleasure,' she could not prevent herself from saying. 'Why tell me that you hated him? Why last night?'

'Because you said you loved him and you've never once said you love me,' he said coldly.

'But that's bloody stupid!' She ran a hand through her short hair. 'You're not going to make me love you by behaving the way you did.'

'Don't swear, darling. It's not ladylike!' There was a sudden seething in Joshua's face as he flung aside the newspaper and grabbed hold of her arm. 'Why did you marry me? One of the reasons I married you was for your money, but you with all your talk of its not being important wouldn't have married me for mine. So why?'

Rebekah suddenly laughed. 'I'm a fool! Aunt Esther said you were marrying me for my money! I should have listened to her but I thought it couldn't be true because you seemed to have plenty of it. I was wrong!'

'The young never listen to their elders the way they should. I'm not broke, my dear, but more money is always useful.' He forced her against him. 'But you still haven't answered my question. Why? If you answer me correctly then we could be happy.'

She stared at him. 'You want me to say that I love you.' He made no answer, just looked at her, and she experienced a feeling of pity. 'I wish I could say I did. I'm sorry.'

For a moment he was silent then he pushed her back against the pillows. 'Don't be sorry for me, my dear,' he growled. 'Be sorry for yourself. I married you because I knew it would make O'Neill mad.'

She scowled. 'He's dead! Why do you have to behave like this? Couldn't we at least try to please each other?'

Joshua opened his mouth and she waited but he did not speak, only shaking his head before sliding over her. 'I'll make you forget him. By Jove, I will!' She tried not to tense as he crushed her beneath him but could not help herself. He began to bite her throat. Her fists clenched and she started to feel angry. Why did he have to hurt her? 'Hit me,' he mumbled. 'Let's make a fight of it.'

'No!'

He stilled and sat back on his heels, frowning down at her. 'Why won't you? You want to hit me, don't you? Emma often wanted to. She threw things. Hit me twice and cut my head open, the little Madam.'

'It must be the Quaker in me coming out that doesn't like fighting,' she said with an edge to her voice.

'Little Miss Quaker.' He laughed and seizing her shoulders, shook her violently, causing her to bite her tongue. 'Respond my sweet, or else!'

Rebekah wiped blood from her mouth. 'No. You've brought Daniel into this, so I will. You want me to pretend in some twisted way that he can still be hurt by what you do. Well, I can pretend too.'

'What do you mean?'

She smiled. 'You're so clever. Think.'

Joshua did not move but his mouth quivered and she thought for a moment he might cry. She waited for him to say something but he just reached for his cheroot case. He lit up and took deep lungfuls of smoke until the end glowed red. Then before she realised what he was about, he stubbed the cheroot several times on her shoulder. She reared up, gasping with pain.

'You will never get pleasure imagining that I am. him. Never! Never!' He got out of bed. 'I think we'll go home today. Get yourself dressed.'

She stared at him, her breasts heaving as she regained her breath. 'But we've only just come.'

'Now!' he yelled.

Rebekah was out of the bed in a trice, scared in case he burnt her again. She was certain her shoulder was blistering but dare not look at it. What was she going to do? Keep her mouth shut and not provoke him would be the wiser course. Be sweet and nice and a dutiful wife. Oh God! What had she done?

She dressed hurriedly, trying to ignore his watching her as she placed a handkerchief over the burn, and thinking all the time that coping with Hannah had been easy compared with the future she now visualised. Why hadn't she given it more consideration? Because she had not been thinking realistically, she supposed, believing Joshua madly in love with her and incapable of hurting someone he loved. Money! He had married her for her money. When she looked back on their life in Ireland, when her mother had always seemed to be penny pinching, she felt slightly hysterical. What good had it done her father being thrifty? Suddenly she wanted to laugh and laugh, but instead she jumped when Joshua snapped. 'What are you stopping and smiling at? You've got nothing to be happy about. Last night was only the beginning. Now move or we'll miss the next train.'

Rebekah did not tell him her thoughts, only slipping her arms into her tan and cream dog-tooth checked jacket. She packed her nightdress and soiled underwear, then stood waiting for him to give his next order. At least, she thought, once back in Liverpool, you'll be out all day. But the nights! The thought of all the nights she would have to spend with him made her fearful. Suddenly she remembered what she had said to Edwina about being miserable in comfort and thought how she seemed to go through life saying stupid things. Why had she not foreseen cruelty and fear? It was not as if she hadn't come in contact with them. Little Mrs Rimmer, she had suffered both. 'And survived,' said a little voice in Rebekah's head. 'You'll come through if you use a little commonsense.'

She stared at her husband as he picked up the suitcase, and smiled.

'What are you smiling at now?' he muttered.

She raised her eyebrows. 'You'd rather I went down weeping? I am a bride and so I'm supposed to be happy.'

'Of course you are.' He smiled unexpectedly. 'Perhaps we should stay?'

'That's up to you.'

'What do you want to do?'

'Whatever you want,' she lied.

He put down the case and took off his coat. Still smiling, he unknotted his tie. 'Take off your clothes. This time let's see some activity. You can stroke, bite, suck – anything! If you hurt me, I don't mind. A bit of pain heightens sensations, don't you think?'

She gave him an uncertain look. 'I don't know – '

'My dear, you do. Now don't waste time. And afterwards I'll take you to the Cathedral. You'll enjoy that. And we must get some ointment for the burn tomorrow. I'm sorry about that.'

With a sick feeling in her stomach Rebekah obeyed him, and he seemed to be satisfied with what she did, although he landed her a couple of blows in her ribs for pulling away too soon. Afterwards she would have preferred being alone and suggested that maybe he would like to read the Sunday papers while she went to the Cathedral, but he said certainly not.

As she sat in a pew staring at the intricately carved stalls in the choir with Joshua beside her, she felt divorced not only from her surroundings but from reality. She was no longer the Rebekah she had been twenty-four hours ago but felt a poor creature unable to stick up for herself. Surely this could not be what God intended when it had been written 'Wives be subject to your husband?' She was confused, deeply unhappy, and filled with dread.

It was just as bad for her that night but this time Joshua too seemed to be feeling no pleasure. 'You're holding back on me,' he muttered, slapping her face. 'You're thinking of him, aren't you?'

'When you're giving me pain, I can't think of anything but that,' she gasped.

'As long as you're not thinking of him,' he said in a satisfied voice, and carried on hurting her. It was then she began to hate him.

The next day he suggested that he went shopping with her. 'You'll be bored,' said Rebekah, powdering her face where a bruise showed, and desperate to be alone.

'You don't bore me, my sweet,' murmured her husband, putting down the morning paper and picking up a silver-handled cane. 'At least, not yet.'

He pulled her hand through his arm and it would seem to an onlooker that they were in harmony as they strolled in the direction of the medieval Rows that ran along Watergate, Bridge, and Eastgate Streets in the centre of the city. One had to go up steps from the street to walk along the covered arcades with shops running along one side. Rebekah was in no mood for shopping but took the money Joshua handed her. Probably hers, she thought resentfully. She bought a new hat in pink straw with a deep crown and a dipping brim at the sides, a magazine and a bar of Fry's chocolate cream. He did not ask for the change and she did not offer it. She decided then that she would save it for a rainy day.

They stayed two more days in Chester and then went back to Liverpool, Rebekah still suffering from a sense of unreality.

'Welcome home, sir, Mam.' The maid, a smile on her red-cheeked face, bobbed a brief curtsey. 'There's a fire in the living room. I'll make some tea and bring it in.'

'Thank you, Janet.' At least, thought Rebekah, she is pleased to see me.

And so it proved. Once Joshua went to work the next morning, the maid came in to discuss what was needed that day and to say how nice it was to have a mistress in the house after all these years. 'One can't count Miss Emma, if you don't mind my saying, mam. She was no good at being in charge, always needed looking after. Very highly strung she was.' She smiled. 'I think, though, you and I can work together.'

'I'm sure we can,' said Rebekah, returning her smile. 'First things first – food. I'm going shopping. You can deal with the clothes we brought home that need washing.'

Janet looked surprised. 'You're not phoning the shops, mam?'

'No, I'll take my car.' Joshua had given her housekeeping money that morning and she planned using Tin Lizzie to go into town and shop at St John's Market, where she had often gone with Brigid. The dinner she planned would not cost as much if she bought there sometimes, and what was saved could be put in her hoard. She thought of Brigid and how she had spoken on the *Samson* of changing husbands characters. Only dynamite, she thought, would change Joshua. At that moment she had every intention of being a dutiful wife and housekeeper but she had vague thoughts about its not being forever.

Chapter Eighteen

Rebekah put petrol in the tank of her car and drove away from her husband's house. Strangely, as she passed familiar streets, the feeling of unreality faded. Impulsively she decided to call on her aunt. The sun was shining and she would not be seeing Joshua for hours.

'So thou's back, is thee?' grunted Hannah on opening the door.

Rebekah looked at her with something akin to affection. 'Thanks for the welcome. Is my aunt in?'

'She's in.' Hannah thrust her face close to hers. 'We've been managing fine without thee. So there's no need for thee to be always showing thy face.'

Rebekah drew back, not wanting anyone to look too closely at her. 'I've come to take her out,' she said promptly. 'I thought we'd go to town and then for a trip in the country.'

'Her knee's bad,' said Hannah, folding her arms across her thin breasts. 'Got to rest it.'

'You told me that she should keep on the move,' retorted Rebekah, and pushing past the maid went up the lobby to steal her aunt from Hannah's clutches.

'This really is good of thee, Becky love,' said Esther, holding on to her hat as her niece drove along a road in Formby-on-Sea which led to the coast. 'I've never been this far out of Liverpool.'

'I thought you'd enjoy it.' Rebekah glanced at her. It was curiosity that had taken her in this direction and they would have to be turning back soon if Joshua's meal was to be on the table by the time he returned home. She glanced about her, not sure what she was looking for, and then suddenly saw it. There was a set of imposing wrought iron gates and through them she could make out a large building. There was a notice which read 'Asylum for Mentally Afflicted Gentlefolk'. She went a little further up the road and then turned round.

Rebekah often thought of Emma in the weeks that followed, questioning what Amelia Green had said to her the day of the wedding, not only about Emma and her mother but Joshua too. War unsettled men, she had said. Had war inflicted on her husband the peculiar fascination he had with pain? There were times when she did not know whether to be glad or sorry that the tweeny slept out and Janet's room was so far from the large bright bedroom overlooking the park that she and Joshua shared.

She did most of what he asked her without comment but she would not use the cat o' nine tails. Something inside her would not allow her to vent her hatred in that way. Perhaps it was because she knew that was exactly what he wanted – for her to show passionate response to his mishandling of her. She suffered his calculated assault on her body without a struggle. Only once did he hit her with the whip and afterwards he astonished her by crying at the sight of her blood and saying he was sorry. She just could not understand him.

There were evenings when they entertained some of his associates and he gave her money for a new dress, telling her just what he expected of her. She would go to Bold Street and buy a new gown, never spending the amount he gave her, and what was over she put away.

If she stayed in, the days seemed endless. Her job had finished when she married but she still went to visit Mrs Dodd. 'You don't look well, girl,' she said, staring at Rebekah. 'Have you been caught?'

'You mean, am I having a baby?' she murmured, bobbing Lily on her knee. 'No.' She would have added, Thank God, but that would have meant explanations and she had no intention of telling anybody what she suffered at Joshua's hands. Not even Edwina, who had been a VAD during the war and was now a member of the Red Cross. She was suggesting that Rebekah, who had been a junior member in Ireland, should come along to the meetings and be useful.

In the end she agreed to go along, and life seemed very real and earnest during the weeks when spring turned to summer. Civil war was threatening in Ireland. Edwina and her father went on holiday. Her aunt also went away on some peace conference. Joshua mentioned that he might have to go to New York on business. She prayed that he would go but the days passed and he did not mention it again.

One afternoon she was in town, having left the car at home because she wanted to save money on petrol, when she noticed that there was an Ethel M. Dell film on at the cinema. Earlier in the year Ethel had got engaged to a Colonel Savage. The paper had said that her books had made her a fortune. Rebekah wished that she could get her hands on her money so that she could leave Joshua.

The film was guaranteed to melt the stoniest hearts and Rebekah came out of the cinema feeling little better for it. She paused to pull on her gloves but a poke in the back caused her to stumble. A hand at her elbow prevented her from hitting the ground.

'Are yer all right, luv?'

It was a voice Rebekah recognised. 'Joe?' She turned and saw him with Brigid. Unexpectedly, tears filled her eyes.

For a moment neither of the women spoke. Then Brigid said faintly, 'Yer not going to cry, are yer? What have you got to cry about? Didn't yer get just what yer wanted when yer married his lordship!'

Rebekah blinked back the tears. 'So you know about that?'

'I saw it in the *Echo*, and I saw it coming anyway.' Brigid squared her shoulders. 'But there wasn't any need for yer to leave Ma's party the way you did without a word of explanation. Although our Pat told us what happened.'

Rebekah's expression froze. 'Your Pat? I suppose that's why you never answered my letter? You took his side.'

'What letter?' said Brigid, frowning.

'The one I sent, saying that Pat was getting too serious and I didn't want that. We'd agreed just to be friends. I supposed he gave his own version of the story so you weren't prepared to believe mine.'

Brigid exchanged glances with Joe, who shrugged. 'Don't look at me. I know nothing about it.'

'I never received any letter,' said Brigid earnestly. 'I would have answered it if I had.'

'Well, I sent one.'

Brigid shook her head. 'I'm sorry I didn't answer it but I thought you'd finished with us because of his lordship.'

Rebekah stared at her. 'We were friends.'

Joe's glance took in Rebekah's expression, then Brigid's. 'Listen, luv, I'll go and have a pint over the road. I think you two have some talking to do. I'll give yer a quarter of an hour and then meet you at the tram stop.'

'All right.' Brigid did not watch him go. Her gaze was fixed on Rebekah. 'Yer can see why I believed our Pat. I knew that his lordship wanted you when we were in New York. When I read about the wedding, I was convinced yer'd chucked Pat and ended our friendship because of him.'

'It's not true!' Rebekah cleared her throat.

There was a short silence before Brigid said fiercely, 'But yer married him! Where does that leave all yer talk about loving Daniel and never forgetting him?'

'I haven't forgotten him! But he's dead.'

Brigid's eyes flashed. 'He's dead but our Veronica thought she saw him the other day.'

'She couldn't have,' said Rebekah, feeling as if her heart had suddenly sunk into her stomach.

'That's what I said. But it's funny all the same.'

'I don't find it funny.' Rebekah suddenly could not bear being still and almost ran across the cobbled road to the tram stop. She turned and stared at Brigid who had followed her. 'I'd like to believe it! If you'd said you'd seen him, I probably would, even though it's impossible.'

'I know.' Brigid sighed. 'I bumped into his brother the other day down at the Pierhead. After all this time I thought that queer. I asked him how he was and whether he'd been living in America. I said how sorry I was about Daniel being drowned and how upset you'd been at the time.'

Rebekah's expression barely concealed her emotions. 'I'm surprised you spared a thought for me if you believed I'd just walk out without a word. Besides, you'd be wasting your time if you expected Shaun to weep for me. He hated me. So you probably made his day!' She dug her fists deep into her jacket pockets. 'What was he doing in Liverpool anyway?'

Brigid shrugged. 'I didn't ask. I presumed he was over here seeing his cousins, but when I mentioned him to Maureen she said that she hadn't seen hide nor tail of him.'

'Probably up to no good,' said Rebekah politely. 'Remember the telegraph wires being cut on the Wirral? They got Sinn Feiners for it? I bet he's been up to something like that! Some Republicans are still at war with the British.'

'You mean – he's a terrorist and was making a quick getaway on the Irish ferry?' Brigid's voice rose to a squeak.

Rebekah stared at her and the hurt that Brigid's words had inflicted caused her to say, 'He's a troublemaker! And for all you know the police might have been watching him and now could be watching you!'

Brigid's mouth fell open and she crossed herself quickly, glancing about her. At the sight of a policeman standing on the other side of the road she darted behind Rebekah. It proved too much for her when she had had nothing to laugh at for ages, and she burst out laughing. 'You idiot! Nobody's going to arrest you!'

For a moment Brigid did not move then she smiled. 'You thing! Yer had me going then!'

Rebekah's eyes still wore a warm expression. 'You hurt my feelings. I do still care for Daniel, but I wanted to please my father and I wanted children. It's all right for you. There's your Pat and your Kath and her kids. Then there's your other sisters and cousins and aunts and uncles. I only have Aunt Esther.'

For a moment Brigid was silent. 'Veronica misses you. Why don't yer come round some time? Our Pat's home at the moment, but he left Green's and does long trips to Australia now. He'll be sailing in a day or so.'

Rebekah's expression softened. 'Thanks. Perhaps I will.'

'Do yer love his lordship?' asked Brigid tentatively.

'Don't ask daft questions.'

Brigid burst out, 'Are you happy?'

'I'm as miserable as sin. If he pops off, I won't grieve.'

Brigid stared at her. 'Yer terrible!' She started to laugh.

'Aren't I just?' Rebekah's laugh was hollow. 'I want to leave him.'

'Yer what?' The laughter died on Brigid's face.

207

'You heard me. He's a real – monster.'

'What d'yer mean, he's a monster?'

Rebekah shrugged. 'I can't tell you everything now. Joe'll be back in a minute.'

Brigid scrutinised her face. 'We'll have to meet again,' she said. 'Soon.'

Rebekah nodded. 'When does Joe go back?'

'In a couple of days. We can meet on Friday. I have a half day.'

'Right.' Rebekah freed a shaky breath. 'You can't know how glad I am that I went to see Ethel M. Dell.'

'I do,' said Brigid, and hugged her. 'Here's yer tram. I'll meet yer outside the new Palladium on West Derby Road at one.'

Rebekah nodded and caught the tram. Her mood was buoyant as she travelled home.

Joshua was there before her and her spirits sank at the sour expression on his face as he looked up from his newspaper. 'You're late.'

'I went to Cooper's in town to get that special cheese you like.' Impulsively she put her arms around his neck and kissed his cheek. 'How are things in the shipyards now that the engineers have returned to work? Will you be getting that ship converted?'

'Probably.' He looked at her, an arrested expression on his face, then folded the newspaper and put his arm round her waist, squeezing it. 'That trip I mentioned to New York – I've got to go in a couple of days. I could be away for a few weeks.'

For a moment Rebekah could not speak for joy but she schooled herself not to show her true feelings. 'I'd go with you but I think I'd find it too upsetting still,' she said, infusing a touch of regret in her voice. 'It's only now that I can think of Mama and Papa without it hurting. Memories would come flooding back and we don't want that, do we, just when I think I might be forgetting the past.'

'You're talking about O'Neill?' He pulled her against him and frowned into her eyes.

'Who?' she said lightly.

Joshua smiled. 'I told you I'd make you forget him.' He stroked her shoulder, and his fingers wandered over her breast. 'He could never give you all what you have here with me.'

'No.' She forced herself to press her lips against his. 'You aren't too angry at me staying at home?'

'I understand. Although you'll have to make up for it tonight. Perhaps tonight will be the night. I would have thought you'd have started having a baby by now.'

'I'm not.'

A disgruntled expression settled over his face and she kissed him quickly, knowing that it was going to be difficult because she had a period.

Rebekah closed the door and her dancing footsteps echoed round the hall as she spun round and round with Moggy in her arms. 'He's gone! He's gone!' she whispered in the cat's flickering ear. 'And he won't be back for weeks!' Perhaps she should leave him now before she did start having his baby? She had saved forty pounds and Joshua had left her money to live on. She could get a job. Any job! And if she pawned a few things that would bring in extra money. The white fox furs could go. They reminded her of that honeymoon in Chester. She thought of how Joshua had spoken of his hatred for Daniel and then shook her head to rid herself of the memory, considering instead how Veronica had believed that she had seen Daniel. Perhaps she had mistaken him for Shaun? They were brothers after all and Shaun might have grown more like Daniel over the last couple of years. She would mention that, and about pawning the furs, to Brigid whom she was meeting in an hour's time.

Brigid shook her head uncomprehendingly and stroked the white fox furs. 'I know men can be cruel, but to hit you and want to beat you . . . I don't understand it.'

Rebekah tucked her arm in Brigid's. 'I haven't told you the half of it, and I'm not going to,' she said lightly. 'But you do see why I want to leave him?'

'Yes. Although – don't you think he'll come after you? The law would be on his side, you know? He could make you go back and he'd be mad at yer, wouldn't he?'

209

'I know.' Rebekah felt cold and sweaty at the thought. 'That's why I have to get away now, before he comes back. Can you pawn the furs for me?'

'Of course I can.' Brigid smiled and her voice was deliberately cheerful. 'I'll take them to Ol' Solly. He'll give you a good price. He's an old Jew but he's fair. Mam always swore by him in the old days.'

Good.' Rebekah placed the furs back in the brown paper bag and they began to walk.

There was a short silence before Brigid said, 'Yer know that yer welcome to come and stay with us. The only thing is, he might find you.'

'I know. It's the same with Aunt Esther.' She cleared her throat. 'I could go to Ireland. I doubt if Joshua would follow me there because he hates the plate. He hates Daniel! One of the reasons he married me was because he thought it would hurt Daniel. Ridiculous, when he's dead.'

Brigid dropped her gaze to the pavement. 'Is he, though?' Her voice sounded strained.

Rebekah stared at her. 'Are you saying that you believe Veronica? Because it could have been Shaun she saw.'

'It's not just Veronica.' Brigid lifted her head. 'It's our Pat. *He* says Daniel's alive.'

For several moments Rebekah could not speak while the words penetrated like sharp knives into her brain. Suddenly she was reliving that terrible time after the disaster. It had seemed incredible that Daniel could be dead and she had not believed it. But Shaun had said he was. Why should he lie to her? *Why*? An hysterical laugh burst inside her. *Why!* Shaun had wanted to break up her relationship with Daniel! And Joshua? She stared at Brigid and her fury exploded into words. 'He lied to me! Joshua must have known Daniel was alive! I could kill him – kill him.' Her fists clenched. 'If I had that Cat now I'd – '

'Shhh!' Brigid dragged on her arm. 'I shouldn't have told you like that.'

Rebekah turned on her. 'When did Pat tell you?'

'Yesterday. I told him about seeing yer and just that yer were unhappy – that his lordship was a bit of a monster. Then I spoke about how besotted yer'd been about Daniel on the ship, and how his death had really broken you up. I mentioned what Veronica had said.' She bit her upper lip. 'He laughed and muttered something about yer making your bed and having to lie on it. That he didn't believe yer cared about anybody but yerself, and that Daniel and him were just pawns in some game you'd played. That he'd seen Daniel last winter in some port or other.'

'He did?' croaked Rebekah. 'Did he say whether Daniel mentioned me?'

'He didn't speak to him. Just caught sight of him in a pub.'

'Oh God!' Rebekah suddenly felt faint. 'Perhaps Pat was imagining things.'

'He seemed pretty definite. What are you going to do?'

Rebekah pulled herself together and was silent for a few seconds. 'You can find out if Daniel is still alive by asking his cousin or aunt. I-I don't mean to sound unkind but I wouldn't put it past your Pat just to make it all up so that you could tell me and hurt me. Does that make sense? Or do I sound completely crazy?'

'I don't think our Pat's lying.'

Rebekah nodded. 'Then ask Daniel's cousin for the truth. She might not have wanted to tell you that Shaun had visited. He's a known rebel. For all we know, Daniel might have been there as well.'

Brigid's eyes narrowed. 'Yer mean she could have thought I'd betray him to the police?'

'Yes!'

Brigid's cheeks puffed and then she blew out a breath. 'That could be it – and yer see what this means? It could have been him that Veronica saw.'

'Yes!' Rebekah's lips quivered. 'Oh, Brigid, I've got to see him.'

'He mightn't want to have anything to do with yer when he knows about his lordship,' said Brigid reluctantly.

'And he might! He loved me! He'll understand,' she stammered. 'I thought he was dead, and he must believe I'm dead or he'd have come looking for me.'

'Not necessarily,' said Brigid. 'Perhaps it was just a shipboard romance on his part. Yer don't know.'

211

A cold shiver raced through Rebekah and for a moment she could not think, then she said, 'I have to find out. You'll ask his cousin?'

Brigid nodded.

'Thanks!' Rebekah hugged her. 'You're my bestest friend.'

'Hmph!' Brigid smiled. 'Yer using me but I'll find out what I can and tell you tomorrow.'

'Bring the kids to Joshua's house and we can go to the park before having tea in the garden.'

'Okay. I'd like to see the house,' said Brigid.

They said no more but parted and went their separate ways.

The sun gleamed on thickly leafed trees and lush grass in Newsham Park. Jimmy had brought a ball with him and was booting it as far as he could with his left foot. Veronica was sent to fetch it every time but did not seem to mind. Rebekah was pleased to see them both but glad to have them out of earshot.

'Well?' she demanded, clutching Brigid's arm. 'I've hardly slept. Tell me – he is alive?'

Her friend nodded. 'He's alive and in Ireland.'

Rebekah felt weak with relief. 'Thank God.'

Brigid shook her head. 'Yer haven't got anything to thank Him for yet. Ireland's a terribly dangerous place at the moment. There's divisions in the Provisional Army and the Dail. There's already fighting and it's almost certain that there'll be open civil war between the Free Irish troops and the Irregulars soon.'

Rebekah nodded. 'It can't be any more dangerous than when the Black and Tans were there. Where in Ireland is he?'

Brigid sighed. 'Yer still going to go?'

'You know I am.'

'He and Shaun are with the Irregulars in Dublin.'

'Dublin!' Rebekah closed her eyes on sudden tears because she knew that she could find her way around the city. 'Have you an address?'

'They seem to move about a bit but Maureen said something about the Four Courts building.'

Rebekah was surprised. 'What's he doing there? Still, I'll be able to find him.'

212

Brigid shook her head. 'Yer crazy. Yer could be killed stone dead.'

'I've got to go.'

'I'll come with yer if yer like.' Brigid looked away across parkland.

Rebekah smiled. 'Don't be daft.'

Her friend looked at her and said awkwardly, 'When the *Samson* went down we said we'd stick together. Cross our hearts! I feel bad about his lordship. If I'd have known about that letter you sent, I've a feeling yer'd have never married him.'

Rebekah shrugged. 'We'll never know. I appreciate what you're saying but I'm going it alone. Joe would never forgive me if anything happened to you.'

'He wants to marry me.'

'And will you?'

'Mam likes him. He's a good steady bloke. I'm not crazy for him but he'd do anything for me and I'm fond of him. There's not many like him around.'

'No.' Rebekah squeezed her arm. 'He's a good bloke, as you say. Now let's call the kids and have tea.'

That evening Rebekah informed Janet that she was going away for a few weeks and that she could take some time off on full pay.

The next day Rebekah visited her aunt and took the cat with her. Unexpectedly she felt sad because she had no idea if she would ever see her again. 'I'm taking a little holiday, Aunt Esther,' she murmured, not looking her straight in the eye. 'I wondered if you would look after Moggy for me?'

'Hannah won't like it but I don't mind,' said Esther, taking the cat on to her knee. It purred as she stroked it. 'Where art thou going?'

'London,' she said quickly. 'I've never been before and I thought it's about time I saw the capital of England.'

Her aunt looked up. 'Will thou be away long?'

'A couple of weeks. Joshua's in America.' She fiddled with her teaspoon. 'I'm going with a friend,' she added, completely perjuring herself. 'I'll write if I'm away longer.'

'Well, look after thyself. Don't overdo it.'

'I won't.' She hugged her aunt before hurrying out.

Hannah followed Rebekah up the lobby. 'London,' she said opening the door for her. 'Right den of iniquity that place is. Thee could fall into all kinds of sin without thy husband.'

'Couldn't I just,' retorted Rebekah, amused. 'And you could get run over by a tram while I'm away. Stop listening at keyholes, Hannah, and take care of Aunt Esther. Don't be putting arsenic in her tea.'

Hannah flushed. 'The very idea,' she said, and slammed the door.

As Rebekah strode up the road she met Edwina. 'Come in and have a chat and a cuppa,' said the older woman.

'Love to,' said Rebekah, flushed with rushing. 'But I can't. I'm going away and have to pack.'

'Where are you going?'

'Joshua's on his way to New York so I thought I'd go to London.'

'London?' Edwina stared at her and grinned. 'Now if you'd said Ireland I wouldn't have been a bit surprised. But maybe you've grown more sensible since marriage.'

'Maybe.' Rebekah smiled. 'Would it be so daft to go to Ireland? The Red Cross go into such situations with their eyes wide open and some would consider them crazy.'

Edwina eyed her thoughtfully. 'You're not bored, are you, and thinking of playing Florence Nightingale? Because if you do, make sure you have a white flag handy.'

Rebekah laughed. 'Of course! But marriage has completely knocked out of me any daft notions I once had.' She lifted a hand in farewell and ran up the road.

A short while later she was on her way to Ireland. It was a calm crossing but her insides churned and her emotions were in turmoil. What would Daniel say? What would he think? Would he believe her when she told him that his brother and Joshua had deceived her? Surely the same thing had happened to him? Her nerves were all strung up and she could not keep still. She paced the deck as if her existence depended on her walking all the way to the Emerald Isle. She considered what she would find in a country swiftly dividing against itself. There was the provisional army and government led by the one time newspaper man Arthur Griffiths and Michael Collins, pro-treaty men both. They were up against a growing army of Irregulars, who believed republican principles had been betrayed by still retaining British sovereignty, and who had among their supporters De Valera, Rory O'Connor, Liam Mellows and many others. Why had Daniel joined them? She could understand Shaun doing so but Daniel had wanted peace. Doubts crowded into her mind. Perhaps Brigid would be proved right and he would not be pleased to see her. Maybe she should not have come? She slumped on a seat and gazed with unseeing eyes across the sea.

Her first glimpse of the Irish coast brought memories flooding back. A faint rattle of gunfire came to her across the water and with it, fear. For a moment it was as if she was back in the past and all that happened since had not taken place. Then she squared her shoulders and prepared to disembark.

Chapter Nineteen

As Rebekah walked the streets of Dublin she was conscious of
a feverish excitement. A number of the shops were closed and
shuttered and Free State troops were stopping and questioning people, while carts were held up and searched. The
Customs House had been damaged since she was last in town
and O'Connell Street with its many hotels was choked by
armoured cars. She had hoped to find a room there but
instead made for a hotel she knew overlooking St Stephen's
Green, away from the centre of activity. She freshened up,
took off her wedding and engagement rings, and dropped
them in the pocket of a large canvas bag. She also placed in
the bag's depths money and – remembering what Edwina had
said – a basic first aid kit, Red Cross armband, and small
bottle of brandy. Then she went in search of refreshment
while she thought about what she was going to do.

Although apprehension had destroyed Rebekah's appetite
she drank two cups of tea and ate a slice of bread and butter.
The firing of heavy artillery soon shattered the tinkle of
teacups and she jumped to her feet, only to sit down when no
notice seemed to be taken of what was happening. She caught
the eye of a youngish man sitting at the next table. He looked
tired and dishevelled. 'What's happening?'

He stubbed out a cigarette. 'Have you been on a desert
island that you don't know?' The accent was English.

'I've just come from Liverpool.'

He grimaced. 'You should have stayed there. Rory O'Connor could be planning on making martyrs out of his Irregular
troops. They've occupied the Four Courts building since
April but now they've been issued with an ultimatum.'

'The Four Courts?' Rebekah gripped the edge of the table.

He nodded. 'The state troops have them surrounded and are telling them to come out. There's a chance that they could be blown sky high if they don't, because there's a cache of ammunition beneath the building. I've been outside all night. There was a dawn raid. Now there are several breaches in the walls – but the Irregulars are refusing to surrender.'

Rebekah's heart began to pound. 'Are all the Irregulars in Four Courts?'

He shook his head. 'They're all over the place. They've taken over several of the hotels in O'Connell Street, so I'd steer clear of that area if I was you.' His voice was kindly. 'In fact, I'd get out of Dublin.' He drained his cup and rose, picking up his trilby from the table. 'Well, duty calls. My editor will have my guts if I miss out on any of the excitement.'

'You're a reporter?'

He nodded and moved away.

The blood seemed to be rushing to Rebekah's head. What were the odds of Daniel still being inside Four Courts? Even fifty-fifty seemed too high and she raced after the reporter. Her fingers fastened on his arm just as he reached the street. He turned with a frown but she smiled disarmingly. 'Can I come with you? I won't get in the way.' She released her hold on his arm.

He stared at her from weary grey eyes. 'You're crazy. It's no place for a woman. You could see some unpleasant sights.'

She made an impatient noise in her throat. 'I was here during the time of the Black and Tans! Besides, I could help. I've done some Red Cross work.'

He shrugged. 'It's a free country. Just don't get in my way.'

Rebekah had no intention of getting in his way. As it was she had difficulty keeping up with him, and if she had not known Dublin well she might have lost him. As they drew nearer the Liffey, the sound of an enormous explosion tore the air. For a moment they froze. Then they were running.

'Press!' shouted the reporter to a group of soldiers clustered around artillery. They both ran on before any one moved to stop them and crossed the bridge.

The gateway to the Four Courts building was blocked by vehicles, and dust and smoke choked the air. The reporter pounced on one of his colleagues and dragged him to one side. Rebekah waited impatiently, getting her breath back as the sound of fire engines came closer. She went over to the journalist. 'What have you found out?'

'They're arranging a truce so the firemen can have a go at getting the fire under control,' he said quietly.

'They'll be some dead?' She had her emotions firmly under control. He pushed back his trilby and took out a packet of cigarettes. 'Sure. But there's some still alive. Otherwise we wouldn't be having a truce.' He scrutinised her face. 'Do you know somebody in there?'

'I might.'

'Hard luck. But they'll probably allow them to bring the wounded out.'

'Can we go closer now the shooting's stopped?'

He shrugged but they made tracks.

It was pandemonium with soldiers shouting and rushing about. Firemen trailed hosepipes. There were sightseers, as well as several vehicles whose drivers had deserted them to have a closer look. There were also a couple of ambulances, and nurses.

Already there were bodies stretched on the ground and several more bloodied figures were being brought out. At the sound of a voice Rebekah stopped and stared at a young Irregular kneeling beside a man on the ground. Then she ran towards him. When a trooper would have stopped her, she pulled an armband from her bag. 'I'm a Red Cross helper!' she blurted out.

'All right, miss.' He allowed her to go through.

She slithered to a halt and knelt down. The young man looked at her but said nothing as she lowered her gaze to the figure on the ground. Her vision blurred and she had to rub her eyes before being able to see the face properly. It was coated with dust and smeared with dried blood from a gash on the side of the head. His eyes were closed. The left shoulder of his battledress was sticky. It was Daniel. She had to fight the wave of dizziness that passed over her.

'Well! Can you do anything for my brother?'

Rebekah bit back what she would have liked to say and looked at Shaun who appeared not to have recognised her.

218

'Give me time to think,' she murmured, glancing around. There was a priest in attendance, and nurses and orderlies were seeing to the loading of some of the wounded into ambulances. They all drove off as she watched. She looked at Daniel and brushed his cheek with the back of her hand. 'Help me to get him over to one of those cars,' she said quietly.

'I can't drive,' said Shaun.

'I can.' She slung her bag over her shoulder. 'Now let's move him.'

'We might be stopped.'

'And we might not,' she said impatiently. 'Let's just do it.'

Daniel groaned as they lifted him to his feet but he did not open his eyes and was a dead weight as they dragged him to the car. Rebekah prayed that the driver of the Morris Oxford four-seater she had her eye on would keep on watching the fire. Water hissed on the flames, causing smoke to billow everywhere. People coughed and blinked their eyes but it was perfect for her plans. 'How the bloody hell am I going to open the door?' gasped Shaun.

'I'll take his weight while you get a hand free,' said Rebekah.

But before Shaun did so, a boy came over and opened the door.

'Thanks,' whispered Rebekah.

They managed with a struggle to get Daniel into the back of the car. She took off her jacket and made a pillow for his head. Shaun got in the front seat and she stared at him in exasperation.

'D'you want me to turn the handle, miss?' asked the boy.

'Yes! Yes!' She smiled and flipped him a florin before getting into the driving seat.

After a couple of false starts the engine came to life and cautiously she drove off. There was a shout followed by shots. She ducked even though it would have probably been too late if the bullets were on target, but they were not and she did not stop. Soon they were out of range. It was then that she felt cold steel against her neck. 'Don't go the hospital.'

'What?' Had Shaun recognised her.

'Keep you eyes on the road,' he ordered. 'People die in hospitals. And I don't know where you've come from but you

219

must know that the Free State troops won't be letting me or Danny go free, *if* he gets better.' His voice quivered. 'Head for O'Connell Street.'

'You can't get through. It's blocked with armoured cars.' She glanced at him. 'The hospital would be better. Unless you want you brother to die?'

'Of course I bloody don't!' he snarled. 'But you can help him, can't you?'

'Yes!' She concealed her trepidation. 'But I'm no doctor. His head and shoulder – what happened?'

A bullet went straight through his shoulder. And he was hit by a brick or something when everything seemed to explode.'

Rebekah was relieved that she wouldn't have to be digging out a bullet. 'I'll need water.'

'I'll get you some,' he muttered.

'In that uniform? If we're stopped – '

'I'll shoot the lousy sods.'

'Dear God,' she groaned. 'Is violence the only way you ever think of dealing with a situation?'

Shaun stared at her. 'Do I know you?'

'Hardly.' She started to slow down despite the barrel of the gun digging in her ribs now. 'I'm not going any further. There's troops ahead.'

'Drive through them,' he ordered. 'I've got our Danny's gun as well as my own.'

She sighed. 'You mean I'm to run them down while you have a gun battle?'

'You've got it.'

'I won't do it.'

'I'll shoot you.'

'Do it then. Then you won't have to explain to your brother why I'm still alive.' Her voice was expressionless.

Shaun's mouth fell open and he scrutinised her carefully before muttering, 'I thought I'd seen you before. It was best for both of you to think the other dead.'

She raised her eyebrows. 'You call the state Daniel's in best for him? You're crazy. I'm turning round.' She spun the wheel and Shaun was flung against the door.

He grappled for a hold. 'You bitch! I'll kill you for this!'

'Save your breath.'

A weak voice behind them said, 'You heard the lady, Shaun. Shut up.'

For a moment Rebekah's muscles seemed to lose strength and the car skidded across the road before she managed to bring it to a halt with the engine still running. Trembling, she rested her head on the steering wheel for several seconds before pulling herself together and looking over the back of her seat.

'They lied,' said Daniel faintly. 'They bloody lied.' He reached out a hand and she took it.

'As soon as I knew you were alive, I came.'

He nodded and closed his eyes, still holding her hand.

'This is great,' muttered Shaun, hunched up against the door, glowering at her. 'Are we going to sit here all bloody day with you two holding hands?'

'We probably wouldn't be in this mess if it wasn't for you,' said Rebekah, her gaze flickering over him before returning to Daniel's face. 'We've got to find somewhere safe to take him. If I could I'd get him on the first boat back to Liverpool. But I suppose that's out of the question?'

'Too bloody right,' said Shaun, shifting to kneel on the seat and stare over the back. 'How about Lily's place, Danny boy? She's be glad to see you.' He smirked.

Daniel's eyes slowly opened and with difficulty he forced himself into a sitting position. 'Find a quiet street to park in, Becky, and give me time to think.'

She nodded and released his hand.

Shaun swore. 'We can't just – '

'You don't have to *just* do anything,' muttered Daniel. 'You can go and find out what's going on. There's places where you'll be welcomed.'

'You just want me out of the bloody way.'

'Too right,' said Daniel.

Shaun slumped in the seat, staring down at the gun on his lap.

Rebekah was wondering who Lily was and how best to keep Daniel out of sight. 'Help me to get the hood up,' she said to Shaun. He muttered something incomprehensible but did as she told him.

She drove around till she found a quiet street and brought the car to a standstill.

221

Shaun got out. 'Are you going to wait for me?'

Rebekah remained silent, waiting for Daniel to say something, but at that moment the air was split by an explosion and Shaun tossed Daniel's gun into the car and began to run back the way they had come.

Before Daniel or Rebekah could speak, the door of the house opposite opened and an elderly woman came out. She crossed the street. 'Did you hear it? Loud enough to wake Old Nick himself.'

'Where d'you think it came from?' Rebekah leaned against the car, hoping the woman could not see inside.

'It'll be Four Courts.' She shook her head and tightened the shawl about her shoulders, peering round Rebekah. 'I worry about them bullets flying about when my son's coming home from work. And the shells! They're making a terrible mess of Dublin. All the fine buildings getting holes in them.'

'It's a shame.' Rebekah hesitated. 'I wonder if I could bother you for some water?'

The woman stared at her. 'You can have a cup of tea, girlie. Two, if you're wanting one for him in the motor as well?'

Rebekah smiled. 'Two cups of tea and some water would be fine. I can pay you.'

The woman fixed her with a look. 'I'm not after having your money, girlie. I'm not on anybody's side. I just want it all to stop. An Irregular, is he, like the one who ran off?'

Rebekah blurted out, 'He's wounded! That's why I need the water. It's best if it's boiled. Would you mind?'

The woman's face creased. 'Once a woman gave our Lord a drink of water. Sure, and shouldn't I do the same? Would you both like to come in?'

Some of the tension went out of Rebekah. 'Thanks. But I think I'm better not moving him at the moment.'

'That's all right.' The woman went back across the street.

Rebekah opened the back door of the car and slid along the back seat. Daniel's eyelids lifted and he stared at her.

'You look a right mess,' she said. Then her fingers covered her chin and mouth in an attempt to stop them quivering, but she could not prevent tears filling her eyes and spilling over and a sob sounding in her throat.

'Shhh!' His expression was a mixture of pain and tenderness as he forced his arm up and grasped her fingers. She kissed his

222

palms before rubbing her wet cheek against the back of his hand.

'The swines!' She sniffed and kissed his hand again.

'You mean Shaun and Green?' His voice sounded terribly weary.

She nodded, unable to speak for the tears that continued to well up in her throat, at the back of her nose and in her eyes. Instead she undid the buttons on his uniform with shaking fingers and fought for control of her emotions. 'I don't think I'll ever forgive them.'

'Me neither. What are you doing?'

'I want your jacket off. I need to see the wound.'

With her help he straightened up and she held his head against her breast while peeling off his jacket. Before she could do anything more, there was a knock on the window. Their Good Samaritan had moved fast and was outside with a tray.

Rebekah took it and thanked her. The woman gazed at Daniel. 'You'll need some different clothes, laddie. If you don't mind my dead husband's, I'll get you them.'

'I'd be grateful,' whispered Daniel, looking paler than before. The woman vanished from his sight.

Rebekah placed the tray on the seat and reached for her bag. She poured two tots of brandy into the tea and held Daniel's cup to his lips while he drank. There were slices of buttered soda bread on a blue and white plate but he could eat no more than two bites.

She downed her tea swiftly, as well as a slice of bread, then set about dampening the bloodied shirt where it was stuck to his skin. To get rid of any dirt as quickly as possible was vital. The wound had to be cleaned and kept clean if septicaemia was not to set in. Knowing that she was hurting him made the task even more difficult.

She talked to try and keep both their minds from the task in hand. 'What are you going to do about Shaun?'

'Can't do anything.' The words were slurred. 'All I care about is us getting out of this alive.' He gritted his teeth as she pulled the fabric away from the wound.

'Sorry,' she whispered. 'I'd get you to Liverpool if I could but I think that's not on at the moment. Out of Dublin will have to do. Somewhere quiet in the country.' She lifted him against her and took off his shirt, letting him rest against her for five minutes or so before going on to the next stage of the treatment which she knew would be difficult for them both.

'Remember me telling you about Grandmama's farm in Wicklow?' She moistened some clean cotton waste as she gazed at the bruised and bloodied skin about the punctured skin.

'Green owns it.' He pressed his lips tightly together as she began to swab the wound.

She kept her head bent. 'He did. But I heard that it was set on fire. It's still standing, though.'

'How d'you know all this?' His voice was faint.

Rebekah hesitated. 'His lordship himself told me. That's what Brigid calls Joshua.'

'So you've been seeing him?' Suddenly his fingers were on her chin, pushing it up so that she had to look into his angry eyes.

'Papa made him my guardian,' she said in clipped tones.

'That explains a few things.' His hand dropped and he leaned back, closing his eyes. 'We've got a lot of catching up to do. Where's Green now?'

'America – on business.'

'Good. We'll go that farm then. I can't think of anywhere else right now.'

She nodded, praying that it would not be too difficult to get out of town if the Good Samaritan came up with those clothes. She put some gentian violet on his back and chest and bandaged him up.

The woman came back with a suitcase. 'I hope they'll fit.'

'I'm grateful,' said Rebekah, holding out a hand, knowing that she dare not offer the woman money again. 'God bless you.'

'And you, girlie. Try and get him to stay out of trouble.'

'I will.' Rebekah smiled and thanked her again.

It was a struggle getting the almost unconscious Daniel out of his uniform trousers and into a tobacco-smelling suit of too large clothes but she managed it, knowing that she would have to move soon because she had noticed several curtains twitching. She got out of the car and turned the starting handle. Her arm ached with the effort and at first the engine would not fire. Then it coughed into life and she raced to her seat.

Rebekah chanced going back to the hotel, paying her bill and picking up her clothes, and it was not so difficult after all.

She smiled brilliantly at whichever troops stopped them on the way out of town and put on a country Irish accent to pass off Daniel, slumped unconscious in the back, as her drunken merchant sailor brother. The fact that he smelt of alcohol gave a realistic touch to her tale.

She did not breath easy, though, until she reached the top of a hill and paused briefly to ease her taut muscles – to look back on Dublin lying far below them and the Irish Sea beyond. Liverpool seemed a very long way away.

Chapter Twenty

Rebekah's memory was good but even so she would not have remembered the way to the farm if in the past her father had not pointed out, on various trips into the country, the roads and narrow lanes which led to his childhood home.

She stopped at Naas and left Daniel sleeping in the car while she filled the tank and the spare can with petrol, and bought food and some essentials. She was glad that the June evenings were long as she coaxed the car up a steep hill. She had put down the hood and the smell of honeysuckle sweetened the air.

Suddenly Daniel spoke. 'Where are we?'

'Nearly there.' She glanced over her shoulder. 'If you want to pinpoint it, Glendalough is a good few miles the other side of those hills to our right. I reckon we've got about a mile and a half to go.'

'Let's hope we don't have any visitors.'

Rebekah wondered what kind of visitors he meant and was apprehensive. Joshua's man might call. She turned the steering wheel and they went up a narrow rutted lane. They bumped along with leafy branches brushing the sides of the car and she prayed they wouldn't lose a wheel. 'It was pony and cart when I was last here,' she called. 'I hope we can go all the way along.'

They could, but had to leave the car in the lane because the turn into the farmyard was too sharp and steep.

Rebekah had to help Daniel down from the running board. She opened a rickety gate and they stood a moment, with him holding on to her, staring at the neglected vegetable garden and a vista of fields where the grass grew tall. There was a grey stone house and a couple of outhouses.

'There doesn't look like there's been a fire,' said Daniel. 'No smoke on the walls and the windows are intact.'

'Perhaps his man lied. Wanted out,' murmured Rebekah, believing that it was Joshua who had been untruthful. 'It looks empty. I don't remember it being so desolate.'

They went towards the house and she remembered that there were no drains, no piped water. The door was not locked and they stepped straight into a kitchen with an open staircase running up one side. It was almost as she remembered. There was a cavern of a fireplace with chains and a hook for the large blackened cooking pot that still stood there. Placed beside the fireplace was a stack of cobwebby peat, chipped wood and newspapers. There were cupboards and a table and two wooden chairs, as well as a dusty, leaking horsehair leather sofa. A couple of shelves with some crockery and a number of books hung above a stone sink with a single tap. Underneath there was a galvanised bucket.

'It's not Paradise.' Her imagination had painted something better.

'It's not Hell either,' said Daniel. 'And it looks like some-times it's occupied.'

'I don't think so.' She led him over to the sofa and he slumped down and closed his eyes. 'I won't be a moment.' She went outside remembering that the privy was the outhouse with the rambling pink roses round the door. It looked like it had been some time since it had last been used. She would have to fetch water from the river unless – She looked up at the roof, remembering the tank to catch rainwater, and went back inside the house.

Daniel opened his eyes. 'Lavatory?'

She showed him and wandered through the garden, gazing at the distant hills, shadowy neglected fields and the trees that shifted and whispered in the evening breeze. She thought of Joshua and was glad that he had never brought her here. Not that he would have stayed in this house. It would have had to be his father's mansion.

Daniel came out of the privy in the borrowed trousers and with a blue shirt flapping about his hips. His lean face was drawn with pain. 'We'll have to do something about that,' he said, indicating the building behind him with his head. 'But right now what are we going to do about food?'

'I bought some in Naas when you were asleep. It's in the car.'

'Good girl.' He managed a smile. 'Lights?'

'Grandmama used to have oil lamps but I didn't see any, did you?'

'No.' He drew nearer, holding his left arm awkwardly. 'At least the nights are short at this time of year.'

'And it's not really cold. We can have a go at lighting the fire tomorrow.'

'You remembered matches?'

'Yes. And firewood and a tin opener and a sharp knife. I even brought several newspapers. Are you hungry?'

'A bit.' He leaned against the house wall. 'I'd forgotten quiet like this existed.'

'I'm not surprised. Do you want me to help you inside or do you want to look at the view while I fetch some things from the car?'

'I'll watch you.'

She smiled faintly and hurried to the car. Daniel was sitting on the ground when she returned with the box of food. She put it down and went over to him.

'My legs aren't as strong as I'd hoped.' He pulled a face as she bent over him. 'Don't try and lift me! Give me another minute and I'll get up.'

'I'm not a weakling,' she said, picking up the box and taking it inside.

'I never thought you were.' He looked up as she came through the doorway. 'But we'd be stuck if your back went. Give me a hand now and I'll get meself up against the wall.'

Rebekah did as he said, and taking it slowly together, soon had him on his feet. They went inside and over to the sofa once more. This time she ordered him to lie down. There was a back to the sofa but only one arm. She put her jacket under his head. 'Now rest.'

She was aware of him watching her as she opened a tin of beef and cut bread, buttered it, opened a jar of mustard, and made thick sandwiches of the lot. Into two cups she poured a bottle of Guinness. Then she took them over to him and sat on the edge of the sofa. They did not speak while they ate and drank, but kept glancing at each other.

He looks older, thought Rebekah. There were tiny wrinkles round his mouth and eyes. His eyes! She had forgotten they were such a beautiful mahogany brown. And his lashes were dark and thick like paint brush bristles. His hair was still curly despite the grey. No, it was dust, and there was blood making the front bit stick together above his nose. She had always liked his nose. Lovely and straight. And his mouth. She remembered how he had kissed her, and looking was not enough.

'I'm sorry about your father and mother,' he said. 'At least, I presume she's dead if Green's your guardian?'

She nodded and drained her cup. 'I was lucky. I had just gone into the cabin. What happened with Papa?'

He put the plate on the floor and told her, adding, 'I'm sorry.' There was a pause. 'Did Shaun really tell you I was dead?'

'He insinuated it.' She laced her fingers in her lap. 'I presume he told you I was dead too?'

'Green had just told me you were, and when I asked Shaun he made out that it was true.' Daniel stared at her and she stared back.

'Your brother was against us going together from the start.' She looked down at her hands.

'And Green hated me as much as I hated him.'

'I could have killed him when Brigid told me you were still alive. All that time – '

'I know.' His head dropped on to her coat and his throat moved.

Her own constricted and it was a minute before she could say, 'Brigid and I threw flowers on the Mersey.'

He cleared his throat. 'Thanks.'

'They were chrysanthemums. Yellow for remembrance.'

'That's nice.' He smiled slightly.

Her fingers twisted round each other. 'I stood on that spot at the end of the landing stage where you took me that first time we met in Liverpool. It wasn't nice at all.'

There was a pause before he said, 'I've stood there since.'

'If only we'd seen each other.'

He nodded. 'You've been living in Liverpool with your aunt?'

'I did. Yes!' She smiled with relief. 'And Hannah! Remember Hannah the gorgon?'

'You mentioned her when we first met.' There was a silence.

'It seems a long time ago.'

'We only knew each other for just over a week.' Her breath shivered in her throat. She wanted to hold him and keep on holding him and could not understand what was preventing her from even touching him.

He stared at her from beneath half closed eyelids. 'I often wished I'd known you longer.'

'So there were more memories.' Her voice was quietly meditative. 'It was such a short time we had.'

'Now we have today.' He stifled a yawn.'

'I hope we have more than today.'

'Mmm!' His lids closed.

Rebekah watched him, listened to his breathing, then rose and went outside to fetch the suitcases. When she returned the room was full of shadows. She covered him with an overcoat and then sat at the table, staring through the small sash window at a silver and apricot-streaked sky being overtaken by the purply plum-coloured mantle of night.

Before it was completely dark she went upstairs and found that in one of the two rooms stood the bed that had been her grandparents'. There was also an old oak wardrobe with a large drawer in the bottom. Inside were a couple of well-worn blankets smelling of lemon balm and lavender. Instantly in her mind's eye she saw her grandmother and memories flooded in. She smiled, remembering how she had always been happy in this house.

Rebekah took out the blankets and had to push the drawer hard to make it shut. It made a noise and strangely she half expected the house to come alive then, but the only thing that happened was that flecks of whitewash fell from the ceiling. She bent to pick them up from the wooden floor but they powdered under her fingernails. When she straightened she winced and put a hand to her back. It struck her suddenly just how much she had crammed into one day.

She dropped the blankets on to the bed and went downstairs feeling her way cautiously in the dark. Daniel was still asleep. She placed the back of her hand against his forehead. It was hot but not burning. For a moment she hesitated, considering whether to wake him and help him upstairs where he would probably be more comfortable. Then she decided against it and went to bed.

Rebekah woke early to the chatter and song of birds in the trees, and her name being called. She yawned, stretched, forced her eyelids open and crawled from beneath the blankets.

Daniel was sitting at the table with his shoulders hunched beneath the overcoat. He faced the window but turned at the sound of her footsteps. There was blood on his shirt and smeared down the side of his eye and on his cheekbone. He looked glad to see her. 'I wasn't sure where you were.'

'You shouldn't have got up.' She tried to keep the worry out of her voice as she touched his face and shirt and was glad that the blood was dry. 'I'll have to get some water.'

'You want the fire lighting.'

'Yes. But you can't do it.'

'Can you?'

A smile twisted her mouth. 'I'll get the water.'

She tried the tap but all that came out was a thin brown trickle. 'The tank must be blocked with leaves. I'll have to go to the river.' She reached for the bucket and went outside.

The air was chilly because the sun was having a struggle to break through the mist that still clung to branches of trees and bushes and wove thin ribbons in the tall grass. She went through the gate, wishing she had paused to put on her jacket, and crossed the lane. She found the footpath that led to the river bank, a five-minute walk away, thinking about Daniel.

When she returned he had lit the fire and there was fresh blood on the shirt. 'You're an idjit.'

He raised his eyebrows but said nothing.

'We'll have to get that shirt off, and the bandage.'

He nodded and started to undo buttons. She looked away and into the blackened cooking pot, which was clean. She poured the water into it and went for more.

231

He was still sitting where she had left him when she returned but the lines about his mouth had deepened. He was in pain and she wished she could bear it for him. She must still love him. She poured half the water into the pot and then went over to him.

They went through almost the same rigmarole as they had yesterday with them both gritting their teeth as she eased lint and bandage away from his skin. Again she talked to try and make it easier. Commonplace things. 'I think it'll be a nice day when the mist lifts completely.'

He nodded, his eyes shut.

'You'll be able to lie outside in the sun.'

'What about you? Are you going to rest?'

'I want to find some spagnum moss.'

He opened his eyes.

'It's supposed to have antiseptic properties, and it's absorbent,' she explained, starting to clean his face. 'The Red Cross used it in the war.'

'I didn't know you were in the Red Cross.'

'I was a junior recruit. Children helped to gather the moss.'

You're going to be poking around bogs then? You could get stuck.'

She smiled. 'That reminds me of a conversation we had once.'

'On Seaforth beach.'

'Yes.'

There was a brief silence before he said, 'I'll come with you.'

'You won't!'

'I will.'

She opened her mouth to argue but changed her mind because of the expression on his face, and instead went and made tea.

They had bread and jam and a scalding sweet brew with tinned milk but she planned to make a good nourishing stew for dinner. After she had gathered some moss.

The mist had cleared, and the air was soft and warm. Bees and flies buzzed amid the sweet-smelling flowers and grass that reached Daniel's shoulders and were level with the top of Rebekah's head. Today seemed to belong to a bygone age. A time of innocence before mankind started making its mark on the earth. If it had not been for worrying about his wound she might have relaxed completely, but she was made anxious by the fear of losing him again.

'Why do you think the house still has furniture in it?' she said, swishing the grass with the arm that carried a bag for the moss.

'The occupier left in a hurry and nobody cares about the house or the land.'

She almost said, Joshua certainly doesn't, but had no desire to bring him into the conversation. 'You think he was threatened?'

'Could have been, in these times. Does it matter? Whoever it was has gone, leaving it for us.'

'You don't think he'll come back?'

'We'll worry about that if it happens.'

'There were no clothes in the wardrobe upstairs.'

He looked at her. 'But there was a bed?'

'Yes. You'd better sleep in it tonight.'

A corner of his mouth twitched slightly but he did not say yes or no. She had trouble keeping her colour down and wondered why she should flush like a virgin at the thought of the two of them in bed together. Although she had not suggested that.

They came to the river where it was shallow and wide. The sun slanted down through trees, dappling the water so that it was a deep mysterious green in places and translucent in others. They could see mud, flowing weed and shiny pebbles beneath.

Daniel stopped and drank from his cupped hand where the river rushed white and foaming around rocks. Rebekah slipped off her shoes and trod carefully in boggy ground where the river had once overflowed its banks and washed over the odd large stone. She found what she was looking for and soaked it to rid it of any mud before putting it in the bag.

Daniel had seated himself on a rock and was staring into the water. 'There's fish.'

'I know. Papa used to bring a rod here.' She perched sideways on a few inches of rock beside him, and was immediately conscious of the warmth of his hip. 'There's a rod in the

233

cupboard back at the house, and a reel with line and hooks and a box of flies.'

'Perhaps I'll try my hand.' He turned his head and their faces were only inches apart. 'Can I kiss you?' he said.

'Yes.' She took his face between her hands.

His lips were cool with the water he had just drunk and he was in need of a shave, but it was the kiss she had been wanting and needing for a long time.

They put an arm round each other and carried on kissing, long and leisurely, rousing latent passions. They could not get enough of each other and desire left them breathing heavily when his mouth lifted from hers.

'Nothing,' he said, holding her close, 'has tasted that good in almost two years.'

'No.' She rested her cheek against his neck. 'This is like a miracle.'

He stroked the back of her head. 'I remember when I first saw you with your hair cut. I'd just been thinking that you'd changed your mind about coming, and it hurt.'

'I remember your face smeared with grease and dirt in the engine room. I wanted to rush over and fling my arms around you – I'd started to believe that I'd never see you again.'

'And now we're here.'

She leaned against his arm and laughed.

Daniel grinned. 'What's so funny?'

'Nothing. I'm just happy.'

'Happy, happy, happy!' He tried to swing her over on to his knee but could not.

He grimaced with painful effort and she scolded. 'Give it time!'

'We've lost enough of that.'

Rebekah stood. 'We'll catch up.' She grasped his hand and he came to his feet.

They walked back, arm in arm, enjoying the peace and being in each other's company.

On exploration of the neglected kitchen garden they found some strawberries and rhubarb. There were potato plants, too, growing among weeds, but they both reckoned it was too early to dig them up yet.

Rebekah put the moss on the windowsill to dry in the sun, then made sandwiches from the remains of the beef. She had a cup of tea and Daniel a bottle of Guinness. 'It's good for you,' she said with a smile.

'So are you.' The kissing this time reminded her of all that was sweet and light. It was honey, sunshine and flowers, and left them both light-headed with joy.

She ordered him to rest in the garden and he told her that she must as well. 'I've got things to do,' she protested, smiling. 'A stew to get ready, and those clothes you were given will need altering. And I'll have to go for some more water and wash a couple of things.

'Later, girl.' He took her hand and led her outside.

They lay in the grass, with his head on her midriff, her arm across him, eyes closed against the sun.

'Less than thirty hours ago I thought you dead,' he murmured. 'I'd been shot in an exchange of gunfire outside Four Courts and by the middle of the morning there was a possibility of my joining you in the great blue yonder. No surrender that's what half of them were saying before the explosion.'

'What about you.'

'I was wondering what the hell I was doing there. Irishmen shooting Irishmen. It's a terrible thing, Becky.'

'Why did you join the Irregulars then?'

'Because I wanted what de Valera wanted: a united Ireland. I'd gone back to sea after the ceasefire, believing it was all over. But it wasn't, and our Shaun got himself involved and went on about me sitting on the fence. He said I had to choose sides. The trouble was I'd been hankering for a fight ever since Green told me you were dead. I wanted to smash his face in because he was crowing, knowing what I was suffering.' The bitterness was in his voice again.

Her arm tightened about him. 'He's not worth thinking about.'

'I know. But that doesn't stop me. Especially now I know he's in charge of your affairs.'

'I can cut the connection. The money doesn't matter.'

There was a pause before he said, 'Was there much?'

She stilled. 'You know, I never asked. He gave me an allowance, but there are the shares in the company too. The trouble is that Papa made it so that I couldn't have control of my affairs until I was twenty-five. I was annoyed about that. Why not twenty-one?'

'What if you married?'

'I don't know. I never asked.'

'I bet it would be different. It could be why he lied to me.'

'He lied to you because he hates you,' she said with a sudden surge of anger. 'It's as you said – he wanted to hurt you. He's that kind of man.' She opened her eyes and pushed herself up on one elbow.

Daniel twisted his head and looked at her. 'You must have got to know him pretty well to have discovered that about him.'

'Pretty well. But I'll never understand him.' She looked across the garden, thinking now was really the time to tell the truth. But suddenly it seemed like the serpent in the Garden of Eden – destructive. 'Can we talk about something else?'

'Suits me.' He closed his eyes. 'Tell me what you've been doing for the last twenty months or so?'

Rebekah breathed easier and lay back. Daniel seemed to have no suspicion about her and Joshua. And why should he? It seemed incredible to her now that she had actually gone and married him, for better or for worse, in sickness and in health, till death do they part. She pushed that thought aside and began to talk about the life she had led in Liverpool that had not involved Joshua.

'This Pat – Brigid's brother,' said Daniel after she had mentioned him several times, 'you went out with him?'

'I was hurting and lonely. It was nothing important. Brigid lost her husband, as you probably know, and it was Pat's way of cheering us up. I never went out with him alone and I stopped seeing him a while ago.' She hesitated before saying, 'What about this Lily Shaun mentioned?'

'Lil has a bike. She was acting as messenger for our units in Dublin.' His head shifted on her stomach.

'That's all?'

'No. Our Shaun told her that there was a woman in my past and that I needed help to get over her.'

'He had a nerve,' said Rebekah indignantly.

'He was never backward in coming forward.' He yawned.

'And?' she prompted.

'And we were friendly.'

'How friendly?'

'Friendly, friendly.'

Rebekah cleared her throat. 'Like we were friendly after a couple of days?'

Daniel turned his head and with difficulty moved to press his face against the fabric covering her breast. She felt the warmth of his breath. 'Never,' he said in a muffled voice.

She wanted to believe him. Then she did not want to believe him. It would lessen her guilt concerning Joshua if he had been with another woman, though she hated the thought. 'I'd better stir myself,' she murmured. 'There's the vegetables to peel.' She sat up and he moved with her.

'You don't believe me.' He stared at her straight in the face.

'Yes I do.'

'You should. It could never be the way it was with you.' His tone was serious.

She swallowed, knowing how true that had been for her. 'I believe you. But I've still got to peel the vegetables.'

There was a short silence, then he smiled. 'Do you want help?'

She shook her head and Daniel pressed his lips against hers briefly, then eased himself down on the grass. When she came back out with some newspaper and the vegetables he appeared to be sleeping. She sat on the step, glancing at him now and again as she peeled potatoes, carrots, onion and turnip, and tried very hard not to think about him and Lil.

'You can cook,' said Daniel in a pleased voice, pushing his empty plate and taking her hand.

She smiled. 'Mama made sure I could. The mutton wasn't too fatty?'

'It wouldn't be your fault if it was – but it was fine.' He kissed her fingers.

'Perhaps we could have fish tomorrow?'

'Sure, if the day's not too sunny I'll take a rod. Will you be coming with me?'

'I might join you after I've been to the village. We'll be needing more bread and I'd like some fresh milk.'

'You'll perhaps need to be careful what you say?'

237

'I know. You don't have to tell me you're an Irregular on the run,' she said lightly, watching him toy with her fingers.

'A deserter.' His expression was grim. 'The danger in a place you don't know, is not knowing which side people sympathise with.'

'I'll be careful.'

He nodded.

She pulled her hand away. 'I'll wash the dishes. You have a rest.'

Daniel frowned, leaning back in the chair so that all the weight was on the back legs. 'All I've done all day is rest. I'm not used to it.'

'You can fix the fire if you're so desperate to start that shoulder bleeding, or there's yesterday's papers you can read.'

'I know what they'll be saying. Will you get me a paper tomorrow?'

Rebekah agreed and got on with her chores. Afterwards they sat on the sofa together and she would have altered a pair of trousers for him but he took them out of her hand and threw them on a chair. She was pulled against him and his mouth came down on hers. His kisses demanded and she responded with a hungry desire that dissolved all sensible thought. Physically he was just as attractive to her as in the past and she was not going to start worrying about the rights and wrongs of the situation she had got herself into. On the *Samson* she had been ready to do anything to stay with him, and she was ready now. They went upstairs. She had to help him undress and did so carefully, conscious that he was watching her every expression. Her fingers checked his bandage before, trembling slightly, they explored his chest and unbuttoned his trousers. She knew better than to arouse him too quickly and just missed touching the source of his manhood, although it was difficult to avoid and she wanted to please him. She knew, though, that she had to pretend that the only sexual experience she possessed had been in his company. Not easy when her subconscious was telling her where to kiss and caress.

Daniel lay on the bed, watching her undress while the final shafts of evening sunlight played over her body. 'It's the first time I've seen you completely naked,' he said quietly. 'I know you had a good shape because it felt right, but – '

238

'Shhh!' She clutched her frock in front of her. 'You'll have me blushing.'

He grinned. 'I should hope so. Now come here.'

She went, with that first time that they had made love on the beach in her thoughts. Her need for him took away any inhibitions. He touched and kissed places that Joshua would never have considered. She was high with breathless excitement by the time he finally took her.

Afterwards she worried as her fingers searched the bandages back and front. He had bled a little. 'I'm all right,' he said drowsily, dragging her arm and pulling it across his chest. 'Go to sleep now.'

Unexpectedly depression spoilt the moment. Joshua had a habit of saying those words when he had finished with her. When was she going to tell Daniel the truth? He would not like it. Wouldn't like it at all! Fear made her feel cold all over. Her arm tightened protectively around him as she tried to shut out a different kind of bedtime memory. She drifted into sleep but the memory followed her and turned it into a nightmare. When she awoke, the decision was made. She was not going to tell Daniel about her marriage.

Chapter Twenty-One

Rebekah came through the gate, spilling water in her haste, but Daniel had already got up and was in the garden, gazing at the roof.

'Don't even think it,' she said, putting down the bucket and rubbing a muscle in her arm.

He turned and came over to her. 'Perhaps tomorrow.' His hand reached for the bucket but she gripped the handle before he could touch it.

'Perhaps in a week,' she said severely. He just looked at her. 'Daniel! I don't want you trying to unblock that pipe while I'm in the village. You'll do some gentle fishing.'

'You don't think I'll be using my shoulder for that, woman?'

She sighed. 'I suppose you will, but not to the same extent as getting up on a roof. I'd say rest completely but I've got a feeling you've no intention of doing that.'

'You're getting to know me.'

'I should say I am.' She smiled. 'Is the fire still in?'

'I've seen to that.' His hand fastened on part of the wooden grip of the handle. 'We'll share.' His voice was determined.

'You're a stubborn man.'

'And you're a bossy woman.'

'Only for your own good,' she protested.

The tiny creases at the outer edges of his eyes deepened. 'And don't they all say that before they start trying to change you?'

'There's nothing about you I want to change,' she murmured, eyeing him carefully and putting her tongue in her cheek. 'Except several days' growth of beard, that terrible shirt with blood on it, and your bandages.'

He rasped his chin with a fingernail. 'They might ask awkward questions in the village if you buy a razor.'

She agreed and kissed him. The next moment the bucket was on the ground and they were lying in the grass making love. It was another two hours before she set out, walking to the village to save petrol.

It was set in a narrow valley with most of the houses spread along either side of a single street. There was a church, the priest's house, a small school, a blacksmith's, and a general store that sold everything and had a bar at one end. Rebekah had considered going to the nearest town about six miles away where she had attended church every Sunday when she had stayed with her grandmother, but had changed her mind, thinking it more probably that she would find out more about Joshua's man in the village.

She reckoned on it being reasonably safe for her to admit to who she was or had been to Mary Lochrane, who kept the shop with her husband. She was a large woman with a mass of soft brown hair that she wore tied with a bootlace.

'It's changing times we're living in, Miss Rhoades,' she said as she sliced bacon. 'You must feel it with your granny gone and the land sold to that man in Liverpool. I'm surprised to see you here, I must admit.' Her fine dark eyes were curious.

'You remember my father?'

'Aye! I remember him fine.'

'He died.' Rebekah told her about the accident but said nothing about Joshua's being her guardian. It seemed that it was not known because the woman only tuttered and expressed her sympathy.

'I've nearly got over it now,' said Rebekah, 'but I had a yen to see the old place. I was surprised to find the house empty, so I thought I might just stay there a while. Is there someone I should see about it?'

Mrs Lochrane's head drew closer to Rebekah's as she wrapped the bacon in greaseproof paper. 'Nobody'll be minding. Mr Dixon, whose wife died from the appendicitis, lived there after your granny. He got drunk in here one night roundsabout Christmas and spoke up for the Treaty. Next day

241

there's a notice pinned to his front door telling him to get out or else. So he upped and left. Seeing as how there's no Mr Green to check up on people, everything's been left pretty much as it was.'

'You don't see Mr Green here at all?'

'Not him.' She tossed her head. 'Not for years. It's rumoured, though, that there's talk of him selling the place. Let's hope it's true. It's not doing anybody any good for things to be left the way they are.'

Rebekah agreed and asked how much she owed. It seemed reasonable considering all she had learnt.

'Is it on your own you'll be staying there?' asked Mrs Lochrane, handling her change.

Rebekah kept her head down as she put the money in her purse. 'I have my cousin from Liverpool with me.' She picked up her purchases and Mrs Lochrane moved to open to door for her.

'Perhaps we'll be seeing you with your cousin next time?'

'My cousin hasn't been well and needs peace and quiet. Some good Irish country air should do the trick.' She nodded and went on up the street, smiling at anyone who looked her way.

Daniel was not in the house when she arrived back so she left everything on the table and went in search of him. He had abandoned fishing and was in the river. 'I thought I might as well get myself cleaned up,' he called.

'You've got your bandage wet, idjit.'

'Stop fussing.' His brown eyes wandered slowly over her in the peach cotton frock and his fingers fastened on her bare ankle. 'Get your clothes off and come in.'

'I have no towel and I can't swim very well,' she murmured, eyeing him below the water line.

'It's not deep, and besides I'll look after you.'

She smiled. 'You can't look after yourself, going and getting yourself shot.'

He pulled on her foot and she lowered herself quickly on to the grassy bank. 'All right! But don't rush me. I bet it's cold.'

'It'll take your breath away.'

She pulled a face but began to undo her frock. 'Mr Dixon, who lived in the house, was threatened. He spoke up for the Treaty.'

Daniel frowned and was silent a moment before saying, 'Did you get a paper?'

'They surrendered at Four Courts.'

'I see.' For a moment he looked grim. 'Anything else?'

'The woman who keeps the shop reckons that it'll be all right for us to stay. I told her that I had my cousin from Liverpool with me.'

'So I'll have to put on a Liverpudlian accent?'

'And be Quaker and female, I think,' she said with a mischievous look.'

'Re-bek-ah!' he groaned, shaking his head and so sprinkling her with a myriad drops of water before pulling her into the river.

She gasped with the cold shock and pretended to hit him but he put his arms round her and kissed her long and hard until she actually did strike him.

He loosened his hold. 'This is the life,' he said against her ear.

'You're easily pleased.' She put her arms round him as the current tugged at her legs.

'The simple life. You, me, food to eat and somewhere to lay our heads. What else do we need?' He nuzzled her neck and then lifted his head. 'What's this scar on your shoulder?'

She hesitated before saying. 'It's where the bed fell on me on the *Samson*.'

'It looks like a burn.' He turned her round. 'You've marks on your back as well.'

'Same thing.'

'They look different.' He pulled her close again and rubbed noses. 'Poor love.'

'I survived. But I'm not sure I won't be having pneumonia when I get out of this river,' she said through chattering teeth. 'A hot bath is what I'll be needing, but I'm sure I'm not going to get it.'

'I'll warm you up.' He smiled into her eyes.

'Is that a promise?'

'You bet.' He kissed her, and set about keeping his word.

Daniel slid down from the roof and entered the house where they had lived for ten days. He stared with satisfaction at the brackish-coloured water coming from the tap. 'You can use that water for washing but don't drink it, love.'

'I've no intention.' Rebekah carried a bucket over to the cooking pot and filled it. 'I suppose I should want it to rain so we can have fresh water in the tank.'

'I can't believe we've been so lucky.' He sat on the sofa, gingerly feeling his shoulder, but the bandage and vest were still dry. 'Becky, we'll have to get married.'

Her legs suddenly felt weak and it was several seconds before she turned and looked at him. 'I'm not bothered about getting married. We'd have to talk religion, and as we're already living in sin, what does it matter?'

He stared at her. 'It matters to me. And I never thought I'd hear you talking of living in mortal sin so lightly!'

'I might talk of it lightly but I don't mean it lightly,' she said, sitting down. 'I was thinking of Adam and Eve the other day and how there was no priest or minister there to marry them. When we leave here, who's to know that we're not married?'

He frowned. 'I know you don't want to be a Catholic, love, but I wouldn't force you to go to our church. But if we could just have the priest say the words over us. I want us to be respectable. I don't want our children being bastards.'

'Children!' She got up and began to sort out the washing, thinking how men thought it was so easy to get you with child.

Daniel came up behind her and wrapped his arms about her waist. 'It might have happened already.'

Rebekah turned in his arms and looked at him. 'And it mightn't have.'

'We make love all the time!' he exclaimed, squeezing her.

She looped her arms around his neck. 'You could be making love to me now instead of talking.'

'Later. Now I want to sort this out. Once my shoulder's healed I'm going back to sea.'

She dropped her arms. 'What's the rush? We're safe here and I've still got money.'

'We feel safe,' he said, slackening his hold. 'But feelings can be deceptive. And there's another thing, I don't like living off you.'

'But that's stupid.' She pulled away from him. 'In Liverpool I know women who have to work to keep a family going. I don't suppose the children care who's earning the money.'

'That's different.'

'But in a way it's the same. You can't earn at the moment and the money I have is enough for us to live on for a while longer. I'm not saying for always, just a few more weeks.'

'And then?' he said quietly. 'I go back to sea and you're left on your own? I want a wife to come home to, Becky, not a mistress.'

She flushed. 'When you say that it makes me sound different to how I see myself. I think of myself as your wife already.'

He drew her close again. 'I want to be sure of you and I want you to be secure. If anything were to happen to me – '

'Don't say it!' She clung to him. 'I don't want you to leave me. I couldn't bear it if – '

'Shhh!' He kissed her and for the moment decision-making about marriage was put aside.

It was to come up again a week later when they were walking in the hills.

'Look at that view.' Rebekah forced Daniel to halt. 'Let's rest and have our sandwiches.'

He did as she asked and they sat gazing down the hillside and across a valley to the tree-massed slope on the other side. A rabbit watched them from a few feet away.

'The view won't keep us, Becky. We have to make some decision.' Daniel screwed up his eyes against the sun. 'I met the priest when I was fishing last evening.'

'Did he ask where you were staying?'

'Yes.'

'Did you tell him?'

'I gave him the impression I was sleeping rough, and from my tramp-like appearance and my talk, he drew the conclusion that I was an Irregular on the run. We discussed the Treaty.'

She bit her lip. 'Do you think he'll report you to the constabulary?'

Daniel's brow creased. 'One lone deserter? He asked me what I thought of Father Albert – who was with us at Four Courts – for urging the men to quit to save more bloodshed.'

She sighed. 'What did you say?'

'I said I was out of it but that I would have gone along with him.'

'Sensible man.' She kissed him. 'What do you think has happened to Shaun?'

Daniel shrugged. 'If he was caught he could be in Mountjoy prison.'

'But if he wasn't? She toyed with a blade of grass. 'Is it possible he could find us?'

'Anything's possible if he really wants to trace us. He has connections and if there's men in the village who sympathise with the cause – ' He shrugged. 'We're not that far from Dublin and he knows the car.'

She was dismayed. 'You don't think we should leave now?'

'Not right now, but soon. We'll have to think about where to live.' He lay down, his hands behind his head.

She felt depressed at the thought of being parted from him in an Ireland that was still at war with itself and unexpectedly had a longing to see Liverpool again. At least there she had friends. 'What about Liverpool?'

'Liverpool!' He pushed himself up and his expression had changed. 'Green's there.'

'It's a big city! Besides, we could live just outside. Seaforth, or somewhere like that.' Her voice was eager.

He scowled. 'I don't want you within ten miles of Green. I don't trust him.'

'How's he to know I'm there? You're not thinking, love. When you're away at least I'll have friends in Liverpool.'

You're thinking of Brigid, whose brother is Pat. Who's a sailor. Talk gets round. Before you know it Green will know exactly where you are. Or you'll go and visit your aunt or that friend of yours, Edwina, and they'll spill the beans. I don't want him pestering you while I'm away. You don't know him like I do. He's ruthless when he wants his own way.'

'I'm sure you're right.' She felt a strong sense of guilt and apprehension, as if the mere mention of Joshua's name could spoil everything between them. 'I'll have to stay in Ireland.'

He frowned at her. 'You don't have to make it sound like a penance.'

'I'm sorry. It's just that I'm going to miss you when you go.'

'I never told you it would be easy being married to a sailor,' he said, and getting to his feet went on down the hill ahead of her. She followed him slowly, trying to cast off a feeling of gloom.

246

'Ugh! I got soaked just coming from the car!' Rebekah shook herself, scattering raindrops, as she closed the kitchen door.

'Did you get a newspaper?' Daniel helped her off with her coat.

'And posted my letter.' She took the newspaper from a shopping bag and handed it to him.

He opened it, and after a minute or so said quietly, 'There's been fighting in Limerick and Waterford. It's been going on for days but now both towns have fallen to State troops.'

'That'll mean more Irregulars on the run.' Rebekah stared at him, her breath coming fast.

'And more filling the prisons.'

'Shaun?' She went over to the fire and dipped a ladle in the stew that was simmering in the pot.

'Who knows?' he said shortly. There was a silence.

'I met the priest today,' she said brightly. 'He was very nice. Enquired after your health and asked how much longer we'd be staying.'

'And what did you say?' He placed two bowls on the table.

'I said we'd be leaving at the end of the summer.'

'Why did you say that?' He sat on a chair and drummed his fingers on the table. 'I've got to be earning, Becky. We'll go to Dublin. I know a few people – '

'Lily.' The name came out without Rebekah even thinking about it.

He stared at her. 'If that's a joke, it's not funny.'

Sorry!' She spooned the stew into the bowls. 'But it seems to me, Daniel, that I'm going to be left alone in a Dublin that's just as dangerous as it was two years ago. I don't believe the Irregulars'll give up on the city. It'll be guerilla warfare again, and wobetide anyone who gets in the way.'

He stirred his stew, frowning down into the bowl. 'You're over-reacting because I've got to leave you. But I did tell you what it would be like married to me.'

'I'm not married to you,' she murmured, hurt because he seemed unable to understand how insecure and scared she felt.

Daniel looked up. 'I did ask you. Is that what this is about?'

'Don't talk stupid,' she said angrily. She sprinkled damp salt on her stew. 'I said the other week I wasn't bothered about being married.'

'So you did. I thought it unlike you.'

'Why?' She met his gaze squarely. 'Did Lily want to marry you?'

'Lily again!' He put down his spoon. 'What the hell's this about? She meant nothing to me!'

'It's easy to say that.' Some devil was driving Rebekah. She dipped her spoon in the stew. 'Did you go to bed with her?'

His eyes hardened. 'I'm not telling you. But I'll say this – she would have been happy to! Perhaps I can still make her happy, the way things are going on!'

'Things!' she banged her spoon down on the table, splattering it with gravy. 'You mean the way *I'm* going on, don't you? Perhaps you'd planned on marrying her? Maybe you're wishing now we'd never met again?'

'Who's talking stupid now?' He stood and rammed his chair against the wall. 'I don't know how you can even think that, never mind say it?' he said vehemently, taking his second-hand coat from a hook on the wall. 'Haven't I asked you to marry me? I'm going for a walk, and perhaps when I come back you'll be talking sense.'

'*Me* talking sense!' Rebekah jumped to her feet, folding her arms across her breast. 'Walking in the pouring rain – you call that sensible?'

Daniel gave her a look and without another word, opened the door and went out.

Rebekah stared after him and burst into tears. She did not know what made her go on about Lily. What would Mama, if she could see her from heaven, be thinking of her now? What was God thinking, her living with Daniel and married to Joshua? She rubbed her wet cheek against her sleeve and tried to control her tears. What was she to do?

A soaked through Daniel returned three hours later. She hurried to help him off with his coat. 'Where've you been? I've been worried sick! I thought you weren't coming back! Come over the fire and get dry.'

He smiled. 'It did me good.' He pulled her towards him and rubbed his wet hair in her face.

She protested but could not help laughing. 'You pig!'

'Grunt, grunt!' He swung her off her feet. 'I'm a selfish swine, Becky love. You've been worrying all the time about us not being married, haven't you?'

'I have?' she stammered.

'Of course you have.' He wrapped his arms round her. 'I went to see the priest. I told him that we'd been living in sin and asked him to marry us as soon as possible.'

'You what?' Rebekah could scarcely believe what she was hearing.

He grinned. 'Don't let's argue religion. I have to make us legal before I go back to sea.'

She swallowed. 'I see.'

'I say you do!' He laughed and swung her around again. 'You will say yes?'

'What about banns?' she said desperately.

'"Tush to that," said Father Donovan, when I told him what Green had done to us in order to get his hands on your money.'

'You said that? Did he believe you?' Rebekah was breathless with the speed of his actions.

'Sure and he believed me! Isn't Green English, a Protestant, and an uncaring landlord to boot?'

'But – but *I'm* Protestant and English. Doesn't he – ?'

'But you're half Irish, polite and pretty! And you came back to Ireland in search of me and rescued me from the jaws of death!'

'You didn't say that?' Rebekah was starting to feel peculiar.

'I did. I told him that we loved each other madly.'

'Mad's the operative word,' she said, sagging against him. 'Oh, Daniel, I don't know what to say! I feel sick.'

He looked anxious and ushered her over to the couch. 'Let's sit down. It's the shock! And we didn't eat our dinner. You'll feel better once you've got some food down you.'

'Food. Yes,' she said faintly. 'Let's have some dinner.'

He hurried over to the fire. She watched him filling the bowls and tried to form the words 'I'm already married', but they would not come. Instead she murmured, 'When is this wedding?'

'Soon. Maybe tomorrow. Or the next day.'

Right,' she said, trying to control the terrible churning in her stomach. 'I'll have to pick out a frock.'

Daniel smiled as he brought her a bowl of stew. 'That pale green crêpe-de-chine. I like that one.'

She returned his smile and ignored the voice in her head that told her that what she was planning was wrong. 'Dum-dum-de-dum,' she murmured.

'There'll be no music,' he said. 'Just a quiet ceremony.'

'That'll do me,' she said, and ate her stew.

That night Rebekah could not sleep. The words 'Bigamist! Liar! Cheat!' kept running through her mind. She had read of a case in the *Liverpool Echo* only a few months ago. A soldier had been brought to court for having one wife in Liverpool and another in Preston. What was she to do? She could not bear hurting Daniel. She considered all they had been through and how they had found each other again. She smiled. They had been happy. Slowly she relaxed. She slept and dreamed her old dream of being locked in the turret, and was afraid. Someone was coming up the stairs and she could not escape.

It was daylight when she woke. Daniel was out of bed and dragging on a shirt.

'Who do you think it is?' she mouthed.

At that moment there was a knock on the door and a voice said, 'Danny! Are you in there?'

She watched him open the door a few inches to reveal Shaun's face.

'Out!' Daniel pushed his brother before him and closed the door, shutting Rebekah in.

She got out of bed quickly and dragged on her dressing gown. Downstairs the two brothers confronted each other, one either end of the table.

'I knew she was here,' said Shaun. 'They told me in the village. Miss Rebekah Rhoades is staying in this house with her Liverpool cousin. But nobody has seen the cousin.' He grinned. 'I found that interesting so I came out here.'

Daniel's eyes narrowed. 'How long have you been here?'

'An hour or so. Stirred up the fire. Had a cuppa tea and some bread and jam. Not a bad place but a good bloody walk to find you.'

'How did you find the village?'

'A couple of the lads are from around here. It was one of the mothers who mentioned Miss Rhoades and her motor.' Shaun smirked. 'It was after that I mentioned that I knew her and the cousin might be my brother. They let on that you and her are the talk of the place since yesterday. A wedding in the offering and her getting married in our church. Quite a romantic tale you made out of it, Danny boy, but you're not married to her yet.'

'I will be soon,' said Daniel. 'What d'you want?'

Shaun looked injured. 'You could be a bit more welcoming. I could have been killed. I thought you'd be glad to see me.'

'Why? You're nothing but trouble.'

'Now that's a fine thing to say! There could be state troopers on my tail.'

'So you go and declare yourself to all and sundry in the village?' Daniel's tones were disbelieving. 'Don't make me laugh!'

Shaun sighed heavily. 'It's a fine thing to be calling your brother a liar. And there's me worrying about you.'

'Come off it! You're a liar.'

'Don't believe me then.' Shaun shrugged. 'I was in the fighting at Waterford. I was lucky to get out.'

Daniel stared at him before walking over to the window. 'It's a bloody shame. It says in the newspaper that de Valera wants to talk peace.'

'So he does – but who's listening? Michael Collins and Griffiths sold us down the river. There'll be no peace.' Shaun's expression was ugly. 'What you've got to decide, Danny, is if you're with us or against us.'

'I'm out of it,' said Daniel. 'I'm going back to sea.'

'You can't quit!'

'You're going to stop me?' A grim smile played around Daniel's mouth.

'Danny! You know they won't let you,' insisted Shaun. 'You're either for or –'

'You know what I'm for.' Daniel held his brother's gaze. 'But I'm not going to be fighting my fellow countrymen for it, and that's my final word on the matter.'

There was a silence during which Rebekah felt faint again and lowered herself on to the bottom stair. Shaun glanced at her. 'It's her fault we're arguing! Mam must be turning in her grave. I tell you, Danny, you could be making a mistake. Guess what I found in that bag over there.'

Involuntarily Daniel looked at Rebekah's canvas bag sitting on the floor in the corner. 'You went nosing in Becky's bag?' he said furiously. 'You've got no right – '

'Hold on,' said Shaun, placing on the table a wedding ring and ruby and diamond engagement ring. 'I found those in it.'

Daniel stared at them and did not speak for a moment. 'So? They're her mother's,' he said at last. 'Aren't they, Rebekah'

She stood up. 'Yes.' She came over to the table and feeling like an old, old woman, sank on to a chair. She did not look at Daniel.

'There,' he said to his brother. 'Now get out.'

Shaun's gaze went from one to the other. Then without another word, he left the house.

Daniel watched him through the window until he was the other side of the gate, then he turned. 'He could be back with others.'

She stared at him. 'But you haven't done anything wrong.'

'You heard me tell him I've quit. You should know what they're like. I think it's best we do go to Liverpool. You've got friends there.'

There was a silence before she murmured, 'You think I'm going to need friends?'

'We all need friends.'

She felt cold to her stomach. 'Has he actually brought any men with him?'

'You heard what he said.'

She nodded and squared her shoulders but her heart was thumping as she reached for the oats and put a cupful in the frying pan. 'Are we leaving today?'

'Yes.' He picked up the rings. 'I didn't know our Shaun had taken to thieving. Are they your mother's?'

Rebekah stared at him and her throat ached and she felt so sick that she could not answer him immediately. He looked at her with a slight pucker between his brows. 'Well?'

She swallowed. 'I'd hardly take them from her dead hand.'

'Your Grandma's then?'

'No.' A splinter of laughter escaped her. 'The Bible says, "Be sure your sins will find you out!" and that's what's happening to me.'

'Becky!' He went pale and moved over to her. 'What is it? Tell me!'

'You won't love me any more! You'll hate me!' A sob shook her throat.

'Tell me!' He shook her.

'I'm married, Daniel!'

She would have found it easier if he had immediately shouted at her but instead he was silent for what seemed an age before his arms slackened and then dropped. There was an expression in his eyes that made her want to cry and cry and when he shouted in a furious voice: 'It's Green, isn't it? It's bloody Green!' she did start crying but he ignored her tears and yelled, 'Why, Rebekah? Why if you loved me?'

'I did love you! I *do* love you!' She scrubbed at the tears on her cheeks and her voice rose, 'But I thought you were *dead*, and he was so persuasive. It was what Papa wanted and I felt so guilty about him because we quarrelled and he died. I wanted to please him even though he was dead! Can you understand that?' Daniel was silent, just staring at her. She continued, 'I realised my mistake as soon as I married him. He changed. It was frightening. He was cruel, calculatingly cruel. That scar on my shoulder you asked about – he did it on our honeymoon with a cigar because I mentioned your name. He knew that I loved you and he told me that one of the reasons he married me was because he hated you.'

'Green told you he hated me on your honeymoon?' His expression was disbelieving.

'Yes!'

'Why?'

'Why on the honeymoon? Or why hate you at all?'

'I know why he hates me.'

Rebekah smiled bitterly. 'You were his friend once. I think he liked you. He kept going on about you. He wanted to know if you'd tried anything on with me. I couldn't understand it, but of course he knew all the time you weren't dead and that I loved you. On our honeymoon I didn't want him to touch me and he raped me. He wanted to be the first with me but of course he wasn't. You were. Not that I told him that. As it was he hurt me. Since then I've lost count of the times he's hurt me. He has a Cat o' Nine Tails.' She choked on the words and stopped.

'Don't tell me any more.' He was white about the mouth. 'I need to think. I'm going for a walk.' Not bothering with a coat he opened the door and went out.

Rebekah ran after him. 'Daniel, you will come back! You won't – '

He pushed her away. 'Just let me be for a while!'

She watched him go with his hands rammed in his trouser pockets, and had to lean against the door jamb. Her head throbbed and she felt sick.

When he was out of sight she staggered inside and sat down on the sofa. She tried to think what to do but could not. Then she smelt burning. She got to her feet and took the frying pan from the fire. She threw the burnt oats on to the peats, watching them blacken even further. Hell's fire. She had thought it terrible when she believed Daniel dead but now she experienced a different kind of loss. Often she had marvelled that he had loved her, but had believed in that love. Now he might not love her any more. She could not bear the thought. She had to speak to him. And without stopping to think any more, she opened the door and went after him.

Chapter Twenty-Two

Daniel was striding along the river bank with visions of violence in his mind. He had wanted to hit Rebekah, that was why he had to get out. His white hot anger had abated somewhat and he was no longer dwelling on her deception but on a childhood memory of his father knocking his mother to the floor, and of her whimpering when her belly was big with Shaun. His brothers had been out and he had put his arms round his father's leg and hung on to prevent him from kicking his mother again. He shuddered even now at the scene. His father had fallen over, and his mother had lumbered to her feet, and grabbing Daniel's hand had fled with him to Old Mary's house.

As he thought of Old Mary, he remembered the day he had walked with Rebekah to the bay. The attraction between them had been strong even then. Holy Mary, why had he had to love her? He paused and gazed down into the water. It was where he normally fished and they had bathed here once or twice. He remembered the marks on Rebekah's back and shoulder and there was a tightness in his chest. A Cat o' Nine Tails! It was a bad moment as he struggled with his emotions. He was about to turn round when he saw his brother running towards him.

'Troopers,' panted Shaun. 'I told you they were after me and when they realise who you are, they'll be after you too. Although with that beard – ' He paused, bending over and resting his hands on his knees, getting his breath back.

'Is this another one of your tricks?' snapped Daniel. 'Because I'm in the mood to biff you one.'

'Don't be like that, Danny,' he protested. 'We've got to get away from here, and quick. You can drive. You can get us out of here.'

'I can what? You're joking if you think I'm going to get involved in anything to do with you! I wouldn't put it past you to be making all this up.'

Shaun laughed. 'I'm not! Why would I do that? I'm telling you, Danny, they'll be up here soon and we've got to get away.'

'We've got to get away!' Daniel's eyes narrowed. 'What about your friends in the village? I bet they've put you up to this to get me back.'

Shaun protested but Daniel did not believe him. 'Go and put your head in a pot and boil it!' He pushed his brother out of the way and began to walk back to the house.

Shaun followed him. 'Were those rings really her mother's?'

'You heard what she said.'

'Why wasn't she wearing them?'

'Would you wear a ring like that fancy one to do chores?'

'She could have worn the wedding ring. I bet she's been deceiving you.'

Daniel turned and his expression was bleak. 'Don't talk to me about deception. You told me she was dead! Green told us both that the other was dead! Now get out of my sight before I forget that I once cared that you'd be born alive.' Shaun stopped in his tracks and Daniel walked away.

He saw Rebekah half a mile further up the river, running towards him, and when she would have flung herself at him he held her off. He gazed into the drawn face that was blotchy with tears.

'You were coming back to me?' she stammered.

'How should I know? You've got me that way I don't know where I am. Let's go before Shaun catches up with us.'

'He's still around?'

Daniel nodded and hurried her along, making her run to keep up with him.

'What are you going to do?' she asked.

He stared at her unhappy expression and dropped her hand. 'You want me to make you feel better by saying I forgive you?' he said in a seething voice. 'Straight away! Just like that!' He snapped his fingers.

'I don't suppose you'll ever forgive me. You hate Joshua too much for that.' Her voice trembled. 'But I thought you loved me enough to stay with me. After all, I left him to find you and it wasn't easy for me to come to Ireland alone. I was scared, not only of the fighting but of what I might find out when I met you again.'

'And what did you find out?' he muttered, looking away from her towards the house.

'That I still loved you,' she cried. 'But I soon realised that I'd been living in a fool's paradise thinking that you would understand why I had married Joshua, so I decided not to tell you. I didn't mean to hurt you.'

He looked at her. 'I'll never understand women. You really thought we could carry on without my ever finding out the truth?'

'I didn't want to think,' she said. 'It seemed simpler just living from day to day and pretending Joshua didn't exist. We were happy.'

'Happy? Living in a fool's paradise?' He shook his head and stared down at the ground.

'What are we going to do?'

He looked up. 'Bloody hell, Rebekah, why keep asking me that? I bloody don't know,' he said savagely. 'Perhaps we should just to go bed and pretend – that – none of this – has happened?' He did not know why he said it.

'Bed?' She stared at him, her eyes twin pools of shock.

Suddenly he wanted to hurt her. 'Do you think it'll be different? Perhaps it will now I know I'm having it with a married woman.'

She flushed. 'You make it sound more sinful.'

'It is more sinful.'

'How can you say that?'

'I just open my mouth – '

'Daniel, don't be cruel.'

'Cruel! Me?' His voice was harsh. 'The way you went on about Lily, and all the time you were married to bloody Green!'

'I know,' she said miserably. 'If you want to know, I was thoroughly ashamed of myself for going on about Lily.'

'You should be.'

'Daniel, I do love you!'

'So you say. You'll have to prove it.'

'I thought I had by leaving Joshua.' She tilted her chin. 'I've given up a lot for you, you know. Perhaps you should think about that.'

For a moment he said nothing, then with some satisfaction he said, 'Green would be bloody mad if he knew we were together. I wonder what he'd say if he found out?' He took hold of her wrist and hurried her into the house. For once he bolted the door before running her up the stairs.

Daniel no longer wanted to strike her but was in no mood to be nice to her. It seemed to him that she had not grieved long for him, but perhaps he would not have minded so much if it had been anyone else but Joshua Green. Then again, he could be kidding himself because he loved and did not want anyone else to have her. He could hazard a guess to how much she had suffered at Joshua's hands and it did occur to him that she had paid for her mistakes. Even so the pain she had inflicted went deep. He wanted to be rough with her but surprisingly she did not seem to mind that and somewhere along the way desire took over and their passion for each other seemed greater than before. He wondered if she believed that this could be the last time they would make love.

'Would you really have gone through with marrying me?' he panted.

'Yes,' she gasped. 'I didn't want to hurt you.'

'Good God!' He was shocked, but incredibly he was flattered at the same time. 'You're more ruthless than I thought.'

'I love you,' she whispered before he kissed her once more.

Afterwards Rebekah fell into an exhausted sleep and Daniel lay watching her, considering what to do. He was still thinking when he heard someone trying the front door. He got up and looked out of the window. As he did so, Shaun called in a loud whisper, 'Danny, open up! You've got to let me in!'

He opened the window. 'I don't want you in here. Go away!'

'Danny, for God's sake!' called Shaun in desperate tones.

Not wanting Rebekah wakened, he turned from the window and crept downstairs.

His brother almost fell over the step in his haste to get inside. He had a gun in his hand. 'Danny, they're here! The troopers! They're just up the lane! We'll have to fight it out, but we've got a chance in here.'

Daniel stared at him. 'I could kill you!' His voice was harsh. 'Why do you always have to come and muck up my life? D'you think I'd risk a fight in here?'

'I wouldn't have thought you'd have cared where we fought.' Shaun licked his lips. 'You're not worrying about her after the way she deceived you, now?'

Daniel said nothing, only shutting the door and going to look out of the window. 'If they get us, they'll get her,' he murmured. 'They mightn't believe she's not in on it. Where about are they? Near the gate or what?'

'Not that close.' Shaun's eyes shifted away from his brother's. 'Why?'

'Because I went to get them away from here.' He moved swiftly over to Rebekah's bag on the floor and took something from it. 'Come on,' he said to his brother.

'What are you going to do?' stammered Shaun.

'You'll find out.' He opened the door and pushed his brother in front of him. 'Give me the gun and over to the car!'

Shaun stared at him and slowly a smile crossed his face. 'You're gonna run the sods down!'

'Not if I can help it. You'll have to turn the starting handle.' Daniel loped across the ground and through the gateway. He glanced up the lane which curved a few hundred yards down. The men could be just round the bend.

He got in and flung the handle to Shaun, who hurriedly inserted it. The engine coughed into life as Daniel, ears straining, tossed the gun inside. Shaun jumped in, slammed the door and picked up the gun on the seat. He pulled another from his belt, only to be flung back against the seat as the car started up the lane.

Rebekah woke, recalling instantaneously the traumas of the day. She reached out for Daniel but he was not there. A twinge of anxiety made itself felt as she clambered out of bed and dressed. There was no one downstairs and the fire was almost out. How long had she slept? Her stomach rumbled.

She had not eaten all day and neither had Daniel. Where was he? Would he have gone fishing? The rod was in the cupboard. A walk?

Opening the door Rebekah went outside. It was quiet except for the sound of birds. She hurried towards the river and walked further than she had ever done until bushes and undergrowth made it impossible to go any further. Her anxiety grew and she felt light-headed with hunger. Had Daniel gone to the village? Retracing her steps she made for the gate and suddenly realised that the car was missing.

For a moment Rebekah just stared at the vacant spot, hardly able to take in the evidence of her eyes. Then she thought of Shaun but remembered he could not drive. Daniel could. Perhaps he had taken his brother to the nearest town? She gnawed at her lip. When? What time? How long would it have taken if he had done so not knowing the roads?

Rebekah meandered along the lane as far as the bend but there was no sign of anyone. She went back to the house and found the fire out. She did not have the heart to attempt to light it again and made do with a slice of bread and jam and a drink of ginger beer. There was a sock to darn so she set to doing that. She checked for Daniel's spare clothing upstairs. It was still there.

She went outside and wandered up the lane again. Her fear was growing. Perhaps he had decided to leave her? Had been so disgusted with her deceit that he had not been able to stand the sight of her any longer. 'Don't be stupid!' She said the words aloud but it did not make her feel any better. She went back to the house. She would light the fire before it became dark because Daniel would want something warm to eat.

It should have been an easy task because she had watched him get the fire going often enough, but it would not light. She could have cried with frustration as the peat smouldered but did not ignore properly. She longed for Daniel to come back but a voice inside her kept saying, 'He's not coming back.'

Again she went outside to the gate. Nothing! It was getting dark and even the birds were silent. Her loneliness was complete. She went back to the house, lay on the couch and pulled a coat over her. It was only just before dawn that she slept.

It was a horse whinnying that roused Rebekah and she sprang up, only to sit down again because everything spun round her. There was a knock on the door but before she could get up, or ask who it was, the door opened.

Joshua, wearing breeches and a tweed jacket, tossed a riding crop down and leaned on the table. 'My dear Rebekah, I'm glad to say that you look bloody awful! It serves you right for making me chase after you to this devilish place. You can get your things together. You're coming home.'

'How did you know where to find me?' Rebekah's voice was barely above a whisper.

'It wasn't easy.' He picked up the crop again and toyed with it. 'A gentleman doesn't expect his new bride to be missing when he returns home after weeks away. The house was empty. There was no Janet. I visited your aunt and she said that you were in London but did not know where. I went to see Edwina and she said the same.' He whacked the table with the crop and his voice rose. 'It was very embarrassing not knowing where my wife had gone!' His eyes glinted. 'I waited a week and still there was no word. Edwina called to see if you were home.' He hit the table again. 'She suggested that you might have gone to Ireland. Something about Florence Nightingale and the Red Cross. I remembered how you'd wanted to come here. What were you thinking of? Where you looking for ghosts? O'Neill's perhaps?'

Rebekah's fear was now so great that it took her a full minute to answer. 'Don't be silly. I just had a yen to see the place again,' she stammered, rising to her feet. 'I knew that you were much too busy to bring me so I came alone.' She crossed her fingers behind her back.

'I see.' He touched her chin with the crop. 'It was naughty of you. Anything could have happened. It's a dangerous country and that's why I didn't bring you in the spring.'

'As you can see I'm perfectly all right.' She pushed the crop away but he immediately touched her face with it again.

'Joshua, please!' She moved out of his reach but he followed her.

'No welcoming kiss for your husband, my precious.' His pale blue eyes rebuked her. 'I would have thought that after six weeks apart you would have missed me. I've missed you.'

He had forced her into a corner and now reached for her. She would have ducked beneath his arm but he was too quick. He attempted to kiss her but she averted her face and his lips touched her cheek instead. He shook her. 'What's changed you, Rebekah?' His tone had altered, was sharp instead of velvety. 'I'd started to believe that we could rub along quite nicely.'

Rebekah wanted to scream at that but thought it wiser to remain silent.

Her husband's expression turned ugly. 'Nothing to say, my dear! I thought you would have had lots to tell me!' He nuzzled her neck and instinctively she braced herself as his teeth nipped her skin hard. The next moment she was struggling with him but he forced her down on to the floor. He straddled her, painfully prising her fingers away when she sought to keep her skirts down. He gratified himself swiftly.

When he rolled away from her, it was several minutes before Rebekah could rise but she managed it. She had to rid herself of the stink of him! The door gave beneath her fingers and she was out and stumbling towards the river. She waded in fully clothed, despite the chill water, and tears rolled down her cheeks. Shaun's coming, and now Joshua's arrival, were death to all her dreams.

'You'll get pneumonia like that,' said Joshua from the river bank. 'Come and get dry and put on a clean frock. Pack your case and let's get going.'

Rebekah ignored him.

His lips thinned. 'Rebekah! You're being utterly stupid. Now come on out of there!' He stepped into the water and seizing a fold of her sodden frock, pulled her towards him. 'Now you'll stop this nonsense or you'll be sorry. Being on your own here has affected your mind.'

A muscle moved in her throat but she did not say anything, only doing what he said. She walked stiffly beside him. He was silent and she knew she was in for trouble but could see no point in trying to run away. It was obvious that Daniel no longer wanted her. What she had done had been terribly wrong and now she was to pay for it.

She changed and then packed her case while Joshua waited downstairs. For that she was grateful, fearing what he would do to her if he saw Daniel's spare clothing. She went down-stairs, sick with misery.

Outside Joshua untethered the horse and told Rebekah to get on its back. 'I'm too tired to ride,' she said.

'You don't *have* to do anything!' He made a swipe at her bottom with the crop and she moved swiftly. 'That's the ticket.' He smiled. 'Just sit and I'll lead him. We'll fetch my bag from the big house. I'm not staying in this place any longer than I have to. They're a sullen lot and it takes all day to get any information out of them.'

Rebekah made no reply but was relieved that nobody seemed to have mentioned Daniel. When they got to the house she paid little attention to her surroundings because she was so depressed. They stayed only half an hour while a pony trap was brought round. Then they left.

Rebekah was sick on the ferry and Joshua told her that it was all in her mind. She thought of her father and how he had said the same thing to her mother, and how because of him she had married Joshua. In that moment she hated them both.

When the Liver birds came in sight she felt a momentary lifting of her misery. At least Daniel had been right in saying that she had friends here.

Chapter Twenty-Three

It was to be several weeks before Rebekah saw either of her friends. With having been away there were matters to be seen to and besides she was unwell and felt lethargic, having no interest in anything. Eventually, though, she decided that she should go and see her aunt. On the way she met Edwina.

'So you're home! Did you go to Ireland? It's been ages. You look terrible,' said the older woman.

'Thanks,' said Rebekah drily, not feeling too friendly to Edwina, partly blaming her for mentioning Ireland to Joshua.

'What's up?' Edwina's smile vanished. 'Is it something I've said?'

Rebekah realised that she could hardly tell her the truth. 'Nobody likes being told they look terrible. My tummy's a bit upset and I feel tired since I got back from Ireland.'

'Tougher than you thought, was it?' Edwina put her hand through Rebekah's arm. 'Was Joshua cross?'

'Yes. You know how he feels about Ireland.'

'By the look of you, you saw more unpleasant sights than you planned on?'

'Yes, I did.' Her smile came and went as she remembered her first sight of the wounded Daniel. 'I really don't want to talk about it.'

Edwina nodded. 'I understand that.'

They walked along the road in silence. Rebekah forced herself to ask, 'Have you spoken to my aunt?'

'You're joking! You know her opinion of me.'

'I was on my way to see her.'

'Come and have a cup of tea with me first. Dad's out.'

Rebekah did not really feel like going but said yes. After all, it was not Edwina's fault that everything had fallen apart.

The cup of tea did Rebekah good and so did Edwina's gossip about the neighbourhood, coupled with her talk of the latest films. In return Rebekah told her a little about Dublin, the house and the village. She had another cup of tea and a couple of scones. Her appetite seemed to have returned and she did not refuse another scone when Edwina attentively offered the plate.

Her friend suddenly blurted out, 'You know, Becky, the more I look at you the more I'm convinced!'

'Convinced about what?' said Rebekah in surprise.

'That you're having a baby!'

'What!'

'You're having a baby,' repeated Edwina. 'There's a look about your face. And you said that your tummy's been upset. Yet you've been tucking into those scones like there's nothing wrong with you. Have you seen your monthlies lately?'

'No!' Rebekah stared at her and a multitude of emotions erupted inside her. 'Are you sure?'

Edwina smiled. 'I can't be sure. I'm not a doctor or a midwife. Would you be pleased?'

'Pleased?' Rebekah pressed a hand to her stomach. Joshua had been going on about a son and heir, but if it was well past two months since her period then . . . Her spirits lifted. 'Yes. I'd be pleased.'

'You'll have to look after yourself. Plenty of good food and rest,' said Edwina.

Rebekah nodded and suddenly wanted to be doing something. It was as if she had suddenly come alive again. 'What should I do?'

'You'll have to see a doctor.' Edwina's eyes twinkled. 'I bet Joshua will be over the moon.'

'Yes.' Rebekah smiled. Hopefully her having a baby would alter matters.

'He'll probably coddle you to death. You'll have to be careful. Lots of babies miscarry in the first few months.'

'I'll tell him that.' Since returning, her husband had taken full advantage of what he called his marital rights. It was very probable that he would consider the child his but she was sure she knew different. Oh Daniel, our baby! There were times when she just could not believe that he had left her without a word. Now she wanted to weep but instead had to smile. 'I'll tell Joshua as soon as I'm sure.'

'You do,' said Edwina. 'The sooner he knows, the sooner you'll be spoilt.'

Rebekah could only hope that was true.

Because she was deep in thought, she would have walked past her aunt's house if Esther had not been leaning on the gate. 'Rebekah!' She pounced on her, seizing her arm. 'Thou must come in. I've missed you so much. Joshua called and didn't seem to know where you were. I didn't tell him about your friend because she told me not to.'

'So Brigid did come to see you?'

Her aunt nodded vigorously. 'She spoke a bit rough but seemed very fond of thee. She told me that thou was well and I wasn't to worry about thee. That you weren't sure when you'd be home. But I have worried, my dear. Hannah kept saying that she knew that thou would just go off and not come back. That thee were kicking thy legs up in London, and giving the men the glad eye.' Her cheeks flushed. 'Thou knows the way she goes on.'

'Who better?' said Rebekah wryly.

'She said it was very odd that thee didn't write to me thyself and I must admit, dear, that I have wondered why.'

'I didn't go to London,' admitted Rebekah. 'I've been in Ireland and I didn't tell you because I knew that would worry you even more.'

Her aunt's look was one of pure disbelief. 'Why on earth did thou go there? So dangerous, Rebekah.'

She shrugged. 'There are lots of places in Ireland that are far more peaceful than Liverpool, Auntie dear. I went to see the farm where Papa was born. I just had a yen. I've been back for weeks but haven't been feeling well. Now shall I come in for that cup of tea or not? I have some news you might be interested in.'

Esther opened the gate and they went inside. Hannah was coming down the stairs as they walked up the lobby and Rebekah was certain she had been spying on them through the upstairs window.

'So thee's back, is thee?' said the maid, giving the shiny knob at the bottom of the stairs a vigorous rub with a duster. 'Just like a bad penny, thou is.'

'I'm pleased to see you, too, Hannah. Killed anybody's character lately?' She smiled.

'What's that?' said the maid, glaring at her. 'I ain't killed nobody. Thee and thee arsenic. Miss Esther's very well.'

'What's this?' said Esther, looking startled.

Rebekah pulled on her arm. 'It's a joke which Hannah didn't get. Let's go and sit down. That knee's still hurting you, I see. I'll have to get you out and about before I won't be able to fit behind the steering wheel.'

'What do you mean?' said her aunt.

Rebekah told her that she could be having a baby.

'But that's lovely!' Esther flung her arms around her. 'I do hope it's a boy.'

Rebekah agreed that a boy would be acceptable.

'Thou'll know thee's born when thee gives birth,' said Hannah, smiling. 'Aye! Thee'll know, me girl.'

Rebekah laughed and wondered just what reception Joshua would give her news.

Startled but pleased, his pale blue eyes fixed on Rebekah's face, and he paused in the act of fastening the last button of his shirt. 'You're having a baby? Well, it's about time! I knew I could do it but I was starting to wonder about you. You've seen the doctor?'

'Yes. It's early days but he's sure I am.' She wished she had the courage to tell him that it was Daniel's child and to wipe the smile off his face.

He sat next to her on the bed, putting his arm round her, and kissed her cheek. 'We'll have to look after you now.'

'Yes. You'll have to be careful,' murmured Rebekah. 'I mean, it might be best – safer – if we don't have relations for a while. I've heard that you can lose a baby that way.' She did her best to infuse regret into her voice.

He frowned. 'Did the doctor say that?'

'Yes.' She smiled and deliberately rested a hand on his trousered thigh. 'I'll need some money.'

His fair brows rose. 'For baby clothes? Don't you think it's a bit early?'

She opened her eyes wide. 'For clothes for me, Joshua. I'm going to grow out of everything I've got and you don't want me looking a frump, do you?'

To her surprise Joshua reddened. 'Of course not. But you won't go buying them in shops,' he said gruffly. 'You'll have them made. There was a woman my sister used to have call. I'll find you her address.' He rose and went over to the walnut dressing table and unlocked a drawer. He came back over to her. She suffered his kiss as he pressed money into her hand and a piece of paper. 'Treat yourself to something nice, Rebekah. Flowers or chocolates. Some new perfume, perhaps? Anything you like.'

She thanked him, although she considered it no more than her due, and planned to save some of it. She would see Brigid, though, and take her out for a slap up meal where she could tell her all her troubles and hope she did not say: 'I told you so!'

'Yer like a bad penny,' said Brigid in a non-nonsense voice but with eyes suspiciously bright. 'Yer keep turning up just when I think I've got rid of yer.' With unnecessary briskness she dusted some non-existent crumbs off the damask cloth on the table between them.

'Hannah said I was a bad penny,' murmured Rebekah. 'I think she still has her eye on my aunt's money.'

Brigid smiled. 'She didn't like me arriving bearing news. She'd rather yer'd just vanished from the face of the earth.'

'I could get a complex,' said Rebekah, looking up from the menu. 'Shaun turned up at the farm after I'd written to you. And, of course, you know how he feels about me.'

'I was wondering when we'd get round to why you're home. Tell me what happened?'

Rebekah told her everything, including what she had not mentioned in the letter.

Brigid's expression was severe. 'Yer're a right pair of sinners and I don't know how many "Hail Marys" yer'd have to say to get yerself forgiveness out of all this.'

'I don't blame you for saying that,' sighed Rebekah. 'Sometimes I wonder if it was really me doing all those things. But I love him and he loved me.'

'And having said that,' said Brigid, 'you think it excuses everything?'

'No. But I'm paying for my sins.'

Brigid shook her head. 'I bet.' She was quiet a moment then said, 'I find it hard to believe that Daniel would just up and leave yer without a word. Although he had every right to be mad with you for lying through your eye teeth.'

'I didn't lie,' said Rebekah with the smallest of smiles. 'I just didn't tell the truth. It was so difficult because Joshua and Daniel hate each other, and we were so happy.' She leaned on one elbow. 'I've thought a lot since being back in Liverpool and wonder now whether Daniel would have come back? Although I can't stop thinking of how he looked when I told him about being married.'

'It's a hard thing for a man to stomach,' said Brigid. 'But I'm inclined to think that it's all down to Shaun, Daniel's going. They must have left together. Weren't there any clues?'

'Clues?'

'Yes! All the best mysteries have clues. Look at Sherlock Holmes and that new writer, Agatha Christie! What was the last thing that Daniel said to yer about Shaun?'

Rebekah considered. 'Not much. Something about him still hanging around, and Daniel not wanting to talk to him.'

Brigid's face brightened. 'There yer are then! He might not have wanted to go with him, but perhaps he had to. You mentioned the troopers – '

Rebekah put down the menu and was silent for several moments. 'I have considered that the troopers or the Irregulars captured him, but I don't like thinking like that. I'd rather he'd just left me than have to start believing all over again that – that he might have been shot by one side or the other.'

Brigid squeezed her hand. 'Don't be thinking of any of it. Yer don't know what's happened. Maybe yer'll see him again?'

Rebekah nervously twisted a strand of hair round her finger. 'I haven't told you all of it – I'm having a baby.'

There was a brief silence before Brigid said, 'Well, there's nothing so surprising about that. Whose do yer think it is?'

'I'm pretty sure it's Daniel's.'

'I wouldn't let his lordship hear yer say that.'

Rebekah gave a tight smile. 'I'm not a complete idiot.' She picked up the menu. 'Now what are we going to have to eat? You can have anything your heart desires.'

Brigid's expression was suddenly upset. 'Oh, Becky, luv, yer really worry me sometimes! Where will it all end?'

She pulled a face. 'I don't know. We'll just have to hope for the best. What are you having?'

Brigid sighed, ordered roast beef and Yorkshire pudding, and changed the subject to talk about Joe and her family, adding that Patrick had been home, had met a girl in Australia and was talking of settling down there. Rebekah was surprised but pleased and wished him all the luck in the world.

The meeting with Brigid made Rebekah feel more settled and although Daniel was never far from her thoughts and she had a continuous aching regret for what might have been, she looked forward to the baby's birth.

Two items of news out of Ireland almost destroyed her determination to get on with life as hopefully as possible. These were the reported deaths of Arthur Griffiths from an apoplexy and the shooting of Michael Collins in an ambush. If Daniel had been captured by the troopers and was in prison, there could be reprisals for the death of such a prominent leader as Collins. For days she fretted but gradually accepted that she was not doing herself or the baby any good.

The months passed slowly and Joshua, who had been irritable at first due to his enforced celibacy, seemed to grow resigned to Rebekah's unavailability. There were days when he arrived home extremely late but Rebekah asked him no questions. He often talked of 'my son' and of the child inheriting Green's one day.

Just before Christmas the death by firing squad of Liam Mellows, who had been at Four Courts, was reported. His was not the first Irregular's death Rebekah had read about but it affected her deeply as the baby was moving inside her. She did not want to think of death when life was so precious. She wished so many things could have been different and that she knew definitely what had happened to Daniel. The Civil War dragged on despite the Irish gaols being full to overflowing with prisoners.

270

The New Year came and went and the pile of tiny garments, that Rebekah and her aunt were making grew to ridiculous proportions as April approached.

'There won't be enough days in the week for the poor thing to wear all these,' said Edwina, when Rebekah showed her the deep drawers full.

Rebekah eased her back. 'I'm making sure I'm well prepared. I feel so enormous that I'm sure this baby's twins and they're playing football.'

Edwina sighed. 'All mums-to-be feel huge at the end. Have you decided whether to be confined at home or in hospital? More mums are opting for a hospital birth these days – nice and sanitary.'

'Joshua says home.' Rebekah grimaced. 'I'm to have the doctor and a nurse afterwards. I must admit to feeling more than a bit nervous. Is it as painful as they say? Because the doctor says that I can have an injection of scopolamine and morphine if the pains get bad.'

'Twilight sleep. I've read about it in a brochure.' Edwina sat on the rocking chair and looked up at Rebekah. 'It's said to shorten labour and help with the milk.'

'Then you think it's worth trying?'

Edwina said softly. 'If things get bad, you'll beg for it.'

Rebekah paled and put a hand over her swollen stomach. 'I'll bear anything as long as he doesn't die.'

'Not as many babies do die these days. But you're sure it's going to be a boy?'

Rebekah laughed suddenly. 'Girls don't play football.'

Edwina smiled. 'There'll come a day when nothing will stop us women doing anything we want.'

'I still think you're a suffragette at heart,' said Rebekah, still smiling as she shut the drawer. 'Come and have a cup of tea.'

Edwina rose from the chair and they went downstairs arm in arm.

Two days later Rebekah went into what she called premature labour and there was no time for twilight sleep. She gave birth to a six pound fourteen ounce son, and a smiling Joshua came into the room as the baby was laid in her arms. 'Michaels says it's a boy.'

'He's beautiful!' A sore but not too exhausted Rebekah marvelled as she gazed into the red little face with the screwed up eyes.

'He's ugly and dark-haired!' exclaimed Joshua, his smile fading slightly. 'I thought he'd be fair – and he hasn't the Greens' nose.'

The nurse looked up at him as she folded a towel. 'I've seen babies with hair as dark as dark can be, sir, end up as fair as Goldilocks. First lot of hair often falls out.'

'I see.' He sat on the edge of the bed and touched the baby's cheek. 'He has blue-grey eyes, though?'

'Yes. But eyes can change colour.'

'Good God!' Joshua stared at the baby. 'I hope he doesn't change into a girl,' he said with deliberate humour.

The nurse smiled condescendingly. 'Now that would be a miracle! It's a fine boy you've got there.'

'He's lovely,' said Rebekah, her arms tightening protectively about her son, and hiding her expression from Joshua. 'Thank you, nurse, for everything. And I must thank Doctor Michaels. I didn't have chance to do so before.'

The nurse smiled. 'He said you were a woman of good sense. No screeching, and you did as you were told.'

Joshua looked gratified. 'I should hope no wife of mine would kick up a fuss. But well done, dear.' He kissed Rebekah's forehead. 'I'll leave you with nurse now and go and phone the good news to a few people.' He added with unaccustomed consideration, 'If you don't mind, I might need to go out for a while?'

'Don't worry about me,' said Rebekah cheerfully. 'I'll be glad to rest.'

'Of course.' He waggled his fingers in her direction before disappearing behind the open door.

Nurse and Rebekah smiled at each other. 'Best place for husbands, out of the way,' said the nurse. 'Now let me take baby and you have your rest.'

Reluctantly Rebekah handed over her child and relaxed against the pillows. Thank God for nurse! But was it true that eyes could change colour? She did not allow the question to plague her. At least she had been safely delivered of Daniel's son. She wondered what he would do if he knew about his child. For a moment she was sad and then her gaze wandered to the baby's crib, and turning over carefully, she was asleep in minutes.

Chapter Twenty-Four

Rebekah's son was christened Adam Joshua David, and as soon as she was fit and Brigid had a day off, she wheeled him in his pram to call on her friend.

'He's gorgeous,' said Brigid, a dreamy expression on her face as she rocked the wide-eyed baby who was sucking his fist.

Rebekah smiled. 'You'll have to get one of your own.'

Brigid turned pink. 'I'll get married first. What does Joshua think of him?'

'He's as proud as Punch.' Rebekah sat in a chair, unbuttoned her blouse and held out her arms for her child. 'Although he still doesn't like David's hair being black. He wants it fair and so it should be fair.' She began to suckle the baby, looking down at him with a gentle expression on her face.

Brigid sat opposite her. 'But David has blue eyes. Isn't he happy with that?'

'They're changing colour,' said Rebekah quietly. 'They're going darker.'

'Oh!' Brigid looked into the baby's face. 'What does he think about that?'

'He hasn't said anything.' She rubbed her cheek against the baby's downy head.

'Perhaps he hasn't noticed?'

'Nurse remarked on it in front of him.'

Brigid's face clouded. 'Do yer think he has any suspicions?"

'If he has he's keeping them to himself for the moment. Just as I kept quiet my suspicions of his going with prostitutes when I was expecting. I discovered some rubber sheaths inside a pair of his socks and he was often out in the evenings. With that sort of woman, he'd be scared of catching something.'

Her friend frowned. 'He hasn't been violent, has he?'

'Raised his hand and his voice.' Rebekah lifted her head. 'He doesn't like the baby crying. Nor does he like me breast feeding. He goes on about me putting David on the bottle but I have nurse on my side.' A smile lifted her mouth. 'She says mother's breast is best and it really embarrasses him.'

'He's jealous of yer giving all yer attention to the baby. But as long as he doesn't suspect that David is Daniel's.'

Rebekah's arm tightened about her son. 'If he attempts to hurt David, I couldn't stay with him. At the moment I'm resigned to living with him, but there might come a time – '

'Well, yer know what to do if things get tough.'

Rebekah's eyes softened. 'I'm a real trial to you, aren't I, love?'

'Yer a right nuisance,' said Brigid in a gruff voice. 'I'll make us a cup of tea.'

Rebekah smiled and no more was said on the subject of Joshua.

David thrived and Rebekah did most things for him except his washing. She found caring for him a joy but worried when Joshua played with him. Sometimes her husband would pick David up, gaze into his face, then toss him into the air. She would hold her breath and start forward because he did not put out his arms to catch the child until he almost reached the ground. Twice she spoke to Joshua sharply and he turned on her. 'Do you think I would drop my own son?'

'No,' she said quietly, conscious of the aggression in his voice.

Often Rebekah was aware of Joshua's eyes on her when she was nursing the baby, and she tensed, waiting for him to make some comment but he never did and she could only feel relief when he took himself off somewhere. The weeks passed and she was as happy as she ever could be parted from Daniel.

It was one May day when Rebekah had been to visit Brigid and was walking home, that Mr McIntyre called to her, waving a newspaper: 'The Civil War's over!'

A smile spread over her face. 'That's good news.'

'Well, everything's been going to pieces, hasn't it?' He leaned on the gate. 'They'll have to sort something workable out.'

Rebekah thought of Daniel. 'Peace in Ireland,' she murmured. 'It seems almost unbelievable.'

'Aye, well, people can't be fighting forever.' He grinned. 'Are you coming in for a cup of tea?'

'Thanks but I better hadn't. I want to call in on my aunt and then I'll have to rush home. I've been out all afternoon.'

He looked disappointed. 'Perhaps next time?'

'Yes.' She waved her hand and went on her way.

Esther was pleased to see her and the baby. 'Where's my precious little boy?' she cooed over the pram. 'Can I have a hold of him?'

'You're precious little boy is wet,' said Rebekah promptly. 'I'll have to change him.'

For a moment her aunt's face showed distaste then she smiled. 'He can't help it, the little love. I'll get Hannah to make us a cup of tea. Then I want to talk to thee, Rebekah.'

She looked at her aunt, wondering what Hannah had been up to this time, but Esther's conversation had nothing to do with the maid.

'I've made a will, Rebekah, and I'm leaving all my money to your son. I know thee must be wondering why I haven't left it to thee, but – ' Her aunt paused and her mouth tightened. 'I'm not the fool thy husband thinks me. I'm not chancing him getting his hands on it – which he might if I left it to thee. I've tied it up so he won't be able to touch it.'

'Good for you, Aunt Esther!' Rebekah could not be annoyed with her, although expectations of her aunt's money had occasionally figured in her own plans. She balanced her half naked son on her hip, rose from her seat and kissed her aunt. 'You can't realise how happy it makes me. At least he'll be secure.'

Esther flushed and said unsteadily, 'Thou might have thy faults, Rebekah, but I've watched thee and thou loves the baby and hast the makings of a good mother. Even Hannah has admitted that and she knows about such things. Sarah would have been proud of thee. If only Papa had lived to see this great-grandson of his, he too would have been proud.'

Rebekah did not know what to say so kissed her aunt again.

She was smiling when she left the house but as she neared the park her expression became sombre. She dreaded facing Joshua. He had started pawing her in bed but she had continued to bind herself underneath, telling him that the bleeding after the birth had not stopped. Surely it would not be long before he realised that she was pretending?

His car was in front of the house but Janet opened the door. 'Mr Green's upstairs,' she answered in response to Rebekah's question.

'Is he in a good mood,' she whispered.

'The cat's in hiding,' muttered Janet. 'That says something.'

Rebekah grimaced. 'Where's Nurse?'

'Gone,' said Janet succinctly.

'Gone where?'

'Gone for good.' Janet jerked her head upwards. 'The master told her to pack her bags and paid her off.'

Rebekah felt a sudden chill. David whimpered. 'Has my husband mentioned anything happening to one of his ships?'

'Never a word. And there's nothing in the *Echo*.'

Rebekah gnawed her lower lip. 'Open the back gate and I'll go into the garden.'

She wheeled the pram round and settled herself in a chair. As she fed David, she gazed unseeingly at the mermaid figurehead, wondering what the dismissal of the nurse meant. Was it money, or was there some deeper reason behind her being sent off?

There was a sound at the french windows and she turned and saw Joshua. He lit a cheroot and came slowly towards her. 'Nurse has gone.'

'Janet told me.'

She determined not to ask why but he answered her unspoken question. 'I didn't see why you needed help with the boy. You spend enough time with him yourself.'

'That's all right.' She flashed him a smile. 'I'll manage. When I was on Outdoor Relief I saw women coping with five and six children without help.'

'Slum children,' he said disparagingly.

Rebekah stared at him. 'I thought you cared about the children and the work of the Seamen's Orphanage?'

His eyes narrowed against the smoke. 'I was taught that it was my duty to show an interest. My father also told me that a man often has to grin and bear things.'

'Men aren't the only ones,' she murmured.

'What's that mean?' He scowled. 'What have you to complain about?'

'Did I complain?'

'It sounded like a complaint.' He looked disgruntled. 'If anyone has cause for complaint, it's me. You're always cuddling that baby. He'll be spoilt. It's not good for children to be picked up all the time.' He moved suddenly and wrenched David out of her arms. The child gave a startled whimper as he was dragged from her breast and she cried with pain and attempted to regain possession of him.

'I'm feeding him,' she said angrily. 'Be careful of that cigar!'

'You're always feeding him,' growled Joshua, pressing David against him and staring at her bared breast. 'There's never any time for me.'

'You'd rather he starved?' She pulled together the edges of her blouse.

'Go on, cover yourself up! Never anything for me these days!'

She looked away from him. 'You wanted a baby.'

'Yes, I did. But I didn't expect it to take you over. Another woman would have been happy to leave it all to the nurse, but not you. You're going to have to learn that I won't put up with it for ever. You can put him to bed now and give me some of your time. And by the way, I've moved his crib out of our room.' He offered David to her then feigned dropping him as she put out her arms.

She caught him quickly. 'Why do you do that?' she said in a seething voice. 'One of these days – '

'One of these days I might drop him, were you going to say?' muttered Joshua, stubbing out his cheroot on the place the mermaid would have had a bottom if she did not have a tail. 'Maybe not if you put him on the bottle and give me some of what he's been getting.'

She flushed. 'I want to feed him myself. He's my son!'

'He might be yours but is he mine?' Joshua lit another cheroot.

'What's that supposed to mean?' Rebekah's voice was cool despite her heart's beginning to race.

'His eyes are changing colour. If I believed – '

'Believed what?'

'He doesn't look like me.'

'He's only a baby.' She placed David in his pram.

'I've often heard people say "Doesn't he look like his father?" of babies.' His eyes glinted. 'And there's another thing. I don't like you calling him David.'

She was ready for that one. 'I prefer it to Adam. Papa and I weren't always on the best of terms.'

'I suppose you prefer David because it's the nearest you dare get to Daniel?' he snapped.

She stared at him, thinking how often she stopped on the brink of an argument. She did so now, saying in a controlled voice: 'David was the old testament hero – and eventually a king. I thought it fitting.'

His face reddened. 'You're pushing your luck, Rebekah. I know my Bible. I'm still king of this castle, not that child. It's something you forget.'

'How could I? You lord it over me whenever you can.'

'I'm your husband! I have rights.' He tossed his cheroot in a flower bed and before she could think of moving away, seized hold of her arms and thrust his face close to hers. 'What were you doing in Ireland last summer? Why did you really go? Did you soothe any rebels' brows? O'Neill's for instance?' It was so sudden that Rebekah could not think what to say for a moment. 'Well?' he demanded.

For a moment she was tempted to fling the truth in his face but commonsense asserted itself. She had David's safety to consider. 'Is this some sick joke? You told me Daniel was dead. Has he suddenly come alive again?'

For a moment he was silent, his fingers digging into her upper arms, then he muttered. 'Put the boy to bed. I want some of your attention for a change.'

Rebekah did as she was told, dreading the hours ahead, but it was not as bad as she feared. A business acquaintance of Joshua's called and the men talked shipping and the slump in trade while the level in a bottle of whisky fell. Rebekah slipped away to feed David and stayed in the nursery. She was still there, gazing out of the open window over the moonlit garden, when Joshua came and stood in the doorway.

'Why aren't you in bed? You should be in bed.' His words were slurred.

'I'm coming.' Rebekah tried to inch past him but he took hold of her and pulled her close. Whisky fumes fanned her cheek and she recoiled. 'How much have you drunk?'

'Not enough not to know what to do with you. You should have had a drink with us, my sweet. The alcohol might make you more friendly.'

'I didn't want a drink,' she murmured, trying to free herself. 'But if it's what makes you happy.'

'I'm not happy.' He swayed as he clung to her and said against her ear, 'You could make me happy if you – ' He whispered a suggestion.

'No!' She tried to pull away but he kept hold of her.

'You did it when we were first married! You did! You did!' he cried petulantly.

Anger stirred inside her. 'Only because you forced me. I'm not doing it now! Now let me go before you wake the baby.'

'Damn and blast the baby,' he shouted, shaking her. 'I've been patient, staying away from you, and now I want what's my right!'

'Keep your voice down,' stuttered Rebekah. 'Do you want to wake the whole neighbourhood?'

'I damn' well don't care!' He slapped her across the face.

Her hand went to her cheek and there was a churning inside her. 'Don't you hit me!'

'And how are you going to stop me?' he sneered.

She kicked his ankle and they began to struggle. He yelled insults at her and she screeched at him, not caring what she said but fighting like one demented, hating him for all he had put her through. The baby's crying brought her back to her senses. 'Now look what you've done,' she panted. 'Let me go to him.'

'No! Let me!' Joshua pushed her against the wall and went over the crib. He snatched up David and went over to the open window and held him out.

Rebekah screamed and darted across the room, hovering around Joshua, terrified to touch him. 'Don't drop him! Please, don't drop him!'

He glanced over his shoulder and there was a triumphant look on his face. 'What'll you give me if I don't?'

She did not hesitate. 'Anything!'

'What I asked before?'

She nodded.

'Give me your word. I don't trust you.'

'I swear it.'

He brought the baby in and gave him to Rebekah. David's screams turned to whimpers as she hushed and rocked him.

'Just put him in his crib,' ordered Joshua, still smiling.

Rebekah wondered if her husband was quite sane to do such a thing but was still too shocked to attempt further rebellion at the moment.

She performed the act Joshua desired, disliking it and him. She vowed that it was for the last time. The risk to David in staying with Joshua was more than she could cope with. Tomorrow she would leave.

The next morning, Janet asked if she was all right, looking with some concern at the bruising on her face. Rebekah did not want to involve her so she just answered that she felt a little unwell and asked her to do the shopping. With the maid out of the way she hoped that there would be nobody concerned enough about her to notice her leaving.

It was no easy task choosing what to take. When she had left for Ireland it had been a simple matter of packing as suitcase for herself. Now she had all the baby's paraphernalia to think about. She loaded her car. It was a struggle and she could not find room for the crib, but the rest she managed with the help of a couple of boys playing in the park. Then she sat in the driving seat a moment while the enormity of what she was doing overwhelmed her. Then, vividly, like something on a screen she pictured Joshua's face as he held David out of the window and she drove off.

Rebekah arrived at Brigid's home just before noon, not expecting to find her friend in but hoping her sister might be there. Not that she had ever been able to get close to Kath.

'I hope you don't mind but could I come in and wait for Brigid?' Despite all her efforts Rebekah's voice trembled.

Kath frowned. 'I suppose yer'd better.'

281

Rebekah felt the colour rise in her cheeks. 'If you'd rather I didn't – I could come back.'

'No. Come in.' Her eyes narrowed as she scrutinised Rebekah's face. 'You look like yer've been in the wars but I'm not going to ask questions. I'm doing the ironing. Our Brigid'll sort yer out.' Her glance passed over the loaded car. 'I'll help yer with the pram and then yer can take it round the back with the baby in.' Rebekah thanked her, hoping that Brigid would not be long.

The children came in first and Veronica fussed over the baby. Brigid was soon after them. 'What is it, Becky luv? I didn't expect to see yer this soon.' She looped her handbag over the door knob and pulled off her gloves. 'Come in the other room and tell me what happened?'

Rebekah told her.

Brigid's mouth tightened. 'The pig! What are yer going to do? Mam'll say that there's a place here as long as yer need it, but it's not what yer used to and I won't always be here.' She toyed with a button on her dress. 'Joe and I have decided to get married at the end of July.'

Rebekah smiled. 'I'm glad for you both. And I'm not planning on staying for ever. Just until I find my feet. I'd have gone to Aunt Esther's only that would be the first place Joshua would look for me. After that it would be Edwina's.'

'He won't think of coming here?' said Brigid.

Rebekah hesitated. 'I don't think he knows that I'm still friends with you.'

'Hmmph! You never know. You'll have to be careful.'

That night David slept in a drawer while Rebekah shared Brigid's double bed. It took some time for Rebekah to sleep as her mind was trying to formulate plans for hers, and David's future. The trouble was that there was a great big 'if' over the weeks and months ahead.

The next few days Rebekah discovered what hard work it really was looking after a baby without nurse's help. Dealing with nappies and wet bedding with no running hot water was a never ending chore, although there was a certain satisfaction in seeing the washing blowing on the line in the yard despite the smuts it collected. But it was not all work and she enjoyed taking David for his walk. She was often stopped by women in the street who, talking nonsense to her son, made comments about his dark curls. In return he favoured a few with a toothless smile.

Ma Maisie doled her out a share of the household tasks and often asked Rebekah to do the shopping. She had some money of her own and would sometimes buy a special treat for the supper table as well as contributing to expenses. It was while shopping that she came out of a shop about a week after leaving Joshua to find the pram with David in it missing. She tried not to panic, but after scouring the road, shops and sidestreets, her anxiety was pitiful. She ran home to Kath and poured out what had happened. She alerted the neighbours and they joined the search but came back empty-handed.

The local bobby was informed and asked Rebekah some pertinent questions about her married status. When she said that she had left her husband, he proved to be unsympathetic. 'Maybe you should go home, Missus,' he said, closing his book. 'Perhaps the little lad's there.'

The idea that Joshua might have snatched David had been at the back of her mind since she had discovered him missing but the thought of returning to his house had caused her to search every other avenue first. Now she had to face facts. Somehow her husband had guessed where she was hiding. Fearing that he might do something to David and not waiting for Brigid to come home, Rebekah got in the car and drove to her former home.

Joshua opened the door to her. 'I want my son,' she demanded, burning flags of colour high on her cheeks. 'What have you done with him?'

His mouth curved in a smile that did not affect the chill light in his eyes. 'Rebekah! I was expecting you. Do come in?'

'I don't want to come in. I want David!'

He scowled. 'I'm not having a wrangling match with you on the doorstep for the neighbours and passers-by to listen to. Haven't you embarrassed me enough, leaving me the way you did? I won't tell you anything unless you come inside. No! Come round the back first.'

Rebekah glared but accompanied him. 'Is David out in the garden in his pram?'

'You'll see,' he said.

She saw all right. No pram but he had chopped off the head of Andromeda. 'Is this another sick joke of yours?' she demanded after several seconds. 'Where is my baby?'

'You don't like it? I think she looks better. Come and have a drink and I will explain all.' He took her elbow and hustled her inside and into the sitting room. 'Do sit down.' He pushed her on the sofa and went over to the drinks cabinet. 'A brandy for your nerves?'

'There's nothing wrong with my nerves.' she retorted, clasping her hands tightly to stop herself from hitting him.

A cup of tea, then?' He rang the bell and a maid entered and took his order. She glanced curiously at Rebekah.

'Where's Janet?' asked Rebekah as soon as she was out of the room.

'I decided to dispense with her services.' He opened a cigar box and offered it to her, sighing heavily when she shook her head. 'I'm sorry,' he murmured. 'I forgot that you didn't. I suppose the tea will help to calm you down.'

'Seeing my son will calm me down.' She rose her feet. 'Is he upstairs? I'll go to him.'

Joshua blocked her way. 'A waste of time. He's not there.'

'Let me see.' She tried to go round him but he only moved with her.

'Believe me, Rebekah, he isn't in the house!' His tone was emphatic.

She stared at him. 'How did you find him? Where is he? What have you done to him?'

'A letter from your common friend inside one of your books.' He exhaled a fragrant cloud. 'The boy's in a safe place. An orphanage actually.'

'I don't believe you,' she stammered. 'Why would you – '

Joshua smiled. 'Why indeed? But don't you think his father might still be alive? Or perhaps he's really dead now?'

Rebekah was silent.

Joshua's left eyelid twitched rapidly and the cheroot smouldered between his lips as he spoke jerkily. '*You* might say his father is very much alive. That I am the father! I would like to believe you, my dear, but – ' He cleared his throat. 'I'm going to Ireland. Someone in that Godforsaken village must have seen something. I have a photograph of O'Neill. Money talks. If he was there – ' He paused expectantly. 'You could save me a journey, Rebekah.'

'And you could tell me the truth.' She was trying her hardest to keep calm. 'Where is my baby?'

Joshua's fist curled and it was obvious that he was struggling for control as much as she was. 'The truth, my sweet, my love, is that you are an adulteress and as such must pay for your sins. Your son, as I said, is in an orphanage.'

Before she could speak there was a knock on the door and Joshua answered it, taking the cup from the maid, shutting the door and turning the key in the lock as Rebekah moved towards the door.

'Joshua, you're crazy!' She clenched her fists. 'Unlock that door. This isn't Victorian times, you know! Let me out!'

He smiled and pocketed the key. 'I'm the king of the castle, remember? You should think before you act.'

She moistened her mouth. 'Joshua, you can't keep me here.'

He said quietly. 'Drink your tea. I'm going to have a brandy.'

'Dear God,' she cried, 'I don't want tea! I don't want brandy! I want my son!'

'The good Lord would agree with what I'm doing,' said her husband, pouring out a generous measure of spirit. 'You're a wicked woman. Drink your tea before it gets cold.'

'You hypocrite! What about you and your prostitutes?'

'It's different for men.'

Her eyes glittered. 'The old excuse! Will you tell me where David is?'

'I might if you calm down and drink your tea.'

She stared at him and then sat down, picking up her cup. 'Well?'

'Well what?' He swirled the brandy, watching her.

'Where's David?' Her mouth was dry so she drank the tea.

'I've told you – I'm not going to have him back here, Rebekah. I'll tell people that he died and that grief turned your brain.'

Suddenly she could not believe that it was all happening. It must be a nightmare. She stared at him as he took a large mouthful of brandy. 'I loved you once, Rebekah. We could have been happy but you turned against me.'

She was starting to feel strange and hysteria rose inside her. 'You caused me to turn against you! You were cruel and you lied to me.'

'Lied to you about what?' He started forward.

'Daniel! You cheated, and cheats never prosper!' She put her hands to hot cheeks. 'This is crazy!'

'No!' Suddenly his face loomed in front of her, large and grotesque. 'It's you that's crazy and I know just the place for you. Only the best asylum for my wife, so it's expensive. If you're good I'll probably let you out in a few months' time. By that time your son will have been put up for adoption.'

'Adoption!' Horror seemed to be paralysing Rebekah's limbs but she managed to fling the cup at him. It hit him on the forehead and then smashed in the fireplace.

'Violence now.' He smiled and tutted. She threw the saucer at his now double image, saw him sidestep before it, too, shattered into pieces. The last words she heard him speak seemed to freeze her mind. 'I think I'll tell the man to bring a straightjacket for you. We didn't need one for poor Emma.'

'She's coming round.' It was a voice Rebekah did not recognise.

She lifted heavy lids and stared up at Joshua and the stranger. 'There now, Mrs Green, you're all right,' he said with a smile.

'David! Where's David? He said – ' Rebekah sat up abruptly. 'Who are you?' She realised that she was lying on top of the bed in the room upstairs. 'Why am I here? Have you taken David away?' she said unsteadily.

'I'm Doctor Gail, and you fainted.'

'I never faint. He must have put something in my tea. My baby!' Her voice broke on a sob. 'Where's my baby?'

The two men exchanged glances and Joshua said in sober tones, 'See what I mean, Doctor, she won't accept the truth.'

Rebekah's eyes sparkled with unshed tears. 'You don't know the meaning of truth! Where's Doctor Michaels?'

'Michaels is away,' said Doctor Gail. 'I'm standing in for him.' He sat on the chair beside the bed and took Rebekah's hand. 'My dear Mrs Green, I'm sorry but your baby is dead.'

'No!' She stared at Joshua. 'My husband stole David from me, to punish me.'

The heavy features of the doctor were sorrowful. 'I've seen your baby. Believe me, he's dead.'

Rebekah had thought she could not feel any worse but she did. 'I don't believe it.' Her mouth quivered. 'Let me see the body.'

'Certainly, Mrs Green, but are you sure this is wise?' His expression was sympathetic. 'It will upset you.'

Rebekah started to wonder if she was going mad. Surely she could not have imagined what had happened between her and Joshua downstairs? She darted a glance at her husband.

'My sweet, you can see the body if you like,' he said gently.

His words scared her but she slid off the bed, unaided.

Joshua attempted to take her elbow but she pushed him away. 'Show me this baby.'

Joshua shrugged and led the way downstairs. Rebekah followed, accompanied by a grave-faced Doctor Gail. At first sight of the baby in the tiny coffin, Rebekah felt faint. Had her husband killed her son? It was a few moments before she dared take a closer look. 'That's not David,' she stated in a relieved voice. 'This baby has fair hair. My husband is trying to trick you.'

'My dear Mrs Green, why should he do that? You're overwrought.' Doctor Gail put his arm about her shoulders. 'The maid said it's your baby and he's got a look of your husband. Grief has affected your mind and so you refuse to accept the truth.'

Rebekah shrugged off his arm and turned on him. 'How could that maid know? She's never seen my baby! Find Janet or nurse! They'd tell you I'm telling the truth.' She saw that he did not believe her, and despaired. She slammed a hand down on the side of the coffin. 'I don't know where my husband found this child but it is not mine! It is not mine!'

'Calm down, dear,' said Joshua in a soothing voice. 'You're getting hysterical.'

'If I am, you're to blame!' She stared at him with wild eyes. 'Where is David? You told me an orphanage! Which orphanage?'

'I told you nothing of the sort. My dear, you're starting to imagine things.'

Rebekah's fists clenched and she tried to gain control of the anger and fear that was rising, rising, threatening to choke her. 'I am not! You're doing this deliberately, Joshua. You want me to suffer. You want to drive me mad.'

'My love, why should I do that?' His voice had that velvety note that she knew so well. 'I love you. I loved our son. Don't you think I'm upset because David's gone?'

'No! No!' She shook her head vehemently. 'You didn't love him and you've never really loved me. You don't want people you love hurt. Where is David? Where is my son?' On the last two words something snapped inside her and she flew at Joshua, hitting out at him with flailing fists. She wanted to smash his smirking face until there was nothing more of him left. He called the doctor and then she was struggling with both of them. Joshua held her face down on the floor. She felt a stabbing pain in her arm and then was swimming through cotton wool.

Chapter Twenty-Five

'It's quite a nice place. I'm sure you'll settle,' said Joshua in conversational tones.

Rebekah made no reply but attempted to free herself from the straightjacket.

'Emma was quite happy here,' he continued. 'The doctor's changed but this one seems quite decent. You'll have lots of sea air . . . nice grounds to wander round once you calm down. You can play tennis. There's a few books and a chapel. You'll be able to confess your sins to Almighty God and perhaps find forgiveness.' He smiled at her and began to peel an orange from the dish on the cream-painted beside cabinet. 'See, I'm not all bad. I've told them you're to have this private room for a few days – it's costing me a fortune but they would expect it from a man of my position. Then you can go into a general ward. I told them you'd probably like company.'

'I don't want company. I want to get out of here! I want my son.' Her voice shook.

'I notice you always say your son, never our son!' His hand tightened on the orange, and juice and flesh oozed between his fingers.

She tried to get a grip on herself and eased her dry throat and tried a different tack. 'Where did you get the baby from?'

'Baby? What baby?'

'You don't have to pretend with me, Joshua.' Her voice was controlled. 'You've been very crafty but you can tell me the truth.'

There was a silence while he took out a handkerchief and wiped his hand as she waited impatiently for an answer. 'You

289

can get anything if you're willing to pay for it. The mother was unmarried. I have influence in certain circles.'

'And where's David?' she said quietly.

'He became the dead baby, but I'm not going to tell you what its name was or where he is.' He leaned back in the chair with his legs stretched out before him. 'If you knew it would make it easier for you. Not knowing is always so much harder to bear. And the fact that you can't do anything makes it even better.'

Rebekah despaired. 'You're evil! Evil!'

His eyebrows rose. 'My dear, it's you who committed adultery, remember?' He leaned over and patted her cheek. 'I won't be seeing you for a couple of weeks. So sweet dreams until then.' And getting up, he left the room.

Rebekah wanted to scream and go on screaming. Her aching breasts were a reminder that somewhere someone else was feeding her son. She had known that Joshua would do something terrible if he ever guessed about her and Daniel, but never anything like this. But at least David was alive. Joshua had not killed him. If only she could get out of this place.

'There now, dear. Are you going to be good?' A buxom middle-aged attendant came in. Her companion, a fresh-faced young girl, smiled in a friendly fashion but Rebekah was too miserable, and also in too much pain, to care.

'My baby. My breasts hurt.'

'Poor lamb. He's in heaven now and as happy as Larry,' said the older attendant. 'You must accept God's will. There'll be other babies.'

'My baby isn't dead,' said Rebekah emphatically. 'And my breasts hurt because of the milk.'

'I know nothing about that,' said the woman. 'Never been married.'

'I do,' said the young girl in a slight Liverpudlian accent. 'My sister had milk fever. Perhaps Mrs Green has it.'

The woman sniffed. 'Have to get one of the nurses. You go, Ada.'

The girl went and returned with a nurse, who ordered the straightjacket taken off and examined Rebekah's breasts. She told her to express the milk herself and that would give her ease. The straightjacket was to stay off, but of course if she were to get violent again –

Rebekah turned her back on them and wept. They left the room, locking the door.

The next couple of days passed in a peculiar haze. A different doctor visited Rebekah and asked questions which she responded to by telling him that David was alive and in some Orphanage where her husband had put him. He spoke to her in a soothing voice, asking why he should do that? She hesitated to tell him, knowing the truth would probably make them side with Joshua. Her nerves grew so taut that she threw an orange at the doctor. He dodged it expertly and told the nurse to give her cold showers.

Rebekah hated the showers which seemed to numb her brain. She felt trapped as if on a bridge of barbed wire with a waterfall beneath, waiting to sweep her sanity away. Perhaps David really was dead and she was mad? Her thoughts raced like scampering squirrels, causing her to press her hands to her head in an attempt to stop them. She yearned for her baby, and desperately needed Daniel. The war was over. Perhaps he would come. If he still cared. If Brigid could get news about her being missing to him through his cousins. If – if – if! She wondered what Brigid had thought when she had not returned, and whether Joshua had told her aunt that David was supposedly dead. Dead! No, she did not believe he was dead as they all kept saying. Even though perhaps life would be easier for her if she said that she did believe it. But she could not accept that. Somewhere he was alive and she had to hold on to that thought. To get out and find him.

Rebekah was moved into one of the four general wards, which gave her something else to worry about. Fortunately men and women were kept separate but nearly all the other women patients were older than she, and preconceived ideas of lunacy filled her mind as she watched one approaching.

The woman stared at her, her tongue lolling on her chin like an overheated dog. She asked Rebekah what her name was. She answered in a flat tone and a minute later the woman repeated her question. This went on, interspersed by the singing of hymns and the cackling of laughter, hour after hour. It was maddening.

There was a woman who believed herself to be Queen Victoria, and gave Rebekah orders. 'Fetch me a cushion and be quick about it.' When she did not obey, the woman pushed her. 'Do as you are told, girl. I don't find your behaviour funny. Albert will see to it that you are punished.' Rebekah moved away but the woman followed her, repeating the order. In the end Rebekah pretended to do whatever she asked, even if it meant pouring out invisible tea and handing a cup to her. This, strangely, seemed to pacify her.

There were several younger women who suffered fits. At first these were frightening but Rebekah soon learnt that they were not to be feared and that the orderlies knew how to handle them, without anyone coming to harm. A couple of women of about her own age were suffering from melancholia, so the young Liverpudlian orderly told her. 'It's due to the war,' she said with concern. 'Poor things. They sunk so low into the doldrums that they haven't been able to drag themselves up again.'

Rebekah knew just how they felt. She was having difficulty keeping hope alive. She would never get out and would go mad, like those patients who never met her gaze but directed their conversations to an invisible someone behind her. They became angry when nobody answered them, or they were given wrong answers by real people, and got violent. They went missing for a few days then. She admitted her fears to the young orderly. 'I'm frightened of going mad.'

'Well, if you're only going, then you're not there,' said the girl in bracing tones.

Her words brought a smile to Rebekah's face. 'I'm on the edge. Do you think people can drive you mad?'

'Me mam was always saying that we drove her mad.'

'You live with your mam?'

The girl shook her head. 'I have a room in the village. It's nice and I enjoy having a room to meself.'   -

Rebekah forced herself to show interest. 'You have brothers and sisters?'

Ada nodded. 'You remind me of one of them. My sister who had milk fever. She was really strange for a while after losing Tommy, her baby. It was the midwife's fault. She came from a sickbed and didn't wash her hands. She's all right now. Had two more babies since. You'll be all right, given time.'

'My baby –' began Rebekah automatically, then stopped at the look in the girl's eyes, and after an inward struggle, continued the conversation. The girl was friendly and she could do with a friend. 'How did you come here?'

'I couldn't get work. Then I saw this advert in the newspaper and decided to have a go at it. I had an interview in Liverpool, and Bob's your uncle, here I am! It's not as bad as I thought – but maybe that's because most of them here aren't what you'd call really dangerous. They have money and because they're a bit soft in the head and can't look after themselves, their families put them in here.'

Rebekah said grimly, 'I don't think all the orderlies think like you. Some of them have no patience. I've seen Doris smacking some of the older ones.'

Ada's mouth tightened. 'Doris should keep her hands to herself! But you can get that way that you look on them like children who need disciplining.' Her expression softened. 'But you're not like that. You're here just for a rest, really. You've had a shock and you need time to get over it.'

'Is that what the doctor says?' Rebekah's voice was unsteady and for the first time in what felt like months she experienced a glimmer of hope.

Ada smiled. 'That's what I say! Now would you like to have a walk in the gardens? It looks like it's going to be a fine day.'

The fresh air did Rebekah good. The gardens were spacious and the flower beds bloomed. Life was real again. She was not going mad. She would get out and find David.

She kept saying the words to herself but as day slowly followed day with no change, and no visit from Joshua or word from anybody else, she struggled against feelings of panic. She asked for writing materials and wrote letters to her aunt, Brigid and Edwina, telling them what had happened, but they were returned to her without explanation.

Her anxiety became so great that remembering how Emma had escaped she tried to climb the locked iron gates but was spotted by one of the patients who was up a tree calling the birds. The attendants were alerted. Rebekah struggled but she was taken back to the house and confined. It was as if she had committed a crime and was in prison. She screamed to be let out but nobody took any notice of her and eventually she sank on to the floor, weeping.

When she was released Ada came to speak to her severely. 'You weren't half silly trying to get out. What was it that made you do a thing like that?'

'I'm mad,' said Rebekah, pushing back a strand of lank hair and staring at her. 'Don't you know.'

Ada sat beside her. 'No, you're not.'

Rebekah lifted her head. 'You say that but perhaps I am.' She paused. 'Has there been any news from my husband?'

'No, and they're annoyed about it. Payment's due.'

Rebekah stared at her with a mixture of uncertainty and hope. 'What will they do if he doesn't pay?'

Ada shrugged. 'Not sure. They might move you somewhere else.'

'Somewhere worse? Would you like to see that happen to me, Ada?' She grasped her hand. 'Or would you like to help me get out of here?'

'Help you get out?' Ada stared at her. 'You're not asking me to unlock the gates? I don't – '

'No, I wouldn't get you into trouble.' Rebekah smiled. 'But could you get me paper and an envelope on the sly? If I write a letter to a friend, will you post it?'

Relief slackened Ada's mouth. 'I don't mind doing that.'

'Thanks.' Rebekah laughed and hugged her.

Daniel's eyes scanned the page yet again and then he placed the letter on the table and looked at Brigid, pouring milk into two cups. He had been released from prison two days ago and a headline in a Dublin newspaper had brought him immediately to Liverpool, and Brigid, in the hope that she would help him to find out exactly where Rebekah was. He had not been disappointed because only that morning Brigid had received a letter from her. Such a letter that it made him want to weep. His hand shook slightly as he took the cup of tea from Brigid. 'I'll have to get that doctor.'

'It's terrible! All these weeks believing his lordship had taken her to Ireland when all the time she's been in a place like that!' Brigid hit the letter with her fist. 'Can you believe anyone could be so cruel as to put a dead baby – '

'I can believe anything of Green,' said Daniel, barely able to control his own anger. 'Where do we find this Dr Michaels?'

'Her aunt might have his address. We could try there.'

He nodded, gulped down his tea, impatient to be on his way. He placed his cup on the table. 'Drink up, Bridie.'

'I'll leave it,' she said with a sigh. 'I can see you're raring to go.' They went.

'Wicked! That's what it is! Wicked!' Rebekah's aunt sat ramrod straight in the armchair next to the fire, gazing up at him. 'Ireland! That's where I was told she was! And all the time – ' Words obviously failed her.

'We'll get her out,' said Daniel. 'If you could tell me Dr Michael's address?'

Her mouth trembled. 'I'm sorry, Mr O'Neill, I can't help thee. Reluctant as I am to suggest it, her friend Miss McIntyre might have the address.'

'Thank you.' Daniel held out his hand.

She hesitated and took it. 'Thou will find the boy and bring them both here?'

'I'll find him.'

'She nodded and called Hannah. 'See Mr O'Neill and the young woman out.'

The maid nodded, eyeing Daniel up and down with obvious satisfaction as she went before them up the lobby. 'I knew Miss Becky had someone in Dublin. Sinful, I calls it! And scandalous! But I suppose thee knows what thee's letting thyself in for if thee's known her that long. And I never did like that toffee-nosed husband of hers. Just get that baby back. We miss him.' She opened the door and shoed them out.

Daniel's eyebrows went up and Brigid giggled. 'Now yer've met her, yer'll never forget her! Come on. I think Miss McIntyre's house is only a few doors up.'

Edwina answered their knock and Daniel introduced himself.

'You're from Ireland,' she said, gazing at him with obvious interest. 'You'd best come in. Although I can tell you now, if you're looking for Rebekah, I don't know exactly where she is.'

'We know where she is, Miss McIntyre,' said Daniel, turning his hat between his hands. 'It's a doctor we want. A Dr Michaels – do you know where we can find him?'

'Is it a doctor you want for Rebekah because of what's happened to Joshua? I was just reading about his death in the *Daily Post*. I can tell you it gave me quite a shock.'

'I'm sure it did.' The news came as no surprise to Daniel. 'But your paper must have more information than the one I saw in Dublin.'

Edwina opened the door wider. 'Do come in and explain yourself. Even if it's only for a few minutes. You can read the report while I make a cup of tea.'

'No tea for me, said Daniel, smiling slightly. 'But Bridie would probably like one.'

Edwina shot Brigid a glance. 'Rebekah's spoken of you. It's nice to meet you,' she said politely. 'Do come in.'

They went in and Edwina handed Daniel the newspaper, placing a finger on a front page headline which blazoned: 'Local shipowner's body found in undergrowth on estate in Ireland'.

Brigid read the words over his shoulder in a muted voice. 'It says they think the body's been there a week.'

'He was shot several times,' said Edwina. 'It'll come as a shock to Rebekah. You say you know where she is, Mr O'Neill?'

'Yes.' He folded the paper and handed it back to her. 'She's in an asylum. He placed her there after stealing my son and putting him in an Orphanage.'

Edwina stared at him and then sat down abruptly 'I don't understand! Why *your* son? And Becky – she wasn't mad.'

'No!' exclaimed Brigid fiercely. 'But he was determined to drive her mad!'

Edwina made a helpless gesture. 'You'll have to explain properly. I know she didn't love Joshua but –' She paused and stared at Daniel, who stared back. 'She loved someone else who died – ' Her voice trailed off.

'The rumours of my death were greatly exaggerated by Mr Green,' said Daniel, smiling unexpectedly. 'Brigid will explain. You're Becky's friend so I don't think she'll mind you knowing the truth. If you can just tell me where I can find Dr Michaels?'

Edwina drew a long breath. 'Rodney Street. I can't remember the number but his name will be on the brass plate outside.' She stayed him with her hand. 'You said Joshua put your son in an orphanage? You do mean – David?'

He nodded.

'Oh, golly! Which one?'

'We don't know.' His mouth tightened. 'I had thought it might be the Seamen's Orphanage.'

'No,' she said, shaking her head. 'Becky told me that the children have to be at least seven years old.' Daniel swore softly and she gave him a look. 'That won't help. Your best bet is a church organised home. Quite a few run places for unmarried mothers. They take the babies and get them adopted. I – ' She stopped and stared at him, and he nodded. 'Golly! Was she with you in Ireland last year? You don't have to answer that! I'll give you the address of the place which, in my opinion, is your best bet. I remember the first time I heard Joshua's name, it was in connection with the orphanage where I placed my baby. I think he was on the board of guardians.' She reached for her handbag and took out a pencil and paper. She wrote down a name and address and handed it to him.

'Thanks,' said Daniel, and left Brigid to do the rest of the talking.

Rebekah was sitting in the asylum chapel, staring down at her hands. That morning she had done basket weaving and the sides of her fingers were sore from twisting cane. She was in a hopeful mood since Ada had posted her letter but had thought that a prayer or two would not go amiss. She laced her fingers, closed her eyes, and asserted all her will to get God on her side. She promised him all sorts of things if only he would get her out of this place.

There were footsteps and Rebekah turned to see one of the attendants, who looked extremely serious. 'You've got visitors, Mrs Green. The doctor said you were to come to his office at once.'

Rebekah was filled with apprehension but she scrambled to her feet and hurried after the nurse, hoping that Joshua had not returned. The corridors had always seemed long but now they seemed endless. The attendant pushed the door open and Rebekah entered a sunlit room.

Her gaze immediately fell on Daniel. She could scarcely believe that she was really seeing him. The beard was gone and he looked a little older. There really were grey hairs in his mop of curls this time – but it was Daniel! Her legs went weak and she had to put a hand on the back of a chair. He rushed forward and lowered her on to a seat, and his face came close to hers. 'I've come to get you out of here, love,' he murmured. 'I've told them I'm your Irish cousin. Understand?'

'Yes,' she whispered, although she did not, and clung to his hand, only taking her eyes off him when Dr Michaels spoke.

The doctor was looking sombre and came straight to the point. 'I had a talk with Dr Gail this afternoon and his description of the baby that died, that he said was yours, did not match the one I remembered. He was far too young for a start. Also I've been in touch with the nurse who tended you. We had a talk about your husband and his attitude towards your child. She mentioned things that convinced me that your husband was extremely jealous of the attention you gave to the baby, and she believes that this could have led him to act in a way that could cause suffering to you and your baby. I can see no reason for you to be kept here any longer.'

'Thank you,' said Rebekah in a quiet voice. 'But what about my husband? Where is he?'

The resident doctor leaned forward. 'Mrs Green, I would hesitate to tell you this news in other circumstances, but as it is, I have to inform you that your husband is dead.'

'Dead!' Rebekah moistened her lips and her gaze switched to Daniel's face for verification, also seeking something else though she did not find it.

His face was expressionless when he said gravely, 'It's true, Becky. He was shot on his estate in Ireland.' I take it that he believed because the civil war was officially over that it was safe for him to visit Ireland, but it wasn't because the fighting hasn't ceased. Some of the Irregulars have sworn to continue the struggle for an united Ireland free from all ties with England. You know that there were such men in that area and that he wasn't liked in the village.'

'Yes, I know,' she whispered, still shocked.

'The police informed us this morning,' said the asylum doctor, toying with an inkstand on his desk. 'We weren't going to tell you yet, but in the light of what has been revealed we think it best you know the truth. You can leave whenever you wish. We'll see that your things are packed.'

She nodded. 'Immediately, please. I have to find my son, you see.'

The doctor flushed and averted his gaze as she thanked Dr Michaels for coming. He offered her and Daniel a lift back to Liverpool and asked if there was anything else he could do. 'I have given Mr O'Neill a letter of explanation and introduction, but if you wish me to go to the orphanage with you, I will.'

'Orphanage! Then you know which one David is in?' Rebekah turned to Daniel. Joy and excitement were suddenly emotions that she could allow herself to indulge in.

He grinned. 'I'm living in hope. Edwina thinks it's a possibility.' He said in a low voice, 'I think we can manage without the good doctor, don't you? We could get the train. There's things we have to say to each other.'

'Yes,' she breathed, wanting nothing more than to be alone with him and to find David.

It was not until they were outside the imposing wrought iron gates that she said in an even voice, 'You didn't kill Joshua, did you?'

He looked amused. 'No. Would you have liked me to?'

She shook her head and said. 'No. He caused us a great deal of suffering but he was an unhappy man and I'd rather not have his murder hanging over our heads. Tell me how you got here? What happened when you left me? And where've you been all this time?'

He told her as they walked hand in hand to the station. 'I came out of prison a couple of days ago and one of the first people I saw was our Shaun, begging on O'Connell Bridge. He'd lost a leg.' He paused and a muscle moved in his cheek.

She waited a few minutes before saying in a soft voice, 'So you were captured? How did Shaun – ?'

'I was getting him as far away from you as possible that last day I saw you. I intended coming back but I crashed the car.'

'You crashed it!' If only she had known. If only. It would have saved her so much heartache. And he had intended coming back.

'I didn't know the roads or the car,' continued Daniel. 'He said there were troopers but there weren't. But after the crash we did meet some. Shaun had broken both legs. I was knocked out and came to in someone's house. They'd called in the troopers because of Shaun's being armed. We were separated and I didn't see him again until yesterday.' He paused and gazed across the road, his expression tight. 'They'd had to amputate one of his legs. Gangrene. But they let him go free. Apparently they didn't consider him a danger any longer.'

'I'm sorry.' She squeezed his hand.

'It's tough on him and at the moment he's blaming me for everything. I brought him to Liverpool to my aunt's because I just couldn't leave him in Ireland.'

'*He's* why you came to Liverpool?' she said lightly.

He looked at her and smiled. 'You know he isn't. After I saw Shaun I read the newspaper headlines about Joshua. I came for you. I went to Brigid thinking she'd know where you were, and she did.'

'You read my letter?'

'Yes. And if Green hadn't already been dead – ' He grimaced. 'He must have believed that David was my son.'

'He did.'

'Is he really like me?'

'I think so.'

Daniel took a deep breath. 'Let's go and find him.'

Chapter Twenty-Six

'We're looking for a baby.' Daniel and Rebekah stood in the open doorway of a large oak-panelled entrance hall, confronting a woman who reminded Rebekah a little of Hannah.

'Go away and come back in the morning,' said Hannah's lookalike.

'No!' Daniel put his foot in the door. 'This is important, Miss.'

She sniffed. 'If you want to adopt you must apply in writing and your situation will be looked into.'

'We're searching for a baby. There was a mix up and we've been directed to you.' Rebekah's tones were haughty. 'Daniel, the note from Dr Michaels.'

He took it from his pocket and handed it to the woman. She opened it, read it, and eyed them with ghoulish interest. 'It says that Mr Green is dead? When? We haven't heard a thing.'

'It's in today's paper,' said Daniel, pushing the door wide and pulling Rebekah inside. 'He was shot in Ireland. So sad about his death. A worthy gentleman.'

'A good man indeed,' said the woman effusively. 'My condolences. He was well thought of, and that must be a consolation to you.'

'Of course,' said Rebekah smoothly. 'He liked children so much. Wanted to help poor mothers.'

'A caring man.' The woman sighed. 'Only a month or so ago he brought the little boy to us. He said it was the child of an unmarried girl – the daughter of one of his sailors washed overboard. We were glad to help and promised to do our best to find the boy a good home.'

Rebekah almost stopped breathing. 'And have you found him one?'

'Not yet.' She sniffed. 'Due to it's being Mr Green's express wishes that we find the boy a home, we've been more particular than usual. Which it seems is just as well in the circumstances. A mix up, Dr Michaels says.' She was obviously curious but they had no intention of enlightening her and causing a scandal.

Daniel squeezed Rebekah's hand. 'Perhaps we can have a look at him?'

The woman hesitated then nodded. 'If you're very quiet you can have a peak. It is late, you understand?'

They said they did and followed her. She led them to a large room with rows of cots and spoke to a nurse who was bottle feeding a baby.

The nurse walked soft-footedly towards them. 'Come with me,' she whispered. 'Jonathan's a lovely baby. He has the most gorgeous curly hair and big brown eyes.'

Rebekah's heartbeat threatened to suffocate her. Brown eyes!

'We had some problems with him at first,' went on the nurse in a low voice. 'Especially feeding him, but he's a good boy now.'

Rebekah remembered her sore breasts and the wasted milk and wanted to cry.

The nurse stopped by a cot which contained a gurgling baby with one of his feet in his mouth. She smiled. 'This is Jonathan.'

Rebekah stared at David and was about to pick him up when something made her look at Daniel. His hand went out and removed the foot from his son's mouth. Immediately the child moved his mouth against the back of his hand and sucked at his knuckle. An indescribable expression crossed Daniel's face and he lifted the baby out of the cot to cradle him awkwardly in his arms.

'You're not supposed to take the babies out of their cots,' said the nurse.

Daniel took no notice, taking a small hand into his own.

'Well?' asked Rebekah, smiling.

'He has a look of our Shaun when he was a baby.'

'Your Shaun!' She groaned. 'You can't mean it! He looks like you. He's a good-looking baby.'

'Please, will you put Jon back?' interrupted the nurse. 'You might think he's yours, sir, but it has to be done legally.'

They both ignored her. 'Our Shaun was okay when he was small,' said Daniel. 'It was only later he got spoilt.'

'I suppose he'd best come and live with us.'

Daniel gave her a look. 'You could both drive each other crazy.'

'Excuse me!' said the nurse in a fierce voice. 'If you don't put that baby back right now I'll have to fetch Matron.'

Daniel took no notice but put his free arm round Rebekah as they walked away from the cot.

'Hey!' Hastily the nurse placed the baby she had been feeding in David's cot. It took only two seconds for it to start screaming.

Rebekah and Daniel passed through an open french window that led on to a terrace. The nurse followed as several more babies started crying.

Rebekah, hearing the noise, turned. 'The other lady will explain. I'm Mrs Green.'

'I don't care if you're Mrs Red, White and Blue,' said the nurse, bristling. 'She didn't say anything about your taking Jon. Only about showing you him. I'll get told off or dismissed!'

'Neither will happen if you do what I say,' insisted Rebekah in a soothing voice.

The nurse stared at her. 'You can't just take a baby like that,' she said weakly. 'Even though him and him have a look of each other. There's rules!'

'They do have a look of each other, don't they?' Rebekah's face lit up. 'Oh, go back, love. Stop those other babies crying! I'll see that you get a great big box of chocolates for being such a help.' She turned and ran to catch up with Daniel and they went out of the gates together.

Epilogue

Rebekah came down the steps of the building where Joshua's solicitor's office was situated near Dale Street. She was wearing an eau-de-nil chiffon frock and a black straw hat with an artificial green gardenia decorating its narrow brim. There was a bounce in her step as she walked. The street sloped downwards towards the river and soon she passed beneath the Overhead Railway, nicknamed the Dockers' Umbrella by Liverpudlians. She narrowly avoided a heavily loaded horse drawn cart.

'Watch it, luv!' The words were accompanied by a wolf whistle. 'Got a date, have yer? I wouldn't mind taking yer on meself.'

Rebekah smiled and felt good.

David was safe with Aunt Esther, who was still in shock after Rebekah had told her that Daniel was David's father and that they were going to get married. Hannah had said with relish: 'Told thee, Miss Esther, she always was one for the men.'

'Men!' Rebekah had retorted. 'There's only ever been one man in my life.'

Now she looked at the man in her life as he gazed over the river at the ships. In the navy pin striped suit, and with his dark brown hair in disarray by the sea breeze, she considered him still the most attractive man she had ever set eyes on. She came up behind him and slipped her hand through his arm. 'Are you wishing yourself on one of them boats?'

'Ships, Becky.' Daniel turned, smiling. 'How did you get on? Did you shock the man in your best green frock?'

'I'm sure I did. He was even more shocked when I told him I was going to a wedding.'

'You're wishing it was your own, perhaps?'

She smiled. 'I thought you might have suggested a double one.'

'I was excommunicated last year.'

Rebekah stared at him. 'You never told me that.'

'Most of us Irregulars were at some time or other. Sure, and I forgot about it in all the excitement. Like you're forgetting to tell me if I was right about Joshua's money.'

'You mean, had he put a clause in his will saying if I married one Daniel O'Neill, then I wasn't to get a penny?' He nodded. 'You were wrong,' she said softly. 'You won't believe this but the shipping line goes to David. Joshua must have made the will after he was born and strangely, considering what he suspected, he never bothered to change it. There's some charitable gifts and a hundred pounds for his cousin. The rest is mine.'

'Odd,' said Daniel, shaking his head. 'I can't understand him. I never could.'

'I don't doubt that he was thinking of his reputation even after death,' murmured Rebekah. 'But after all, what is he giving me? He told me that he married me for my money.'

'It doesn't make sense.' Daniel shook his head.

'Some old aunt of his reckoned there was mental instability from his mother's side of the family.'

Daniel stopped. 'You've had a lucky escape.'

She nodded, remembering. 'What are we going to do about the business? Someone will have to look after it until David is old enough. I know you fought for a free Ireland, but – '

'But it's not the way I dreamed it,' he said quietly.

'Is anywhere?' Her voice softened. 'If you ask me, the pictures of places people carry in their minds have no reality. They're like that Land of the Ever Young you spoke of.'

He shrugged and looked over the river. 'Dreams die hard.'

'You have to dream new dreams. We have to think of David and he has a future here. We'll have to become respectable.'

'Respectable?' he murmured. 'Is Liverpool a city full of respectable people then?'

Her lips twitched. 'It has its share of rogues. But what do you expect? It's a seaport! Its ships go all round the world and you can hear ten different languages in a day!'

He stared at her then smiled. 'You don't have to convince me. I know the place. I thought we might go on a cruise.' He brought out two tickets with all the panache of a magician successfully pulling a donkey from a hat. 'I was thinking that the captain could marry us without any fuss.'

'It sounds a good idea.'

'I thought so. In the morning do?'

She nodded. They kissed, and arm in arm went off to Brigid's wedding.

Epigraph

Set me as a seal upon your heart . . . for love is strong as death, jealousy is cruel as the grave . . . many waters cannot quench love, neither can the floods drown it. If a man offered for love all the wealth of his house, it would be utterly scorned.
Song of Solomon

A SPARROW DOESN'T FALL
by June Francis

For young Flora Cooke the misery of the Second World War
and the hardship it brings is both real and unrelenting. When
her husband Tom is reported missing, presumed dead, Flora
is left to raise her family alone amidst the ruins of war-torn
Liverpool.

As she struggles to come to terms with the tragic news, Flora
attracts the attention of two very different men. One offers
security whilst the other offers the prospect of a new life in
California. Both promise her love.

But it takes another great tragedy before Flora finally listens to
the promptings of her heart and seizes a second chance at the
happiness that has for so long eluded her.

0 553 40364 8

THE GREEN OF THE SPRING
by Jane Gurney

A heartwarming saga of love and separation during wartime.

The carefree days of lazy picnics and house parties end abruptly with the outbreak of war in 1914.

Separation and the testing of young promises form the trials of war as much as trench casualties and Zeppelin raids. Whether from the 'Upstairs' world of the Brownlowes or the 'Downstairs' domain of Mrs Driver's kitchen, each of the inhabitants of Maple Grange is affected by the conflict in Belgium and France, and in ways that they could never have foreseen . . .

0 553 40407 5

IN SUNSHINE OR IN SHADOW
by Charlotte Bingham

Brougham is an imposing and beautiful house, the stateliest of stately homes, but to Lady Artemis Deverill it brings only sorrow and a lonely, crippled childhood. For Eleanor Milligan, born in downtown Boston of a poor Irish immigrant family, childhood means a continual battle against her bullying brothers and cruel father. When they meet on a liner sailing to Ireland, Artemis and Ellie couldn't have less in common or be more different in looks or temperament. But in spite of this they become friends, and when Ellie's Cousin Rose asks Artemis to stay on at Strand House, County Cork, for a few weeks of an idyllic pre-war summer, Artemis has little difficulty in accepting. It is there that Hugo Tanner meets both girls and is posed a question that will haunt him for the rest of his life.

0 553 40296 X

THE FAIRFIELDS CHRONICLES
by Sarah Shears

Set in the heart of the Kent countryside and spanning the period from the turn of the century to the end of the second World War, Sarah Shears introduces us to the inhabitants of Fairfields Village. As we follow the changing fortunes of the villagers we see how their lives and loves become irrevocably entwined over the years and watch the changing patterns of one of our best-loved novelists.

THE VILLAGE
FAMILY FORTUNES
THE YOUNG GENERATION
and now, the long-awaited conclusion:
RETURN TO RUSSETS

Published by Bantam Books

A SELECTION OF FINE NOVELS
AVAILABLE FROM BANTAM BOOKS

THE PRICES SHOWN BELOW WERE CORRECT AT THE TIME OF GOING
TO PRESS. HOWEVER TRANSWORLD PUBLISHERS RESERVE THE RIGHT
TO SHOW NEW RETAIL PRICES ON COVERS WHICH MAY DIFFER FROM
THOSE PREVIOUSLY ADVERTISED IN THE TEXT OR ELSEWHERE.

☐	17632 3	**DARK ANGEL**	*Sally Beauman*	£4.99
☐	17352 9	**DESTINY**	*Sally Beauman*	£4.99
☐	40296 X	**IN SUNSHINE OR IN SHADOW**	*Charlotte Bingham*	£4.99
☐	40163 7	**THE BUSINESS**	*Charlotte Bingham*	£4.99
☐	17635 8	**TO HEAR A NIGHTINGALE**	*Charlotte Bingham*	£4.99
☐	40427 X	**BELGRAVIA**	*Charlotte Bingham*	£4.99
☐	40428 8	**COUNTRY LIFE**	*Charlotte Bingham*	£3.99
☐	40298 6	**SCARLET RIBBONS**	*Emma Blair*	£4.99
☐	40072 X	**MAGGIE JORDAN**	*Emma Blair*	£4.99
☐	40321 4	**AN INCONVENIENT WOMAN**	*Dominic Dunne*	£4.99
☐	17676 5	**PEOPLE LIKE US**	*Dominic Dunne*	£3.99
☐	17189 5	**THE TWO MRS GRENVILLES**	*Dominic Dunne*	£3.50
☐	40364 8	**A SPARROW DOESN'T FALL**	*June Francis*	£3.99
☐	40407 5	**THE GREEN OF SPRING**	*Jane Gurney*	£4.99
☐	17539 4	**TREASURES**	*Johanna Kingsley*	£4.99
☐	17207 7	**FACES**	*Johanna Kingsley*	£4.99
☐	17151 8	**SCENTS**	*Johanna Kingsley*	£4.99
☐	40405 5	**GREED**	*Lis Leigh*	£4.99
☐	40206 4	**FAST FRIENDS**	*Jill Mansell*	£3.99
☐	40360 5	**SOLO**	*Jill Mansell*	£3.99
☐	40363 X	**RICHMAN'S FLOWERS**	*Madeleine Polland*	£4.99
☐	17209 3	**THE CLASS**	*Erich Segal*	£2.95
☐	17630 7	**DOCTORS**	*Erich Segal*	£3.99
☐	40261 7	**THE VILLAGE**	*Sarah Shears*	£3.99
☐	40262 5	**FAMILY FORTUNES**	*Sarah Shears*	£3.99
☐	40263 3	**THE YOUNG GENERATION**	*Sarah Shears*	£3.99

All Corgi/Bantam Books are available at your bookshop or newsagent, or can be
ordered from the following address:
Corgi/Bantam Books,
Cash Sales Department,
P.O. Box 11, Falmouth, Cornwall TR10 9EN

UK and B.F.P.O. customers please send a cheque or postal order (no currency)
and allow £1.00 for postage and packing for the first book plus 50p for the second
book and 30p for each additional book to a maximum charge of £3.00 (7 books
plus).

Overseas customers, including Eire, please allow £2.00 for postage and packing for
the first book plus £1.00 for the second book and 50p for each subsequent title
ordered.

NAME (Block Letters) ....

ADDRESS ....

....